MARCUS RHODES IN
OPERATIONAL NIGHTMARE

M. J. JURAND

1

LILLEHAMMER

Marcus Rhodes Tier 1 Special Forces Operator felt equally comfortable and uneasy as he journeyed by train towards Lillehammer Norway. The reason behind this was that the Intel given to him was scanty and it made him feel rather apprehensive, plus there was the lingering unanswered question as to why he had been selected given his disastrous past record of dealing with the X chromosome that invariably led to the collapse of any relationship be it professional or private.

"I fuck up every time I deal with a woman" He quietly cursed.

'Is there anything I can get you Sir?" A very voluptuous railway female attendant asked as he stared into space

"Not another temptation!" Marcus mentally sighed as he visibly rolled his eyes "Err………black coffee and one of your Danish…..I mean Norwegian scrolls would be lovely…thank you"

"With pleasure Sir" She answered with a wink of her vivid blue eye. Marcus watched her lecherously as she turned on the spot and wiggled her nicely rounded buttocks down the passageway.

The landscape outside was bleak and uneventful. Marcus hoped that his present mission was not one of rescuing the train he was on from any terrorists that might have come aboard given that most countries had adopted a global attitude towards immigration.

"I can do bugger all if there's more than three…there is only so much that my trusty Glock 19 and I can do!" he muttered to himself as he recalled how easy it had been for him to smuggle his weapon through the European Union's customs in bits and pieces.

With that in mind Marcus Rhodes decided to do a quick reconnaissance of the carriages so as to give him peace of mind or would it be more than that because being paranoid had kept him alive for all of his active years.

"Is everything all right Mr Rhodes" The pretty female railway attendant asked as he passed her by.

"Just stretching my legs"

"Not too long now…about 45 minutes left to go" She warmly replied in an erotic tone of voice.

"Thank you"

"You're next"

"Pardon….?"

"Your coffee and cake…….. Or would you prefer breakfast in bed?" She seductively asked.

"Are all Norwegian girls so easy…….." He wondered and returned to his seat.

The remainder of the journey was uneventful downright disappointing one might say made worse by the fact that the pretty railway attendant was not further forthcoming in any shape, form or manner.

"Just another flirtatious bitch…!" Marcus thought to himself as the train rolled into the once famous town of Lillehammer home of the 1994 Winter Olympics.

Marcus collected his backpack, cautiously left the train and casually walked towards the tourist information booth to ask for the best method of transport for the next part of his journey.

The middle aged Norwegian male who was a little hard of hearing thanks to years of listening to heavy metal rock bands and not at all fluent in English grunted and roughly pointed to a taxi stand which was populated by a motley group of nefarious looking taxi drivers, as Marcus approached them he was set upon by a several foreign individuals offering a variety of private services.

"You want guide….I show you around…give you special price…love you long time"

"Not now…..later" He roughly replied as he waved the annoyances away and allowed his body language to shout 'bugger off'.

A suspicious looking Afghan with gold capped teeth who had obviously managed to convince the naïve Norwegian authorities into believing that he was worthy of refugee status thrust himself at Marcus and said "Come this way…. proper taxi for you…where you go….I take you there…no problems"

The last two words cut deeply into Marcus, elevated his suspicions and sent a shiver down his spine. Marcus put his hand inside his jacket and felt for his Glock which was tucked in his trousers and held in place by his belt. The Afghan meanwhile opened the front passenger door but Marcus refused and seated himself in the rear of the cab which resembled a poor copy of a traditional London Cab.

The Afghan pretended to punch in the coordinates of their destination into his GPS; the doors automatically locked once he started the engine and did not unlock each time they stopped which Marcus found a little unnerving. About fifteen minutes later the Afghan asked.

"You here for business or pleasure…..?"

"Business" Marcus abruptly answered.

"Very good….I have certain items that can help you and your friends feel good….make for better, bigger business…everyone like that….it is the Afghan way" The taxi driver slyly answered.

"What do you mean?" Marcus asked playing dumb.

"I think good idea if you bring Aunt Emma or maybe a Black Russian or maybe a few Dutchies along and introduce them to your business friends, I have plenty in glove box" The Afghan replied using the urban slang to describe opium and marihuana.

"No thank you, I think we will stick to Norwegian Vodka" An answer the Afghan did not particularly like and he floored the accelerator and drove like a jilted lover who was intent on taking his life.

The taxi came to a screeching halt outside of Hakon's Hall situated in Lillehammer's Olympic complex. Marcus paid the man, took no notice of his ranting or ravings and walked towards reception where he hoped someone knew where he was supposed to go thankfully one such individual existed who cheerfully produced a map of the complex and pencilled it in.

"If you go to the Luge and Bob track behind it is the forest where paintball is played. We are in between seasons so it is empty. It is about a twenty five minute walk through the forest in a straight line and then you will find the campsite you want."

Marcus thanked the clerk and took his leave. It was early afternoon. Within minutes he was at the edge of a forest of paint splattered trees that bore the hallmarks of numerous fierce battles and thousands of rounds of spent paintballs.

Dressed in brown cargo pants, a long sleeved loose fitting jacket and wearing rugged hi-tech mountaineering boots Marcus made a steady beeline towards the designated meeting place. As he carefully drudged his way through the forest and its undergrowth the ice and snow beneath his feet cracked with anticipation which heightened his senses and he stopped momentarily to assess his circumstances.

Marcus slowed his breathing, opened his mouth to accentuate his hearing and looked meticulously around for any available cover, standard paranoiac response, never underestimate anything, always look and listen, identify something that does not fit!

The animals, insects and birds of the forest knew something was amiss; it wasn't their responsibility to warn Marcus, he was just another traveller, a stranger to these parts, of no consequence or had the years of combat caused him to imagine that the world was a dangerous place no matter where he found himself. These thoughts were answered in a flash as the trees that weren't trees stood up, took aim and started firing at him.

Marcus instinctively drew his weapon and dropped to the ground. He landed heavily, rolled into a tight prone firing position to minimize his body's surface area. High velocity and accurate "paint balls" whizzed straight past his head from three positions; the left, the right and from in front of him.

"Amateurs or amateurs in disguise….? Only one way to find out….!" Marcus asked himself as his years of advanced Ops training kicked in and he took careful aim at one of the heavily camouflaged individuals and fired three warning shots in rapid succession that hit and splintered the tree that the shooter stood next to, his tactical response was quickly answered by two deafening and blinding explosions.

"Flash bangs! These Norwegians take their paintball seriously" Marcus painfully groaned. He played 'dead' so as to allow his senses to reset themselves which gave his 'assassins' sufficient time to escape leaving Marcus somewhat confused and momentarily disorientated.

Marcus decided to remain motionless for at least fifteen minutes and continuously assess his position whilst his mind repeatedly asked "Have they gone or are they playing the same waiting game as well?"

"It's now or never" Marcus grunted at the end of the time. He promptly raised himself into a kneeling position and expertly covered his forward 180° arcs with Glock in hand. Satisfied that all appeared normal he stood up to his full height, quickly turned around and noticed out of the corner of his eye that an unidentified being of sorts was shadowing him. Each time Marcus moved so did the being ever so slightly and cleverly until it could not bear the suspense of it any longer and it let out a blood curdling cruel and mischievous laugh that made Marcus bolt for safety.

The Tier 1 Special Forces Operator cleverly sprinted and zigzagged at break neck speed through the forest until he reached a lush green meadow where he took refuge and hid in the tall grass.

"What the fuck was that!?" He cursed as he caught his breath "And where's the fucking Olympic Committee when you need one, I must have cracked a new world record for the 800m dash!" He complained as his heart continued to race wildly.

"Well done Mr Rhodes…welcome aboard" A voice from out of the blue beckoned.

"Welcome aboard what?" He questioned as he tried to locate the source of the voice.

"Over here"

"Stop fucking with my head! Just tell me where you are and what the fuck you want" Markus barked as he surveyed his surroundings with Glock in hand and assumed that he was still dealing with one of those who had just attacked him in the forest.

"A bit touchy are we?"

"I have no reason to feel that way" Marcus sarcastically replied.

"Well if that is the case I suppose it might be safe for me to introduce myself" A solid well built man in his mid fifties and a wearing a gillie suit warmly responded as he stood up from his hiding spot not five feet away from Marcus.

Marcus looked him up and down for any suspicious movements or armaments and did not relax his guard nor lower his weapon which he kept fully trained on the stranger who smiled and offered his hand as a gesture that indicated that he was friend and not foe. Marcus remained unmoved and unimpressed considering what he had just endured.

"Come now my friend….so far so good" The fifty year old Scott softly said in a broad accent as he removed his head gear.

"I'm not a mind reader…what do you want of me?" Marcus insolently replied as he realized that he was possibly dealing with a military type, most probably an ex-Rupert in fact.

"Well you obviously don't do drugs so my learned taxi driver tells me. You dealt with the incident in the forest which we call 'Our warm welcome to Lillehammer' exceptionally well and as a bonus you even attracted the attention of our favourite troll"

"What's her name I've dated a few in my time"

"Perhaps we can arrange a meeting"

"I can hardly wait" Marcus sarcastically replied as he started to relax.

"Very good, shall we start walking? My name by the way is Major David Weir ex British Royal Marine" The red headed Scotsman replied as he turned and lead the way to the camp site that was the final intended destination.

As they walked in single file Marcus remained silent and closely followed the Major who took a path that passed through places heavily steeped in local folklore. The scenery was one of rebirth as winter reluctantly gave way to spring with the countryside becoming dotted with alpine flowers.

The camp that they would finally reach was an accumulation of single storey timber chalets which had housed past Olympic competitors from all over the world. These were neatly arranged to fit into the surrounding topography.

Major Weir picked up the pace as they neared the site and he stormed his way towards the largest building which was the community centre.

Inside a man and two women were patiently waiting and engaged in idle chit chat until the Major burst through the doors and rashly said "Okay shut the fuck up and listen"

The trio instantly went silent, the two 'ladies' considered the major somewhat coarse if not downright obnoxious whereas the males smiled and thought "I like this man's attitude"

Before Marcus has a chance to size up any one of the three the Major continued to issue orders. "Right then follow me, we're going into another room that's more secure!"

Marcus expected that it was likely to be well guarded and filled with hi-tech equipment, large screens, monitors, satellite up links, covert listening devices etc. However when the Major opened the door and switched the lights on nothing but emptiness greeted him.

"Welcome ladies and gentlemen to the Room of Frustrations, no windows, other doors, just lots of empty egg cartons as far as the eye can see!"

"No kidding what's fucking next" Marcus thought as he saw thousands of the packaging simply stapled to the walls and ceiling but not the floor which was covered by standard judo mats.

"Right then introduction time; I am Major David Weir the devilishly handsome man you were instructed to meet, this is Marcus, Nicoli, Anya and Brit" He said as he pointed to each one of them in turn and then allowed each to acknowledge the others by way of a simple nod of the head.

"I take it your journeys were uneventful, nice and smooth and you had no trouble finding the place" He asked and whilst the majority agreed Marcus frowned and thought "Uneventful my ass!"

"Except Mr Rhodes you were not so lucky but then that is the story of your life. Polish mother, worked as a domestic for a prominent widowed aristocrat who managed to make her pregnant making you half Polish half British. Your father used his substantial contacts and influence allowing you entry into Sandhurst Military Academy where the snobbery and class distinction got the better of you. You didn't particularly like the running man game in which you were taken completely naked and blindfolded to a remote location, dumped, given nothing more than a pair of urine filled runners and expected to make you way back to the barracks under freezing conditions. It seems your penchant for stealing and wearing women's clothing landed you in hot water with the local constabulary. Needless to say your commander was not impressed and disciplined you accordingly, but true to form you retaliated by breaking his jaw. Luckily you held dual citizenship with Poland which allowed you admission into the Polish army after your discharge from Sandhurst. You excelled and rose through the ranks as a general enlisted soldier. Your physical, analytical and tactical skills did not go unnoticed and you were preselected for the elite Grom unit which you passed easily even though some outside experts argued that you had failed the psychological assessment in relation to respecting authority which had previously cast its disapproval of you for performing security work during your holidays for prostitutes and during the Sochi Winter Olympics for even though the Polish officials were and continue to be on good terms with the Russians it is not for public knowledge, hence the reasons for you being here. Nicoli on the other hand does not have your pedigree; he hails from Cobras a supposedly advanced Serbian Military Police unit of no consequence in my mind whereas Anya and Brit are much more interesting" The Major slowly and deliberating said as a matter of fact which made neither Marcus nor Nicoli particularly comfortable.

"Both are from the FSK the Norwegian crack unit" he continued after taking a brief pause for the benefit of his listeners.

"You must be fucking joking" Marcus doubted as he was well aware of its stringent entry requirements and physical demands.

"I see you doubt me Mr Rhodes" the Major said as he picked up on Marcus's negativity.

"45 push ups, 50 sit ups in 2 minutes, 8 pull ups, swim 400 meters in 11 minutes. March 30 kilometres carrying 25 kilos in 4 hours and 50 minutes, I fucking doubt it" Marcus rudely rattled off as he looked and considered Anya to be nothing more than a puny runt.

"Would you care to spar with the young lady Mr Rhodes? The floor is yours" The Major asked as he mischievously smiled, gestured and invited the couple to engage in physical combat.

2

A.R.S.E. FIELD

Before he took a step forward Marcus Rhodes without any hesitation or regard for political correctness boldly said "I don't like hitting women unless they deserve it"

His somewhat chauvinist statement caused Brit to place her hand over her mouth so as to suppress her laughter, Anya simply smiled and said "So you don't hit women, how chivalrous of you, but then again what are you afraid of? A big strong Sandhurst outcast shouldn't even raise a sweat dealing with the likes of me"

"I think she's got the better of you already Mr Rhodes" the Major concluded and watched Marcus carefully remove his jacket, roll up his sleeves and divorce himself of any loose items including his Glock 19 which he cocked and locked.

Anya meanwhile stepped away from him and performed a series of stretch exercises as though she was preparing to perform in a gymnastic event. The two combatants then walked into the center of the room, squared off and stood two meters apart. Marcus stared coldly at Anya and thought "I still don't know why I am here unless it is to demonstrate my gladiator skills, no matter, if it's a fight they want, then a fight I will give them. This runt in front of me as far as I am concerned is sexless, six inches shorter, reach also about six inches less than mine, thirty kilo lighter, short but sharp fingernails, would have to come in quick and close to do any harm, doesn't look like a biter, eye gouger or anything vicious like that. Only visible weapon so far is her double edged tongue, has a preoccupation with counting her fingertips using the thumb on the same hand, probably a nervous habit, she's scared and rightly so she has less than a forty percent chance of hitting me never mind winning, don't be cocky remember… always expect the unexpected…..Time to engage ….. Let's fight!"

"You don't like hitting women! Are you afraid of the consequences? Are you afraid that I might actually beat you?" Come on Mr Rhodes let's dance show me what you've got!" Anya mercilessly taunted as she casually walked towards him just before she slightly dropped her left shoulder faking that she was about to hit him with her right fist. Marcus instinctively put up his hands to block the punch and protect his head allowing Anya to outwit him and she kicked him forcibly in the abdomen with her left foot winding him in the process and propelling him backwards. Marcus landed heavily on his back and hit the back of his head on the floor with an almighty thud that would have rendered many a man unconscious. Stunned by the quickness and force of her actions he rapidly reassessed his capabilities and his adversary.

"This bitch means business, no more Mr Nice Guy" he thought as he scrambled to his feet, ignored Brit's cheers and applause and took up a defensive position in readiness for Anya's next move.

The FSK agent did not disappoint him and launched another attack. As Anya neared him, Marcus took the initiative; he took one step forward, pivoted on his right foot and attempted a knockout blow with a straight punch to her jaw line. Anya quick as a flash side stepped his manoeuvre deflected the punch and brought the full force of her right leg to his exposed rib cage dropping him instantly. Marcus winched with pain and was about to pass out but his advanced training and determination to succeed and survive prevented this from happening.

"So you want more Mr Rhodes? Aren't two strikes enough for you?" Anya ruthlessly teased as she continued to 'count fingertips' with the thumb on her left hand.

"Annoying little bitch, she must have an Achilles heel somewhere" Marcus mentally cursed as his mind raced to find a solution to his immediate psychological problem.

Marcus staggered to his feet and pretended to struggle to breathe as he gasped for air. He remained doubled over and clutched his side as though one or more of his ribs had been broken. Sensing that she may have exceeded her authority Anya out of compassion and a sense of duty flew to his side only to be greeted with a vicious upper cut to her solar plexus.

"You utter bastard!" she screamed as she dropped to her knees but that was not the end of it, she recovered in an instant, jumped over Marcus and kneed him in the back propelling him across the room. Not intent on showing any further mercy Anya stormed towards Marcus grabbed him by the ankles and pulled his pants down to expose his naked buttocks.

"Welcome to ARSE field" she flippantly said as she towered over him.

"Well done Miss Betts, stand down" The Major ordered in a congratulating fashion ending the one sided conflict.

Nicoli walked over to where Marcus lay as a crumpled mess and offered him a hand up whilst Brit embraced Anya and examined her for any injuries.

"Tidy yourself up Mr Rhodes you're stalling proceedings" the major impatiently barked at Marcus who was slow to respond.

"That's alright for you to say I've just had my ass kicked by some biological freak. Now I understand my purpose, nothing more than a convenient punching bag to highlight women's superiority over men. At least I got one good punch in" Marcus incoherently mumbled to himself.

"Did you hear me Mr Rhodes; you're not impressing anybody

with your naked exhibition now tidy yourself up that's an order"
The Major bellowed.

"I've never had any complaints" Marcus insolently replied as he
scrambled to his feet, tucked his shirt into his trousers and dusted
himself off.

"Perhaps we should let the troll decide" the Major teased.

"Looking forward to that as always" Marcus carelessly replied as
he gritted his teeth.

"Well then, what we have witnessed today is a practical demonstration of what the human body is capable of once it is fully
activated. Anya here is a fine example having mastered the unique
ultra secret technology that we have surgically implanted into her.
It is officially known as Activated Rapid Systemic Enhancement or
ARSE for short.

"ARSE hey......where exactly is this technology implanted?"
Marcus jeered

"Bit homophobic are we Mr Rhodes afraid of where the implant
is likely to be inserted?"

"You must admit it has it connotations, how do I know that
ARSE doesn't stand for Another Rectal Symphony where the person
shits all over you?"

"I thought that had already happened" the Major cuttingly
replied.

"Point taken" Marcus meekly agreed and remained silent

"Good then let us continue, first of all Mr Rhodes you were very
fortunate that Brit was not chosen to engage you otherwise I dare
say you would have most likely have been admitted into intensive
care. Scary stuff I hear you say. Not really, it's perfectly natural and
completely drug free. What we have done is develop a highly sophisticated integrated bio-electric circuitry consisting of a small
rectangular graphene master chip surgically positioned half way
along the brain stem's exterior; five smaller chips have been individually imbedded just below the skin in each of the fingertips of the

dominant hand. After a period of time usually about three months these become part of the body's nervous system and can be manually operated at will. The master chip responds to signals generated by the thumb touching the fingertips of the same hand corresponding to a unique numerical sequence that causes the master chip to stimulate the activity of the brain stem thus amplifying the individual's ability to survive under extreme circumstances, namely the classic fight or flight, fright has been taken out of the equation. Consequently the individual achieves higher sensory performance, an exponential increase in muscle strength and cognitive function. Anya and Brit are our most successful candidates so far. Sadly we have had a few casualties along the way until we fine tuned the system"

"Like broken bones, brain storms and psychosis" Brit unexpectedly butted in

"Thank you but we don't want to scare off these two fine gentlemen just yet" The major cautioned

"I thought they should know what they are getting themselves into" Brit apologized

"Yes Major that was and still is the foremost thought in my mind" Marcus said in a confronting tone of voice

"Very well perhaps I should explain. Certain members of NATO are very unhappy about the way that the Americans continue to bully and railroad NATO policies and their enactment. They are quite rightly tired of being puppets and would like to cut a string or two. These members who will remain anonymous have decided to form a small squad to monitor the Yank's intelligence activities, form conclusions and make appropriate recommendations so as to achieve a better balance in international political outcomes, something that the UN repeatedly fails to do. Each one of you after much exhaustive research has been chosen and is invited to become part of this highly dangerous operation. What sorts each one of you out from the rest is your ability to question and not blindly follow orders. You will in effect be answerable to yourselves only. Your outcomes will either please or displease your faceless employers"

"When do we get the ARSE?" Nicoli keenly asked whilst Marcus remained disapproving and tight lipped

"Afraid not soldier, you're active from this moment on, the advanced bioelectric graphene circuitry takes at least three months to harmonise itself with your nervous system during which time certain neurological disturbances may occur. We want you fully operational not dysfunctional" The Major explained

"In other words this squad is experimental" Marcus quickly deduced

"Precisely"

"Two Amazonian woman babysitting two males, makes me feel quite insignificant!" Marcus said with a degree of annoyance

"I'm sure you have hidden talents that will impress the ladies" The Major ambiguously said making light of the situation

"Providing they don't break them off" Marcus crudely replied

"You can always pursue the troll"

"I forgot about her" Marcus insolently replied

"How unfortunate, shame on you soldier, I think you should send flowers"

"Where and when do we start" Marcus asked cutting to the chase

"I'm glad you asked that question, but before I give you the answer I take it Shadow 1 is a go?" the Major asked feeling a little apprehensive

Everyone nodded in the affirmative except Marcus who cast some doubt by asking "This freedom that we have been given, who do we answer to, we can't just go running around killing people as we please"

"Quite moral of you soldier, for now you answer to me only, leave it at that otherwise we will become bogged down in a needless philosophical debate that will achieve absolutely nothing! Deal with every situation as you see fit, survival is paramount...do I make myself clear?" the Major firmly said in a fashion befitting his rank

"Yes Sir" Nicoli, Brit and Anya smartly replied except for Marcus who remained neutral

"Excellent…I'm going to step out for a while to arrange transport to our next destination this should give you ample opportunity to get to know each other" The Major replied and took his leave

"Well then who is going first?" Marcus asked taking the initiative

"I will" Anya brightly answered still gloating in her victory

"What's your story then?" Marcus inquired bearing no grudges towards the young woman

"I graduated from Oslo University with a Masters in Criminal Psychology and Forensics, after two years in private practice which I found dissatisfying I enlisted in the general army even though I was entitled to officer status, shortly after FSK was undergoing a restructuring process in which it was looking for a new breed of talented individuals and that is how I met Brit" Anya replied as she gave a thumb nail sketch of herself

"What she says is true; my background is a little different. I come from a family of 'shrinks' There was the expectation that I should follow suit except when I saw how distorted their view of reality was I decided not to have any part of it, I wanted to be normal, consequently I studied to become a primary school teacher which gave way to library studies" Brit shyly answered

"So you're a lexicographer" Marcus asked tongue in cheek as he visualized Brit doing it doggy-style over a pile of books.

Nicoli thought otherwise as he preferred a hot Hungarian woman in contrast to the outspoken Nordic types.

"That leaves you to impress us with your talents" Marcus joked as he gestured for the Hungarian born Serbian to say something

"I…err…am quite a simple man with simple tastes and pleasures"

"Does it involve women?" Brit asked out of curiosity

"Sometimes if I am in the mood"

"Otherwise?"

"I like playing chess…it lasts longer"

"I see" Brit replied trying to sound disappointed but before she had a chance to interrogate Nicoli any further the Major returned and loudly announced

"It's almost time to go, but first afternoon tea is being served!"

"What…where and when…?" Marcus thought

"Where is right here, what is a choice of Russian Caravan tea or English Breakfast, cake is in the form of high protein energy bars especially developed for long distance cyclists, no you're not going to bicycle to Trondheim you each have the luxury of a BMW G 310 R motorcycle which I believe after reading your individual profiles are more than capable of handling. Now that Shadow 1 is when, I have an important announcement to make, I am the fifth active operative, I do not believe in being a desk jockey giving orders of a dubious nature, I will be with you in the field otherwise how can I gain your respect? In my left hand I hold a thermos full of Russians, in my right a thermos full of English, one for Anya, one for Brit, I shall leave you to make your selections whilst I fetch your individual documentation" The Major announced as he handed over the two thermos flasks, a tube of disposable paper cups, a basket of high protein bars but no sugar or milk.

Marcus allowed everyone else to go first and hoped that they did not all prefer the Russian tea as it was his favourite. He found the protein bars which were coated in thick dark chocolate particularly palatable which came as no surprise as they were made in Germany something that the group immediately made into small talk.

Major Weir returned in a matter of minutes.

"Right it's down to brass tacks, ID, cover stories, Anya Betts alias Bree Andersen nurse; Britt Lund alias Lee Brex paramedic" He said as he handed out their respective drivers licenses which they eagerly accepted without any qualms having done it many times before on numerous operations for the FSK

"Nicoli Bartok now known as Bart Nyers your EU passport… fashion photographer and lastly our illustrious Mr Marcus Rhodes or should I correctly say Mr Ralph Martine BMW executive field salesman, I detect you are all flattered by our choices, no thanks nor applause necessary, I also see by your facial expressions that you are thinking what's next. Our first job will be to monitor the on goings at Trondheim airport where the Americans courtesy of a change of mind by the Norwegian government have set up a military base as part of the USA's marines' winter training program, which we suspect is more sinister than that as our Intel suggests it is part of their Anaconda strategy which involves encircling Russia. The base is located 380km north of here it will take approximately five hours via highway E6 to reach, however that is not our initial destination we have a safe house located in 'Hell'. Ladies and gentleman when you have had your fill of tea and 'cakes' taken a toilet break, please assemble outside and I shall give you the appropriate directions" Major Weir said in no uncertain terms before he turned on the spot and marched outside.

Marcus knew his place in the world, it was about six paces behind women and lengthening accordingly he disposed of all of the rubbish before attending to his own needs consequently he was the last to join the group, it was his way of secretly assessing the other operatives as to their suitability with respect to being fully trusted.

"Helmets, maps…disposable Norwegian phones… for each one of you, saddle bags are appropriately packed as per your job description" The Major barked as he assigned each one their respective motor bike

"Unfortunately I cannot join you for the ride I will meet you later at the farmhouse, if one or more of you does not arrive I will assume you have deviated to the alternate safe house. I will know where to find you as each bike is fitted with a pre-programmed GPS that sends out a distress signal in the event of a deviation. That's about all, travel safe and I will see you later this evening for dinner, any questions?" The Major bluntly asked as he watched the members of the newly formed Shadow 1 spring into action

Both Anya and Britt had no time for the formalities of getting to know their bikes, it was simply a matter of mount, insert and turn it on! The boys on the other hand were a little more respectful and gently eased themselves into the saddle. Anya was the first to tear away with Britt in hot pursuit leaving Nicoli and Marcus to duck for cover as a hail of stones came flying their way.

"Fast flashy moves will get you nowhere my lovelies when you cross swords with a master chess player" Nicoli grunted as he briefly watched the two girls speed away down the dusty back road and not one to shy away from a challenge he quickly donned his crash helmet and powered up his bike.

"So what are you going to do? Stand there like a dumb polak or give chase" Nicoli rudely bellowed just before he engaged the clutch, opened the throttle to full and desperately tried to hold onto and control the mechanical beast between his legs that threatened to slide sideways and kick him off

"Having trouble?" Marcus dryly replied as he watched the Serb make an utter fool of himself

"Just teaching her who is boss…!"

"Good luck with that…" Marcus answered and waved Nicoli away as the Serb snaked his way down the dusty back road

Unlike the other three the BMW motor cycle that was assigned to Marcus was subtly different something that did not go unnoticed by him

"What do we have here? Off road tyres and no GPS" Marcus observed as he carefully examined the motor cycle "I wonder what else is missing" He thought as he unfolded the road map that Major weir had provided.

"A map of Iceland… that will come in handy…means only one thing…I have been abandoned unless I can make up for lost time by sprinting after them. Well my little German fraulein show me what you are capable of" Marcus calmly mumbled as he turned the ignition key and heard "click…click…clunk" without anything further happening

"Status report…I have been officially elevated from abandoned to stranded…bloody marvellous…what's next?" He cursed as his mind entertained the prospect of ambush whilst his body automatically dismounted, searched the saddle bags for tools and a solution

"At least my equipment lives up to its reputation of 'in the field executive sales' add service to that" He quietly thought as he located a miniature socket, spanner and screwdriver set which he intended using. Once again he turned the ignition key and heard "click…click…clunk" followed by nothing

"Fuel, air, electrical, three things to consider, systematic approach using process of elimination, first fuel…tank full…lines patent…no petrol odour…no leakages…all intact, move onto air, filter clean, no obstacles, check, lastly electrical…battery terminals secure… nice and tight…no breaks in line until we reach the distributor and what do we find? Connection apparently secure until you pull it out and find plug in covered with non conductive material…scrape it off…reconnect…problem solved, right, let's try again" He muttered to himself as he put his repair to the test

"Click…click…boom…vroom" the bike boomed as it exploded into life and quickly found its rhythm

"That's better…question is what bastard set me up and where to from here?…I recall the Major mentioning Hell…I wonder if such a place exists given the way Norwegians spell…bet the guy at Hakon's Hall might know" Marcus concluded feeling rather pleased with his handy work and deductive reasoning.

Nicoli meanwhile had caught up with the experienced FSK speedsters who played a cat and mouse game with him weaving in and out of traffic along the E6 motorway which they knew well having travelled on it numerous times. The trio frequently reached dangerous speeds upwards of 140km/hr in the 90-110km speed zones and used heavy transport trucks, lost tourists and the occasional deer or boar as decoys to block, harass and delay each other and to demonstrate their superior handling skills but try as hard as they may the FSK operatives were no match for Nicoli who simply outwitted them on every occasion. After ninety minutes of intense battling Anya and Britt unexpectedly slowed down and decided to take a coffee break at one of the numerous well equipped service stations along the motor way. Nicoli offered no resistance and happily joined them for as far as he was concerned they had been check mated. The trio parked their BMW superbikes at the rear of the complex away from prying eyes, the girls turned their jackets inside out to give a sense of new identity and advised Nicoli to leave his behind securely stored in one of his saddle bags.

Marcus although he thought about a refreshing cup of freshly brewed coffee had other pressing matter to attend to, namely locating 'Hell'. Unfortunately the man who had previously assisted him earlier that day was not on duty at Hakon's Hall.

"Hello my name is Gunnar" another cheery attendant called out to Marcus who looked rather lost when he entered the sparsely populated reception area.

"Err…yes…I am hoping you can…is there such a place as Hell in Norway" Marcus replied vacantly

"You foreigners are all the same…quite funny…we have many sir" Gunnar somewhat campily replied with a flick of his wrist and wink of his eye

"Whereabouts…?" Marcus asked all ears

"Well…we have one in the south, one in the north and some people call the 'Pulpit' hell especially those afraid of heights and steep cliffs. So…the one south of here is Helvete Nature Park…it is an extraordinary experience, you have to watch your step because it has Northern Europe's biggest potholes" Gunnar said with a nod of his head

"Really…?" Marcus sublimely scoffed

"Oh yes sir! 25 meter wide and a minimum of 40 meter deep!

One minute you're walking around the trees in the undergrowth without a care in the world…the next minute…you're a goner!"

"I see…so you really need to watch your step…any houses around there?"

"Only one a mountain farm with grazing animals managed by a very quiet reclusive couple"

"How far is southern hell" Marcus asked in order to get his bearings

"68 kilometre from here"

"What about northern hell"

"Ah that sir is the famous one especially for tourists…there are many jokes about it!

"Like" Marcus asked attempting to show interest

"I had an ice cream in Hell is one of the popular ones, the Hell railway station has a really good much photographed sign it reads 'Hell God's Expedition' Not many people want to go inside never mind visit the village"

"How far away is this one?"

"Approximately 380 kilometre near Trondheim"

"Sounds like the place to be" Marcus dryly said as if he was the kind who enjoyed the bizarre and macabre "How do I get there" he then asked

"I recommend you avoid highway E6 as there has been some commotion on it and it is blocked…better you back track to Hamer, deviate to Elverum and drive north to Tynset followed by Roros before rejoining the E6 at Storen. Then it is a smooth ride to Trondheim which you avoid and continue onto Hell. It will take you at least six hours as you are new to the area and you will most likely drive slowly out of courtesy for the wild life and trolls. Driving at night can be very scary I suggest bedding down in one of the small towns I mentioned before it becomes too dark. We Norwegians want our tourists to stay happy and healthy, so they come back for more adventures. Here I give you a road map for you to follow"

Gunnar the very happy gay cheerfully replied in a theatrical fashion

Marcus thanked him for his help, accepted the map and briskly walked away thinking that he was on the right track. It was 4pm in the afternoon which meant that Marcus only had around three hours of sunlight left, an insufficient time to make it as far as Storen as the journey was longer and technically more demanding than the E6 motorway. He hoped that the commotion Gunnar spoke about did not involve the rest of the newly formed squad considering the reckless way in which all three had driven off earlier that afternoon. Marcus decided to contact them via phone for peace of mind but when he retrieved the device he found its battery to be completely flat.

"Abandoned and isolated just ducky…oh well just another day in paradise" he resolutely accepted before he mounted his BMW motorcycle and drove leisurely along the route mapped out for him by Gunnar.

The journey was uneventful until he reached the outskirts of Roros where a bunch of what he thought were redneck signs warning travellers that they were about to enter a UFO hot spot attracted his attention. The signs were nailed to a string of trees along the road and read "Do not go into the mountains" "Report missing people" "Keep your dog close" each bearing the skull and crossbones symbol plus the occasional alien

"Fact or fiction or is it due to the fact that the Americans have set up base nearby, perhaps it's part of their scare mongering tactics to keep unwelcome visitors away" Marcus thought as he passed them by. He stopped at a roadside convenience store further along to purchase two one litre bottles of spring water, cotton wool balls and a tub of Vaseline.

As he stood waiting in line to pay for his goods Marcus struck up a conversation with one of the locals.

"Is it true what I read on those road signs coming into town" he asked the middle aged man who had seen better days

"You mean about the aliens and missing people?"

"Yes I do" Marcus confirmed

"Very true, we are very scared, worried and don't know what to do. The police aren't much help"

"That's a pity" Marcus answered and quickly thought that they were part of the equation

"You're not thinking of going trekking through the mountains" The local asked

"No I'm on a motorbike…but out of curiosity if I was looking for trouble which road would I take?" Marcus asked tongue in cheek which the local thought was quite strange

"If you must know once you leave here, travel for about three kilometres towards Storen, on the right hand side of the road you will see an old dilapidated fire station built in the 1940's which is surrounded by a rusty fence and barbed wire, it is unwise for anyone to go anywhere near it, never mind walk up the track next to it that leads into the forest and mountains. We have erected a sign with 'problemer' as a warning to spare peoples' lives" The local grimly said in a low voice

"Sounds serious…I'll keep that in mind"

"Please do…that is the place where people and dogs have gone missing" The local strongly emphasized

Marcus thanked the local, paid for his goods and then threw caution to the wind and headed in the direction of trouble. It was nearing 6.30pm in the evening by the time Marcus reached 'problemer' the road was very quiet not a soul about which heighten his paranoia. Marcus parked his bike in front of the fire station and proceeded to idly walk about its perimeter. He causally stopped now and then to inspect bits and pieces and make out as if he was interested in taking a photograph or two. He noticed that the fence was not as ancient as the locals thought, it was in fact quite new and spray painted to make it look old furthermore it was made from a highly sophisticated wire used in high tech surveillance.

"Point of entry…no sentinels…must look as though I am a tourist, behave like one who is lost but you're not, so where in this dilapidated fire station are you hiding I ask you?" Marcus thought as he scratched his head and made his way back to his motorbike and then decided to return to Roros and find a place to eat and hopefully more locals to interact with and provide him with additional Intel about 'problemer'

Luckily the Hiort Pub an English style sports pub was open and bustling with activity as it was the local Troll Hunters fortnightly meeting.

Marcus parked his motorbike outside, grabbed his backpack and followed his nose, inside it was a hive of activity with a group of rowdy people watching a national soccer game on the big television, others playing darts or pool, some engaged in deep philosophical debates, many enjoying a hearty roast dinner and then there was the Troll Hunters all huddled together swapping experiences, locations and visual proof of their encounters with the mystical creatures.

After ordering and paying for his meal at the main bar Marcus decided to sit close to the Troll Hunters and listen in on their conversation which was relatively boring until one of them introduced the subject of the redneck warning signs on the outskirts of the village

"Look Nils…we have to put a stop to this visual pollution right now!" A solidly built local demanded

"I understand what you are saying but all of our attempts have failed. As soon as we take them down, they're back again" Nils equally loudly answered

"That's not good enough! I've said it before we have to keep watch 24 hours a day"

"That's not possible, the road is too long and they do it in a flash, we don't have the manpower or electronic resources and we don't know from what direction they come from" Nils strongly argued

"Excuse me for interrupting but are you gentlemen talking about the warning signs about aliens as you drive into Roros?" Marcus politely asked as he stood up and approached the Troll Hunters who suddenly went silent

"This is a private and exclusive discussion group, we don't entertain strangers requests, perhaps if you went through the proper channels we might accommodate you" Nils very abruptly and rudely answered and gave instructions for his compatriots to continue debating in Norwegian leaving Marcus well and truly out in the cold

"Sorry to have bothered you" Marcus apologized as he thought "Well at least I know who is working for the Americans"

But it did not end there, the Troll Hunters appeared frightened by Marcus's presence and they decided to end their meeting. They quickly dispersed but one of them however remained behind on the pretext of having another quiet drink and when the coast was clear introduced himself to Marcus

"Good evening my name is Odd"

"I'm sure we all are in one way or another…it's not that unusual" Marcus replied

"You misunderstand me… my name is Odd spelt O…D…D"

"Mr Odd is it?" Marcus asked trying to clarify his understanding

"My first name is Odd and you are?" Odd asked

"Ralph Martine…pleased to make your acquaintance…I hope your surname isn't balls"

"It's Frank" Odd replied as he brushed aside Marcus's attempt at humour

"Well Mr Frank can I buy you a drink?" Marcus kindly asked the odd looking Norwegian who looked as though he had met his fair share of trolls or imagined he had

"Later…the answer to the question you asked my group earlier is yes; the signs started appearing shortly after the devious Americans set up base in Trondheim. Quite a few of us want the Yanks out but the politicians are deaf to our demands. Our club name Troll

Hunters is a bit misleading because we do not hunt trolls we are more of a preservation society that looks after the trolls' habitats which are being badly disrupted. Someone wants to keep us out of the mountains" Odd slowly explained as he repeatedly looked over his shoulder

"Is the old fire station a good starting point?" Marcus asked the distraught Norwegian

"Better than where the alien warning signs exist"

"Why is that?" Marcus asked probing for more details

"From personal experience" Odd vaguely answered

"Can you be a little more specific?" Marcus insisted

"The warning signs act like a magnet, the majority of people deviate off the road where the signs are located and trek into the forest for two to three kilometres until they find a 'convenient' open field that has a nice view of the night sky where numerous 'stray' lights appear, some say it is rare but when they happen it resembles an orchestrated light show without the music" The odd troll hunter cynically answered

"As spasmodic as the Northern Lights or are they more regular or erratic?

"I would say regular to keep the attendances up and prevent people from scouting about where they are not welcomed"

"I feel as though you know something but are afraid to reveal it" Marcus cleverly deduced

"One mustn't upset the apple cart; we have to keep the tourists happy, we being the local authorities who have their strings pulled by the Americans. This however is not the place to discuss such sensitive matters, the walls have ears, perhaps we should retire to my cosy wooden cottage it's not far from here, let's walk, I've recently lost 50 kilos"

"Though exercise?" Marcus inquired

"No my wife left me six weeks ago. We both had our obsessions, once again not the place to discuss these, let's go" Odd replied with a mixture of sadness and happiness and then he abruptly spun on the spot and walked out

They spent the next hour trying to gauge each other over generous amounts of homemade schnapps which Odd had expertly distilled from local cloudberries found in a secret part the forest. When Odd was sufficiently inebriated so that he could walk in a straight line without error he decided it was time to go.

"Where to now...?"

"Into the mountains where the fire station stands and the cloudberries grow in profusion, here one flashlight for you and one for me" Odd said as he produced two palm-sized high powered bicycle lights.

Marcus insisted on walking in order to sober up and use the green toilet if need be, Odd on the other hand couldn't stop drinking and brought along a hip flask for added measure which did nothing more than accentuate the dark side of his sense of humour

"So Mr Ralph Martine...what did you say you did for a living?

"BMW field sales executive, I am meeting a consortium of clients looking to purchase significant numbers of our bikes; I specialise in practical demonstrations and accompany them on field trips" Marcus convincingly bluffed

"'Why the interest in UFO's"

"It's been a passion of mine for a long time, in other words wanting to know the unknown if you know what I mean" Marcus ambiguously replied

"I think you will be disappointed"

"Oh I don't know something odd might still happen" Marcus optimistically said and allowed Odd to lead the way

"Odd Frank...a strange name...perhaps it's a shortened nick name and you Odd are commonly known as frankly odd by the locals after they considered your obsessions whatever they might be" Marcus thought as he kept up with Odd who it appeared was well and truly on a mission "The more you drink the sharper you become..." Marcus observed each time Odd sipped from his hip flask

"Sure you wouldn't like some?" Odd offered

"No I'm quite alright...need to keep my wits about me"

"Very well" Odd replied and slowed his pace to compensate for the increasingly rough terrain

"Is this the way to the fire station?" Marcus asked feeling a little disorientated

"Not exactly...we are walking in an oblique fashion to end up far behind it and about seven kilometres away from the alien warning signs into my favourite part of the countryside where the cloudberries grow profusely and the trolls dance to the rhythms of nature or at least they once did before the drones arrived"

"And now...?"

"They sulk and scheme of ways to oust the intruders from their caves" Odd replied and he started to whistle Grieg's music from Peer Gynt

"Is that where you come in?" Marcus asked

"I cannot do much other than offer solace to these magical creatures. Careful you almost stepped on one" Odd erratically said as he side stepped a clump of rocks which to Marcus was nothing more than a clump of rocks

"This man is definitely odd" Marcus mumbled and then apologised by saying "Sorry...won't do it again"

"Better not...evening...nice to see you again...how are things... still...oh that's a shame...tomorrow will be a better day..." Odd haphazardly said as he looked left and right repeatedly and acted as though he was interacting with familiar people that he knew along the way

"What are you doing?" Marcus asked becoming increasingly paranoiac and disturbed by Odd's eccentric behaviour

"Just saying hello..."

"How come they don't say anything in return?" Marcus asked

"They do...but you probably mistake it for being the wind"

"This is becoming increasingly bizarre" Marcus thought and he seriously entertained the idea of aborting the mission

"Enjoying yourself...?" Odd cheerfully asked

"Not as yet...haven't seen any UFO's" Marcus pretended to grumble

"Give it time, once they finish their aerial display they'll be heading in our direction" Odd confidently replied before stopping to examine the topography of their surroundings

"Are we in the right place?" Marcus asked

"We are...except...something's different...something's not quite right" Odd sounding very concerned answered in a hushed whisper

"How do you know...?"

The trolls are agitated... this is not a good sign"

"What are you saying?" Marcus asked as his senses went on red alert

"There is death in the air...better we take cover and wait for whatever is causing the disturbance to reveal itself" Odd calmly replied whilst Marcus on the opposite hand reached for his Glock. After twenty minutes of waiting and standing quite still to no avail Odd decided that they should move once again, this time a little slower and a little more alert. Marcus resorted to stealth mode whereas Odd relied on his cloudberry concoction. It took half an hour for them to navigate the intensely eerie forest which emotionally drained both of them before Odd and Marcus reached the first of their destinations namely a field of flowering cloudberries.

"This is strange...very strange indeed" Odd remarked as they came to a halt

"Explain" Marcus asked short and sharp to the point as he strained his eyes to pick up the slightest indication of anyone's presence that might do them harm.

"The trolls have abandoned the cloudberry patch and appear to be in hiding. They don't usually behave this way"

"Can you talk to any one of them and find out what is wrong?" Marcus said playing along whilst his true self went into defensive mode and did a meticulous 360 degree sweep of their surroundings.

"I can't even see one...usually what happens is after the orches- trated 'alien UFO' light show the custom made matt black drones fly past here on their way back to base without causing us any disturbance, but tonight it is different and it worries me. I feel as though we shouldn't be here" Odd nervously replied as he struggled to decide whether to proceed or turn back. Marcus on the other hand feared not and played the waiting game.

"I wish I had a pair of night vision goggles or a Sophie" Marcus mentally sighed as he continued to strain his eyes so as to catch a glimmer of anything unusual but nothing on the ground revealed itself instead an ominous shape appeared in the distance over the mountain range that separated Norway from Sweden.

"Odd...over there...what do you think it is?" Marcus quietly attracted Odd's attention as he pointed to the object which was coming their way in a menacing fashion.

"Nothing like I've ever seen before...it's too big for a drone and it's silent and I feel it's looking for trouble" Odd replied panic stricken a reaction which Marcus had seen many a time before in the field in those who could not handle the perils of war

"Stand your ground until it passes...no better still lay down flat and pretend you're dead" Marcus whispered as he huddled up to a tree in such a way that it completely hid his presence from any form of prying eyes.

"I can't...I don't feel safe out here...in the open. There's an opening to a cave on the other side of the patch...that's where I think we should hold up" Odd anxiously and without thinking stuttered dismissing Marcus's invaluable advice.

Without waiting for Marcus to respond Odd sprinted for what he thought was salvation, the cave entrance was a good 200 meters away a distance that would under normal circumstances have taken a good ten minutes to traverse given the density and thorny nature of the cloudberry bushes. Odd however was not in a stable frame of mind which caused him to stumble and yelp as he got caught up in the bushes which ripped his clothes and tore at his flesh causing him to scream with pain. Marcus watched helplessly as his military training and personal reasoning prevented him from rendering any assistance. Odd bravely soldiered on until the black object hovered over him deciding what to do, it also had no choice given Odd's proximity to the treasure that it had been sent out to protect and without any indication to the contrary it lashed out and fried the odd Norwegian to a crisp leaving nothing more behind than a pile of ashes.

"What the fuck!" Marcus blasphemed as he witnessed the cruel execution and realised that his Glock was completely useless against this mighty adversary.

"Anti gravity technology coupled with advanced Tesla plasma ray courtesy of the Nazi's and WW2" Marcus quickly surmised as he decided to remain motionless until the black object was satisfied that no further threats to its cache of 'treasures' existed. Under such circumstances time dragged on very slowly and even it seemed stopped now and then whilst in total contrast Marcus's heart sped up fed and urged on by his rampant paranoia which in turn was nourished by his desire to know what and how sensitive and advanced the detecting devices were on board the black sinister object.

When everything had finally settled down including his heart rate Marcus very cautiously emerged from his hiding spot and wondered what was so important that it necessitated killing innocent people.

"You don't scare me for one minute" Marcus convinced himself having seen grittier times in the past which he briefly reflected on after which he fearlessly made a bee line for the mountains where Odd claimed there was an opening to a cave. Unlike Odd Marcus stepped carefully, silently and avoided being tangled up by the thorny bushes. He even entertained the thought that he might encounter a helpful troll to show him the way. "Strange how the trauma's of war play tricks on your mind" he thought as he remembered encountering demons and ghosts in the past that either protected or scooped up wounded souls.

As Marcus neared the steep mountain range he tripped on a rock and heard a yelp, wondering what he might have kicked he paused to see if it was an animal like a squirrel or baby deer. Two glowing red eyes greeted him instead followed by a strange language that made no sense to him at all and then as quickly as they mysteriously appeared they disappeared.

"This is becoming increasingly bizarre" Marcus muttered to himself and started to question his own sanity.

But then the phenomenon happened once again, this time without a yelp or so he thought. Two red eyes to his left repeatedly flashed at him and then vanished as soon as he neared them. Marcus concluded that these were not random occurrences and that in fact he was being guided to where someone wanted him to be. Bit by bit Marcus carefully followed the eyes in the night and made his way up the steep escarpment ever vigilant that the black object might return and consequently he continually calculated where he would hide should such an event occur?

The route up the mountain that was 'mapped out' for him was simultaneously tortuous and relatively easy. The 'helpers' guided Marcus in a fashion that provided ample foot holds and hand grips. After an hour of exhausting climbing Marcus reached a narrow opening which he realised was not the same as that which Odd spoke of and had run towards. Marcus gingerly peered inside and hoped that he was not venturing into the lair of a flesh eating animal such as a lynx, he withdrew his flashlight that Odd had provided and shone it down the length of the empty tunnel that had been sculptured by ice and time. Satisfied that all was clear he stepped inside and slowly made his way along it. He found that it sloped downwards and he speculated that in all probability it would most likely open up into a cavern. Marcus's prediction proved to be correct and within minutes of squeezing his way through the tight slit in the mountain side he felt the freedom of the expanse that greeted him even though it was drenched in darkness.

Never the fool that rushes in Marcus turned off his flashlight cautiously stepped forward and lowered himself to sit cross legged on the platform that overlooked the vast cave below. He patiently waited for his eyes to accustom themselves to the dark and allow him to locate the position of the motion detectors that were present on the cave walls six feet above its floor. These electronic devices bathed their surroundings with a mixture of red and green light. Marcus could quite plainly see that the caves floor was covered with an array of American made weaponry and its corresponding ammunition which he spied included depleted uranium armour piercing shells.

One pallet in particular attracted his attention as it emitted a blue light which automatically made Marcus think 'dirty bomb' and that he should limit his exposure to its harmful radiation especially if it contained caesium 137. Bearing that in mind Marcus became convinced that this arsenal of sophisticated weapons was meant to be and remain secret to both friend and foe and sealed shut until further notice.

"No wonder the trolls are mad...if I had this in my backyard I would feel the same" he quipped as he pondered his next move. Marcus's dilemma was answered in a heartbeat when a male dressed in black clothes appeared from nowhere and staggered about clutching at his chest in obvious extreme pain.

It was a twenty foot drop to the cave floor below something that Marcus was reluctant to undertake, he looked around to see if there was another avenue of descent but his rational mind exerted itself and decided that it was better to observe than engage.

Marcus watched intensely as the man struggled to hold onto life and without any warning Marcus felt a bead of heat run down the back of his head and neck which he instinctively recognised as originating from an infra red beam of light that sought to lock onto its prey and extinguish it forever. Marcus instantly rolled onto his left side, misjudged the width of the platform that he sat upon and fell fifteen feet, luckily it was not a vertical drop but a succession of steep narrow steps that repeatedly punched and kicked him in synch with explosions on the wall opposite him followed by more that appeared to occur outside until he landed heavily with at thud then everything went quiet. Badly bruised and winded Marcus shakily scrambled to his feet found his bearings and stealthily followed the unidentified man outside.

"Allah... forgive me...Allah...I am sorry...I shouldn't have listened to David" Marcus heard the man scream as he watched him vomit copious amounts of fresh blood.

Sensing that the depot of illegal weapons was not guarded and out of a sense of duty to alleviate suffering Marcus caught up with the man to see what he could do. By then both Marcus and the man realised that he was at death's door which had opened and was ready to accept the man's soul.

"Here...take this...show the world what assholes the Americans are....Allah's greatness will bring peace to the world..." The dying man said in a garbled fashion as he thrust a digital camera into Marcus's hand and died without any struggle. Marcus pocketed the electronic device, checked the unidentified man's vital signs for signs of life but he had well and truly passed back into the world from which he came.

Marcus stood up to reassess his situation and the likely cause of the outside explosions. Fifty meters to his right he detected the faint glow of burning metal and the outline of what he thought was the dark object that had previously vapourised Odd.

"Who, why and how...?" He thought as he breathed slowly and

deeply to alleviate his anxieties and then he concluded that someone had been shadowing them all along and he suddenly feared for his life.

Marcus reached for his trusty Glock, released its safety and attempted to load it but it failed. The weapon had jammed, under different circumstances he would have disassembled and reassembled the weapon, there was no time for that, survival was of the essence; whoever was present was expert and perfectly disguised to the point of being invisible.

"What's the matter Mr Rhodes having difficulty recognising me?" Major David Weir whispered from his hiding spot.

"What...?" Marcus replied somewhat startled

"I am the local who spoke to you earlier today at the convenience store, remember... cotton wool, water and Vaseline"

"How did you...?" Marcus asked as he secretly chastised himself for failing in his line of duty.

"You didn't think for one moment that I would allow you to proceed without backup" David Weir answered as he remained in his hiding spot.

"You knew all along" Marcus answered finally realising that he was conversing with the Major.

"I had my suspicions or should I more correctly say suspicions that belong to others which your movements proved correct"

"Movements that were cleverly orchestrated" Marcus deduced as it dawned on him that he had been manipulated from the very moment that his newly acquired colleagues left him.

"Perhaps it's time to compare notes...shall I or will you go first?" The Major asked still remaining in his hiding spot, something that started to irritate Marcus.

"I would prefer face to face" Marcus rightfully grizzled.

"Come over here then" The Major beckoned as he activated a small pocket torch and flashed it three times.

"Cosy spot" Marcus quipped once he reached the Major.

"It has its advantages" The Major replied and handed over a thin hooded jacket and a pair of pants.

"What are these for?" Marcus frowned.

"Prevents detection by thermal imaging"

"Clever" Marcus replied as he quickly donned the non reflective hi-tech garments which the Major also wore.

"Well just don't stand there looking oh so pretty, tell me what you found" The Major impatiently barked to which Marcus handed over the digital camera that the dying man had given him as he detailed his own personal eye witness account and then remained silent as the major replayed the camera's footage.

"Looks to me as though someone wants to play nasty, I think we should call in the troops"

"Surely not the Americans" Marcus seriously questioned.

"I thought about that meaning if they are the guilty party then most probably they are on their way which gives us about one to three hours depending upon what they send out to retrieve the downed drone. We are approximately 150 kilometres from Trondheim, a helicopter could reach us in forty five minutes depending on how fast they scramble without drawing attention to themselves, failing that a truck or van plus trekking through the forest will take much longer. I was considering alerting the Norwegian emergency services namely Police and Rescue" The major replied as he retrieved his highly sophisticated phone reserved purely for military use.

But before he could use it Marcus roughly snatched it from his hand and said "A strategic move perhaps but not a particularly wise geo-political one"

"I think you are exceeding your authority soldier"

"Not if we are working as a team" Marcus wisely countered which caused the Major to reconsider his position.

"Very well soldier over to you"

"With respect Sir...what is our current location in relation to the Norwegian Swedish border?" Marcus bluntly asked as he returned the Major's phone.

"We are well and truly inside the Swedish side" Major Weir replied rather surprised with the result once he had activated the device.

"Then....?" Marcus smartly asked

"We contact the Swedish authorities" The Major wisely answered.

"Precisely...thereby side stepping any attempt by the Americans or highly ranked corrupt Norwegian politicians to squash any thorough investigations and the discovery of the cache of weapons that are illegally parked according to international law"

3

SWEDISH RHAPSODY

Within thirty minutes of the Major making the call and giving the co-ordinates of his position the ever vigilant and highly efficient Swedish Mountain Rescue was the first to arrive at the 'accident scene' where the Major pretended he was administering first aid by keeping the fallen 'rock climber' warm by covering him with a blanket.

"What do we have here?" A very athletic middle aged male Swede who carried a comprehensive medical kit asked as he briskly strode towards the Major.

"I came across this man about forty minutes ago and immediately raised the alarm"

"You were lucky to get through, reception is quite poor in these parts which makes it difficult sometimes for us to locate badly injured victims" The Swede answered as he gestured for his colleagues to bring the stretcher.

"It would seem so" The Major answered even though he knew better and watched as the Swede went about his work expertly with torch in hand

"Quite a lot of blood, did you see what happened?"

"I remember seeing him stumble down the side of the mountain and vomit profusely. Being dark I thought it was food that he brought up. He then staggered about and shouted something about others being stranded above or elsewhere or in danger, I am not quite sure it was all so sudden and unexpected" The Major replied in a distressed tone of voice

"I am afraid it's too late for this man"

"What do you mean?" The Major asked pretending to be shocked

"He is dead no doubt about that and by the looks of it did not die as a result of a fall" The Swede seriously answered as he effortlessly turned the deceased man over to reveal a horrific radiation burn across his upper back "We will need to wait for the police and coroner" He then said as he continued to examine the corpse

"Goodness me...I've never seen anything like that before" The major said as the Swede shone his torch over the deceased's injuries

"Not unless you have worked in a nuclear facility" The Swede grimly answered before he stood up to greet the warming rays of the early morning sun which had just started to peer over the distant horizon.

"Death gives way to life just like night precedes day" The Major prophetically said as he also stood up

Marcus meanwhile was becoming increasingly restless in his hiding spot and wondered whether he should make his presence felt especially when the Police arrived even though he had been given strict instructions to stay put.

It wasn't long thereafter that a solitary heavy duty Swedish automobile with four occupants pulled up at the scene. The middle aged paramedic promptly engaged them and within minutes the group had formulated an investigative plan which they would all follow that fitted in with the deceased's location and surrounding area. They showed no interest in the Major who to them was nothing more than a passerby of no particular note apart from taking down a brief statement from him and recording his address details they preferred him to depart the scene in case he contaminated it further.

Major David Weir left without a whimper confident in the knowledge that the pedantic Swedes would follow the blood trail and discover the exit point in the mountain that would ultimately lead them to the stash of illegal weapons. He also believed that forensics would discover Odd's remnants and the downed black object which would further intensify the magnitude and importance of the killing zone. With those thoughts in mind David Weir nonchalantly disappeared from view and nestled next to Marcus in the well camouflaged hidden location that overlooked the crime scene to while away the time until the troops arrived all of which he would record by using the dead man's digital camera.

"This is beautiful" The Major cheerfully said

"You're crazy! I'm tired, miserable, cold and hungry and dying for a crap!" Marcus replied in contrast

"There's nothing stopping you...off you go then"

"Won't I expose myself?"

"Only if you want to...but I somehow think they are too preoccupied down there to notice anything that you might have to offer" The Major replied tongue in cheek as he produced a small folded up carry bag

"What's this for?" Marcus asked frustrated by the Major's sense of humour

"Go use the green toilet and then find plenty of berries...there must be lots around"

"Berries...?"

"Yes berries...high in sugars, antioxidants and water, instant energy in every little bugger...forgotten your survival skills already...?" The Major flippantly replied and waved Marcus away, which made him wonder how long the Major intended keeping the Swedes under surveillance.

David Weir came well equipped with a small but powerful set of binoculars which he used judiciously to spy on those below

"Come on my cunning conquering Vikings, do your stuff, take

the bait, it's not that difficult, there's seven of you, let's get on with it, you're close, very close, that's right, slightly more to your left and you're in!" The Major mumbled as he observed and mentally directed one of the policemen to discover the well disguised exit point.

"Go on...say it"

"The blood trail stops here...the wall is solid" The policeman shouted to his colleagues

"That's not I wanted to hear...damn Americans made the fucking exit door seamless...damn...damn...damn!" The Major bitterly cursed until he heard

"We might have to investigate the ridge above us, I can see traces of blood up there and there appears to be a faint outline of an opening about 50 meters further up" The Swedish policeman said as he stepped back and shielded his eyes from the intense early morning sun.

"That's better...now you're starting to do your job" David Weir mumbled under his breath and watched as the policeman looked for a way to scale the mountain side. As he studied the terrain he was joined by one of the Swedish Mountain Rescue men who was more experienced in these tasks

"What are you wanting to do?" He asked in Swedish

"See that faint outline up there I think it is an entrance to a cave"

"Is that where you think we will find the nuclear bomb?" The mountain rescue man joked

"Either that or Thor's hammer"

"In that case it's a simple skip, hop and jump up the well trodden path"

"What path? There is no path it's a maze of rocks, cracks and fissures"

"That's because all you policemen have blinkers on, you're all about black and white, no grey areas for you, I wonder about your lot sometimes" The mountain rescue man cuttingly remarked and set off to scale the steep ascent without any tools.

"Fucking smart arsed goat...!" The policemen swore as he watched the rescue man easily ascend the treacherous mountain side. He was followed shortly after as if on cue by his colleague who wisely brought along ropes and the appropriate climbing gear.

Marcus meanwhile after having relieved himself started to hunt for berries. He was familiar with blueberries, raspberries and strawberries, anything else would require passing the skin, lips, and gums allergy test before being consumed.

"I suppose one or two handfuls per person will keep us going until we return to civilization" He convinced himself as he merrily picked away and sampled the forest's fresh produce not realising that he had encroached on someone else's territory.

Suddenly without any warning Marcus was violently hit from behind and bowled over. Dazed and disorientated he scrambled to his feet as best as he could in readiness to face his assailant but it came at him once again from his blind side and sent him sprawling. Not knowing what he was dealing with Marcus picked up the most readily available weapon namely a length of broken branch and swung it wildly in all different directions hoping that he would make contact with his attacker.

After a few minutes of frantic and fruitless effort everything went silent, Marcus stood his ground and held the branch high in readiness to strike, from the corner of his eye he caught a glimpse of a wild boar smugly strolling away with five piglets in tow and he sensed it was thinking "Job done time to move on"

Afraid that he had been gorged by a tusk Marcus checked his anatomy for any signs of injury before picking up his bag of berries and limping his way back to the Major.

"What the hell happened to you?" The Major asked as he gazed upon Marcus's dishevelled appearance and awkward gait

"Had an encounter with a pig"

'You certainly know how to have fun" The Major glibly replied as he avoided eye contact and suppressed his laughter

43

"Any activity...?"

"Plenty...our mountain rescue team it appears has discovered the illegal depot of arms which caused quite a stir. I suspect they have alerted CBN which as you know is the Swedish armed forces centre for protection against chemical, biological, radiation and nuclear treats. I predict an advanced team will be flown in within the next two hours to secure the area, additional ground equipment and staff will follow by road around mid afternoon; which means it's time for us to leave, I don't particularly want to become implicated and needlessly detained and questioned by any one of those down there. How did you go with breakfast? I suppose bacon and eggs are out of the question?"

"Berries as requested Sir...!" Marcus replied somewhat insolently

"That will have to do...remember the way back?"

"Yes I marked my passage....."

"With a broken twig or two...." the Major interrupted

"Correct" Marcus answered feeling somewhat annoyed and inadequate

"Change of plan, we'll go this way instead" The Major said as he helped himself to a handful of dew covered fruits of the forest.

"What about my motor bike?"

"Probably stolen by now" The Major dryly said

"What...!"

"Can't trust the locals especially when the keys are left in the ignition" The Major whimsically answered as he strode along.

"Why do something so silly?" Marcus asked a little irritated by the revelation as he felt for the motorcycles keys which he knew were in his trouser pocket

"To avoid being confronted by the locals as to the last known whereabouts of one burnt out alcoholic" David Weir cleverly suggested.

"We wouldn't want that now would we?" Marcus answered playing along

"Especially if we are meant to be a covert undercover operation"

"Then let's keep it that way" Marcus almost sarcastically replied as he doubled his pace to keep up with the Major

"Good berries by the way"

"Grew them myself, handpicked you know" Marcus quietly fibbed

"I would never have guessed" The Major answered as he helped himself to another handful and then offered the remainder to his subordinate officer who gladly accepted them.

It became obvious to Marcus as they walked along that the Major had prior knowledge of the area in which they trudged because it wasn't very long before they reached a well trodden dirt track that offered a straight forward and clean exit from the forest and its thick undergrowth. Marcus could see that the track was used by all manner of people, animals and vehicles, for he spotted horse, dog and deer droppings, wooden cart, off road four wheel drive trucks and motor cycle tyre tracks.

"Mind your step...don't want you stepping into any shit" The Major cheerfully said as he guided Marcus along

"I've had enough of that for one day" Marcus metaphorically replied as he struggled to keep pace with the Major

"Better days ahead, I can feel it in my bones" The Major optimistically said as he briefly looked around to make certain that they were in the correct place and that their transport was not far away.

Marcus then realised that he had gone without sleep since the early hours of the previous morning and he suddenly felt more tired than he previously imagined.

"I think it's bedtime for you soldier, you can stretch out once we reach my car, not far now" The Major confirmed in an effort to make Marcus feel better and encourage him to continue soldiering on.

Within fifteen minutes much to Marcus's relief they reached a dilapidated Land Rover Defender which had seen better days. It appeared as though it had over the years been used as a target for battering rams as it was severely dented but remained functional

"Don't worry it looks worse than it actually is much like yourself, here climb on board, I'll just take my tool kit away and you can stretch yourself out, there's plenty of room in the back" The Major politely said as he opened the tailgate and rearranged a few bulky items so as to allow Marcus to make himself comfortable. David Weir smiled as he watched Marcus's body rapidly go limp as his mind descended into a deep much deserved sleep "You have done a good day's work soldier, rest now because you will bloody well need it" the Major whispered and then set about preparing the next phase of his project which he knew would more than likely shake the gates of hell. He then climbed into the Land Rovers driver's seat and closed the door.

"You might look beaten up but you certainly have a big heart" David Weir whispered as he turned the ignition key to fire up the land Rovers motor, a simple yet powerful act that signifies mans incredible ability to create. The Major then selected first gear, released the handbrake and made a U turn to drive to the main road that joined highway FV30 which would take them to Storen, a ninety minute journey at the speed limit or longer if you wished to take your time and enjoy the countryside, on this occasion David Weir drove as if he had a baby on board, one that needed a good rest.

After two hours the Major deviated from FV30 and entered Storen where he knew he would find a substantial breakfast and a retail post office in which to drop off his package, so he thought, Marcus however had other ideas and remained non responsive. The Major out of respect changed the order of his preferences by dropping off the parcel and then deciding to drive to Trondheim which he estimated would give Marcus an additional hour to sleep if not more, perhaps then he would wake up and join the Major for brunch or an early lunch whichever one suited him.

The Major's reasoning proved correct, Marcus did indeed stir once they entered Trondheim's city limits.

"Where are we?" He blearily asked

"Trondheim"

"Oh brilliant...another day in paradise...!"

"You must be hungry" The Major deduced ignoring Marcus's sarcasm

"Me... not at all...! How could I be? I've feasted on berries that are full of antioxidants, sugars, water, instant energy in every one of the little fuckers" Marcus acidly replied

"Well if that's the case there's no point in me shouting you bacon and eggs, waffles with jam and cream and a pot of freshly brewed Jamaican coffee"

"Make that hot chocolate and I'll reconsider your offer" Marcus replied playing along

"Agreed"

"Any idea where or what the others are doing?"

"They should have stayed at the safe house last night and this morning be mingling with the anti American protestors outside of the military base"

"Does that mean they had dinner at the safe house?"

"No... Lodgings only" The Major replied

"What about breakfast?" Marcus asked out of curiosity

"That is included"

"Let me guess, tea and coffee making facilities, toaster, frozen croissants"

"How astute of you Mr Rhodes"

"I get around"

"So it would seem" The Major replied

"Will they be joining us?"

"That is a good idea" The Major agreed

"Will you make them privy to what we found?" Marcus seriously asked

"Not as yet, it might complicate things"

"Why?"

"I can't say at this stage, give it a day or two" The Major mysteriously answered

"Very well" Marcus replied and took what the Major had just said to be an indirect order

David Weir had no difficulty in locating the swarm of protestors as he drove through the streets of Trondheim as they had provided more than adequate road signage which pointed the way to where they had set up camp much to the authorities' sanguine. Anya and Brit were present in the crowd and appeared to have made many new friends and looked as though they had been readily accepted by members of the group which surprisingly was made up of some serious looking people.

Once the Major had parked the battered Land Rover Marcus walked over to where the girls were standing and behaved as if he was their beloved relative by hugging and kissing them affectionately to which the girls responded in kind. After being introduced to several members of the Keep Norway Neutral party Marcus excused himself and invited his 'sisters' to join him and their 'uncle' for morning tea somewhere warm and cosy which many of the protestors overheard and they immediately invited themselves along for a change of scenery. This played perfectly into the girls hand and they warmly invited everyone willing in the group to join them.

"Where's a good place to eat?" Marcus openly asked those around him

"The city is a little too far from here, there is a nice Italian cafe in the airport terminal, we can walk and talk along the way and get to know each other better" One of the protestors warmly replied as he smiled broadly and pointed to the terminal.

"Excellent I'll just go and fetch our uncle" Marcus convincingly said

"Get him to leave his car where it is, it will be safe there and attract no parking tickets, this is neutral ground" The same protestor proudly answered in a manner that suggested they had put it up the authorities.

"Shall do"

"Hey wait for me" Brit enthusiastically pleaded as she grabbed hold of Marcus's arm and slowed his progress

"Always" Marcus replied in a sincere tone of voice, a response that caught Brit slightly off guard

Anya and the others meanwhile waited patiently as Marcus and Brit collected their 'uncle' who was rather curious as to the where-abouts of Nicoli which was the very first thing that he asked Brit in a low voice whilst he embraced her.

'I honestly don't know. We lost contact with him last night after we left the hotel where we had dinner. Nicoli became very friendly with two men who claimed to be Serbs on holiday in Norway. They were getting on like a house on fire downing one drink after another, telling stories, laughing and joking around and asked Nicoli to join them for one drink, Nicoli said he would follow later but he didn't come home and we haven't been able to raise him on his phone. We even returned to the hotel early this morning to see if he spent the night there or if his motorbike was still around, but no trace and not much help from the staff" Brit explained feeling guilty for not providing better news and allowing Nicoli to break ranks.

"You did well under the circumstances, I am sure he will turn up one way or another" The Major softy reassured her and then went about the business of securing the Land Rover before they all strolled over to where Anya and her newly acquired friends were standing.

4

SINS OF YOUR FOREFATHERS

As they walked along towards the terminal Major Weir slowed his pace to distance himself from the protestors who lead the way. It was clear to Anya and Brit that he was preoccupied and distressed about Nicoli's whereabouts which was further magnified as the Major was unable to raise him on his ultra sophisticated mobile phone.

"No luck either?" Brit commented as she looked over the Major's shoulder and watched as he tried all manner of avenues to locate the missing operative

"Afraid not, it appears as if his phone is dead"

"Flat battery...?"

"Far worse than that I'm afraid to say"

"Explain" Brit asked rather curious by the Major's response

"Each one of the mobile phones I gave you is fitted with a highly advanced locational circuitry imbedded in the phones makeup making it virtually undetectable. It even has its own independent power supply so that in the event of power failure it will continue to broadcast its location for up to a week"

"In other words you are suggesting Nicoli's phone has been destroyed"

"Deliberately" The Major grimly affirmed

"Why?"

"I imagine to obliterate his existence..."

"Oh dear" Brit sighed whilst Marcus thought "Is that how you kept tabs on me"

"Precisely which leads me to ask did either one of you remember seeing the 'Serbs' that Nicoli agreed to have a drink with prior to last night's dinner?"

"I don't" Brit was quick to answer whereas Anya mulled the question over for a moment before committing herself.

"I see you think otherwise" Major Weir observed.

"Yes it was at the petrol station when we were standing in line waiting to order coffees. Nicoli had unzipped his jacket and was next to me when a stranger who resembled one of the 'Serbs' said 'nice lucky charm'. He wasn't referring to me but to the four leaf clover that Nicoli had hanging around his neck. I remember thinking later on in the hotel 'haven't I seen you before and you don't look Serbian to me more Middle Eastern if anything'"

"How did Nicoli react?"

"He simply grunted and avoided looking at the man who said nothing further"

"I see...so was it a coincidence that they crossed paths at the hotel? Do you remember anything about their transportation?" The Major asked seeking more detail

"Nothing at all"

"Where were they seated in the petrol station's cafe?"

"I can't remember largely because they were of no interest to us, as far as I am concerned it was a casual encounter"

"Did they follow you out when you left" The major persisted in his line of questioning

"Not that I can recall"

"What about being shadowed by any sort of vehicle as you travelled towards Trondheim?" The Major asked as a test of Anya's observational skills

"I hardly think so"

"Why is that?" The Major calmly asked

"We played a high speed cat and mouse game along the highway" Anya answered with a blank face in an attempt to hide her embarrassment

"Nothing untoward at the safe house or its surrounding...?"

"Nothing"

"What she says is true" Brit interrupted

"It would appear so but I also conclude that whilst you played your games you dropped your guard but then again I suppose you wanted to fit in and not appear to be undercover cops"

"Correct" Brit answered on behalf of both of them and kept walking with Anya in tow leaving the Major to ponder their situation and the unanswered questions namely was this newly formed unit already under surveillance and if so by whom?

Twelve hours earlier Nicoli had similar thoughts once he realised that his drink had been spiked and that his body was sliding into a zombie like state. He cursed himself for being less than vigilant but then how was he to know that his family's past had caught up with him and he would ultimately pay the price.

The 'devil's breath' tasteless and odourless is the world's scariest drug so potent that it causes its victims to give up their free will and even their memory. Its active ingredient scopolamine plays havoc with neurotransmitters in the brain, used as a truth serum by the Nazi's during WW2; it was later employed by the CIA during controversial behavioural engineering experiments in the 1960's. Since then it has become one of the favourite tools for the Colombian drug lords, but it has a downside, namely that the victims can become unpredictably agitated, super aggressive and violently turn on their perpetrators.

Once the 'Serbs' had discreetly smuggled Nicoli out of the hotel and transported him into the depths of their sound proof black house, they with the use of suitable instruments went about prodding and probing his family's memories.

"Well Mr Bizica who would have thought that standing in line waiting to buy a cup of coffee would have yielded such a magnificent result" One of the 'Serbs' arrogantly boasted as he approached Nicoli who was well and truly strapped down in an seemingly immovable steel chair.

"I don't know what you are talking about" Nicoli weakly replied as he struggled to keep his mental faculties intact

"Let me enlighten you" The same 'Serb' said as he grabbed hold of Nicoli's amulet and ripped it from his body cutting the back of Nicoli's neck

"That hurt" He whimpered as he felt flesh warm blood trickle down his spine

"That's minor compared to what awaits you Mr Bizica!" the false 'Serb' barked as he dangled the amulet before Nicoli's eyes.

"I still don't know what you are talking about"

"What's this?" The false 'Serb' shouted

'A four leaf clover"

"A what...?"

"Four leaf clover"

"But it's more than that isn't it Mr Bizica?"

"Why do you keep calling me that name?" Nicoli answered changing the subject

"Because Mr Bizica that is your real name!"

"My name....my name......is..." Nicoli struggled to remember

"Is Bizica....bi...zi...ca...! The false 'Serb' repeatedly shouted as spittle flew from his mouth and his eyes bulged with uncontrollable anger. Meanwhile the other false 'Serb' left his post at the gas fuelled blacksmiths forge that he had fired up and joined his comrade "what's in the middle of this four leaf clover?" He calmly asked in contrast

"A large diamond" Nicoli replied in a slurred manner

"What's around the diamond?"

"I don't know some arty- farty mishmash, it doesn't mean anything to me" Nicoli responded

"But it matters to us Mr Bizica!"

"I'm so happy for you" Nicoli taunted his fanatical captors as a pawn might threaten a Queen on the chessboard

"How did you come by this?"

"I can't remember" Nicoli falsely answered as he felt his body starting to respond to his higher control

"We can and we will instruct you how to remember and we encourage you to confirm what we are about to tell you" The second 'Serb' arrogantly said as he pointed for his colleague to fetch the nail gun, it was then that Nicoli realised that his hands and fingers were splayed out on wooden boards and held firmly in place with Velcro straps.

"Firstly this is one of a kind, a unique Hamsa fashioned by a high class jeweller for a very rich Croatian Jew whose wealth was unlawfully acquired by the Ustashe under the command of one Myron Bizica who operated in the Jasenovac concentration camp during WW2"

"Fuck....they're fucking Mossad Nazi hunters...Fuck!" Nicoli mentally screamed as terror flooded his body and his mind went blank with fear.

"Are you listening to me.....?" The Mossad agent violently shouted as he attempted to physically shake Nicoli out of his stupor but to no avail "How much Devil's Breath did you give this Goyim?" He asked as he turned to face his accomplice

"Enough"

"Try too much....now what?" He asked frustrated by the progress of their interrogation

"We bring him around with this" The first Mossad agent sadistically replied with a wry smile as he stuck a needle into Nicoli's vein and administered the contents of the syringe which contained a mixture of physostigmine and amphetamine

"Fuck...where the hell am I?" Nicoli roared with pain as he wildly thrashed about and attempted to break free

"Might have given him too much" The same agent said as he battled to control Nicoli's rages which appeared to be increasing in strength

"Can you fucking get it right you fucking dumb ass!" The second agent angrily scolded his partner and impatiently waited until it appeared that Nicoli had settled down and then he started to grill Nicoli once again "Now where were we? That's right...remember the fabulously rich Jew and how his treasures were stolen from him, well it so happens that we came across a photographic inventory courtesy of the jeweller who took immense pride in his work, and what belonged to our rich Croatian Jew. It appears that Ustashe did the same and it also mentions who was in charge of keeping them safe. It seems your Grandfather Myron Bizica generously distributed many items amongst his family members which means it points to you Mr Bizica"

"Fuck off! I'm not telling you nothing and you can tell that to all of your shits standing around you! Nicoli blurted out like a possessed madman

"Oops" the other Mossad agent said

"What do you mean oops?"

"Might have given him too much...I think he is having a psychotic attack"

"For the last fucking time can you get it right?"

"Alright...alright...what works in these circumstances is a little pain...one nail here and one nail there should do it" The Mossad agent gingerly replied as he used the nail gun to drive a nail into the first knuckle of Nicoli's left index and middle fingers shattering the bones in the process.

"You fucking Jew scumbags now you're crucifying me...You... you...fucking Jews!"

Nicoli screamed with rage as his body went into overdrive and developed an immense drug fuelled strength that enabled him to partially break free. With his free leg he brutally kicked the agent that stood in front of him in the groin propelling him backwards and causing him to collide with the blacksmiths forge and with his free hand Nicoli grabbed hold of the nail gun that the other agent was holding turned it on him and drove two nails into his face.

Nicoli then wrenched the chair free from its housings and attempted to rid himself of it entirely and as he did so yelled at the top of his voice "You money loving scum I will teach you what it means to pick on the wrong person as he first kicked the Mossad agent who was down with nails in his face squarely in the rib cage breaking three ribs two of which pierced one of his lungs before he stormed towards the other Mossad agent who had collided with the blacksmith furnace in such a way that it scattered white hot coals and pokers all over the place before it collapsed on top of him and burnt him severely. Smoke, dust and the smell of impending death and burnt flesh filled the air as the two highly trained killers called on their physical reserves in order to survive. If this was a case of mistaken identity it had gone horribly wrong, perhaps he was nothing more than a mercenary a soldier of war the spoils of which were his to keep, no matter what, it was time to do or die and with such thoughts in mind the agent whose lung had been punctured remained prostrate he could not breathe as he was drowning in his own blood whereas his colleague scrambled to his feet grabbed a white hot poker that lay close to him and challenged Marcus for the right to life.

"This will be one fucking chess game in which there will be no winners" Nicoli had already predetermined in his mind, with his left hand nailed to the armrest, his leg tied to one chair leg and his waist firmly roped in Nicoli was unable to free himself completely nevertheless he spun on the spot and used the chair as a weapon to protect himself by pushing its legs into the Mossad agent's back as he flew past. The Israeli tried to compensate for the shove but was unable to do so; he lost his balance and crashed heavily to the floor.

"So what's does it feel like to be on the receiving end you bag of shit?" Nicoli roughly asked as he towered over his victim with nail gun in hand and used his pain to drive him on.

"I will kill you" The Israeli violently threatened

"First you have to be able to walk!" Nicoli shouted as he fired two nails into the Israeli's lower spine instantly paralysing his legs

"You bastard....I'll...."

"Do nothing...your days are over...Zionist pig!" Nicoli mercilessly shouted back as he spat on the man and fired another two nails into the apex of his spine rendering him a complete quadriplegic

Relieved that it was over Nicoli then sat down to admire his handiwork before attempting to set himself free once and for all, the other Mossad agent meanwhile started to laugh in between coughing which Nicoli callously took no notice off until the Israeli starting counting down as if there was an imminent launch.

"Counting your last seconds...?" Nicoli sarcastically commented as he looked around for a way out of the basement come dungeon that he had been so crudely deposited into, but none made themselves visible.

"Air tight, water tight and sound proof, a chamber of horrors for horrors run by horrible ugly people" Nicoli painfully muttered whilst the dying Israeli switched from counting to repeatedly saying tick tock in an increasingly louder voice which made Nicoli realise his situation namely one of living on borrowed time which came to a sudden and abrupt end which started with a spark, then a flash of blinding light followed by intense heat, deafening noise and finally never ending darkness for all concerned.

5

NOT EVERYONE IS CHICKEN

Robert Larssen or 'chook' as he was affectionately known, was enjoying his customary 1am romp with his latest girlfriend Svetlana who was meant to be nothing more than payment in lieu of a trumped up traffic violation but it turned out to be something completely else.

"I'm glad you booked me for 'speeding'" she purred as Robert stroked the inside of her exposed thigh

"Me too"

"Are we using hand cuffs tonight?" Svetlana teased as she ran her tongue over her teeth

"How bad a girl have you been?" Robert asked

"Very..."

"Then we must do something about it" he erotically replied in a low voice as he placed one hand over one of her naked breasts and was about to kiss her fully on the mouth when his mobile phone started chattering incessantly. Robert reluctantly let go of Svetlana and answered the call as it was expected of him to be on call 24 hours of the day no matter what.

"Yes...what is it?" he roughly barked sounding quite annoyed

"Good morning to you too...." Marianne his long time colleague who manned the communications desk at Trondheim municipal police station brightly said

"Alright fill me in" He sighed knowing full well that his extended love making session had come to an abrupt end

"I thought that was your job" Svetlana mischievously whispered as she nibbled on his ear lobe and reached around to grab hold of his erect penis which had decided to stand down

"There has been numerous reports of an explosion near Hell on one of the converted farming estates, I think by the sounds of it, it's that exclusive resort David's Camp you know the one that I mean" Marianne slowly explained as she made reference to the notes in front of her

"I'll meander over there and report my findings" Robert said without any further ado

"It shouldn't take you long judging by the GPS location of your phone; by the way what's your friend's name again?" Marianne asked with a tinge of jealousy in her voice

"Barbara..." Robert abruptly said as he struggled to remember Svetlana's Christian name, an answer that earned him a very quick smack to the head from his 'jilted' lover

"Guess it's time to leave" he said as he nursed his sore head

"Pig...!" Svetlana cursed as she covered her naked body and stormed into the bathroom to return moments later with her electric toothbrush.

"You're going to brush your teeth in bed?" Robert asked both surprised and confused by her actions.

"Not at all...this is my male substitute...off you go and do your Polis duties...I might think about you as I pleasure myself" Svetlana coldly remarked and waved Robert away who simply shook his head and resigned himself to the fact that he would never fully understand women something that was not uncommon amongst those who served to protect their nation's security.

Robert Larssen knew the way to David's Camp very well as he had spent many years as a youngster playing hide and seek in the surrounding fields and forests during school holidays and summer vacation with his friends and their dogs. He felt sad that it had become a weekend retreat for the political elite but then that was the way of the world money brought favours and friendships something that he did not approve of having seen plenty of it during his stint in the Norwegian armed forces where he acquired his nick name 'chook'. He would have preferred rooster or cock for that matter but people believed he and his appendage were not up to the mark.

Not knowing the source of the explosion Robert decided to park his police van some distance from the timber lodge and use the cover of darkness to his advantage. He very quietly exited the van, donned a bullet proof vest; made certain his telecommunications equipment was fully functional, removed his pistol from its holster and slowly walked towards the lodge whilst he held a powerful LED torch in one hand.

The night was still except for a faint breeze that carried the slightest suggestion that a fire or explosion had indeed occurred on the premises. As he neared the house he detected smoke rising from the basement vents and he noticed that the windows above these were distorted and broken. Instead of storming into the house Robert decided to walk around and check the exterior of the building and as he did so he came across Nicoli's BMW motorcycle parked next to the latest high powered Jeep AWD off road vehicle. He immediately contacted Marianne for a vehicle licence check and then he set about looking for any signs of life by firstly shining his torch through the windows before entering the house through the rear door which was unlocked.

Robert gingerly stepped inside with his revolver at the ready for this as far as he was concerned was another case of expect the unexpected. The building groaned as he walked on its polished floor boards indicating that it had clearly been injured and struggled to keep itself together. Each room that he entered was a shambles, stuff lay strewn about, furniture had been shifted, there was no power, all electrical devices stood dormant, the only light that he detected was that which had filtered past the door to the basement and even then it was erratic.

Robert decided against his better judgement to investigate what awaited him in the basement as all other rooms had yielded nothing except for one which was not meant to be found namely a priest's hole filled with highly advanced long range telecommunications devices. Being ex army he was able to identify some of the equipment but luckily curiosity got the better of him and he telephoned his long standing friend Morten to help him with the rest.

"Hi Morten...'chook' here...I know it's late but then I also know what you get up to most mornings around this time... you randy bastard...I've just sent you some images to your phone...mind telling me what they are?" Robert warmly said as soon as his friend answered the call but did not expect his friend to react as violently as he did.

"You stupid fucker have you any idea of what you've stumbled on...get out of where ever you are right now!" Morten screamed with the utmost urgency

Realising that Morten was deadly serious and not waiting for any further explanations Robert instantly bolted out of the secret hiding place and sprinted towards the rear door which he knew was open, as soon as he reached it he heard the chilling sound of a detonator go off followed by the inevitable catastrophic kaboom that blew the priest's hole into hundreds of pieces of debris that flew in all directions shredding anything in their path. Robert flew through the door assisted by the explosion's pressure wave and he instinctively dived to the ground as the deluge of fragments whizzed past him at supersonic speed. Momentarily deafened and dazed by the loudness of the bang he looked back to see the building on fire and he mentally thanked Morten for saving his life even though he was miles away.

"Well Chook...what have you found?" Marianne cheerfully said as she answered his call minutes later when he had regained his senses.

"A bit of a mess...might be a good idea to send the fire brigade and an ambulance'" he answered in an understated fashion

"Are there many casualties?"

"Only me..." he answered in dead pan fashion

"How badly are you hurt?"

"I'll live...perhaps you could organise Geir and Havard to assist me with the crime scene"

"Is it that serious?" Marianne inquired as her switch board lit up with many people reporting the incident

"Yes I think we're in for a surprise as to what the occupants got up to at David's Camp" Robert answered and then laughed at what he had just said

"What's so funny?"

"Guess I'm glad just to be alive" Robert suggested but in reality he saw the funny side of David's camp as meaning that David was gay

It didn't take very long for the emergency services to arrive, the ambulance was first whilst the fire brigade took its time after all it wasn't a forest fire or the height of summer and David's Camp from memory was a small isolated wooden cottage that was in need of some repair, their presence was more for mopping up, making the place relatively safe for investigators and filling in paperwork.

Although Robert had assumed that he was physically fine in actually fact he wasn't. The blast had ruptured his left ear drum and inflicted several shrapnel wounds to the back of his unprotected arms, legs and embarrassingly his buttocks, but not sufficiently serious enough to hospitalize him; once Geir and Havard arrived the three of them roped off the perimeter of the remnants of the building while the firemen continued with their work. It was now an official crime scene that necessitated 24 hours police presence until their investigations were completed.

"It's quite a mess, what do you think we will find inside?" Geir asked Robert who looked at him sideways

"There are no insides as you can plainly see!" Robert sternly corrected his junior officer

"I meant inside the basement"

"What basement?" Robert sharply asked

"Every Norwegian house has a basement, this is no exception; look you can see its vents in the walls just below floor level" Havard quickly answered on behalf of Geir who felt a little awkward as this was his first major investigation

"Good observation, bear that in mind both of you, be meticulous, thorough to the extreme, look for anything unusual as to explain what this place was being used for. The firemen will report on the likely causes of the fire and list the number of casualties if any. Remember wear gloves at all times, do not contaminate anything, bag and number all relevant items of interest" Robert briefed his fellow policemen who stood at attention, listened carefully and watched as the firemen made certain that the site was free of any dangers.

Robert Larssen had a slight inkling from his army days that the explosion that he survived was probably caused by a military grade explosive, C4 or HMX perhaps specifically chosen to obliterate the contents of the priest's hole when it had been penetrated by unauthorized individuals who sought to discover its darkest secrets. This notion was confirmed by Morten who telephoned Robert well before the emergency services arrived to make certain he was intact and to explain the harshness of his previous response. Robert was both eternally grateful and understanding. Morten then went onto to identify what Robert had photographed and confirm that it was signature Mossad long range equipment which raised the question as to what were they doing on Norwegian soil? Was it not bad enough that the Americans were already spying on the Norwegians? Secretively Robert was very supportive and sympathetic to the Keep

Norway Neutral action group.

"I see we have been given the all clear" Havard eagerly announced as he acknowledged the fireman who gave him the thumbs up.

"Very well gentleman let us proceed, grab your equipment and go find me that needle in the haystack" Robert metaphorically commanded as he directed Geir to concentrate on inspecting the debris outside of the house whilst he and Havard would attempt to locate the entrance to and enter the basement

"What do I look for?" Geir nervously asked not wishing to look naive nor make a mistake

"Intact CD's, thumb drives, external hard drives, storage devices would be very useful" Robert bluntly said

"Thank you Sir" Geir politely replied and set about doing his duty

Havard meanwhile had already scaled the remnants of the cottage like a blood hound and easily located the entrance to the basement after shifting a number of planks and beams that obstructed their way.

"Ready for a gruesome scene...?" Robert asked making light of the situation

"Horror movies are my forte!" Havard boldly replied

"Very good.....after you" Robert smiled as he allowed his junior officer to descend the stairs with torch in hand while he held back and waited for the inevitable three phase outcome.

First "What fucking satanic monster did this...." second the sound of violent vomiting followed by the thud of a person hitting the ground once they had fainted.

"Guess he'll have to watch smell'o'vision in future" Robert chuckled as he entered the death filled chamber of horrors and shone his torch around to reveal three badly charred bodies lying in distorted positions.

"A cannibal's barbeque delight, not a pretty sight, I wonder who did what to whom?" Robert thought out aloud and realised it was time to call the experts in namely the coroner and his forensic team. He left Havard behind so that he could savour and immerse himself in the ambiance whilst he summoned the firemen and paramedics to look after Havard and record what he had just uncovered. Then Robert joined Geir to search for that elusive needle in the haystack after he had telephoned Marianne and requested meals on wheels.

"Found anything yet?" Robert asked Geir with a straight face as his mind tussled with the information that Morten had provided which didn't sit quite right with him and therefore out of curiosity and before Geir had a chance of presenting Robert with his findings, Robert dialled up the images that he had taken on his mobile phone and thrust them at Geir saying "See anything unusual in these photo's?"

"Err...what...give me a moment" Geir replied and dropped everything that he was doing and accepted Robert's phone. The young officer enlarged each image in turn and carefully scanned them before asking the obvious question "Was anything blinking at the time when you took these?"

"Not that I can remember why?"

"Because nothing catch's my eye, it all looks pretty ordinary"

"Are you absolutely certain about that?" Robert asked rather angry with the young officer's finding

"Yes Sir"

"Get on with your work then!" Robert abruptly said and dismissed the young officer

"Wouldn't you like to see what I've found?" Geir innocently beckoned

"Not now...I'm busy" Robert roughly snapped and stormed off

"God has he got a bee in his boggle" Geir thought and returned to his somewhat fruitful pastime

Robert meanwhile walked back to where he had parked the police van and wasted considerable time attempting to contact Morten whose mobile phone was switched off. "Does he have to sleep, what's the matter with him" Robert cursed as he was rather frustrated, tired and in need of a strong cup of coffee and a fresh apple Danish. Instinctively he knew something was not quite right with the story that Morten had spun him and he suspected that Morten was in danger even though he was an experienced army officer on active duty, but without any hard evidence Robert could do nothing, under these circumstances he was required to perform his duty at the crime scene, Robert reluctantly rejoined Havard to see if he was physically and mentally capable of continuing.

By 10am that morning the entire area had turned into a circus. A veritable flotilla of experts had arrived and set up their equipment, tents and amenities. The hungry paparazzi were soon buzzing around on land and in the air once the story had been leaked by the local residents who exaggerated the events by suggesting it was a terrorist attack on Norwegian soil in response to the Israeli treatment of the Palestinians' in the Gaza strip. This inevitably led to a sensitive political situation in which the Israeli government demanded answers as to why the Norwegian authorities could not guarantee the safety of two innocent embassy clerks who had decided to spend a restful weekend in Hell. Predicatively the American government also intervened, condemned the Norwegian lack of security and attempted by various means to assist or conduct its own investigations into the events of the crime scene.

At around 11am the explosive events at David's Camp once sufficient editorial evidence had been found were broadcast firstly by the local radio station and then by the local and national television channels. The story until a formal police statement was issued remained brief and sketchy but nonetheless wildly entertaining, it presented the facts as being two separate explosions occurring in the early hours of the morning that rocked the surrounding countryside and alarmed its residents. The holiday cottage had burnt down and three badly charred bodies had been retrieved from its basement, the location was an Israeli diplomat's weekend retreat known as David's Camp which was used by embassy staff from Oslo and visiting dignitaries.

Interviews with a cross section of Hell's long standing residents provided ample controversy and speculation as to the likely causes of the crime scene.

Major Weir, Marcus and the girls did not take much notice of the latest breaking news as it flashed across the wall mounted television screen in the quaint Italian cafe that they had settled in at Vaernes airport whilst they enjoyed a hearty late breakfast with their newly acquired friends from the Keep Norway Neutral action party until Anya caught a glimpse of an aerial view that featured Nicoli's BMW motorcycle, it was only then that she decided to pay more attention to the associated televised text and intuitively reach the grim decision that Nicoli was dead which didn't faze her in the slightest and she remained calm and composed throughout.

"This was a very nice break from our normal duties at out protest point. But we must be returning to relieve the others...perhaps you will join us later?" One of the more flamboyant protestors said as he stood up to take his leave along with his fellow friends.

"Yes that would be nice" Britt sweetly answered and remained seated whilst she nursed her hot cup of coffee with both hands

"Good then we will see you later" The flamboyant protestor said and quickly departed leaving the foursome to dwell on Nicoli's demise

"Is that what you think?" The Major asked Anya in a low voice after she had informed him of her woes.

"There's no doubt in my mind" She confidently and unemotionally replied and watched as he studied the breaking news even though he could not read the Norwegian text. Britt and Marcus although non committal seemed to agree with Anya's conclusion judging by their combined body language

"If this is the case I suggest you three continue to gather information as best you can but no mention of Nicoli" The Major sternly gave the order

"On what...?" Marcus asked feeling a little frustrated as he felt as though he had already done quite enough

"We need to know what the protestors know"

"Hardly anything I would imagine, they're protestors for God's sake, noise makers, nothing of substance, a bloody waste of time" Marcus vehemently argued raising his voice

"Everyone has a purpose"

"Good, mind explaining what theirs might be" Marcus sarcastically asked the Major who understood Marcus's point of view and hoped that he would keep secret what they had discovered the previous day

"Perhaps later...I have to go" The Major hurriedly answered and briskly departed leaving the threesome to ponder their nebulous task and pay the bill.

With the heavy military presence at Vaernes air base the Major thought it highly likely that all phones in and about the facility would be monitored by the hugely insecure Americans and even though his phone was of the most sophisticated kind he decided not to risk using it until he was well and truly somewhere isolated. Having found such a spot one hour later the Major contacted his superior for further information on the crime scene and his group's safety.

"Good day Sir, rather delicate here, thought you might be in the know as to how hot is Hell" David Weir cryptically asked once he made contact

"Presently your heat shields are intact" His superior coldly answered before terminating the call leaving the Major in no doubt as to his group's safety

"Well that was short and sweet, but it doesn't mean we lower our guards" The Major contently sighed as he gazed upon the tranquil pastures that surrounded him and wondered how many feathers would be ruffled once the Keep Norway Neutral commander acted on the contents of the package that was coming his way.

Early next morning 'Chook' Larssen sat at his office desk and started carefully shifting though the preliminary evidence that he and his deputies had gathered from the crime site as well as the results of Marianne's vehicle number plate checks, nothing of any significance leap out except for a dust covered and slightly singed USB stick that he without thinking automatically pocketed. Robert felt that he should track down his friend Morten as he thought it was a matter of urgency but before he could make a move the Station Chief burst through his office door accompanied by two sinister looking individuals who 'Chook' took an instant dislike to.

"Gentlemen this is Police Inspector Larssen who is presently heading the investigation into yesterday's unfortunate events at David's Camp" The Station Chief sharply said as he allowed his visitors to rudely brush past him and tower over Robert who calmly stared at them and thought "who and what the fuck do you want?"

They were about to meddle with the exhibits when Robert started throwing his hands in the air and loudly swearing in Norwegian for everyone to hear.

"Apologies...Robert here gets a little over protective at times" The Station Chief said as he grimaced for Robert to settle down which Robert did not take kindly to and gave the Station Chief the two fingers sign in return.

"Let us explain the situation to you I am Isaac Ropeman from the Israeli Secret Service and Mr Emmanuel Silverman is from the CIA. We are here to conduct our own investigations into the tragedy and would appreciate your co-operation one way or the other, having already secured your politicians' approval" The Mossad agent menacingly stated as a matter of fact which Robert took no notice of and simply stood up to his full one metre 90cm height, swept his hands over the exhibits signifying 'here take them' and left the room without saying a word much to the embarrassment of the Station Chief

"I think he mean's it's all yours" The Station Chief quickly responded and left to catch Robert before he departed the police station

"What's gotten into you?" The Station Chief angrily asked once they were outside

"It comes as no surprise to me that they are here...let's say that I saw what was in that 'holiday house' and leave it at that!" Robert abruptly answered leaving his Chief stunned, speechless and wanting to know more, Robert however was not forthcoming and silently walked away.

"All in good time" The Station Chief resigned himself into accepting for he knew full well that Robert's thorough approach would reveal the raw truth in all of its brutality

Instead of taking one of the official police cars Robert opted to drive his own after all the nature of his immediate business was to some extent personal and he felt it inappropriate to use government property under those circumstances. Once inside his car he first contacted the military base to determine if Morten was there only to learn that he had taken sick leave which Robert felt was rather unusual, next he tried Morten's home and mobile phone with no success, in desperation he switched on the car radio for a little relaxation and guidance only to hear that the Jewish Embassy in Oslo had suffered an explosion which had destroyed half of the building and severely injured several people including the Ambassador himself.

Robert remembered that Morten had an office in the Israeli Embassy as the official liaison officer following the 2006 'terrorist' attack on the synagogue in Oslo and he hoped that Morten was not amongst the injured. In keeping with Morten's status one of Robert's more banal duties was to monitor the daily activities of the Keep Norway Neutral action group to make certain it remained law abiding, the events of the past day meant he was required to question the groups' members as part of his check list, given that he wasn't having much luck raising Morten, Robert reluctantly gunned his car's engine and instead of driving to where the protest group were outside Vaernes military base he made his way to the groups' headquarters which was located in a discrete part of Trondheim's outer countryside.

Robert had only visited it twice before and had never been inside the building therefore he didn't know what to expect, accordingly he contacted Marianne to advise her of his whereabouts in order to satisfy security protocol.

"It's back to the hen house where new ideas are laid and hatched, no telling what the KNN (Keep Norway Neutral) are up to, perhaps they are behind the two bombings" 'Chook' thought as he exited his vehicle and gingerly walked towards KNN's command center which appeared deserted but then it always looked that way, not a soul nor car in sight, only the wind to remind you otherwise as it obediently carried the voices of those who were inside the center.

"Low key meeting it would seem on the other hand perhaps a high profile one restricted to the top brass" 'Chook' thought as he detected faint murmurings from within the building he neared and before he had a chance to rap on the door to announce his presence it magically opened of its own accord to reveal Morten who stood at attention and looked as though he was on official business and wished not to be disturbed.

"Well fancy meeting you here" 'Chook' happily greeted his old friend

"What brings you here?" Morten unemotionally asked as he folded his arms across his chest

"Same as you I think, seeing if KNN is linked to the recent bombings" 'Chook' suggested as he thought that it was also part of Morten's duties to do the same as he was the liaison officer attached to the Israeli embassy but then again that did not make sense as the Israeli's had already sent in two field agents, one from Mossad and one from the CIA which everyone considered was in effect Mossad in disguise.

"Who's at the door?" A voice rang out from behind Morten

"My friend 'Chook'" Morten responded

"The policeman...?"

"Yes" Morten as a matter of fact answered

"Invite him in...I've heard a lot about him from our members"

"Very well" Morten reluctantly obeyed and gestured for Robert to follow him down a corridor and into the discussion room to meet Alf KNN's duly elected president

"Alf this is my friend Robert Larssen, he served with me in the army for many years as a telecommunications officer before joining the police force" Morten briefly explained as he introduced 'Chook' to the KNN president

"Good to know and make your acquaintance" Alf replied as he stood up and offered his withered hand as a gesture of good will which Robert freely accepted whilst he thought "Alf short for alien life form an inescapable conclusion as the president's upper body and face resembled a genetic experiment gone wrong which had left him physically distorted but cerebrally enhanced".

"Likewise" Robert said as he tried to determine Alf's age

"Excellent....I was wondering if you could assist us...I understand this will come as an unusual request bearing in mind that you keep us under constant surveillance in order to protect our Israeli population" Alf warmly asked

"Depends" Robert cautiously answered

"Today we received a disturbing video claiming that a huge cache of weapons including 'dirty' bombs has been secretly stored by the American armed forces in Norway's mountain range bordering Sweden. We consider this to be a blatant underhanded violation of our nation's willingness to accept American soldiers on our soil for training purposes only" Alf replied sounding quite disgusted by the controversial arrangement

"Anaconda" Robert cryptically said

"Pardon...?"

"The training of their soldiers under Artic winter conditions was a smoke screen, a diversion a clever move to allow the yanks to implement Operation Anaconda"

"Which is...?" Alf responded all ears

"To encircle Russia with military bases" Robert coldly answered

"I knew they weren't to be trusted, putting that aside in this age of fake news and computer generated images nothing is sacred, I propose you accompany Morten to the co-ordinates supplied namely 62.64272N 11-8669E to verify the authenticity of these allegations. There is a subtle difference between being trained and preparing for imminent war" Alf politely but firmly put forward in the hope that Robert would readily agree with his proposal

"Some would say that this has nothing to do with my investigations into the recent bombings, I disagree for if the video evidence is indeed one hundred percent factual it provides a motive for the attacks" Robert wisely answered with a broad smile

"Excellent I am glad you see it our way" Alf gushed with excitement

"Before we set off perhaps I might be allowed to view the video footage" Robert asked

"But of course the USB stick is still in the computer and here is the package it arrived in" Alf replied as he handed the padded bag to Robert who examined it carefully

"Very professionally done, computer generated label, prepaid postal sachet, no return address and probably no fingerprints, posted in a public mailbox, virtually traceless, whoever did this fears for their life" Robert concluded and then proceeded to study the video footage to determine its true nature, namely fact or fiction. He did this by turning up the volume and adjusting the computer screen's contrast settings which impressed Alf no end. After a few minutes of twiddling the controls and freezing one picture after another Robert declared the footage to be raw in other words filmed on location.

"All that matters now is the accuracy of the vital statistics namely the location's latitude and longitude in relation to the Norwegian border" Alf suggested

"We're onto it" Robert acknowledged and stood up to take his leave together with Morten

"Call me as soon as you know" Alf almost begged as he saluted his 'troops' farewell and safe journey

"Copy that" Morten replied and marched outside

They decided to take Morten's car as it was fitted with sophisticated electronic devices for in the field operations and as they drove along the opportunity arose for Robert to resolve the niggling question namely the extent of Morten's involvement in the recent bombings.

"You know what I find strange is how quickly you reacted last night when I asked you to identify the equipment in the photographs I sent you. For a moment I thought you knew something that was exceedingly sensitive and secret" Robert tactfully asked as he nervously fiddled with the USB stick that he had inadvertently taken from the police station.

"It was a guess on my part"

"A guess...?" Robert questioned in a disbelieving fashion

"Well actually it was more than that; you could say it was more of a calculated decision based on recent terrorist activity"

Would you mind explaining" Robert asked seeking further clarification

Only too pleased to, the latest reported techniques that terrorists are using abroad is the mobile phone. They remove the battery and replace it with compacted pentaerythritol trinitrate or PETN for short which when placed in a sealed container is undetectable, just 100gm of it will destroy a large automobile. The terrorists rig the phones with a piezo crystal that creates a spark sufficient to cause the PETN to explode. The time of the detonation is determined by the phone's alarm clock which sends a signal to the crystal instead of the ring tone on reaching the set time. When you were in the communications room did you vaguely remember seeing a mobile phone lying about?" Morten asked

"No not really"

"Well I did it was in plain sight in the photo you sent me and that is why I shouted for you to make a run for it as I realised it didn't belong to you"

"Okay but how did the phone get there and why did it explode at that moment?" Robert asked sensing that Morten was not telling the truth.

"Someone with a high level security clearance would have to be a likely candidate and as for the hour of detonation the early hours of the morning is perfect as everyone is most probably still asleep" Morten replied attempting to sound convincing

"Very well, what about the Israeli Embassy, was this another phone bomb planted by a person with high level security clearance" Robert asked straight to the point

"That is a possibility" Morten replied sounding a little shaken

"In my mind there can only be one of two possible explanations either the Israeli's unknowingly had a double agent working in their midst or a goyim that they openly trusted" Robert aggressively replied in a way that pointed the finger directly at Morten

"Are you suggesting it was me" Morten defensively replied as his face went blank

"Let us say that I think your relationship with Alf compromises your capacity as liaison officer with the Israeli's"

"Baseless suppositions using circumstantial evidence and contrived theories" Morten cleverly retorted

"Well said by a professional who knows how to cover his tracks" Robert philosophically answered as he continued to nervously fiddle with the USB stick

"You're starting to annoy me with your badly disguised accusations. What you need to appreciate is that I saved your life" Morten emotionally countered

"Only because I was in the wrong place at the wrong time, in some respects I think I may have saved myself by telephoning you yesterday morning" Robert argued

"What's on the USB stick you keep playing with?" Morten asked changing the subject

"I don't know I pocketed it by mistake"

"Mistake or intuitive reasoning" Morten asked

"Are you suggesting I judged its contents by its cover?"

"Yes" Morten replied and pointed for Robert to insert the device into one of the on board computer ports.

The on board computer moaned and groaned as it attempted to seduce the USB stick into giving up its secrets but it refused to do so and sat idle waiting for the computer's next move.

"Looks as though we have a problem" Robert deduced as he gazed upon the computer screen that reluctantly displayed a request for more information

"Which is" Morten asked as he concentrated on his driving and the road ahead

"We need an encrypted password" Robert replied knowing full well that this was an important piece of information

"That shouldn't be a problem, what is it asking for?" Morten replied

"A ten character or greater entry" Robert answered feely somewhat dejected

"Most likely a combination of numbers and letters, challenging but not impossible, try 14, 1, 26, 9 followed by hunter all in lower case and see what happens" Morten slowly replied and waited silently for the result as he navigated his vehicle along the winding road towards Roros

"Are you psychic?" Robert asked rather astonished by Morten's 'guesses'

"Let us say that 'liaison' is not a one way street when it comes to diplomacy"

"I'll keep that in mind" Robert acknowledged and proceeded to examine the abundance of personal files that contained private and sensitive information dealing with their individual wealth and whether it was 'stolen' from Jews during the Nazi occupation of Norway during WW2. Robert found the investigations abhorrent, nauseating and deemed it obscenely fanatical

"Found anything interesting?" Morten brightly asked

"Plenty of motive here for an assassin, but nothing as yet that alludes to the identities of the deceased found at David's Camp" Robert replied as he opened and closed one file after another

"Perhaps you need to look for the unusual" Morten suggested which Robert took on board and started to think laterally

"You're just full of it today!"

"What do you mean?" Morten asked

"Good ideas...in fact too many for my liking.....!" Robert replied

"Don't like being upstaged?"

"Something like that" Robert partially agreed as he searched for that elusive unusual that Morten had referred to

"Found it yet?" Morten teased after a brief moment

"Getting close"

"How close?" Morten continued to tease

"Closer than you are to Roros" Robert cuttingly replied as he searched through the files and clicked on 'renovations' which opened up a host of possibilities, listed under that heading were a list of sub files such as, suppliers, workmen and unusually metal thread which he clicked on to reveal the identities and contact details of Isaac Ropeman and Emmanuel Silverman amongst others including the Israeli Ambassador and the names of two high ranking Norwegians namely the Minister for the Interior and the Minister for Social Justice

"You seem pleased all of a sudden" Morten observed

"Two of the deceased were Mossad agents, the third their detainee it would be fair to say judging from what is on this USB stick and from what I determined at the crime scene before forensics arrived" Robert thoughtfully explained

"Anything else...?"

"That depends on what we find in the mountains and how it will be reported" Robert tactfully answered having been 'double crossed' by ruthless politicians in the past who pretended to be acting in the public good. Morten did not labour the topic any further and decided to allow Robert to mull over the evidence in his mind until they reached their final destination which they did in relative silence

At around noon Morten turned off the road that lead to Roros and drove down a dirt track that would take them close to their designated end point, it was abundantly clear to both that as they ventured deeper into the forest they were being closely monitored.

"How many sets of eyes have you noticed?" Morten asked Robert as a test of his observational skills

"Two so far, the dot above the 'I' on the warning sign that we just passed and one inside the birdhouse a moment ago"

"Very good" Morten replied as he brought his car to a stop, turned the engine off and listened intensely to the murmurings of their surroundings.

"Map or directional GPS...?" Morten asked after a while

"How accurate is the latter?" Robert answered not knowing how advanced military equipment had become or how suited it was to the terrain that they were in and then he un-expectantly feared for the safety of the all revealing USB stick something that Morten picked up on.

"It's already been duplicated in triplicate"

"What has?" Robert asked as he faced his friend

"The USB, one copy for you, me and the KNN neatly packaged and discreetly sent as a sales promotion via email to your private email address at home"

"Anything else I should know?" Robert calmly asked

"Yes I think we should go they are expecting us after all" Morten confidently said as he undid his safety belt secured the vehicle's electronics and retrieved his multifunctional GPS device from its resting place. Once outside Morten punched in the co-ordinates and waited for its display to show the way. Robert meanwhile studied a map of the region which Morten together with an old fashioned compass had provided earlier. Seeing that Morten's GPS was playing the fool Robert suggested that they take a hybrid approach namely map first GPS later or vice versa. Robert had clearly not lost his orienteering skills and he quickly chartered a course for them to follow. Within 35 minutes of setting off they found themselves on the outskirts of the cloudberry field which Robert found both pleasing and disturbing at the same time.

"Something bothering you...?" Morten quizzically asked

"The cloudberries grow unevenly there are patches of unexplained intense growth"

"Variations in soil fertility" Morten casually postulated

"Caused by...?" Robert asked pursuing the point

"Bird droppings, dead decaying animals, who knows, in any case what does it have to do with what we have come here to see, stop being the annoying detective who constantly looks for trouble!" Morten insisted which Robert found to be rather insulting so that he stubbornly marched off to examine the soil beneath the bushes.

"Fucking, determined hard headed bastard!" Morten blasphemed as he watched Robert go about his business.

Now that they were out in the open Morten's GPS decided to perk up and inform him that they were situated a scantly six hundred meters from the designated co-ordinates and it even pointed the way. Seeing that it was fruitless to dissuade 'Chook' from scratching on the ground Morten decided to leave him pecking away whilst he made a bee line for their end point.

Morten had barely covered 100 meters when two burly foot soldiers dressed in forest green gillie outfits halted his progress.

"Stay where you are this is a restricted military zone!" One of the Swedish soldiers politely but firmly said as he stepped in front of Morten whilst his partner covered Morten from the rear.

"I thought that might be the case given the information I was provided with" Morten replied as he faced the young Swedish soldier

"Even so, you are not permitted to enter the area without proper authorisation, please turn around and return to where you came from" The soldier said in a no nonsense fashion showing no regard for Morten even though he was dressed in his full military attire.

"Is Captain Nils Nilsson from the tactical response unit present?" Morten asked taking advantage of the soldier's pedantic attitude

"That is none of your concern, please return to where you came from, you have entered a restricted Swedish military zone" the Swedish soldier barked quite irritated by Morten's persistence

"Are you saying that I have strayed onto the Swedish side of the border?"

"Yes you have, please depart otherwise we will be forced to arrest you!"

"Thank you, I fully understand, give me a moment" Morten authoritatively replied as he began to exert himself. The Swedish soldiers although heavily armed looked nervously on as Morten switched his GPS to communications mode and dialled Captain Nils Nilsson direct

"Nilsson" The Captain abruptly answered

"Good to hear your voice again, how busy are you?" Morten inquired with a sense of urgency

"Not particularly a good time to call" Nilsson coldly answered

"Even if I said 62.6472N 11-8669E..?"

"Where are you?" Nilsson asked sounded preoccupied

"Not far from there being held hostage by two of your men"

"Stay where you are, I'll come and collect you personally, hand the phone to one of the TRT men" Nilsson succinctly ordered which Morten gladly obeyed

Within 15 minutes Captain Nils Nilsson arrived and embraced

Morten who had become a close friend over the years whilst Morten performed his duty as a co-tactical defence officer during combined Norwegian and Swedish military exercises.

"So they decided to change their minds after all and send you" Nilsson commented once he let go of Morten

"I've come of my own accord" Morten blankly replied

"How did you know of this place?" Nilsson asked rather surprised

"I am conducting an investigation into two separate bombings that are most probably linked to each other, in the course of collecting evidence we came across an intact USB stick that contained raw footage of a large depot of American manufactured weapons that were alleged to be at the co-ordinates I previously mentioned to you. We think that this is most likely the next target and we suspect that the radical far right Keep Norway Neutral party has something to do with it" Morten explained as though he was in fact the chief investigator

"That's very interesting however I remain confused about your government's reaction to my telephone call inviting them to view our findings, your Minister for the Interior denied any knowledge, ownership or involvement with the arms and categorically stated that no further action will be taken by his department even though your government has allowed four thousand American troops to be stationed on Norway's sovereign soil for supposed training purposes.

"I agree with you, it doesn't make any sense at all" Morten replied and decided then and there that 'Chook' would be the ideal person to investigate, research, document and reveal who was involved in or behind a government conspiracy

"That is for you to sort out, meanwhile let us go and see what hides in the mountains" Nilsson warmly said as he saluted to his soldiers for a job well done

"How did this find come about?" Morten asked out of curiosity

"It started with a distress call by a lonely hiker who discovered an injured climber and rapidly escalated into what you are about to see once a senior paramedic confirmed the man had suffered extensive exposure to radioactive material. We have since found a number of 'dirty' bombs amongst the weapons, something we Swedes are not particularly happy about hence the telephone to your government as the greater proportion of the weaponry lays on the Norwegian side of the border, the question is was it ferried in from the Swedish side and spilt over onto the Norwegian side or vice versa? We have scoured the Swedish side up and down the length of the mountain chain and discovered no evidence of heavy haulage to confirm the former, hence we conclude it was from your side and yet your government wishes to do nothing about it" Nils answered as they walked through the dense vegetation

"Have you by any chance contacted the American's for answers?"

"Not as yet, we are in two minds about that as we suspect they will deny ownership and claim that some obscure terrorist group located in Belgium or Germany has secretly purchased the weapons on the black market and stockpiled them on our territory, which once again suggests an official conspiracy on your end"

"Having said that what do you think the Swedish government will do about the weapons especially the 'dirty' bombs?" Morten asked

"That is an interesting question which might be answered if we can determine who owns and maintains the surveillance equipment we found inside the cave and since it has been breached will there occur an orchestrated response? I think not, everyone I feel will see, hear and speak no evil!"

"You don't suppose the fallen mountaineer was after some sort of long lost Viking treasure?"

"He certainly received more than he bargained for"

"How is he by the way?"

"Quite dead" Nils replied in dead pan fashion

"Did the fall kill him?" Morten guessed

"No it was the radiation, we think he fell asleep in the cave not realising that where he slept lurked a silent killer"

"That's a shame"

"Before you go in you will need to wear a dosimeter and limit your exposure time to no more than 90 minutes" Nils said as they neared the hot zone where all manner of important people dressed in biological hazard suits were walking about.

"Copy that" Morten replied

"Weren't there two of you who entered the forest?" Nils then casually remarked

"My policeman friend 'Chook' came with me, he thought there was something seriously sinister to be found a the cloudberry patch not far from here and he decided to investigate"

"A combined civil-military operation" Nils suggested

"Something along those lines" Morten coyly answered knowing full well that Nils would not allow anything to slip past him

"Allow me to introduce you to Erik our efficiency expert. Erik will outfit and guide you around, once inside feel free to take as many photos as you wish, and remember to exit before 90 minutes has expired" Nils very strictly said as a scruffy individual with long greasy hair who appeared to have seen better days approached them. Erik without saying a word whipped out a dressmaker's tape measure and proceeded with adept agility to determine Morten's needs which he retrieved from a nearby supply tent. Once Morten had dressed Erik escorted him to the previously undiscovered cave exit which had been physically restrained from closing.

As soon as he stepped inside the cavernous interior Morten realised that someone was intentionally preparing for war as there was enough ammunition to satisfy four thousand megalomaniacs with itchy trigger fingers and sufficient shells and bombs to devastate a medium sized city.

Nils meanwhile back tracked to where he had collected Morten and continued on to where 'Chook" was busily rummaging around in the cloudberry patch

"Find anything interesting?" He asked once he laid eyes on 'Chook' who was busily examining bone fragments

"Yes and no depending upon whether these are animal or human in origin" Robert answered straight to the point without stopping what he was doing

"Why are you bothering?" Nils asked

"To satisfy my observant curiosity and determine whether or not the missing people in these parts lay here"

"Well that's something for you to do" Nils sharply replied as the location was well and truly on the Norwegian side of the border

"Yes it is" Robert dryly answered as he finally stood up to face his inquisitor whom he recognised from a photograph that he saw in Alf's conference room

"Nils Nilsson"

"Robert Larssen" 'Chook' answered as he accepted Nils' handshake

"Care to join us over there?" Nils politely asked

"Not really can't see much point in it, the video evidence I saw was convincing enough, I would prefer to read your findings"

"Such as...?"

"Full inventory of items discovered, identification of responsible individuals based on fingerprint and DNA evidence"

"You don't want much do you?"

"I beg to differ when it comes to matters of national security!"

"An idealist" Nils proposed as an apt description of Robert's character

"Just doing my job of protecting the public" Robert as a matter of fact unemotionally replied

"Let's hope they appreciate your efforts" Nils almost cynically answered and left Robert to go about his duty as he felt it fruitless to engage in any further conversation with the preoccupied Norwegian policeman

"Your friend is decidedly odd!" Nils remarked once he and Morten crossed paths once again

"And you lied to me about limiting my exposure time to 90 minutes" Morten roughly retorted

"How did you find out?"

"Your friend Erik couldn't stop himself from boasting about his innovation"

"Dumb bastard I keep telling him to keep his mouth shut!" Nils grumbled with a shake of his head

"So it's true" Morten concluded

"Presently undergoing field trials prior to commercialisation that is why I limited you to 90 minutes in order to statistically prove the superiority of the fabric's concept" Nils confirmed in a low voice

"From two aspects" Morten put forward

"Which you were quick to deduce; interesting stuff graphene, very versatile, little understood, yet Erik through his quirkiness was able to weave it into such a unique three dimensional fashion that it arrests radioactive emissions. We decided to cover all radioactive material in the cave with a blanket of it and wear suits made out of it for added protection. But this is not the reason why we are here, is it?" Nils explained

"Not really

"So Mr Morten besides the KNN party who else will you be informing" Nils bluntly asked making reference to the illegal storehouse of American weapons

6

HEADS WILL ROLL

Morten managed to get them both back safely to KNN head-quarters by 7.30pm that evening thanks to his advanced driving skills.

"Well that was a bit of a blur, I think I might call it a day and return home" Chook said sounding quite weary once they came to a stop

"Pity you didn't join me in the cave" Morten replied in an attempt to make 'Chook' feel guilty

"It would have been a waste of my time"

"If you say so" Morten coldly answered in a disapproving tone of voice and watched as 'Chook' took his bag of evidence and left without saying another word

"Perhaps Nils is right after all, Robert has become a little strange" Morten thought as he also grabbed his belongings and made his way towards KNN's house which appeared docile as ever.

"Welcome back my friend... successful trip...?" Alf warmly said as he greeted Morten on the front door step

"You could say that"

"Excellent, come inside and enjoy a warm bowl of lentil soup followed by roasted pork knuckle and a glass of cold Norwegian beer"

"Sounds heavenly" Morten replied as he dusted himself off and handed his sophisticated GPS device to Alf who responded by saying 'When only the best will do"

"Both accurate and damning" Morten ambiguously replied

"I am looking forward to it. Come let us feast before we celebrate your hard work" Alf cheerfully said as he led the way towards the kitchen which stood ready to deliver

As they 'broke bread' Morten briefed Alf on what he had seen and the conclusions he drew but it was to no avail for Alf had already conceived a game plan that he hoped would set Norway free

"These images are brilliant, nice and sharp and most importantly each has imprinted on it the date and precise longitude and latitude co-ordinates leaving no doubt in the viewers mind as to the location of the weapons. I see you were also very careful not to photograph any personnel, a wise decision on your part"

"No need for unnecessary complications" Morten replied as he took a sip of his heart warming beer

"I totally agree" Alf replied and was about to reach for his mobile phone when Morten stopped him

"What are you doing?" Alf nervously asked rather surprised

"Saving your soul"

"From..." Alf asked feeling uncertain of Morten's actions and reply

"Uncle Sam and his cronies, Nils Nilsson made it abundantly clear to me that he had already contacted our government about the weapons and was fobbed off by the Minister for the Interior who denied any knowledge or involvement"

"Never did like that man" Alf truthfully remarked

"I think the Americans have been alerted and there is no telling what they might be up to consequently it might be prudent to use my phone for the time being" Morten intelligently reasoned and switched his GPS device to phone mode which Alf freely accepted to contact KNN's counter intelligence officer

"Solver one...Libertas here...need urgent confirmation of authenticity relating to a series of sketches by well known artist prior to sale" Alf said once his contact answered the call

"Very well, usual means; will do. Auribus teneo lupum" his contact replied and signed off using a Latin phrase which meant 'holding a wolf by the ears'

Alf replied by saying "Barba tenus sapientes"

"What was that all about?" Morten asked all ears

"Wise as far as his beard"

"Are you suggesting that clean shaven men are stupid?"

"No comment...we have work to do" Alf abruptly replied and quickly left to print off selected GPS images in another room leaving Morten where his was to reflect on the day's activities, rest for a while and pick away at the pork knuckle. Twenty minutes later his peaceful solitude was rudely interrupted by a pounding at the front door which Alf promptly attended to by running down the hallway. Morten rose from his chair and gingerly looked down the corridor to see Alf exchange an A4 sized envelope for what appeared to be a stack of Uncle Tony's pizzas.

"Are you expecting guests"? Morten inquired once Alf had closed and secured the front door

"Just stocking up the larder"

"Don't you mean arsenal?" Morten countered as he knew that using pizza delivery services was one method that the KNN party used to communicate with its seen and unseen members.

"You're very astute"

"Who's doing what and where?" Morten insisted on knowing

"You have probably already met him, greasy hair, seen better days and rants on about graphene"

"Erik?"

"Brilliant analytical mind, possibly the world's finest hacker, so brilliant in fact that he has permanently embedded himself in the Pentagon and has access to all of its files. The Swedes are equally as keen to cause the Americans to move on so that Scandinavia as such can be left free to conduct its own defence strategies amongst other things. We don't need the West's constant irritating interference and absurd rhetoric" Alf passionately explained

"But he doesn't have a beard" Morten comically remembered

"That's another person, but he can wait" Alf replied

"And I suppose that's exactly what we will be doing for the next few days"

"Not necessarily, the evidence you provided us with today have set things in motion, by tomorrow afternoon the fur should start flying" Alf poetically suggested before he stored Uncle Tony's frozen pizzas in the freezer

"That's what I should be doing, putting myself on ice until tomorrow" Morten secretly thought as he watched Alf rearrange his freezer

"Fancy some raspberry sorbet?" Alf brightly asked as he turned around

"Bit too sweet for me I prefer dark chocolate to round off a meal" Morten replied

"Most intellectuals do" Alf said as he returned the ice confectionary to the freezer

"I might call it a day, thank you for everything" Morten politely excused and fair welled himself with a handshake

"No....... thank you" Alf warmly responded and showed Morten out

"Once in his car Morten was besieged by a barrage of telephone calls on his official mobile phone as well as on his private one both of which he had deliberately left behind in the glove box since the early hours of the morning. The first to vent his anger and concern was Morten's commanding officer.

"Where the hell have you been? We have been worried sick about you!"

"I decided to lie low" Morten convincingly lied

"That's strange because when we learnt that your phone and car trackers didn't work we suspected the worse namely that you had been killed in the Israeli embassy blast in Oslo. We even sent out numerous teams to check on your whereabouts with no success" Morten's chief angrily bellowed

"My sincerest apologies, I thought I might have been one of the targets, you can't be too careful these days"

"At least you're safe and sound, present yourself for duty tomorrow morning at my offices at 8.30am sharp, we need to devise new strategies, the Israelis are behaving like real whingeing bitches"

"Yes Sir" Morten obediently replied and terminated the call, he nervously wondered if he had been spotted elsewhere during the day and if Nils had reported his presence to the Norwegians. The other callers were frantic family members and close concerned friends but not a whisper from the Israelis which he didn't expect as he knew full well that he was considered by them to be nothing more than meaningless expendable goyim.

Morten was no fool he was fully aware that they would go to extraordinary lengths to find those who had bombed their precious David's Camp and embassy and would assign Mossad's ruthless Caesarea unit to conduct the investigation and subsequent assassinations. From this point in time he had to be extremely careful as to what he said and to whom for there was no room for error nor misinterpretation of any sort in anything that he said or did, no suspicion must fall on him, with those thoughts in mind Morten once he made certain that he was not being followed by an automobile, motorcycle or drone and that his vehicle was tracker free drove his car in a secluded remote lane where he parked and proceeded to make structural changes to both his GPS device and on board computer by firstly replacing then destroying the memory cards followed by reprogramming both to time zero. Satisfied that everything was squeaky clean Morten drove home to enjoy a good night's sleep.

'Chook' on the other hand was not so fortunate although some might say he was extremely lucky. Svetlana had 'burgled' his home a few moments earlier for a specific purpose and when she realised that he had returned sooner than expected she decided to improvise and pounce on him as soon as he opened the front door. Completely naked except for a dressing gown that was loosely wrapped around her voluptuous body Svetlana passionately French kissed 'chook' whilst she stroked his eager manhood before luring him into the bedroom where she proceeded to seduce him in no uncertain manner to the point of sexual exhaustion causing each one of them to climax not less than three times. Not satisfied with that she continued to pleasure herself with her ever reliable electric toothbrush whilst 'Chook' slept soundly oblivious to her rampant activities. Svetlana's enthusiasm for mischievous action did not end there, she gathered her clothes, quickly exited the bedroom and went in search of 'chook's' computer to learn what he had been up to. Clever to the extreme Svetlana easily side stepped his computer's password protected login and began browsing through his personal and work files before investigating his internet history even though it had been supposedly deleted, from there she proceeded to his email accounts which revealed that the police investigations so far had drawn a blank with respect to the proper identities of the three deceased individuals found at David's Camp. The only positive evidence was that the devastation was caused by a military grade explosive widely used by both official and unofficial organisations.

The only email that caught her eye was one entitled 'you'll have to hold your breath for this one' sent by Morten who enigmatically wrote 'you will have to dive deeply into dark places to access my knowledge', to Svetlana this only meant one thing, the Deep Dark Web where all manner of shady, unmentionable and unpalatable things proliferate. Certain that 'chook' was more than fast asleep judging by his loud snoring Svetlana decided to try her luck and locate Morten's knowledge. She hoped that Robert's computer was not the property of the police department as this would have rendered it unusable as more than likely it was constantly being monitored for inappropriate content. 'Chook's history of porn site addiction easily negated this fear. She dwelled on the words 'dive deeply' as the key where to look and realised that it was a file of sorts that she sought, a file stored on the Dark Web in a library that contained and protected a great many revealing secrets not for public viewing.

Svetlana was no stranger to the Dark Web or the library as both were part and parcel of her daily activities. Soon she was riffling through the library's index searching for the journals that might interest 'Chook' all that eluded her were their specific titles and then it dawned on her that poultry was the way to go.

First she attempted 'Chook12854' which was a combination of Robert's nickname and his police identification number but that drew a blank even though she tried numerous variations of its presentation, then she hit on the idea that it just might be 'deepdivingchicken' but that also failed, frustrated but not defeated Svetlana knew that she was close so she contemplated long and hard to arrive at 'deepdivingrooster' 'deepdivingcock' which brought a smile to her face and lastly 'deepdivingchook' which proved to be the answer she sought.

"To think that yesterday you were nothing more than a casual encounter to satisfy my penis addiction and today thanks to the Israeli's you have become a person of interest, what a twist" Svetlana whispered to herself in her native language as she perused the contents of the file that Morten had uploaded from the USB stick found at David's Camp. "I hope you have destroyed the USB otherwise it might just be the death of you" she continued to whisper as she pondered on why the Israeli's possessed all of the contact details both private and public for the Norwegian Minister of the Interior and the Minister for Social Justice

"My purpose is not to reason why but just to do or die" She

resigned herself to that fact after which she shut down the computer and quietly left.

'Chook' had also become a person of great interest in the minds of the Mossad-CIA partnership once the USB stick listed as a prime piece of evidence in the crime scene inventory went missing from his desk earlier that day. Agent Ropeman one could say had become obsessed with its recovery as though it was the most precious thing in the world and as a consequence he together with Agent Silverman literally turned Trondheim's police station upside down in an effort to locate it before pursuing the belief that 'Chook' had deliberately absconded with it.

Having determined his private home address and the fact that 'Chook' lived alone Silverman decided that they should pay him a visit around 10pm that night when he was less alert. 'Chook' lived in the municipality of Leinstand, 12km from Trondheim's town centre in a modest Norwegian bungalow located in a quiet well mannered neighbourhood where its inhabitants largely kept to themselves.

The deadly duo arrived just after 9pm and parked their conspicuous black Chevrolet Orlando SUV fifty meters away from 'Chook's' house in front of a rental vehicle that they took no notice of, equipped with state of the art telescopic night vision binoculars they sat motionless and kept a vigilant eye on 'Chook's' activities.

"Man she's hot, she's really hot and boy is she dressed to kill!" Silverman frothed at the mouth as Svetlana exited the front door in a manner that revealed her long legs and ample cleavage.

"I bet you that stupid policeman is probably half dead by now" Ropeman added in jest

"What are you saying?'

'She's shagged him stupid" Ropeman erotically suggested

"Do you think she's a hooker?"

"Well he does live alone" Ropeman put forward and whilst they were contained within a soundproof cabin neither their presence nor their words went unnoticed by Svetlana who mumbled under her breath "You crazy Americans, think you can go unnoticed? Who do you think you are fooling? Your black Chevrolet with Swedish number plates stands out like a limp dick flapping in the wind!" as she confidently strutted towards them in her high heels much like a high class hooker down a catwalk.

Ropeman and Silverman sat open mouthed and watched Svetlana deliberately cross the street and walk directly towards their vehicle as though they had done something wrong. Expecting that she was about to attract their attention they hurriedly hid their state of the art night vision binoculars and pretended to appear relaxed Svetlana however glided past them and got into the rental car that was parked closely behind them.

"Definitely a hooker" Silverman softly whispered

"Probably a high class fifo" Ropeman suggested as he wondered whether or not 'Chook's' salary afforded him such luxuries

"Do you think we could factor her into our overseas expense account?" Silverman asked as his manhood began to stir

"Under what description.....?"

"How about anal....lyst" Silverman crudely replied as his trousers strained to contain his eager manhood

"Sounds reasonable under the circumstances" Ropeman lecherously agreed as he shoved his hand down the front of his trousers and squeezed his meat and two vegetables so as to stay focused on the job at hand "20 minutes and we go in" He then said changing the subject

"Copy that" Silverman replied as he reluctantly returned his mind to surveillance mode but not quickly enough as he was suddenly jolted out of his sexual fantasy by Svetlana unexpectedly rapping on the driver's side window which he wound down

"Besides the fact that you have boxed me in, it appears that my car's battery is dead as is my mobile phone....... can you help me?" Svetlana asked in a bitter sweet tone of voice that caught Silverman completely off guard and made Ropeman somewhat embarrassed

"Err....sure thing..." Silverman sheepishly answered as he reached to open his car door but Svetlana was far too quick for him and he felt a slight sting beneath his left ear near the carotid artery as she jabbed what appeared to be a ball point pen into the side of his neck. Silverman's head and neck became instantly paralysed, he struggled to breathe never mind talk as the toxin rapidly spread throughout his body, his entire nervous system shut down, the last two horrific things that he would ever experience seeing in slow motion were Svetlana expertly withdrawing his gun from his shoulder holster, shooting Ropeman at point blank range though his temple before she shot Silverman through the roof of his mouth with his own gun. Immensely satisfied with her handy work Svetlana then forced Silverman's revolver into his clenched right hand and secured her Botox filled ball point pen courtesy of the defunct bioweapons complex unit 731 Manchuria Japan. She left the vehicle as it was so as not to raise any suspicion of any sort before swiftly disappearing into the night, all of which occurred in less than 70 seconds and went completely unnoticed until dawn broke and the early morning mist had cleared the next day when a curious jogger unlike those who had preceded him earlier concluded that Ropeman and Silverman were occupying the front seats of the black Chevrolet quite unnaturally. Only then when it was reported to the police did the wail of approaching sirens wake up the inhabitants of the sleepy hollow all except 'Chook' who was both physically and mentally exhausted and as consequence remained sound asleep and dead to the world.

It wasn't until 8am that morning when one of the attending police officers was told that 'Chook' lived a few doors down from the crime scene that things took a nasty turn.

Completely oblivious to what was happening outside 'Chook" was happily washing away his cares and worries and vigorously re-energising his soul and sore penis in the confines of his warm and cosy shower. His early morning bathroom ritual was no longer than eight minutes at the end of which time both his programmed toaster and coffee percolator would had performed their respective tasks allowing 'Chook' to enjoy a simple breakfast of two lightly browned pieces of toast smothered in strawberry jam with a mug of hot Ethiopian coffee. Feeling refreshed and somewhat revived 'Chook' strolled into his kitchen to find the station chief and Marianne casually eating his breakfast.

"By the look of surprise on your face you are most probably wondering what we are doing here and how did we get in" The station chief abruptly said in between bites of Chook's toast

"The thought had crossed my mind" 'Chook' replied in a manner that clearly displayed his disdain at having his house and food violated

"Good then we will explain but before we do so, is there anything that you wish to tell us?"

"About?" 'Chook' defensively answered

"You whereabouts yesterday for example"

"Not really"

"Very well then, judging by your behaviour yesterday it became obvious to those present that you resented the presence of agents Ropeman and Silverman, some even thought that you may have encountered them previously and as a consequence you harboured a grudge and that is why you deliberately took the USB not only to frustrate their investigation but lure them into your street where under the cover of darkness you vented your anger and made it look as though Silverman had committed a murder suicide" The station chief grimly accused 'Chook' who stood speechless and wondered if his superior had lost all sense of reason.

"I trust you have some hard evidence to back up your speculations and wild imaginings because all of this is new to me" 'Chook' coldly replied as he gritted his teeth and clenched his fists.

"That is why we are here; if you have no objections the forensics team will conduct a standard examination of your body and clothing"

"Not in the slightest, care for more toast or coffee" 'Chook' dryly answered and proceeded to reload his toaster and coffee percolator whilst he thought of office politics, power struggles and those who might be secretly knifing him in the back for he knew for a long time that whilst his army training had allowed him to solve many cases it had caused unnecessary rivalry, jealousy and contempt.

"No thank you it was quite delicious" Marianne sweetly answered and nodded her head to indicate that she recognised his innocence

"Do you still have the USB?" The station chief bluntly asked

"Yes I think it is in one of my trouser pockets, I'll get it for you"

"No need, stay where you are, I'll attend to it" The station chief commanded

"Very well, you'll find them draped over the chair opposite my bed" 'Chook' replied knowing full well that his superior officer was behaving according to police protocol

"Where were you yesterday" Marianne whispered once the station chief had left the room

"KNN headquarters questioning the president and various members"

"That wouldn't have taken you all day" Marianne said doubting his answer

"I'm very thorough"

"I'm sure Barbara would agree with that statement" Marianne teased 'Chook' who remained un-phased by her taunt even though he bore multiple love bites on his neck.

"Possibly" 'Chook' replied admitting to nothing whilst he buttered his toast, spread lashings of strawberry jam on it and waited for the station chief to return which he did quite promptly

"No problem finding it?" Chook politely asked

"Not at all, but it's of no use to us anymore" The station chief sadly replied as he played with the device

"Why is that?" Marianne asked a little baffled as there had been so much ado about recovering it

"I've just been informed by the Minister of the Interior that all further investigations into the bombings at David's Camp and the Jewish Embassy in Oslo plus the mysterious deaths of Ropeman and Silverman have been placed into the hands of Kripos the national criminal investigation service who will work with Interpol and Europol, we have been officially relieved our services are no longer required" The station chief reluctantly announced which Chook thought to be most suspicious as it was meant to have been a joint operation with one department benefiting from the other. Something to him intuitively didn't sound right and that something Major David Weir was made keenly aware of during a covert telephone conversation with his NATO superiors at the same time that the station chief and Marianne had confronted 'Chook'

7
STRATEGIES

They often say that one man's trash is another man's treasure; it could therefore be argued that one man's frustration can also be another man's joy. In this case whilst 'Chook' had his wings savagely clipped Marcus Rhodes on the other hand was given the freedom to soar.

The trio thought that it would be another day in paradise mingling with the ever so friendly members of KNN getting to know their individual idiosyncrasies and keeping tab on the movements of the American marines stationed at Vaernes. By 8.30am that glorious expectation would be well and truly shattered by Major David Weir who returned to their safe house from his shopping expedition laden with fresh produce and invigorating news that would not suit everyone.

"Change of plan this morning ladies and gentleman" The Major brightly announced as he burst into the kitchen where Brit, Anya and Marcus were huddled together enjoying freshly brewed coffee and wondering when there would be something to eat.

"Why?" Anya asked rather irritated as she was hungry and looking forward to fraternising with certain members of KNN

"Our surveillance mission has been upgraded to something a

little more challenging. Let me explain. It was all meant to be a walk in the park once Marcus had located the secret arsenal of American weapons and the Swedish authorities had been alerted in a round-about fashion. It was my expectation that a political storm would eventuate aided and abetted by the Keep Norway Neutral party publically agitating for explanations once they had received concrete photographic evidence of the arsenal and acted upon it. Our NATO superiors informed me this morning that the Norwegian Government specifically the Minister for the Interior and the Minister for Justice denied any knowledge or involvement with respect to the arsenal of weapons which included a significant number of dirty bombs and spent uranium coated munitions furthermore the Minister for Justice acted very swiftly and gave orders for all members of the KNN to be detained, questioned and if need be arrested until further notice. The media has been banned from reporting or discussing any aspect of the arsenal's discovery which I find unusual as Norway is meant to be a country for free press. The investigations into the bombings at David's Camp and Israeli Embassy in Oslo have been transferred from local police to the National Criminal Investigation Service which will also undertake yesterday's mysterious deaths of a CIA and Mossad agent who had been working together. Initially it was thought to be a murder suicide, rumour has it that the CIA agent fancied the Mossad agent who shunned the CIA agent's advances, needless to say the CIA blames Mossad and vice versa, nothing more than a storm in a teacup as the Israeli's need the Americans more than the Americans need the Israeli's for various reasons. The reluctance of the Norwegians to admit any knowledge or involvement in relation to the arsenal of weapons has caused our NATO superiors to become increasingly suspicious as to the true nature of the relationship between the Norwegians and Americans. The Russians are also puzzled one senior diplomat was heard to say "Taking into account multiple statements of Norwegian officials about the absence of threat from Russia to Norway, we would like to understand what purposes is Norway so willing to increase its military potential in particular through the stationing of American forces in Vaernes. Furthermore Norway pledged not to host foreign troops on its soil in 1945 once Soviet troops left the country after driving out the Nazis this commitment lasted until recently, the question is why? Our superiors suspect that the Americans have in one way or another managed to manipulate one or both of these Ministers in the American interests. This is our new mission namely to expose the nature of the manipulation" David Weir slowly said as he walked about the room distributing freshly baked Danish pastries whilst he quietly gauged the individual reactions of Anya, Brit and Marcus who was the first to respond

"It came as no surprise to me that KNN has been singled out as it represents a very convenient scapegoat thanks to its past history, unfortunately this may have compromised the effectiveness of our unit. Both Brit and Anya by publically associating with members of KNN would have most probably come under scrutiny and most probably already had their identities checked out. Question is what did the Americans discover? Was it a paramedic and a nurse or two FSK operatives?"

"The latter" David Weir grimly confirmed

"Is it to our advantage or disadvantage?" Marcus asked

"Depends on what sorts of questions they ask"

"Who...?" Marcus answered clearly confused by David Weir's ambiguous statement

"Either"

"Meaning the Americans and the National Criminal Investigation Service" Marcus guessed

"Precisely"

"Then I believe it matters not for the latter has been given full responsibility for the investigations all other agencies are thereby required to step down which means both Anya and Brit cannot be seen to be nosing around"

"Surely there must be something that we can help with" Anya said feeling somewhat abandoned and dejected

"You can be our body guards after all you are well versed in using all manner of weapons up to and including anti-tank missiles plus you both have a good arse" David Weir answered with a wry smile

"Wait a minute the FSK is a highly secret, highly skilled, anti terrorist squad which means they can play a role in the ongoing investigations........" Marcus started to say contradicting his earlier statement

"Correct but these two are on special leave, just like you, I think it is prudent to limit their exposure" David Weir interrupted

"What do you suggest we do?" Anya insisted on knowing as she was feeling further alienated than before

"Depends upon what other skills you can bring to the table" Major Weir replied which made Anya feel awkward

"I am very good at reading body language" She defiantly said as she folded her arms across her chest

"I thought that applied to all women" David Weir cuttingly answered suggesting that it was generally impossible for men to lie to women

"I think she means something else" Marcus said coming to Anya's defence

"Really and what might that be?" The Major replied in a conde-scending fashion

"They start with the obvious, namely that both Ministers are guilty or only one is and the other is protecting him or both or one of them is protecting a third party. Anya will enlist Brit's exceptional library skills that extend beyond books, magazines and newspapers to include obscure television interviews on delicate subjects; they will avoid sanitised national news to seek out websites that specialise in bizarre and seemingly illogical accusations that appear to have no apparent foundation" Marcus confidently suggested without knowing what the pair were truly capable of

"Your argument has some merit, I tell you what, I'll give them five hours to prove themselves" The Major almost cynically replied as a means of egging them on

"Exceedingly generous of you, it wouldn't by any chance coincide with the time taken to drive to Oslo?" Marcus postulated

"How astute of you Mr Rhodes, nothing like a drive in the fresh country air to clear the mind, it is in fact one of my favourite past times, beats golf anytime" The Major replied as he betrayed his national sport for which he had no regard.

Whilst they all sat in relative silence devouring their food it dawned on Marcus that Major Weir was no fool who merely putted around the greens and that the organisation which he was part of had at its fingertips the latest Intel on whatever matter was at hand a distinct advantage as it allowed the Major to act quickly and swiftly leaving his opposition flat footed. The knowledge that the Americans had positively identified Anya and Brit as FSK agents worried Marcus. What if the hair brained Yanks vaguely considered the girls as double agents and that they were not acting in their capacities as anti-terrorist specialists, did it mean that the trio was already under surveillance? Was it time to continually look over one's shoulder? Would the journey to Oslo be eventful or uneventful? With those agonising thoughts in mind Marcus decided to ensure that his Glock was in proper working order and that he had sufficient spare magazines. Even though he attempted to contain his paranoia and remain outwardly calm, his thoughts painted another picture which did not escape the Major.

"Something bothering you soldier?" David Weir asked as he looked directly at Marcus

"The murder suicide you spoke of earlier, if it wasn't one of them who committed the crime then who ever did is highly proficient and possibly restricted to the top one percent of paid assassins in the world" Marcus nervously answered

"Point taken but why the hit; was it to sour relations between the Israeli's and Americans or was it personal? Irrespective of that perhaps there is another player, question is what is their game and does it have anything to do with us or what we are about to accomplish? Yes I know it is becoming complicated, best not to think too much about it and just get on with the task at hand. Having said that can we be ready to move out in twenty minutes?" The Major calmly asked with a broad reassuring smile as he stood up to leave the table

Marcus allowed the girls to attend to their toiletries first which he knew wouldn't take them very long; after all it was business rather than pleasure which they were preparing for. The Major being the eternal early bird had already shaved and showered by six am. Marcus decided to shower only and remain rugged looking for the rest of the day.

As the trio assembled in the corridor with their scant belongings the safe house's walls, windows and roof began to shake uncontrollably as a loud repetitive thump, thump noise approached and relentlessly battered the building from above. Marcus immediately feared the worst, he dropped his duffle bag, withdrew and primed his Glock, instinctively commanded everyone to fall to the floor as he imagined that they were about to come under an aerial attack of some sorts. He was about to exit the safe house through the rear door and sacrifice his life when the Major appeared and asked with a look of surprise on his face "What are you doing soldier?"

"Protecting them Sir" Marcus shakily responded as his body filled itself with copious amounts of adrenaline

"Very noble of you soldier but there is no need for that, it's all very innocent, come let me show you" The Major reassured Marcus who remained on full alert

"Look outside the window, it's our transport"

"But we were meant to drive...."

"Yes I know but do you really want to go through needless road blocks and be interrogated by half wits looking for trouble?" The Major answered as Marcus peered outside to identify two HEMS labelled Airbus helicopters that had landed close by and were idling ready for takeoff.

"HEMS......" Marcus feebly said

"Stands for helicopter emergency medical service"

"Who's sick?" Marcus stupidly asked

"We will be if we stay around here any longer, so stand down soldier and climb on board we have some serious work to do" The Major firmly said as he guided Marcus through the open front door and into the waiting helicopter.

The low level flight to Oslo was smooth and relaxed a clever way of avoiding the authorities so Marcus thought as he allowed the journey and passing scenery to dispel his unwarranted anxieties. Marcus travelled with Brit whom he considered to be more attractive than Anya, accordingly he engaged in small talk with the highly accomplished FSK agent who had from the beginning taken a liking to him. They both would have preferred more intimate quieter surroundings and even a glass of wine to spur things along but roughing it often produces better unexpected results. As they neared the heavily forested outskirts of Oslo the pilot slowed his aircraft to a crawl and began searching for a suitable place to land his helicopter which happened to be in the middle of a large freshly mowed paddock situated next to a car park that belonged to Norwegian Ice, a distillery which specialised in producing an extra fine Vodka from potatoes and used as its motto the phrase 'set your spirit free'

Once they had landed the pilot signalled for Brit and Marcus to vacate the cabin and pointed to where they should assemble. Marcus thanked the pilot and took his leave closely followed by Brit, when they were sufficiently clear both HEMS helicopters took to the skies to resume their official duties.

"Well that was pleasant joy ride, I wonder what awaits us next" Marcus feeling at ease merrily chirped as he looked around to locate the Major

"Dangerous stuff I hope, I could do with a dose of excitement" Brit eagerly answered as she licked her lips in anticipation.

"Let's see what the Major has to offer now that he has changed the game"

"I'm having trouble working him out" Brit reluctantly admitted

"Because he is Scottish...?"

"Something like that" Brit answered as she remembered how the Major belittled Anya earlier that day

"I'm sure you will settle your cultural differences, just give it time"

"I guess you're right" Brit agreed as she kept up with Marcus who decided to walk at a brisk pace

"Hurry along you two we have serious work to do!" The Major bellowed from a distance

"Yes Sir" Marcus yelled back and doubled his walking speed "Is this what you had in mind?" He then asked Brit

"Not really" The attractive FSK female agent replied in between taking deep breaths of air

"Neither did I" Marcus mutually agreed as they rapidly approached where the Major, Anya and a tall stranger stood next to an electric golf buggy.

"Sorry we're late, it seems our pilot had some difficulty locating a suitable landing spot" Brit said by way of explanation.

"Apologies accepted as long as you're comfortable with having fewer hours to do your investigative work" The Major barked

"Always up for a challenge Sir...!"

"Good then we can be on our way, but before we do so, this is Nils, he will be your concierge so to speak while we are stationed here. We will set up camp in the potato processing plant where Nils has conveniently provided us with a quiet room but don't expect any luxuries or free vodka for that matter, we are strictly here on business!" David Weir said in reply which came as no surprise to Marcus as he had encountered this sort of behaviour before, what did unsettle him was the fact that Nils did not acknowledge Marcus even though they had briefly exchanged words in Roros. Nils Marcus was convinced was the head of the Troll Hunters group that he had met in the Hiort pub.

"Right if there are no further questions not that one of you has asked any, seat yourself in one of the golf buggies and we can make tracks" The Major sharply said before he clambered into the buggy nearest to him and waited for Anya to join him.

Brit and Marcus followed suit with Marcus allowing Brit to drive as he expected it would be at a slow and steady pace however that was not the case. The Major without any warning sped away in the blink of an eye leaving them in cloud of dust.

"Fasten your seat belt this is going to be fun!" Brit happily exclaimed accepting the challenge as she floored the accelerator and gave chase

"Bloody hell what is this?" Marcus shrieked as he was thrown back

"German built electric rocket!" Brit knowledgeably answered as she revelled in the excitement of the moment

"Definitely not for grannies" Marcus quipped

"Oh I don't know some remain very active in their old age" Brit erotically purred as she cornered the buggy on two wheels out of the car park and onto a dirt road

"Really...?" Marcus said raising an eyebrow or two

"That's why men prefer them" Brit answered it seemed out of firsthand experience as she looked for a way of making the buggy go even faster

"I'll keep that in mind when I'm desperate" Marcus said swallowing hard

"Nervous?"

"Not in the least" Marcus foolishly pretended as the scenery whizzed past and the road bounced them about with its rocks and craters which caused Brit no end of trouble in keeping the buggy stable

"Are you certain we're not on the road to San Jose?" Marcus dryly asked

"What do you mean?" Brit answered somewhat indignantly

"I think you should have zigged instead of zagged there's no Major in front of us"

"What the fuck?" Brit loudly swore and instantly stopped the buggy by taking her foot off the accelerator "Where did he disappear to?"

"Actually he never left the car park" Marcus calmly replied with a wry smile

"Bollocks!"

"My sentiments precisely" Marcus answered and wondered how Brit would reverse her embarrassment

The attractive FSK agent shook her finger in disgust at something else that apparently had annoyed her and without saying anything she left the buggy walked to the rear, lifted it up by its rear bumper turned it a full 180 degrees and then casually climbed back in.

"Feeling better now?" Markus flippantly asked once she had finished

"Not yet I'll tell you when" Brit coldly answered before she sped them away to reach Norwegian Ice car park a few moments later

"We started over there, then he went straight ahead, I took my eyes off him briefly and I assumed he turned left, but if he didn't where did he go" Brit analytically mumbled as she traced their moments with her hand

"He simply dropped out of sight" Marcus said as he remembered

"Why didn't you tell me" Brit asked quite annoyed

"I thought you knew"

"Exactly where did he drop out of sight?" Brit reluctantly asked

"Over there by the mountain of wooden barrels basking in the sun" Marcus politely answered as he pointed to the spot

"Nothing unusual about it but I suppose a closer examination might reveal something' Brit said in a doubting voice that challenged Marcus's observational skills

"Nothing here, nothing there, nothing anywhere; where exactly would you position a potato processing plant...? Brit asked as they slowly drove past an assortment of colourful buildings with a sea of bikes parked in front of them.

"I have no idea except my BMW motorcycle is parked over there" Marcus replied once it can into view and he positively identified it

"What's it doing there?" Brit asked not knowing that Marcus had left it behind in Roros and had expected it to be misappropriated.

"Good question, perhaps it's all part of one giant plot that we have been dragged into" Marcus speculated as his mind raced to find answers and his paranoia raised its ugly head

"Something we can quiz the Major about later" Brit suggested

"Good Luck" Marcus pessimistically responded as he wondered where the Major had disappeared to. Brit continued to drive the golf cart until they passed the mountain of wooden barrels and reached the end of the parking lot.

"This is impossible!" She said in frustration as she brought the cart to a stop

"Actually no, but almost, just keep driving" Marcus replied as he deduced otherwise

"There's nothing there, it's an open field, nothing else!" Brit angrily argued as she stared into space trying to make sense of all of it.

"Just drive!" Marcus said quite assertively

"Yes boss!" Brit reluctantly obliged and drove forward straight into a black hole.

"Where are we?" Brit nervously asked once the noise of a large door shutting behind them had died down.

"Inside the potato processing plant"

"Not possible I saw a field" Brit replied a little disorientated

"It was an illusion, the building has been painted to match its surroundings on all sides using reactive paint which changes in colour and shading according to the time of day and lighting conditions making it imperceptible, a brilliant deception and a clever way of protecting one's intellectual property" Marcus explained and waited for the interior lights to switch on which they did one by one "Park the buggy over there we will walk the rest of the way" He then told Brit

"Not a good idea Soldier soon this place will be awash with freshly harvested potatoes, you should have left the cart outside and entered via the tree trunk" Major Weir said as he appeared by their side catching both off guard.

"We were just about to do that" Marcus boldly replied not admitting to any degree of incompetence on his part

"Your suspicions about Nils I take it caused you to undertake extra surveillance" The Major said playing along

"One can never be too careful"

"Or observant" David Weir cuttingly remarked as his way of saying "you missed the obvious, my buggy was parked outside in plain view"

Once they had squared the golf cart away and entered the potato processing plant via the tree trunk, Major Weir escorted Marcus and Brit through a series of convoluted passage ways and turn offs to access a spacious storeroom which was filled with cleaning equipment and seemingly discarded obsolete computers.

"Make yourselves at home; you have all the necessary tools at your disposal to start your thorough investigations, unisex toilets are down the corridor to your right, opposite that is a small kitchen where you will find coffee/tea making facilities plus an assortment of elegant sandwiches in the refrigerator. There's no need for me to go over what we have discussed earlier. Your task is to uncover what hold if any the Americans have over the Norwegians. You have just over three hours to complete your assignment. See you then" The Major succinctly said and swiftly departed the building leaving Marcus, Brit and Anya to sort out the mess.

"What's the matter Soldier? Don't know where to begin?" Anya asked as she started to fossick about

"What am I supposed to do with prehistoric junk?" Marcus grumbled looking quite bewildered

"That's where you are wrong. Grab that bulky computer over there and connect it to a power supply using an extension cable whilst I find a mouse, keypad and television monitor to suit. Brit can fend for herself, she's more than capable" Anya said taking charge which Marcus admired for it had been a while since he had taken orders from a woman.

Brit meanwhile went about clearing a space and assembling fold up tables and chairs. Within ten minutes Anya had proudly assembled and dusted clean a makeshift operational computer system which Marcus thought stood very little chance of working for any length of time.

"What shall we call this beast?" Anya happily asked

"BMC 1 before modern computers sounds appropriate" Brit suggested as she admired Anya's efforts.

"1 B.C. would be more appropriate" Marcus cynically replied as he seriously questioned the computers capabilities

"Let's boot up and see what we get?" Anya proposed without entering into the argument.

Marcus expected it to flicker once, twice and then go up in a puff of smoke instead the cumbersome desk top computer emitted a powerful hum whilst the ancient looking monitor merrily blazed away

"Who would have thought?" Anya sounded surprised as she read out the computers vital statistics which caused her companions to crowd around her

"Dual 980 quad-core processors, high definition 830 graphics card, 32 GB Ran and 4 terabyte memory, not bad for something that is 1 B.C." She commented which Marcus took squarely on the chin "Universal open source operating system, completely naked, untraceable, no pass words, no encryptions, no programs apart

from internet which is accessed via Wi-Fi in other words we are in"
Anya continued to babble whilst the thought crossed her mind that
there was another consequently she suggested "Brit it must have a
twin, look for it will you then we can start in earnest!"

"No problem, I think I saw it earlier on when I was shifting stuff
around" Brit responded and walked over to where she thought it
was resting. Marcus followed her helped transport it onto the table
and then assisted with its set up and cleaning. Not one for computers
he sat idly by and watched patiently as Brit and Anya went about
intensely delving into all sorts of archives to retrieve any damaging
information.

In Marcus's mind past political diplomatic attempts to find a
solution rarely achieved anything apart from unnecessarily dragging
things out. A prompt military action was a far better choice and
he wondered whether the present assignment would end up that
way. After an hour of looking over the girl's shoulders as they busily
worked away Marcus had reached the limits of his patience and
he decided it was time for a coffee and sandwich break which he
offered to bring to his fellow colleagues but they declined as they
were intent on getting the job done before the Major returned unlike
Marcus who obeyed his stomach first. Accordingly he made his way
to the kitchen where he made himself very comfortable after he had
brewed two mugs of coffee and selected several sandwiches filled
with gravlax smothered in sweet mustard. Reluctant to return to
the storeroom and under no strict instructions to stay put Marcus
decided that it might be worthwhile to become conversant with the
layout of the potato processing plant in the event of an emergency.

As he walked about the facility he realised that it was largely
unoccupied and completely computer controlled with all of the
secretive potato processing occurring underground in secure
tanks and chambers. There were only two ways in and out of the
building namely the tree trunk and the black hole for trucks. Bored

by the sterility of his surroundings Marcus decided to return to the storeroom where he hoped Brit and Anya had lived up to the Major's expectations.

8
EMPTY FINDINGS

As soon as Marcus opened the door to the storeroom he was greeted by the sounds of happy voices and the smell of freshly brewed aromatic coffee. The Major, Anya and Brit were enjoying a lively conversation as though they were celebrating a happy event.

"Come join us" David Weir jovially invited the more serious Grom operative who appeared quite restless

"Good news?" Marcus optimistically asked

"Not exactly, as hard as they tried neither Anya nor Brit in the time allocated were able to provide any concrete evidence as to how the Americans were able to seduce the Norwegian government into stationing in excess of four thousand of their troops on Norwegian soil"

"That's disappointing how did they may I ask conduct their investigations" Marcus politely enquired

"I'll let Anya report on that" The Major now a little more formal in attitude replied

"Being Norwegians we are well and truly aware of the political situation surrounding the controversial decision made some time ago and how tight the final voting was in granting the Americans access. Besides extensively reviewing the numerous newspaper articles and television reports on the events we accessed the public record of all of the parliamentary debates on the topic. The chief advocates for the yes vote we believe were the Minister for the Interior and the Minister for Justice. The Minister for the Interior it appears became rather influential as he had successfully investigated and exposed a 78 strong paedophile ring within Norway that operated to satisfy local and international clients. This elevated his status and credibility no end making him extremely popular and well respected. The minister extended his popularity by creating his own social media page titled 'The Champion and Protector of Abused Children' he is now quite the Scandinavian hero. We believe that as a result of this the yes campaign managed to scrape over the winning line by 52% to 48% of votes cast" Anya slowly explained

"Exactly when did the Minister post his social media page and when did he carry out his paedophile sting?" Marcus asked seeking precise clarification of the events' time line

"Actually that's something we hadn't investigated due to time constraints, ours was one of developing an overview rather than going into specifics"

"Perhaps you could answer the gentleman's pertinent question by doing some extra detective work whilst I make him a cup of coffee" The Major abruptly said as he stood up and signalled for Marcus to join him and aimlessly walk about the complex in silence for the next ten minutes. Marcus knew to keep his mouth shut as he concluded that he and the girls were being closely monitored and evaluated hence it was prudent at this time to remain professional.

"What do you have to report...?" The Major barked upon their return

"Marcus's 'suspicions' were correct. The Minister's social media page had been in existence two years prior to Operation Dungeon the paedophile sting that he instigated and co-ordinated with the help of numerous police districts. The social media page is part of his involvement with Child Protection Services which supposedly safeguard the safety of children under the age of sixteen years, rumour has it that a disproportionate number of children between the ages of three to nine years were taken into care without valid reasons two years ago" Brit answered as her way of predicting what Marcus was likely to say

Major Weir picked up on Brit's intention and coldly stared at Marcus in a way that shouted "Well soldier what do you have to say?"

"It is a pity you did not fully brief Anya and Brit before they had started their investigations" Marcus boldly stated without batting an eye lid

"Careful soldier must I remind you that you are talking to a superior office?"

"That's all well and good but I think you might agree the situation is more complicated than you or your anonymous superiors realise. I would have thought it was a good idea to have shown the girls the video footage that we retrieved some days ago, not only does it raise questions but it will change Brit and Anya's focus"

"I thought mentioning the cache of weapons was sufficient. Obviously it isn't. Have it your way soldier gather around everyone its show time" The Major cuttingly bellowed as he produced a USB stick that contained an exact copy of that which the Islamic man had filmed. As they viewed the extensive photographic evidence which lasted thirty minutes, it became apparent that the cache of weapons exceeded that required to equip four thousand troops.

"Anyone would think the Americans were preparing for war instead of being trained to adapt to extreme winter conditions" The Major loosely commented

"That's the last thing we wanted to hear" Brit answered in a fiercely nationalistic tone of voice which suggested that she wanted to protect Norway and its people from any military conflict.

"That's one probable explanation that cannot be discounted. What does the Islamic man's raving tell us, but more importantly how did he manage to discover the weapons and their location?"

Marcus asked as he prodded for further plausible explanations.

"He mentions David, a bit of useless information without a surname; then he rubbishes the Americans calling them assholes and suggests that Allah is the bringer of peace almost as if it is the Americans who are at fault. Question is what was he doing there, was it to expose the depot of weapons or was it to steal or accept delivery of a consignment, the latter is questionable as he died of radiation poisoning" Major Weir replied which made Marcus a little suspicious as he momentarily considered that the Major was in fact the David that the Islamic man had referred to.

"Are you suggesting that the cache of weapons is for the black market?" Anya asked in a disgusted tone of voice

"Possibly" The Major grimly responded

"Quiet, neutral Norway, full of fun loving unsuspecting citizens, manipulated by greedy corrupt politicians to become a powder keg of destruction" Brit cynically denounced

"We can't let this continue as it is we have to do something about it we owe it to our people!" Anya proudly said in a determined frame of mind

"However we must tread carefully for I feel that there are many players, the Islamic man I fear was a casualty of an arms deal gone wrong, the bombings of the Israeli embassy and holiday home payback for non delivery" Marcus quietly postulated

"What a twist, usually conspirators blame the CIA for such things, no one has ever pointed the finger at Mossad, welcome to the brave new world of imaginary arms dealings" David Weir ambiguously said

"Where do we start?" Brit asked somewhat bewildered by the situation at hand

"Some say that it's not what you know but who you know that advances one's ambitions, supposing it's neither of the two individually but a combination but not one based on fact but fiction" Marcus philosophically answered

"What has this got to do with the matter at hand?" David Weir sharply asked

"Denial by the Norwegians I believe represents stalling tactics to enable them to relocate their merchandise, your friend Nils our concierge is a secret KNN operative stationed in Roros under the disguise of head of the Troll Hunters and David is perhaps not a person but the Star of David which is in keeping with your con-spiracy theory"

"Interesting deductions but no real strategies for us to proceed on" Major Weir jeered

"I thought they were self evident" Marcus calmly retorted

"Perhaps you would like to itemize them?"

"With pleasure Major, you and I will both return to Roros under the cover of darkness and explore the caves where the cache of weapons is located. If time permits we will attempt to find the entry and exit points and report our findings, Brit and Anya meanwhile with the help of KNN's technical team which in all probability is in hiding but can be contacted by Nils they will attempt to hack the personal lines of communication of both Ministers going back at least three years. The agreement between Norway and the USA to host rotational marines on Norwegian soil did not happen on the spur of the moment it was a well orchestrated event. It's not as if Norway needs the almighty American dollar as Norway is presently the richest country in the world according to the World Bank rankings. Failing that I suggest Brit and Anya do it the old fashioned way and penetrate the Ministers' offices one way or another to see what they can retrieve"

"Not bad for a novice. Your ideas bear some fleeting hallmarks of a gripping political thriller but supposing they are not enough what then?" The Major seriously asked

"We blow up the storehouse of weapons" Marcus dryly answered.

"If that is your attitude soldier I suppose we had better kit you up" Major Weir abruptly said as he stood up to greet Nils who it appeared had pre-empted their needs and was ready to assist.

"Welcome Nils I think you already know Marcus from a previous brief encounter, he will require the usual night stuff plus the latest Russian inspired full body armour code named 'croissant' that can easily withstand explosions. Anya and Brit are eager to meet your technical man stationed in Sweden so if you could arrange suitable transport for them we can get things moving."

Nils simply nodded his head to indicate he fully understood and gestured for Marcus to follow him.

9

IS NOTHING SECRET?

Once Marcus was suitably dressed with an array of 'cafe' items as he affectionately thought of them the Major signalled that it was time for them to depart.

"My idea or yours....?" Marcus asked straight to the point.

"Yours of course, Nils is quite the character, just love the code names he has attached to his sophisticated equipment"

"Rather colourful, who would have thought a croissant was in fact body armour and a ham sandwich is two layers of plastic explosive separated by a denoting substance"

"Only those in the know which reminds me put this jacket on will you, we need to look the part" The Major answered as he handed an official 'Norwegian Ice' employees coat to Marcus.

"Is this our cover? Doing deliveries to liquor stores and restaurants"

"Only as far as Oslo's International airport where we will board a SAS jet and fly to Sundsvall, a brief two hour flight"

"And then...?" Marcus inquired

"We travel by car along Route 315 before deviating onto Route 84 to Fjallnäs where we will leave the main road and drive into the mountains until we reach 62.6472N 11-8669E"

"Just in time for dinner, which I hope will not be a mixture of croissants and ham sandwiches! You have organised dinner?" Marcus flippantly asked

"Actually no, in all of the excitement I got rather carried away"

"Lack of attention to detail had better not be one of your failings" Marcus acidly replied with a cold stare.

"I don't suppose a selection of high protein energy bars is going to suffice?"

"Not in the least I would prefer something a little more substantial that I can sink my teeth into!"

"Quite the action man" The Major dryly answered

"That is what I was trained for"

"We can search the Internet once we board the plane and see what Fjallnäs has to offer" The Major suggested

"If not before, by my reckoning it will take us eight to ten hours to reach our final destination" Marcus correctly determined which made the Major realise that he had miscalculated their arrival time in the mountains.

"Yes I agree perhaps we should consider dining in Sundsvall and packing some emergency supplies"

"But not cotton wool, bottled water or Vaseline" Marcus replied tongue in cheek which made the Major smile.

Within the hour they were at Oslo's compact International Airport standing in line to board SAS flight 825 to Sundsvall Sweden.

"Welcome on board, thank you for flying with SAS, pleasant flight" the attractive middle aged female flight attendant with flaxen hair repeatedly said as she greeted one traveller after another.

"Thank you" Marcus warmly replied as he displayed his boarding pass.

"Mr Davidson how nice to see you once again, is everything okay, business doing well?" She asked as she instantly recognised Major Weir

"Thank you, it's mutual, we must catch up for coffee sometime, perhaps next week"

"I'd like that" The attractive female flight attendant purred with a sparkle in her eye.

"It's a date then" The Major whispered in her ear.

"The usual spot" She replied in a hushed voice.

"But of course it has all the comforts of home" The Major confirmed as he passed her by.

"One of your many conquests...?" Marcus bluntly asked once the Major was seated next to him.

"Let's say she is a source of invaluable information and needs to be rewarded in numerous ways"

"How thoughtful of you" Marcus ambiguously answered as he wiggled and fiddled until he was finally comfortable and then closed his eyes to explore the future which the Major didn't particularly worry about but as hard as he could try Marcus was unable to stop his mind from imagining the attractive female flight attendant naked and performing all manner of oral delights whilst the Major repeatedly said "Lick my liquorice, cause its black and twisted" a phrase that would have future ramifications not only for Marcus but Britt and Anya as well.

Unlike Marcus things did not go smoothly for the two highly trained FSK agents as Nils was unable to contact KNN's computer whizz as he had truly gone to ground which meant Anya and Britt would have to resort to 'cleaning' the two Minister's offices in order to obtain the vital information they sought something that they would not do until 8pm that night which allowed them sufficient time to get their resources together, unlike Marcus who for all intents and purposes was the complete package having trained himself in the art of remote viewing which had allowed him at times to gain the advantage over others. So immersed was he in determining the imminent future that Marcus was unaware that they had landed, two hours in real time represented nothing in the dream world.

"Wake up soldier you'll miss the best bits" the Major urged Marcus as he prodded him in the ribs.

"What are we there?"

"Time to get the show on the road"

"Doing a presentation Mr Davidson?" the attractive female flight attendant asked as she passed them by.

"Always seeking new ways of livening things up" the Major joked

"Pity I can't be there" the female flight attendant sighed and sweetly smiled

"You can always come along as a SAS purchasing officer" the Major suggested even though he knew that would be quite impossible.

"I don't have the necessary certificate"

"Damn bureaucracy we'll just have to make it a private affair" the Major lecherously suggested which made the lady blush and quickly take her leave.

"You really are gun ho" Marcus quipped as he stood up to stretch his back.

"Like I said she deserves to be rewarded in numerous ways"

Whatever" Marcus replied disapprovingly and followed the Major out. Once they had stepped onto the airport's tarmac the Major made a bee line to where the baggage handlers were stationed and collected a picnic basket and a set of keys from an unassuming person with distinctive features.

"This way the car is over there" He then said as he nodded for Marcus to follow closely behind.

"Not another dilapidated obsolete Defender!"

"Outwardly but very reliable still packs a punch or two"

"If you say so" Marcus grumbled as he thought the Major to be quite mad.

"First things first, off with the 'Norwegian Ice' and on with the latest innovation in gillie suits" the Major enthusiastically said as he produced a jacket that reflected its surroundings.

"What, how....?" Marcus asked in astonishment

"Borrowed it from an octopus"

"How does the octopus feel about that?"

"Naked and cold I should imagine" the Major dryly answered

"Anything I should know about this?"

"Stay close to your background otherwise it becomes confused and....."

"Makes you look ridiculous"

"Something like that" the Major replied before opening the picnic basket to reveal and assortment of weaponry.

"Croissants and ham sandwiches not good enough"

"Only when it comes to boarding airplanes" the Major dryly explained

"No other food?" Marcus pretended to groan with hunger

"That's down the road can't have a soldier marching on an empty stomach"

"How thoughtful of you" Marcus politely replied and wondered what the Major had in store.

"Right now let's get this stuff squared away and enjoy an early dinner" the Major calmly said as he went about the business of discretely securing the weapons into their various hiding compartments before locking and arming the Defender.

"One last thing before we leave, take off your jacket and turn it inside out. Don't want people thinking you're some sort of freak! That's it, now let's taxi it in" The Major cheerfully said as though he thought they were in for a good night out.

"Where are we going?" Marcus asked

"Sven's Place, good wholesome traditional Swedish food, none of this new age stuff where the food is made to look important by the size of the plate it's on, Sven is an excellent place to relax and plot our evening's activities" The Major brightly said

"Music to my ears because I am famished" Marcus replied as he kept pace with the energetic Major who had already signalled a taxi to transport them.

Sven's Place was a delightfully decorated restaurant situated in the main street of Sundsvall with a mini mart conveniently situated across the road from it one that the Major hinted they would purchase an assortment of provisions for their five hour journey into the mountains. The restaurant was busy to say the least as it continuously provided food from 7am in the morning until midnight to cater for all sorts of folk. Major Weir had reserved a table that afforded views of the street outside and broad views of the restaurant's interior.

The numerous patrons were relaxed but Marcus noticed that members of the staff were somewhat edgy especially the duty managers and it had nothing to do with the pressure of work something else bothered them and he wondered if it had anything to do with something that was black and twisted. Once they had entered Sven's Place they were quickly ushered to their table for two complete with a small vase of flowers and flickering candle.

"How romantic" Marcus joked once they were seated.

"I thought you might appreciate it considering that you are half Polish"

"In what way...?" Marcus asked as to the best of his knowledge there was no such thing as a string of world famous Polish restaurants or Polish cuisine.

"A bit of European flavour getting away from pizza, burgers, Chinese and Mexican"

"In other words sophistication" Marcus suggested

"Precisely" The Major agreed.

"The menu looks very extensive" Marcus commented as he flicked though its contents.

"And simple, a minimum of ingredients for maximum flavour" The Major put forward

"The mark of an accomplished chef" Marcus concluded as he thoughtfully decided what to order considering the time of day, the emptiness of his stomach and the long journey ahead.

"Well what will it be?"

"How can one possibly ignore the meat balls, mash potato with cream sauce and lingonberries followed by princess cake?" Marcus replied.

"I agree an excellent choice, when in Sweden....."

"Do as the Swedes do"

"Precisely" The Major warmly agreed

"Anything to drink gentlemen....?" A spritely waitress asked as she suddenly appeared from nowhere catching both off guard.

"Nothing alcoholic thank you, we have night duty" The Major replied

"Sparkling water perhaps...?"

"Sounds nice, what do you have"

"Norwegian sparkling glacier water, Finnish still and Danish half and half" the spritely waitress answered

"Quite a selection, what do you say Marcus" The Major asked

"I like the sound of glacier"

"Then we shall have two bottles of your finest, slightly chilled thank you" The Major replied as though he was ordering a bottle of fine French wine.

"Straight away Sir" the spritely waitress said and took her leave.

"She is nice" Marcus commented

"In contrast to those across the street" Major Weir disapprovingly said as he noticed two undesirable black Africans park their up market sports car outside the mini mart and emerge as though they owned the place. After briefly exchanging words one went inside the mini mart whilst the other adjusted his attire and strutted across the street to enter the restaurant.

"Black and twisted" Marcus mumbled

"What was that?" the Major inquired.

"Nothing Sir just a premonition I had earlier"

"On route"

"It did not escape you?"

"Not much does" the Major confirmed as he watched the black

African arrogantly approach the restaurants main counter and rudely demand to see the manager whom it seemed was familiar with the African.

"This is more than take away" the Major remarked as he watched the African impatiently pace up and down once he gave his order.

"At least Poland got it right!" Marcus acidly said in a racist way as he stared at the African

"By refusing them entry?" the Major asked

"What better way to minimise gangs, leeches and drug lords?" Marcus quietly whispered as he continued to intensify his menacing stare

"A sensitive subject" the Major diplomatically replied in a hushed voice

"Not to my way of thinking" Marcus bluntly answered without altering his stare something that began to irritate and make the African feel uneasy. The Major could feel a confrontation brewing.

"Perhaps you could change your point of view?" he politely asked in order to defuse the situation.

"Good idea, back in a minute" Marcus quickly replied and abruptly left. The Major watched as Marcus marched out of the restaurant, fearlessly passed within centimetres of the obnoxious African and crossed the street in a manner that suggested he had lost something earlier and that he needed to search the road and pavement adjacent to the parked sports car.

Pretending that he had retrieved the lost object from under the car Marcus returned in time to witness the African accept his take away goodies and subtly flash a ribbon of Belgium made hand grenades that dangled around his waist which the manager acknowledged as a sign which meant "play the game or otherwise"

"Bastard...!" Marcus mumbled under his breath as he walked through the front door and returned to his table.

"I took the liberty of ordering for both of us. Find what you were looking for?" The Major subtly asked as he poured a glass of chilled

Norwegian glacier water and handed it to Marcus.

"Phase 2 complete"

"An object....?"

"No a concept...?'" Marcus answered

"What is phase 1...?"

"Reconnaissance"

"And Phase 3...?" The Major asked even though he knew the answer.

"Dismember preceded by disarm" Marcus unemotionally answered straight to the point.

"I look forward to seeing how well it pans out" The Major replied knowing full well that Marcus had referred to a well tried and tested military procedure.

"So am I" Marcus answered with a wry smile as he kept one eye trained on the black Africans movements something that the Major did as well. They both sat in silence and waited for the inevitable commotion to begin.

The two black African extortionists ecstatic with the size of the protection monies they had just acquired congratulated each other with the high five greeting before climbing into their opulent sports car. Completely oblivious to everything about them the black African who had stolen from Sven's Place turned the car's ignition to on, selected drive and attempted to gun the engine and make a speedy get away. But the car refused to budge instead it groaned as several tyres burst their side walls and the rims dug into the roads bitumen.

Utterly baffled by what had just unexpectedly happened both Africans exited the car and stared at the damage in complete disbelief before they profusely swore and idiotically pranced about demanding answers. They argued with each other as to what had happened and what to do next now that they were stranded and standing in the middle of a crime scene. One produced his answer to everything the almighty and powerful mobile phone for he believed it would solve anything. He would call for backup, no problem but before he had a chance to dial out much to the surprise of one and all they were surrounded by seen and unseen commandos belonging to the city's police tactical response.

Thinking that they could bluff their way out of their predicament both Africans undid their jackets to reveal numerous grenades which they threatened to throw into the mini mart, Sven's Place and at the innocent civilians who walked along the street unless they were allowed to escape. But the tactical response commandos had been given strict instructions on how to behave under such circumstances and they wasted no time in disposing of both Africans killing them with silent and deadly head shots. The time for arresting such criminals, wasting public monies on meaningless prosecutions and housing them in maximum security hotels known as jails until they died was over. Body bags were the cheaper solution.

"That was quick! Did you have anything to do with this?" Marcus asked the Major as he imagined that he could have played a greater role in dealing with the Africans.

"Perhaps" The Major softly answered

"When...?" Marcus asked rather perplexed

"As soon as that stupid African revealed his wares when you passed him by on your way out I recognised your resolve to rid Sweden of this vermin I could not risk losing you or having you injured so I called in the troops. This was nothing more than a distraction we have much bigger fish to fry"

"Thank you Sir" Marcus replied as he began to see the Major in a different light and concluded that they made a good team.

The young spritely waitress all in a fluster rushed to where Marcus and the Major were seated and apologetically interrupted them.

"I'm so sorry to have seated you here! I hope you haven't been too distressed by the happenings outside perhaps I can seat you in a more secluded area?" she nervously said.

"No need to trouble yourself Miss we are both in the rubbish disposal business and have seen far worse grotesque things over the years" the Major convincingly replied.

"Oh thank you Sir for being so understanding. Your meals shouldn't be too much longer the police slowed us down a little"

"We well and truly understand they have to follow procedure at least they haven't closed the restaurant" the Major answered as he observed two plain clothed detectives calmly interviewing the ruffled duty manager who understandably wished for his shift to end.

Meanwhile across the road the mini mart had been sealed off as it was a serious crime scene. Ambulances had arrived and paramedics were inside the store attending to its owner and female employee both of whom had been repeatedly pistol whipped and sustained serious head injuries. Forensics was also present inside and outside to document the evening's events and make certain every bullet fired was accounted for. Several marked patrol cars had also arrived, the occupants instructed to patrol the surrounding areas for any suspicious characters and locate, intercept and arrest on suspicion if need be everyone of the contacts that the black African had on his mobile phone. This was one gang that was about to be liquidated very quickly in Sundsvall.

"The chef must be used to working under pressure" Major Weir flippantly said once their meals had arrived.

"I agree nothing untoward about it at all. Nicely balanced, nothing over or undercooked, flavours intact" Marcus said once he had sampled the dish

"Probably worked in the French Foreign Legion" the Major suggested.

"Or worse" Marcus counted as he eagerly satisfied his hunger.

"Let's hope it goes as smoothly in the mountains" the Major whispered in a low voice

"Don't tell me you have commandos stationed there as well"

"Only us" the Major truthfully confirmed as he smiled and nodded in the affirmative

The rest of the evening went uninterrupted allowing the Major to engage in idle chit chat, people watch and pass the occasional lewd comment about certain anatomical aspects of any attractive woman that caught his eye. The only interruption early on was when the plain clothed detectives asked if the Major or Marcus saw who might have tampered with the Africans get away sports car as three of its tyres it appeared had been deliberately punctured. The only assistance that the duo had to offer was coffee at their expense for the hard working detectives. They readily accepted the offer but passed up on cake as they had to stay at or below regulation weight according to their height.

The journey along Route 315 was uneventful and boring in contrast to Sundsvall but it gave Marcus the opportunity to once again remote view what they might find in the mountain caves and how well Britt and Anya were doing earlier that day.

The government quarter known as Regjeringskvartalet in Norwegian is a collection of nine buildings located in the centre of Oslo. On the 22nd July 2011 it was the site of a car bombing which caused the deaths of eight people and the injury of two hundred others. Several buildings were heavily damaged and as a consequence Regjeringskvartalet was reconstructed to satisfy the elevated standards of security, working space and environmental considerations. In order to prevent another attack eyes seen and unseen, human, electronic or canine were everywhere making it almost impossible to go about the complex undetected no matter what time of day. Only those who worked there on a continuous basis and had undergone vigorous security checks and psychological testing were above suspicion, everyone else was deemed a threat and closely monitored using the latest facial recognition software and intent to harm technology that determined the magnitude of the harm by analysing the individual's body language, facial expressions and body temperature. Even stone faced individuals could not elude being analysed and categorised. These were some of the thoughts and considerations that both Anya and Brit reflected upon before they collectively decided to act upon Marcus's suggestion of 'burgling' the ministers' offices.

"Going in as cleaners even with the best ID and clearance will not guarantee our entry facial recognition technology will expose us. Going in as FSK agents on a pretend mission or otherwise is risky, once our visit is logged all those involved will start asking questions" Brit glumly said as she thought the Major would discipline them for inaction. Anya thought the opposite namely that he would praise them for their caution. Nils who was present said very little as he was preoccupied with locating KNN's electronic whizz kid.

"I think we need to take a different tact, investigate something which is not blatantly obvious but explains everything in full detail" Anya thoughtfully suggested.

"Like....?"

"I honestly don't know" Anya replied scratching her head.

"You might want to investigate paedophilia" Nils said without giving any warning

"What are you suggesting?" Brit asked rather confused as she couldn't see any connection between that and their present investigation.

"It might be worthwhile interviewing the condemned" Nils calmly said as he produced a list of names and their place of 'residence' which he handed to Anya who readily accepted it.

"What is your interest in this?" Brit asked sensing that Nils knew something.

"Let us say that the witch hunt and its subsequent trial were a little too clean and orchestrated. The evidence against the accused was overwhelmingly damning, no public access to the accused was ever granted"

"Then the list is useless!" Brit angrily concluded as she pointed to the list that Anya held in her hand.

"Under the circumstances one could argue yes, but things change and opportunities arise" Nils replied.

"Explain"

"KNN has been fortunate in securing the services of a sympathiser to its cause, a rather vocal psychiatrist who is employed by the federal health department in the capacity of caring for the long term mental well being of prisoners in jail especially those kept in isolation"

"That must be tough for them" Brit answered as she was well acquainted with mental agony which she endured during her FSK psychological training.

"Especially if you are innocent" Nils answered in dead pan fashion

"What do you suggest? I feel we are both powerless" Anya stated

"Subject to change in appearance I thought one of you might join the physician on his rounds this afternoon and make notes, you never know what you might uncover"

It was obvious to Brit that Anya would accompany the sympathetic psychiatrist as she was well qualified in psychology and forensics this was after all a job for the experts, Brit also intuitively reasoned that if indeed the 'paedophiles' were innocent there were faceless individuals who wished to keep the innocents locked away and silent forever. Anya would have to use the subtlest of means to extract further information as more than likely Anya's visit would be closely monitored and recorded in detail. Nils and Anya both agreed with Brit's reasoning and suggested she assist Nils with his efforts to contact Erik KNN's expert computer hacker.

Norwegian Ice distillery's complex was self sufficient for it contained everything necessary to promote itself including makeup, marketing and photographic rooms where everything was made to be not as it was. Once comfortably seated in makeup Anya was physically transformed through the application of different types of prosthesis to resemble a Finnish undergraduate student on academic placement in Norway. When all was said and done Brit had trouble recognising the attractive Anya as not only had her facial features changed but eye and hair colour as well.

"Well don't you look the part" She complimented Anya who had some difficulty adjusting to the new me.

"Compliments aside I must get a move on, I have an important date with the doctor" Anya jokingly replied before she was about to be whisked away by Nils.

"Just a few more finishing touches, student photo ID, authentic duplicated Finnish driver's licence, keys to the rental car, foolscap note book, handbag with female essentials, lip balm, chewing gum, touch up face powder, comb, cheap mobile phone, bobby pins, facial tissues, one emergency tampon, emery board, nail varnish and I think young lady you are set to go. Let me escort you to the car and then you can be on your way. The car's GPS has been programmed to guide you to your first destination, try to be back no later than 10pm tonight" Nils brightly said with a reassuring smile.

Once Anya had exited the grounds of Norwegian Ice and activated the rental car's GPS she knew exactly where to go as she had previously frequented Ullersmo high security prison on numerous occasions.

The prison located 32km NE of Oslo caters for long term inmates, its capacity is limited to two hundred and fifty males, one third of whom are foreigners as a result radicalisation became a problem even though the authorities denied it.

The weather had suddenly changed it became rainy and quite chilly making driving conditions hazardous especially in a rental car which was a far cry from the high pursuit vehicles Anya was accustomed to driving, nevertheless she drove sedately and safely much like a tourist in a foreign land.

Anya's cover was Aino Koskinen a Finnish final year under-graduate psychology student writing a comparative study of mental health outcomes in prisoners with jail sentences between five to seven years in Norway, Sweden and Finland. Her assigned mentor in Norway was Dr Gabriel Retterstol a middle aged unmarried state appointed independent psychiatrist who not only closely monitored the well being of prisoners from a mental and physical point of view but prison guards as well for he considered neither benefited from their prison confines. Dr Gabriel was above all a free thinker who did not accept any of the theoretical explanations nor arguments put forward supporting the use of psychiatric drugs in the absence of proper and accurate laboratory tests the fundamental principle underlying peoples 'psychotic' behaviour as far as he was concerned was that the individual was basically unhappy. Unlike his medical friends who specialised in different areas of practice and would surely die of the very disease they sought to control Dr Gabriel always imagined he would leave planet Earth a happy man.

Nils had arranged for Anya and the Doctor to meet in Ullersmo's public car park and to make recognition easier he provided each with a photograph of the other being chaperoned by the Doctor made it easy for Anya to enter the prison complex.

"How many inmates will we be assessing today?" Anya respectfully asked as though she was in a public library.

"Only those in isolation or solitary confinement, the rest in groups of eight submit a monthly questionnaire electronically which we assess in our offices, I will provide you with a copy" the Doctor answered.

"Does it include a mini mental test?" Anya asked

"Not at all, you will be surprised by its content it's novel it's new unlike anything seen before, in fact it reads like a comic book" Doctor Gabriel answered as he lead the way towards the interview rooms where seven self confessed 'paedophiles' were seated in a circle. There were no guards in the room as the prisoners were considered low risk but 'fair game' should their misdemeanours be unintentionally circulated.

Doctor Gabriel stopped at the door and whispered in Anya's ear "All of these are self confessed convicted paedophiles serving a six year sentence, do not mention their crime, it's a very delicate subject and could lead to confrontations"

"I'll keep that in mind" Anya replied as she thought "You play your games I'll play mine"

"Excellent! How are you at pricking fingers?"

"Haven't done one in a while, why do you ask?"

"As part of the exercise I perform a series of in situ blood tests designed to identify physiological changes as a result of stress, I look at blood glucose, high and low density lipids, sedimentation rates, cortisol levels with my trusty portable machine hence I need a few drops of blood from each individual before I progress to measuring blood pressures, weight, muscle tone etcetera etcetera" Dr Gabriel explained.

"Don't you use a prick like the diabetics do?"

"Yes I do I was just testing your abilities" Dr Gabriel light heartedly replied and opened the door to usher Anya inside where seven males of all ages sat it seemed in a state of acceptance meaning that what happened to them was in keeping with their code namely deliver others from harm, ruin or loss.

"Good afternoon gentlemen nice to see you once again, hope you are all well, this is Aino an attractive student from Finland on assignment here to study how well we threat prisoners in confinement. She will assist me today and may ask you a question or two, if you are comfortable with that. I think we should make a start" Dr Gabriel cheerfully said as he unloaded his gear, placed it on a table in front of him and arranged it in readiness for Anya to take blood.

Anya seated herself, thoroughly washed her hands with a sanitizer and gestured for the first male to come forward which happened quite naturally as if a pecking order existed amongst the inmates.

"Hello" Anya warmly said as the man gingerly approached her.

"Hello" he said in return and sat down.

"What is your name?"

"Stefan" the male nervously answered.

"Do all of you occupy one large cell?" Anya asked as she looked around.

"No each one of us is kept in solitary confinement, we get together for meals, when we have our showers and do our outdoor exercise"

"That must give you quite a lot of time in which to reflect" Anya concluded.

"Often it is too much" Stefan ambiguously replied as he extended his hand.

"So how do you manage to keep on an even keel?"

"I have my creed"

"Daily rituals...?" Anya guessed

"A little more philosophical" Stefan firmly answered

"Something that you might argue with the others....?" Anya asked mindful that everything they discussed was being recorded

"Not really..."

"Why not...?"

"Because we share common ground" Stefan replied without giving anything away.

"Would you like to enlarge on that?"

"Not really" Stefan answered in a defensive tone of voice.

"Perhaps another time" Anya suggested as she lanced his finger and squeezed it firmly so as to signify who was boss, Stefan remained silently calm throughout.

Once she had finished Stefan abruptly stood up and allowed the next in line to occupy his seat.

"Hi" Anya brightly said.

"Hi I am Jebbe" the fresh faced man answered.

"You seem more alive than Stefan, are you always this happy?" Anya asked as she took his hand.

"But of course everything is going fine"

"Your blood seems to reflect that, very bright and vibrant" Anya said once she drew blood and placed it on a test strip "What strategies do you use to cope with the confinement?"

"I draw a lot" Jebbe answered with a twinkle in his eye

"Nothing to do with Stefan's creed...?"

"It's a little too intense for me, I'm over Tyr if you know what I mean" Jebbe confided however Anya misheard Jebbe's over Tyr as being over tired and consequently thought he was not one for serious debating of any sort more of a happy go lucky artist who belonged on the streets of Paris selling his art and before Anya had a chance to ask if she could view them Jebbe scampered away to join his friends.

Male number three was a different kettle of fish largely because he smelt of fish, rotting fish in fact.

"Unusual body odour on second thought it's absolutely awful!" Anya thought as he sat down before her.

"Yes I know I am a genetic freak, my FMO3 gene is on the blink! Comes in useful sometimes, thugs and criminals avoid me, holding down a relationship with the opposite sex is challenging" Martin confessed as he studied Anya's reaction which he found rather amusing.

"Can't you do anything about it?" Anya asked as she struggled for fresh air.

"Sorry got carried away this morning at breakfast and had an extra serving of eggs"

"What's that got to do with it?" Anya asked turning blue in the face.

"My body can't breakdown trimethylamine which causes a fish like odour but if I follow a strict diet I can minimize the amount, however stress worsens it and under the circumstances I am stressed to the max! My name is Martin by the way"

"Pleased to meet you I think....so what you are saying is that you're not coping with imprisonment"

"Not in the slightest, even the creed is not helping" Martin reluctantly confessed.

"Why not....?"

"It's only idealistic I don't think life is meant to be that way"

"Can you explain further?" Anya asked

"Would you willingly put your arm into a lion's mouth knowing full well that it be bitten off?"

"I suppose not"

"Well then I rest my case" Martin answered and waited for Anya to prick his swollen finger.

"I am a little confused, are you suggesting the creed has worsened your situation?"

"Actually it caused it"

"How....?" Anya asked out of curiosity

"In my quest for personal salvation I embraced the creed hoping it would rid me of my afflictions. But it went the other way and I found myself in the wrong place at the wrong time, the rest is history" Martin regretfully answered which left Anya somewhat lost for words as she was instructed to avoid all references to paedophilia. Anya hoped Dr Gabriel might say something to rescue her and diffuse the situation.

"Not bad for a novice, you kept up rather well" Dr Gabriel openly congratulated Anya as he reached over and collected her labelled test strips. "This won't take long" he then said and proceeded to activate his multi tester which responded in kind.

"While I do this perhaps you could distribute this month's story booklet" Dr Gabriel suggested and Anya gladly obliged.

The booklet consisted of twelve back and front pages which depicted two cartoon characters, one of which had something to say whilst the other's was dependent upon the reader who could choose from six different responses applicable to the scene. In such a way the reader determined the text and outcome of the story which reflected the reader's psychological mood at that point in time.

"Clever, imaginative and highly accurate" Anya concluded as she flicked through a spare copy.

"Probably has more applications than just in here" Dr Gabriel commented once he had finished the various test results.

"I agree and I would also argue that it may redefine mental diseases as such and improve our understanding of cognitive functions"

"I am flattered....Martin alias the whinger your test results are normal, so you can skip the poor me act!" Dr Gabriel replied in a loud voice which caused Martin to moan and groan in defeat it also signalled that the session and all of its entertainment was over "That's us done for the day, time to leave, until next month keep well I bid you adieu" Dr Gabriel announced before gathering up all of his sophisticated equipment and waited for the prisoners to hand in their completed booklets.

"They haven't any names on them" Anya observed as she helped the Dr Gabriel

"No problem I know each one by their handwriting"

"Ticks and crosses?"

"Not difficult it's all in the angle" Dr Gabriel replied as he ushered Anya out.

Dr Gabriel's words left a lasting impression on Anya and it made her think what angle was there that imprisoned seven unlikely 'paedophiles' who outwardly did not fit the behavioural profile. A question that Nils would most certainly ask her once she returned to Norwegian Ice where she hoped comfortable lodgings and a hearty meal awaited her.

In that respect Nils did not disappoint in fact once Anya returned he left her alone to discuss her observations with Brit whilst he attended to preparing dinner, a good strategy for some argue that people think better on a full stomach whilst others believe otherwise arguing that hunger makes one more cunning, the portions that

Nils served fell mid-way between the two.

"What conclusions if any have you reached?" Nils politely asked as he delivered two cups of freshly brewed coffee at the end of the meal.

"Stefan was severely withdrawn, Jebbe completely away with the fairies and as for Martin who in their right mind would go anywhere near him? Not one of them possessed that leery, lecherous deviant look in their eyes and by that I mean the entire group as such. I wanted to investigate the creed they spoke of, I got the impression it caused more harm than good. In addition to this Dr Gabriel informed me that each inmate chose to admit guilt without entering a plea" Anya answered.

"Which is to be expected" Nils grunted

"What do you mean by that?" Brit asked

"I thought Anya would have detected the common thread amongst the inmates" Nils responded

"I only interviewed three, apart from paedophilia and a common survival creed I found no other and without talking to the remaining four I cannot extrapolate my findings" Anya firmly retorted

"This creed, what do you know about it?" Nils asked

"Not much"

"Did the word Tyr enter anyone of your conversations?"

"Only over tired" Anya wrongly responded

"Anything else...?"

"Only the dangers associated with it"

"Which were...?"

"Akin to losing one's arm in the mouth of a lion" Anya vaguely remembered

"Then you have your answers" Nils put forward

"Sounds more like a vague basis for assumption"

"Not really, a sacrificial belief system designed to protect others from harm, ruin or loss; all of the inmates the ones on the list that I gave you I believe belong to the same religious order known as the Creed of Tyr, a Germanic mythological God who sacrificed his arm in upholding law and justice. The order came into being in the early 1900's and only accepted the most ardent zealous followers. Its operation remained largely secret it was never seen to be anything else than a benevolent organisation doing good behind the scenes" Nils explained

"Are you suggesting it was deliberately targeted?" Brit asked

"At this stage that remains speculative, something for you to investigate" Nils replied

"Even though it remains secretive....?"

"Women have ways of extracting information out of men which I am certain Anya has done on numerous occasions both in the line of duty and privately" Nils suggested with a wry smile

"Tomorrow's project" Brit concluded with a nod of her head

"Precisely" Nils confirmed as he took a long sip of his hot chocolate in preparation for a solid night's sleep something that Anya would not enjoy as all of a sudden it became her urgent duty to dig up the dirt that the Creed of Tyr was concealing.

Anya's cover would remain the same her purpose of visiting the Creed of Tyr's pastor would be to present her findings with respect to the Creed's imprisoned followers' mental well being. Anya would go alone but for security reasons Brit would shadow her every move. The Creed of Tyr's church and administrative offices were located on the outskirts of Fredrikstad 90km south of Oslo easily accessed by road along highway E6 or via train or bus. The trio thought it best and safest for Anya to drive in the hire car that was fitted with a tracking device, Brit would follow at a safe distance using Marcus's BMW motorcycle.

10
CREED

Early next day after a restless night's sleep Anya was informed that Dr Gabriel's receptionist had arranged for her to meet with the Creed of Tyr's pastor at 9am that morning to discuss the inmates mental well being, to help with this Anya was provided with a full set of patient medical notes should the discussion become technical in nature.

"Feeling nervous...?" Nils asked as Anya glanced at the notes

"A little" she answered rather bleary eyed

"Why is that?"

"I suppose because I don't know how the pastor will react, what's his name by the way?" Anya asked

"Kristiasen"

"Seems appropriate" Anya replied as she shuffled the papers together in readiness to depart

"Know where you are going?" Nils asked

"Is that a rhetorical question?"

"Brit's already gone"

"Why, I thought she would follow?"

"Making certain the roads were clear I think she said" Nils grunted

"How thoughtful of her" Anya roughly mumbled and proceeded to leave

"No breakfast...?" Nils asked

"Thought I might arrive looking stressed out and test his Christian charity"

"You're halfway there" Nils cuttingly remarked and left it at that

The Creed of Tyr buildings were located in picturesque parklands that boarded the Glomma River ideal surroundings in which to meditate and reflect in silence whether inside or out. The only access to the complex was via a private road that allowed vehicles to creep in and park inconspicuously without disturbing the peace.

"Smells of old money and good taste" Anya thought as she looked about, gathered her briefs in readiness to exit the car.

As soon as she stepped outside a hand grabbed her shoulder from behind which caused Anya to instinctively spin around, drop to one knee and prepare to punch her would be assailant in the groin followed by a vicious uppercut to the jaw.

"Steady on I mean you no harm, after all I am a priest" Pastor Kristiasen said a little shaken by Anya's self defence moves

"Apologies force of habit"

"Someone trained you well" Kristiasen nervously replied as Anya relaxed her stance

"I once had a bad encounter with a bunch of immigrants some time ago in Stockholm" Anya falsely explained

"If I didn't know any better I would have guessed you were military" Kristiasen replied as he studied Anya's body language which remained neutral

"Very thoughtful of you to greet me out here" Anya said changing the subject

"Nothing chivalrous about it.....shall we walk and talk?"

"I need a moment to organise my notes"

"You can add Kristiasen to them, Pastor Kristiasen I am the director of the Creed and as such prefer off the cuff comments and impressions" The Pastor replied as he continued to study Anya's body language

"Very well" Anya responded as it became obvious to her that the Creed of Tyr's buildings had been compromised, under such circumstances she decided to remain alert and employ her observational skills to detect anything that could remotely see or listen.

The Pastor signalled for them to take a path hidden from view that would lead them towards the river through lush grasslands. The path was located behind a two meter high hedge that flanked the car park.

"Quite a contrast to the parklands" the Pastor commented once they set foot on the pathway

"In all respects and well concealed" Anya replied as she surveyed the scenery before them

"How are my troops doing by the way?" the Pastor asked once they had travelled at least two hundred meters away from the car park

"Don't you mean disciples?" Anya asked as a way of correcting him

"Not really, you do realise they have seen active duty in Yemen and Syria?"

"Providing food and water?" Anya indirectly asked

"Amongst other things" the Pastor answered which Anya interpreted as meaning killing people in the pursuit of justice

"I didn't know that, I was asked to avoid such questions"

"So what are your impressions?" Pastor Kristiasen firmly asked

"Based on my observations and what you have just told me, none of them fit the paedophile profile, they suffer in silence!"

"There is more to the story which I will reveal once we find ourselves somewhere warm and cosy" Kristiasen slowly said which Anya found quite absurd as the weather wasn't exactly bright and sunny, the wind was bitterly cold as it barrelled down the river, apart from castle ruins in the distance there wasn't anything that remotely resembled warm and cosy, all of which was becoming a little too much for Anya to bear. They walked in single file along the river foreshore with Kristiasen leading the way downstream, within the hour they had reached the castle ruins the appearance of which was misleading as they were the remaining rampart of a bridge long gone. Parked next to the rampart on the opposite side was a launch expertly painted to match its surroundings making it virtually impossible to detect.

"Climb on board we are safe here" Kristiasen quietly said as he clambered up a ladder which resembled an outcrop of fallen rocks, once at the top he helped Anya do the same before the duo descended another set of stairs and disappeared from view.

"Warm and cosy at last, sorry to have exposed you to the elements, can't be too careful these days considering what the Creed has been through" Kristiasen genuinely apologised as he unlocked a door, switched on several lights to illuminate a well appointed executive suite and ushered Anya in.

"Make yourself comfortable, I'll fetch us a mug of mulled wine before seeing what's in the larder" the Pastor said leaving Anya to familiarise herself with her surroundings; Anya started to relax but refused to let her guard down until she was convinced that she was in safe hands which was difficult for her to initially accept as the walls were adorned with what she thought to be occult stuff. Pastor Kristiasen made every effort to win her over by offering generous portions of food and wine.

"You've excelled yourself" Anya cautiously complimented the pastor as he placed a breakfast tray ladened with goodies upon her lap

"Just the bare necessities, smoked Norwegian salmon gently resting on rye crisp bread smothered in cream cheese and garnished with dill mustard, perfect for a lady who hasn't had breakfast"

"You noticed" Anya replied

"From the moment we met"

"What else did you notice?" Anya asked

"Your cover is excellent and whoever you are working for also believes in justice" The pastor emotionally responded

"Just like the many items that adorn the walls" Anya replied making reference to the mythological equipment, spells and relics that were scattered about

"Purely fantasy stuff some of which has found its way into the workings of our creed" Kristiasen freely admitted before he finished his sandwich and proceeded to explain further "Over there we have the Priest's vestments, a blue and purple robe complete with white sash and left handed glove, the right glove is black symbolising the loss of Tyr's hand then the floating brass scales aptly named Balance of Belaros quite the optical illusion, my favourite is the Hammer of Tyr nothing to look at yet capable of emitting a powerful sunray and returning to its wielder on command. Finally we have a smattering of spells written in gibberish to the untrained eye"

"Are those the weapons your troops used in Yemen and Syria?" Anya asked as she wiped her mouth clean

"We do not fight the soldiers instead we go after the cowards who gave the orders for them to sacrifice their lives. Our strategy is to reveal the truth and punish the guilty"

"Your intel must be very good"

"Yemen we determined to be a chaotic proxy war involving the English and Americans both under Jewish control, the Saudi's and French. It became our undoing, the seven operatives you visited in prison had just returned home when they were pounced upon by our Minister of Justice and his cronies seeking to break up a paedophile ring, needless to say I was shocked!"

"Why...?" Anya asked

"One has to work exceptionally hard to achieve that level within the Creed"

"How many levels are there?" Anya asked growing increasingly interested in the Creed's infrastructure

"We start at the bottom with brothers and sisters who have come voluntarily with a desire to return the world into law and order. It is a rigorous process with prayers at dawn, prayers that do not beseech the help of deities nor praise them but seek to awaken the Master within followed by library time in which texts and scholarly articles are studied and critically analysed with a view to improving law and order. The middle ground is for the disciples who have achieved a certain level of enlightenment that allows each one to 'see' from there they are directed to the secret library where they have access to the most provocative truths imagined by mankind. Having said that knighthood is only achieved by a relatively few as the process taxes one's senses to the point that it dramatically frightens individuals away as they cannot embrace what they are capable of"

"Is your congregation very large" Anya asked

"Not at all, it only attracts the idealist and those who are brave enough to protect others from harm, ruin or loss"

"Ironically they could not protect themselves" Anya concluded making reference to those imprisoned

"Which causes me great pain as I could not protect them....?"

"What are you saying?"

"Every member's personal computer is required to be registered with and monitored by the Creed's central computer for any deviant behaviour. Access to the central computer is via encryption which is the same for very member's personal computer meaning you have to access the main computer first before accessing member's computer providing you have the necessary encryption codes. How pornographic material of the paedophile variety found its way onto those imprisoned troops computers is a mystery to me" Kristiasen sadly explained

"Obviously you were too successful in Yemen and Syria" Anya bluntly suggested which caused Kristiasen to momentarily reflect on the various theatres of war that the Creed's troops had been active in

"Nothing out of the ordinary, expose's of official corruption, thwarted arms deals, weapons and cash redirected into the wrong hands" Kristiasen proudly replied

"That's more than enough to piss anyone off!"

"Do you really think so?" Kristiasen asked tongue in cheek

"Yes the question is who?"

"Perhaps you could find out for us?"

"Not without further information" Anya replied

"Such as...?"

"All of the computer access codes" Anya coldly answered as a matter of fact

"Only at the Creed's premises" Kristiasen retorted

"Not Possible! Your facilities have been compromised it needs to be done remotely!"

"You're asking too much!"

"Then we will leave it at that, nice to have met you Pastor Kristiasen" Anya abruptly replied as she stood up in readiness to take her leave

"I need proof!" Kristiasen firmly stated as he blocked Anya's path

"Check your computer records for power failures during your troops' absence and have your security company perform a routine service on your security system, you might be surprised as to what they find" Anya expertly replied with confident smile

"Very well then what?" Kristiasen nervously asked

"Meet me this afternoon 2pm sharp at Oslo's main public library, biblical section make certain you are not followed!"

"It's a date" Kristiasen eagerly replied as he was unattached and in the hunt for a lifelong soul mate with that in mind he raised his cup of mulled wine and saluted their joint venture.

Nine hours earlier and 530km away Major Weir and Marcus had just passed through Fjallnas en route to finding an access point into the mountains, much to Marcus's surprise the Major continued to drive north on the sealed road towards Vastra Malmagen where they would cross the stream and then head eastwards.

"Pleasant snooze soldier?" the Major asked

"Should see me through until daybreak" Marcus aptly responded

"Anything symbolic to report...?"

"Negative Sir" Marcus assured the Major knowing full well that his question related to dreams

"Good then we are clear to proceed"

"Where are we going?" Marcus asked as he thought they would have been off road by now

"Thought we might try the rare earths venture, mountains are full of them, give the Chinese a run for their money"

"Nothing like a bit of competition" Marcus commented and wondered what the Major really knew and how much security was present at the mine site.

"Shouldn't be long now, I understand the works are in the exploratory stage, no serious mining as such, quality, quantity and feasibility are yet to be properly determined, hopefully no trigger happy guards around to make life unpleasant, no matter we will take all necessary precautions" the Major explained as though he had just read Marcus's mind.

"Copy that" Marcus sharply replied as he looked out of the window and studied the eerie shadows that occupied the landscape. They sat in relative silence until they crossed the stream and the Major stopped the ancient Defender to check his GPS co-ordinates.

"Almost there, watch for any signage that makes reference to Rareswede"

"Copy that" Marcus obediently answered as the Major released the car's brakes, dimmed its headlights and drove slowly so as not to miss anything.

"Nothing out here apart from trees, shrubs, flowers and wildlife" Marcus grimly reported as he swept his eyes back and forth so as to detect something meaningful.

"Except for several dirt trails that appear to lead nowhere or do they....?" the Major analytically asked.

"Time to leg it" Marcus suggested

"My thoughts precisely, let's hide beastie, grab our equipment and play Sherlock Holmes" the Major added with an ounce of determination. A few moments later with the vehicle squared away both Marcus and the Major were ready to scout the area. They decided to walk along the edge of the road and examine each trail that they encountered for anything unusual such as heavy duty lorry tracks, nothing of significance caught their eye until the forth trail that appeared to have been compacted by such equipment in addition to a road sign bearing the letters RSM in reflective red tape.

"Rare Swedish Minerals" the Major deduced as he pointed to the sign post

"Only for those in the know" Marcus deduced as he surveyed the area anticipating trouble. The Major used sign language to indicate that they should remain silent and walk along the edge of the dirt track so as not to leave any incriminating shoe prints, feeling uneasy and somewhat paranoiac Marcus signalled a request for a pair of night vision goggles which the Major gladly handed over once he had retrieved them from his backpack. They were state of the art capable of detecting all sorts of light sources in the infra red and beyond. The Major also provided a silencer for Marcus to fit onto his trusty Glock, both provided some measure of comfort but not excessively as to make Marcus complacent for the memory of the black object frying Odd into oblivion haunted him.

Marcus reasoned that the interior of the mountains represented a warehouse of illegal goods which the arms dealers would protect at all costs meaning he and the Major would more than likely encounter some form of electronic surveillance that monitored movement on or near the entrance to the caves, it was a matter of moving stealth fully and keeping one's eyes open furthermore they would need to keep two meters apart otherwise their gillie suits which were based on octopus technology would reflect each other bringing immediate attention and exposing their position.

Marcus calculated it was at least two kilometres walk to the edge of the mountain escarpment initially out in the open they were easy targets before becoming immersed in a heavily wooded pathway which meant plenty of coverage not only for them but deadly assassins as well. The night was still very still, Marcus went first he stepped carefully so as not to disturb anything or make a crackling noise, he walked at a slow and steady pace with the Major bringing up the rear, Marcus did not bother to look back for he knew the Major had become one with the landscape. Nothing out of the ordinary occurred until they were five hundred meters from the escarpment when the eerie shadows that occupied the landscape came alive as the Black Death from above appeared.

'How the fuck did it find us?" Marcus cursed as he immediately stopped in his tracks, remained absolutely still and prayed that his gillie suit would do its job.

Marcus realised that his Glock was useless against the well armed drone; he wondered what weaponry the Major had brought along to counter any attack but as there was nothing but silence to go by Marcus concluded the best method of defence was to remain motionless which he did for an agonising six minutes as the drone went through its paces and performed a series of predetermined sweeps of the area according to a computerised grid pattern. Once satisfied that neither friend nor foe existed the drone sped away to return at an unspecified time. Marcus looked about to see if he had broken any light beam that might have summonsed the monster but nothing was apparent, feeling drained he cautiously set off once again only to be arrested by the sound of a lorry coming up behind them.

Marcus instinctively stepped off the path and fell to the ground where he lay face down amongst the shrubbery, his heart quickened as he heard many foreign voices speaking of things he could not understand but one thing was certain as the lorry passed him by the occupants had come to collect and not deliver. He thought that once the lorry was out of earshot it would be safe for him to resume walking but it unexpectedly stopped and six of its occupants jumped off guns in hand.

"Fuck! What are they looking for?" he coarsely thought as they disappeared one by one into the bushes and then after a brief silence he heard the sound of urine splattering on the ground "Better not piss on me otherwise I'll cut your balls off!" He angrily thought as he recalled being humiliated by senior officers during his brief stint at Sandhurst.

"Must be serious this meeting they're going to" He postulated as he remembered being taught that it was vitally important for a soldier to have his bowels and bladder empty before going into combat. The six men once they had finished and joked about the size of their manhood climbed back onto the lorry to be greeted by three others who remained seated throughout. The lorry then continued on leaving Marcus relieved that an exchange of gunfire had not happened.

"I didn't expect this" the Major whispered once he joined Marcus's side

"Neither did I, the lorry must be known to the Drone"

"Good observation...anything else?" the Major asked

"Negative"

"Then we proceed on full alert" the Major said as he looked back to make certain another lorry was not coming up behind them.

"The road ahead twists and turns; too many blind spots and ambush points, suggest we take an alternate route"

"Very good soldier, I'll check my GPS for one" the Major whispered and whipped out his electronic marvel making certain the screen was dimmed and overshadowed by Marcus's presence. A few moments later he said "There's a stream and what appears to be a waterfall"

"To wash away evidence of recent visitors" Marcus whispered

"So you think it's behind the waterfall" the Major asked suggesting that the waterfall disguised an opening in the mountain side

"For outward goods only"

"Let's get closer and see if you are right" Major Weir replied as he put away his GPS and headed in the direction of the stream. Although it appeared they were going away from their target the stream offered direct access albeit with limited cover. The lorry on the other hand had to take more of a convoluted path before it arrived close to the same point namely the waterfall which fortunately was not in full flood consequently the stream was shallow but its waters were still icy cold.

Once there the Major decided they should avoid walking in the centre of the stream and instead keep to its edges so as to prevent frostbite which meant walking at a slower pace. Marcus disagreed as there were too many loose rocks and he defiantly chose to follow the well worn track that paralleled the stream, he also ditched his night vision goggles and decided to rely on his senses.

"Dumb Polack" he heard the Major say but responded not instead he focused on the job at hand and pricked up his ears to locate the position of the lorry in relation to his. The pathway it turned out was the better way to go; soon he was within meters of the lorry whereas the Major was further back and battling an uneven terrain with wet soggy boots.

Marcus advanced very slowly stopping now and then to make certain he hadn't been noticed. The lorry was parked next to a docking bay which was serviced by a retractable ramp that stretched into the mountain side. There was only one heavily armed thug standing guard next to the driver's door. Marcus reasoned he needed to distract the thug in such a way that it allowed him sufficient time to bypass the thug and silently slip inside the mountain. Explosions were out of the question as was taking down the Black Death from above, a wild animal gave insufficient time but deflating a tyre or two would prove advantageous especially if the thug's duty involved maintaining the lorry in good condition. Marcus crept closer, withdrew his silenced Glock took careful aim and fired a single shot into the rear right hand tyre. The lorry instantly lurched as the tyre deflated much to the annoyance of the thug who thought the night's mission would be routinely uneventful. The thug produced a small but powerful torch and examined the deflated tyre for any structural damage in the hope that it was nothing more than a defective valve.

Marcus watched as the thug grumbled and fumbled his way through the tool kit that hung underneath the chassis which took him a good five minutes to locate the tools he needed, then and only then when the thug had secured the lorry and positioned the jack did Marcus make his move. In a skip and a heartbeat Marcus sprung to his feet and using the available cover noiselessly sprinted on his tippy toes past the lorry, onto the platform, along the ramp, through the waterfall before halting at the entrance to the cave to collect his thoughts and bearings. Marcus's head pounded with the sound of his thumping heart and laboured breathing which he consciously deepened in an attempt to quell his overactive sympathomimetic` system. He stayed put until his eyes accustomed themselves to the dark and then he gingerly advanced inside the cave to look for any stray light.

"Robbers delight" he concluded once he realised how complex the cave system was especially when it came to voices.

"Someone's not happy! Question is... where is she...?" Marcus pondered as he turned his body full circle to identify the likely source of the female voice which angrily reverberated around the cave's interior.

Frustrated by his failure Marcus resorted to other means at his disposal and he sniffed the air for the scent of a woman.

"There you are my lovely, rose, sandalwood, jasmine with a tinge of spice, dangerous but nice" Marcus thought as he detected a faint breeze ladened with perfume that gently caressed his left cheek.

"Are you close or far away" He wondered as he turned in the direction of the breeze and let his nose lead the way through a maze of large tunnels until he reached a hive of activity.

With his back to the wall and his gillie suit working overtime Marcus was completely undetectable, he watched as the nine men from the lorry went about stacking an array of military hardware onto a convoy of carts much like those used by baggage handlers at international airports. Meanwhile an attractive female was fiercely arguing with two shady characters demanding that they return her 'leaf' both however played dumb and denied any knowledge. Marcus sensed that they were blatantly lying and that unless the woman had backup or was exceptionally good at self defence she would most likely end up dead. Marcus retreated into the shadows and retrieved his mobile phone photographs were paramount, of people, of the set up for identification purposes, tonight was not the night to blow things up. With the camera lens set to telephoto Marcus inched forward and took a series of photographs in rapid succession capturing most of the thugs and things except for the woman who decided to abort her campaign and leave threatening to return with reinforcements. The two shady characters did not take kindly to her ravings and followed at a distance but before they could catch up and do her in she simply vanished leaving them rather frustrated and confused. They returned to complete their business at which point Marcus left to explore the remainder of the tunnels at no time during the entire exercise did Marcus worry about the Major in the slightest.

There was no scent to guide him nothing but darkness in all of its sinister forms, nothing sacred about the place, no wondering what devious creatures roamed about, better to be forearmed than dead, night goggles and Glock the order of the day but then something else as the sound of doors closing meant entrapment in a dark and gloomy place. Marcus hadn't previously noticed the folding doors on either side of the entrance into the caves when he first gained entry, doors that guaranteed security and the utmost sophisticated secrecy.

"No point going back nor relying on my phone nothing electronic penetrates into here, better to search for clues, deduce and act intuitively" Marcus thought as he stood still and calmly assessed his situation.

"I entered from the East, Norway lies to the West a few kilometres away and yet the thugs were able to collect their order from over there, question is how was it transported and furthermore is the route patent or sealed at both ends, only one way to find out, about face....march!" Marcus whispered to himself before returning to the chamber where the thugs had collected their weapons.

It was empty, no incriminating evidence of any kind left behind only the faintest hint of tyre tracks, no obvious access points apart from the man made tunnel that Marcus and the others had used.

"Is it all smoke and mirrors and the art of deception that confuses me, surely it was all internally orchestrated, cleverly crafted illusions, master magicians at play intended to fool all of the people all of the time except for one dumb Polack who realises that it is the absence of light that reveals all" Marcus deliberated out loud as he wandered away from the chamber into the darkness of the tunnel to locate its deception that led back to the cache of weapons which he had discovered days before. It was not an easy task for one wrong choice would result in harm meaning becoming lost in a maze that offered no salvation apart from death. Marcus used the hint of tyre tracks plus paint scrapings on the walls of a narrow tunnel as a means of determining which route the electric carts used to navigate their way inside the mountain. His progress was slow, he allowed himself six hours to cover the distance which he estimated to be at least five kilometres, luckily the internal temperature was warm, the air relatively fresh although somewhat damp.

Initially Marcus could see as there was sufficient stray light for his night vision goggles to work with however as he proceeded further they soon became useless, luckily Marcus had brought along a small compact powerful torch which he set onto pulse thereby extending the life of its battery which he hoped would last the distance otherwise he would have to rely on his phone's light as a backup irrespective of that the final result would be tight as only short sections of the access tunnel were straight the remainder were convoluted interrupted by complex junctions that defied reason as the floor of these were invariably covered with water preventing Marcus from making a bee line to the cache of weapons. All was not lost for along the way he discovered that minor deviations exposed pockets where additional weapons were stored which made Marcus realise that they were dealing with a well oiled organisation.

Marcus checked his watch periodically to gauge how well he was advancing but with no bearings to guide him Marcus was literally lost in the dark which at times caused him to mildly panic, relive painful childhood memories and doubt his capabilities. By the fifth hour Marcus reckoned that dawn had surely broken and with it the chance that sufficient sunlight would enter the caves by one way or another sparing his dependence on his torch and phone. Sadly his position within the cave complex prevented light from reaching him and he continued to carefully meander his way about the maze seeking salvation which taunted the soldier with its elusiveness and desire to make him suffer by first cancelling his torch and then by short circuiting his phone, not willing to partake in such games Marcus closed his eyes and by using the 'hands of a blind man' felt his way along the tunnel until he realised that he was not alone as voices and blazing headlights filled the void behind him.

"They never left!" Marcus quickly deduced as an electric cart carrying two distasteful occupants steadily advanced towards him.

"Must pick up the pace now that I can see, need to stay ahead of the headlamps otherwise I'll reflect the light and be spotted" he further reasoned as he increased his walking speed and hoped the next junction if it existed was not too far away. However he was unable to maintain an adequate pace largely because he was in unfamiliar territory whereas the cart having made dozens of trips before powered along.

Ten seconds separated the victim from its hunter, ten precious seconds that represented the difference between life and death, ten seconds in which to decide whether it was better to run and hide or turn around and attack. No telling how many more awaited him at the end of the tunnel but that didn't matter Marcus had faced similar situations before. The highly trained Grom operative pulled out his Glock, stopped on the spot, turned, took careful aim and fired two rounds that shattered both of the electric carts headlights plunging the tunnel into total darkness causing the driver to crash into the wall bringing them to an abrupt halt.

Both occupants were dazed but unhurt both questioned what had happened the more astute of the pair produced a flashlight and proceeded to examine the damage giving Marcus extended time in which to make his escape. Soon he found himself back in the unattended unlit depository and was surprised to find that most of the weapons were still there apart from the entry and exit points that he had previously used, Marcus had reached a dead end.

11

RELIGIOUS EXPERIENCE

Anya hoped that she had made it quite clear which library Pastor Kristiasen was meant to have met her as there were many in Oslo even though she referred to it as being the main meaning Deichman Bjorvika situated on Western Light Place 1 Oslo a beautifully designed six storey building that embodied the pursuit of knowledge.

Anya was deliberately early she patiently waited on the steps leading up to the library's main entrance and casually observed people coming and going whilst she looked for Kristiasen expecting him to stand out from the rest. 2pm came and went, 2.15 quickly passed and by 2.30pm she gave up hope and decided that perhaps those she had been introduced to in prison were in fact paedophiles and deserved the punishments they had received, Kristiasen she deduced was most probably the mastermind and on the run with those thoughts in mind Anya decided to return to Onepark Oslo SP-hus where she had parked the hire car a brief six minute scenic walk where art lovers of all ages congregated. As she approached the opera house a rather dishevelled and distraught Pastor Kristiasen rushed out of the adjacent underground Metro exit and ran towards her.

"I'm so so sorry, I confused myself, to me the main library will always be the National Library of Norway which preserves the past for the future!" he nervously gushed as he tried to make sense and justify his awkward mistake. Anya coldly looked at him and said nothing which further embarrassed Kristiasen who struggled to maintain his composure.

"I brought everything we need perhaps we could go somewhere quiet?" Kristiasen submissively pleaded.

"I had a study room booked at the library" Anya stated matter of fact.

"Perhaps it's still available" Kristiasen optimistically answered

"Perhaps"

"Well then let's go and investigate" Kristiasen suggested as he boldly took hold of Anya's arm and escorted her to the library. Luckily for him the demand for study and conference rooms was very low which meant they could discuss matters in private away from prying eyes and nosey ears of any sort. Furthermore three of the study room's four partition walls were made of double glass which added to its security, fixtures, fittings and soft furnishings further enhanced it, overall Anya was satisfied with its makeup as it allowed her to determine whether or not Kristiasen had been followed and furthermore was under constant surveillance.

While Anya made herself comfortable Kristiasen produced an old tattered leather bound copy of the Bible, a Dictionary and Handbook of Northern Mythology plus a printed hard copy of a power point presentation whereas Anya on the other hand skilfully took careful note of all those seated around them on the outside.

"I understand you have taken an interest in certain aspects of our Creed in relation to its ability that helps our disgraced members cope with their imprisonment" Pastor Kristiasen authoritatively said in complete contrast to his previous behaviour.

"Correct I feel it will make an invaluable contribution to the paper I am writing on the various Scandinavian penal systems" Anya replied as she felt that one or two outside of their room did not belong.

"Instead of praising the Creed of Tyr's virtues I thought it more appropriate to contrast the numerological differences between certain numbers found in the Bible with those in Norse Mythology, of particular interest to Biblical scholars is the number 33 as it is supposedly connected to certain promises made by God in relation to not destroying the entire world with another flood, strangely enough 33 is the numeric equivalent of the word 'Amen' and Jesus died at the age of 33. There are many other examples but one wonders if they are nothing more than mere folly designed to amplify the importance of the number 33"

"Bit cynical on your part" Anya replied pretending to be interested whilst she focused on one particular individual who constantly rocked on his chair.

"Shall I continue?"

"Please do I'm all ears" Anya responded as she furiously jotted down a series of notes.

"Whilst the number 3 is significant in Norse Mythology and paganism special emphasis is placed on number 9, interestingly it together with number 27 figure in the Germanic Lunar calendar but that is by the way, what is important and represents the foundation of the Creed of Tyr are the nine heavenly realms that elevate the student from everything to nothing, these are provided in a book of poetic language the Skaldskaparmal written by the Icelandic historian Snorri. Vindblain is the nethermost where everything is provided in abundance according to the wishes of the individual then as one ascends in stepwise progression to Andlang, Vidblain, Vidfedmir, Hrjod, Hlyrnir, Gimir, Vet-Mimir and finally Skatyrnir which stands higher than the clouds beyond all worlds were nothing exists does the individual fall in love with and fully appreciate what richness nothing has to offer. In front of you are power points detailing how the parameters change from one heavenly realm to the next, as you can plainly see Vindblain possesses one hundred per cent materialism in all of its wealth and glory which diminishes at the rate of 11.11111% recurring until Skatyrnir where it ceases to exist, compensating for its loss is access to 'secret knowledge' which nurtures, enriches and replaces one hundred fold what materialism has failed to provide" Kristiasen solemnly explained but did not claim to have reached the ninth level. He could see by the expression on Anya's face that something needed further clarification.

"What determines how and when a person ascends to the next level? Is it by written examination or practical demonstration? Is it before a panel of judges or a single mentor and what is the nature of the secret knowledge?" Anya rattled off

"The individual decides, no one else, by the process of letting go of everything that he or she has learnt and believes in and accepting the unknown irrespective of how bizarre, foreign, upsetting or unpalatable it might seem, in other words it becomes a measure of how open minded an individual is how adaptable he or she is prepared to be. I hope this answers your questions"

"Partly" Anya answered as she wanted to learn more about secret knowledge.

"Perhaps that's enough for one day, study the power point presentation it contains everything you need to know and if you feel you have the capacity to sacrifice yourself for the benefit of your fellow man then contact me and we can proceed further" Kristiasen warmly responded with a broad smile and the offer of a handshake.

"Give me time these things can't be rushed" Anya answered as she packed away all of the papers that Kristiasen had provided into her attaché case.

"I agree, it is better to be thorough than foolhardy" Kristiasen replied

"Until next time" Anya politely answered and left to go the ladies toilet which was discretely located next to the elevators on the other side of the floor.

Anya took careful note of those seated outside of the study room and expected to make eye contact with the man who constantly rocked on his chair but he had gone and was not to be seen anywhere which made Anya a little apprehensive. Apart from him everyone else on the floor appeared to diligently go about their business whether they were staff, students of all ages or members of the general public.

The female public toilet was unoccupied one would assume as it was pitch black inside when Anya opened its door, but to Anya it only meant all was still and not necessarily vacant under such circumstances she would scan its interior, select a cubicle enter and lock it then quickly perform a costume change before exiting in under thirty seconds. Unfortunately as soon as she did two unsavoury characters pounced on her propelling Anya backwards to land heavily on the toilet seat and jar her spine. Anya instinctively rolled herself into a ball making it difficult for her assailants to keep their balance grab or inflict any further damage in the confined space, knowing full well that the only likely weapons available to them were string, drug filled plastic syringe or sharp object Anya by using her thumb and fingertips activated her A.R.S.E system to give her an enormous amount of brute strength. With both fists clenched Anya when the time was right violently sprung out of her foetal position like a Jack in the box and delivered two viscous uppercuts to both of her would be killers' jaws. The sound of bones breaking and teeth shattering plus the moans of despair filled the air for an instant and then all became silent once again.

"You picked on the wrong piece of arse" Anya triumphantly said as she towered over her assailants crumbled bodies, one of whom was a woman, the other a male.

"Someone doesn't like Kristiasen having visitors" She thought and then wondered if the Pastor was safe.

Her question was answered once she vacated the toilet, several security guards bolted past and headed towards the study room they were closely followed by a senior librarian carrying a defibrillator plus the sound of an advancing ambulance siren all pointed to one thing someone was seriously ill and in the midst of all this the man who constantly rocked on his chair stood quite still with a sinister smirk on his face.

Anya knew only too well it was not safe to return to where she had parked the rental car, she wondered if her change of disguise was sufficient to make a clean get away regretfully no as the man easily recognised the attaché case she was carrying. The cat and mouse game had begun question was how many players were there? What were they after? Was it Anya or what Kristiasen had given her? Anya had two options running and hiding versus hiding in plain sight, the former required a diversion or two, the latter nothing more than raw nerve and the ability to blend into one's surroundings. Anya briefly considered calling for help but that option was pointless as the library on all levels had mobile phone jamming technology in place, it was a sanctuary in which to retreat and study without distraction or interruption. Under such circumstances Anya decided it was prudent to continue to play the role of the avid biblical scholar and accordingly she approached the help desk to inquire where she could find a copy of Snorri's classic work "Skaldskaparmal". The librarian on duty pointed Anya in the direction of the reserve section where multiple copies were available.

The man who constantly rocked on his chair meanwhile kept one eye trained on Anya whilst the other searched for the whereabouts of his extraction team namely the man and woman who unbeknownst to him lay comatose on the floor of the ladies toilet. As time ticked away the man grew increasingly impatient, thinking that Anya would stay put as she appeared to be heavily engrossed in her work he left his station and roamed about the complex in an attempt to locate his fellow operatives only to come up empty handed. His last port of call was the public toilets which had been sealed off and designated a crime scene. Two burley heavily armed policemen kept the public at bay and redirected traffic whilst a team of paramedics worked tirelessly to ensure their patients survival.

Frustrated by his lack of success and the time spent away the man hurriedly returned to the reserve section and was relieved to see the likes of Anya wearing the same coat seated with her back to him, the attaché case by her side.

"At least you didn't go AWOL" He thought and wondered where his two highly trained operatives had wandered off to and then he speculated they had most probably left to check on the other agents stationed within and outside of the building. The man then found a work station favourably positioned and sat down to idly pass the time of day until his prey was ready to depart. Forty minutes later the likes of Anya stood up, gathered her belongings and turned around much to the shock and horror of the man.

"Fuck... who the hell are you..?" The man cursed as the young fresh faced female left the reserve area and he madly barged in only to discover it occupied by two ardent males openly displaying their affection for each other.

Disgusted by his failure the man realising the consequences of his short comings stormed out of the building onto the streets and immersed himself into a sea of restless humanity.

Anya through an act of random charity had secured her freedom by giving her coat to the fresh faced girl not dissimilar in appearance to herself. The girl was jobless, always cold and searching for meaning in her life. She often frequented the library; it was warm and offered salvation in the form of knowledge. Anya's coat plus the offer of fifty Norwegian Kroner brought a measure of relief and hope that things would surely improve for the young girl, for Anya it was a convenient way out, subtle changes in attire and no attaché case guaranteed an easy passage back to Norwegian Ice.

Marcus on the other hand faced a more difficult task as there was only one entry and exit to the chamber that he accessed which he soon realised was not the one he had discovered at 62-6472N 11-8669E even though it stored military weapons. With no light source nor effective night goggles Marcus found it hard to silently move about, he also sensed the two shady characters would be soon upon him and therefore he needed to find somewhere in which to conceal himself and plot a way out but that wouldn't happen before flashes of light entered the chamber as the shady duo used torches to guide their stricken electric cart along only then did Marcus appreciate the size of the chamber and the sheer magnitude of the weapons stored within.

"Someone's been very busy" He thought as he furiously scanned his surroundings in order to locate a convincing hiding spot. "Sticks and stones may break my bones but bombs will always hide me" He quickly concluded as possibly being the least sought after weaponry and he hurriedly made a bee line towards a stack of American made MK-84 2000lb aerial bombs that offered much protection.

The shady duo stopped their electric cart at the entrance to the chamber, one of them then left the cart and walked to a lever that jutted out of the wall. He causally depressed the lever and within moments the chamber became illuminated throughout by banks of LED lights that hung from the ceiling. From the corner of his eye Marcus postulated that electricity was being generated by gravity feed via descending weights, drive sprockets and polymer gear trains that caused the LED globes to glow brightly and Marcus to cringe with fear that he might be exposed, however that was not to be the case as the two shady characters it appeared were more preoccupied with getting the next shipment out. One parked the damaged electric cart whilst the other consulted his phone as to the details of the order submitted on the dark web.

"I hope this doesn't take long" Marcus sighed as he adjusted his position in anticipation of a lengthy stay which on the bright side would provide him with sufficient time in which to eat the high energy protein bars he had bought along and carefully formulate his next moves. As hard as he tried Marcus was unable to make any sense of the shady pair's foreign gibberish and it frustrated him that his mobile phone was inoperative otherwise he would have recorded much of their conversation for future reference. At all times Marcus remained vigilant and monitored the shady pair's movements in relation to his location as they went about assembling the weaponry that the latest American funded 'terrorist' group requested. Marcus without any further evidence deduced that the chamber he found himself in was where the heavy stuff was being stored and he wondered how big the international demand for the MK-84 aerial bombs was.

"What manner of men sells such weapons of mass destruction? Is there no law prohibiting this? How many innocent women and children need to die before any one acts? Is life that cheap? Is money that important? Who are these immoral ruthless people that dare to undermine the safety of mankind?" Marcus thought as he considered unleashing his Glock and ending the lives of the two shady characters that enjoyed inflicting pain and suffering on the poor and destitute. Such a move however would not be damaging enough and of little consequence.

A ham sandwich left in a strategic place for something to nibble on was a far better solution and that place would only be determined once the shady duo had left which was not anytime soon as their task at hand was labour intensive which meant that Marcus needed to stay awake even though he was immensely tired. Sleep would become the death of him as he was occasionally prone to heavy snoring. What kept Marcus awake besides the shady duo's incessant dialogue was the switching off and on of the overhead lights every twenty minutes. Once the weights that drove the gravity feed reached the floor and the lights dimmed a series of direct current battery operated electric motors became activated and lifted the weights back to their starting position and as they descended not only did they generate light but they recharged the batteries that powered the electric motors as well.

Seven cycles passed before the shady duo called it a day and proceeded to leave with their completed order, two hours and twenty minutes of not knowing whether or not MK-84's were part of the order as footsteps ebbed and flowed, two hours and twenty minutes in which to devise a plan to catch the rats. Marcus listened with strained ears as the shady duo drove their spare electric cart to the chamber's entrance and stopped. Marcus cautiously slithered on his belly to observe one of the shady duo leave the cart and reset the lever that controlled the overhead lights and hoped it wasn't an off position which meant instant darkness. Luckily the system had two settings, locked and unlocked the former allowing the cycle to run its course before ceasing the operation. Marcus determined he had at least ten minutes of light to work under less five minutes to allow for the shady duo to distance themselves from him and then and only then would he emerge and build his fat rat trap.

When all was remarkably still and the dust had settled Marcus emerged from his cramped hiding spot and silently walked towards an unlocked steel cabinet that offered tools of repair amongst other things. Inside he found two fully charged LED torches plus an array of firing pins and detonators suited to arming the MK-84 aerial bombs. Marcus carefully selected a sensitive variant that indicated when installed the slightest vibration would cause the bomb to detonate, with tools in hand and with the utmost respect and delicacy Marcus returned to the pile of MK-84 aerial bombs and expertly installed the devices into one of the bombs that allowed easy access to its forward and rear chambers. He then gingerly tiptoed away just before the LED lights started to slowly dim and then quickly returned to the cabinet to retrieve the two fully charged torches, this time he took careful note of what lay inside the cabinet and to his surprise discovered a folded map that detailed all of the passages, pathways and locations of weapon depots within the mountain which meant Marcus could finally navigate his way out of the sinister complex.

Most soldiers would have left it at that and relied on chance to determine when the armed MK-84 bomb might explode however Marcus was more deviously clever than that and decided to use the very machinery that powered the LED lights to fire things up. Being observant he previously noticed several rectangular open wooden boxes containing anti-personnel land mines near the pile of MK-84 bombs, using his torch he scanned the chambers ceiling to locate the weights nearest the pile of MK-84 bombs that drove the LED machinery and their points of contact with the ground. There were three quite hidden in total Marcus placed a number of land mines in and around these in such a way that the land mines would explode once the descending weights came into contact with them, the resulting shock waves and shrapnel would cause the armed MK-84 bomb to explode in one way or another. What would follow was anyone's guess.

Pleased with his handiwork Marcus decided it was time to leave and find his way home to report his findings. The map that he had acquired once it was held up the right way showed quite clearly that it would not be difficult for him to navigate his way out providing there were no further hidden surprises, booby traps or other personnel. The two shady characters had well and truly departed which meant Marcus could use his torch freely to make a mental note of all that was stored within the chamber. Once he had accomplished that Marcus left the chamber without activating the gravity fed LED apparatus even though it was very tempting for him to do so.

"Your next order should go out with a bang" He righteously thought as he despised the illegal arms trade and all those involved in it.

In order to access the great outdoors Marcus needed to 'march' diligently and cautiously along the passages according to the pattern, right, left, right, left, right left, left, in other words whenever he encountered a junction that bifurcated into two arms he would need to select the correct passage according to the map. The first two proved tricky as they stored piles of boxed ammunition in a circular fashion which hid the opening to the correct tunnel, once he had overcome these obstacles the rest was plain sailing and evident that it was an escape route should things go wrong within the complex, however there were moments during his journey in which he doubted his navigation skills to the point that Marcus fleetingly thought he might perish through misadventure after all the map that he found could have been deliberately left behind to foil invaders which made Marcus even more wary of his circumstances. Being alone makes a warrior astute more determined, although there is safety in numbers it is fraught with weakness unlike the warrior who stands strong and resolute with razor sharp senses that detect the slightest ripple in a teardrop. It was at the third and fourth junctions that Marcus seriously questioned the accurateness and validity of his map's instructions which did not fit in with the mountain's desire to help Marcus.

The gentle breeze that previously helped locate the shady duo and their nefarious dealings presented itself once again to correct the map's misdirection; Marcus nervously accepted its assistance and followed obediently through the challenging convoluted tunnels until he found himself in the chamber that he had entered days before. Marcus initially did not recognise it as it was completely empty and devoid of any artificial light and surveillance equipment. Sensing that he was out of danger Marcus took off his jacket and turned it inside out to return to more of a civilian look and then continued to follow the breeze until it was complimented by sunlight entering the chamber.

Once outside Marcus stood quite still, closed his eyes and let out an enormous sigh of relief as his body eagerly drank in the warm reviving sunshine. He had survived another mission which could have gone horribly wrong and he had gathered some scanty information that might prove useful but more importantly he had left behind a mechanism which once activated would purge the mountain of the parasites that dwelled in its bowels. The world would once again become a beautiful place.

Feeling rather refreshed but somewhat hungry Marcus opened his eyes and took in the glory of the seemingly peaceful cloudberry patch before him and then briefly scanned its backdrop so as to identify the path that he and the Major had previously used to access the battered Land Rover Defender. Knowing full well that no such vehicle awaited him Marcus nevertheless decided to follow the path through the forest, access a major road and hitchhike back to civilisation. He had gone about halfway through the cloudberry patch when a gruff voice from behind commanded him to stop.

"Halt you have entered a crime site, please return to your starting point!"

Marcus not wishing to inflame the situation he immediately turned about only to be confronted by the imposing figure of Robert 'Chook' Larssen

"Did you not see the warning signs?" 'Chook' roughly barked visibly annoyed

"I must have missed them" Marcus innocently replied as he sized up the policeman and determined the best spots to hit him should a confrontation arise.

"Not possible, the cloudberry perimeter has been secured, no civilians are allowed to enter, warning signs are everywhere, are you under the influence of an illicit substance?" 'Chook' succinctly asked as he grew increasingly suspicious of Marcus.

"Negative on all accounts" Marcus firmly answered.

"ID and mobile phone" 'Chook' loudly demanded as he took one step back and watched as Marcus searched his mind before retrieving his mobile phone and European drivers licence which he duly presented.

"Well Mr Ralph Martine what brings you to these parts?" 'Chook' asked as he closely examined both items.

"UFO sightings"

"Bit far north for that I would have thought" 'Chook' remarked as he dismissed the reason that Marcus gave.

"Very often the well patronised sites are fake!" Marcus countered.

"Without adequate photographic evidence your testimony will be nothing more than hearsay especially as you have no decent photographic equipment apart from your mediocre phone which appears to be well and truly dead"

"An unfortunate set of circumstances especially when one is reliant on its GPS" Marcus agreed.

"Are you telling me that you are lost?"

"That and sleep deprived" Marcus added

"Am I meant to feel sorry for you?"

"Not in the slightest, however directions to Roros would be nice" Marcus sweetly bluffed as he already knew the way.

"Is that where you came from Mr Amateur?" 'Chook' bluntly asked to which Marcus nodded his head in the affirmative.

"Back to the perimeter without disturbing the evidence underfoot, follow it to the tree line, walk due west into and through the forest until you reach the paved road at which point turn left, Roros is five clicks down the road" 'Chook' replied as he handed Marcus his driver's licence and mobile phone.

"Very kind of you, sorry to have disturbed your diggings" Marcus quietly said and turned to take his leave.

'Chook' did not immediately return to what he was previously doing but continued to observe Marcus follow the secured perimeter until he reached the tree line. 'Chook' did not think twice about Marcus removing his Gillie jacket, turning it inside out and donning it until Marcus in the blink of an eye disappeared from view. Marcus was no fool, he guessed 'Chook' had something in store for him along the lines of forceful arrest and rigged interrogation and even though Marcus was expert in self defence blending into the forest using octopus technology was the preferred option.

Marcus quickly found a nest of saplings in which to nestle into and then waited as the forest around him came alive with half a dozen burly municipal policemen equipped with CB radios who combed the area for his whereabouts based on the premise that he would most likely be walking due west but they did not know whether he was already in front of them or behind, consequently they continuously performed 360 degree visual sweeps of the area and would often look directly at Marcus without realising he was there.

"Octopus 5 police nil" Marcus quipped as the policemen lost any sense of co-ordinated play and started to scramble in desperation as it was clear that a violent change in the weather was soon upon them. Marcus hoped that his Gillie suit was waterproof and unaffected by rain otherwise he would be easily spotted. There was no time to idly stand by and find out as the icy cold wind from the north picked up its pace and threatened to mercilessly unleash its cargo of ice on everything.

Marcus secured his Gillie jacket at the wrists and waist before covering his head with its hood. He then took a south westerly direction which he hoped would end up near Odd's shack from there he would travel by whatever means possible back to Oslo and Norwegian Ice. Within fifteen minutes of starting his journey Marcus was pelted by hailstones the size of golf balls that pummelled everything in their path both flora and fauna braced themselves for its onslaught 'Chook' and his band of municipal policemen abandoned their respective tasks and fled back to the relative safety of their parked vehicles all of which had their windows smashed and interiors filled with ice.

The ambient temperature fell by twenty odd degrees Celsius; it became bitterly cold Marcus felt it on his face as he trudged through an ice covered landscape that became increasingly difficult to traverse. The only thing that gave Marcus's presence away was shoeprints that mysteriously appeared in the snow as he walked along. Even though the conditions were bleak Marcus managed to locate Odd's shack which had been roped off by the police as a crime scene due to the fact that Odd had gone missing under suspicious circumstances whilst in the company of a stranger.

So as not to attract attention to himself Marcus made certain that he only walked in puddles and where there was no snow, journeying back to Oslo meant travelling either by car, bus, train or plane. The latter was out of the question as all flights had been grounded thanks to the freak storm, car and buses were delayed awaiting clear roads which left only trains to consider.

The train station was vacant apart from the station master and one ticket attendant both of whom huddled in front of an electric heater that struggled to keep itself warm, the passenger train to Oslo had been cancelled according to the electronic billboard but a freight train was still running according to the timetable with a scheduled five minute stop at Roros to collect the all important mail. It was the station master's duty to load the carriage once the train arrived which couldn't come quick enough as the cold started to bite into Marcus.

Luckily the male toilet was unlocked which allowed Marcus the luxury of warming himself by using the hand dryer. The last comfort he would enjoy as there were no vending machines offering neither hot coffee nor snacks of any description at the station. The five hour trip to Oslo would prove taxing but then if the carriage was devoid of humans at least Marcus could sleep a while. The screech of brakes being applied plus the rumbling of the mail trolley being wheeled along the platform heralded the arrival of the freight train. Marcus very quickly dispensed what he was doing and carefully slipped out of the male toilet and into the wooden carriage marked Polsen just as the station master had finished loading and was about to lock its door.

"Refuge at last!" He sighed as he stepped into a world filled with peace and tranquillity "Quite warm for an old girl, guess timber construction is still superior to metal" He concluded as he explored the length of the dimly lit carriage to find a heavily worn leather arm chair covered with a tattered woollen blanket in a remote dusty corner at the other end of the carriage. "Hope you don't belong to a grumpy old bear especially a Russian one" Marcus whispered as he recalled defending himself against a particularly aggressive adolescent brown bear during the mating season when he was taking part in a two week Siberian survival course that tested one's physical and mental capabilities to the max and even though the previous twelve hours had exhausted him to some degree it was nothing in comparison to what he had experienced in Siberia.

"This will do nicely" Marcus declared as he allowed the chair to mould itself around him and keep him warm for the uneventful five hour journey back to Oslo.

12

SURPRISING NEWS

The next day found all of the field operatives rather refreshed and revived after being 'pampered' the previous night by Nils and Brit who greeted them warmly on their return, made certain each was washed, refuelled and tucked into a warm cosy bed to enjoy a restful night's sleep. Fresh minds and fresh bodies was the order of the day.

"Good morning ladies and gentlemen, good to see you safe and sound, I suspect we have much gathered evidence to get through, perhaps the ladies should make the start and present their findings" Major Weir warmly said with a broad smile as he surveyed the faces of those seated at the oval table before him.

"Thank you Major, ours did not go as we had anticipated largely due to tight security measures both electronic and personal but that does not mean that we came empty handed, we and by that I largely mean Anya brought home the bacon so to speak. Instead of taking the direct approach and breaking into the ministers' offices Nils suggested we target the imprisoned victims of the paedophile sting. Anya was suitably qualified for this type of operation she accompanied one Doctor Retterstol a KNN sympathiser on his prison rounds to ascertain how guilty each inmate was. The common denominator amongst them was the Creed of Tyr a quasi religious group led by Pastor Kristiasen whom Anya interviewed under covert conditions which did not prove completely successful as we now believe he might have been assassinated shortly after their last meeting. Anya did come away with some useful information in the form of a power point presentation" Brit replied and waited for Anya to load her portable mini projector with the all important data.

"Do you think you were closely shadowed?" The Major asked Anya directly

"Not me specifically, more the Creed than anything else" Anya answered as she fumbled with her device "I would consider myself to be collateral damage"

"Or a person of interest" The Major countered

"A very short lived one, Aino Koskinen has returned to Finland"

"Your cover name"

"Precisely"

"With theatrical make up to boot?" The Major inquired

"But of course"

"I'm impressed"

"Let's hope it continues with what Kristiasen has given us" Anya optimistically replied as she switched on her device and shone the first image entitled An Introduction to Skaldskaparmal on the opposite wall whilst she referred to notes that Kristiasen had scribbled in pencil on the printed copy that he had provided. The image both mystified and confused everyone present including Anya.

"A recruiting drive or an introductory history of the order" The Major asked after a moment of silence.

"I cannot answer that question"

"Very well let us skim through the material and make up our minds" The Major suggested a little disappointed with Anya's efforts.

"As you wish" Anya responded and proceeded to flick through the slides.

First up was the Creed's interpretation of the meaning of Skaldskaparmal as it applied to its strict moral code, the nine heavenly realms were presented as before but contained icons buried included icons buried in the narrative which when clicked upon revealed in greater detail the important teachings of certain mental and physical lessons associated with that particular realm which would guarantee the advancement of the student to the next level culminating in Skatyrnir which very few attained. The final slide simply stated Snorri.

"To me this represents nothing more than an ancient Scandinavian approach to warfare" Marcus commented.

"I agree" Anya sadly answered.

"I think we have missed something, go back to Skatyrnir" The Major intuitively reasoned "Look carefully at the text for any anomalies" He then instructed with little result from the group.

"Enlarge the text to 300%, use the mouse to scan every line and word, there above the letter I not a dot but a sad face, click on it" Marcus suggested and watched as a series of photographs depicted an aerial view of Kristiasen's office from three angles, the most important from behind that clearly showed his computer screen.

"Someone has eyes in his office and I bet ears as well" Marcus concluded

"Very good soldier, however what is the significance of this finding" The Major bluntly asked.

"I can explain" Anya gladly responded.

"That would be helpful" The Major replied

"All of the inmates that I visited in prison according to Pastor Kristiasen had pornographic material of the paedophile variety stored on their personal computers, which Kristiasen argues is impossible as once they joined the creed they were thoroughly vetted and everything belonging to them thoroughly cleansed. From that point on their computers were constantly monitored by the Creed's central computer for content"

"Someone simply hacked their computers" Marcus casually remarked as he thought it common practice in this day and age.

"Not that simple as each member's computer requires a separate password after the main computer which is password protected is accessed. The only way was for someone to constantly monitor Kristiasen's activities in his office in other words constantly look over his shoulder"

"For what reason...?" The Major asked.

"The philosophy of the Creed is to protect others from ruin, harm or loss, all of those imprisoned had seen active duty in Yemen's proxy war prior to their arrest, in other words they were in Yemen promoting an end to the war and establishing peace for the long term much to the disgust of those who fuelled the war"

"This is becoming very interesting" The Major surmised

"There is more" Brit interrupted

"What might that be?"

"My investigations reveal that Pastor Kristiasen had started a friendship with the Minister of the Interior some time ago"

"Let me guess, before the paedophile sting"

"Correct Major, approximately ten months prior" Brit confirmed.

"Someone was either very clever or just a lucky opportunist. Eliminate all opponents in the Middle East and establish a military base in Norway at the same time. Question is who?" The Major said.

"Can we finish examining the text" Marcus interrupted as he felt there was more to be discovered.

"Oblige the soldier will you Anya?" The Major beckoned as he admired Marcus's determination to succeed.

"There in the word 'their' the letter I's dot is a smiley face" Marcus quickly observed and waited in anticipation for Anaya to click on the icon.

"Snorri answers for all, four places plus seventy seven summons the troops" The Major read out aloud.

"I believe these are the log in passwords which means with the help of an expert we can determine who incriminated the Creed of Tyr's agents" Brit argued.

"First we gorge their eyes out and rupture the ears of those who have infiltrated Kristiasen's private domain, this is how we will rid Norway of its vermin" The Major forcibly said as he gritted his teeth.

"On that score what did you discover?" Marcus asked the Major.

"I should ask you the very same question as we I remember went our separate ways" The Major acidly replied as though Marcus had acted in an disobedient manner. Marcus reacted by thinking that what the Major had just said was utter nonsense and furthermore that the Major lacked the tactical skills in the field that made a difference. To the casual observer it might have appeared so but to the astute military mind it was a clever use of resources to acquire as much Intel as possible.

"Unintentionally due to circumstances" Marcus recalled

"Explanation accepted anything of significance to report?"

"The truck that we intercepted was there to collect arms which were supplied by two foreign sounding dealers"

"What language did they speak?" Brit asked

"Broken Swedish interspersed with fluent English, once the deal was completed and they were alone their mother tongue sounded Arabic; I managed to take photos which I will provide copies of once my phone is revived"

"Anything else soldier...?" The Major roughly asked.

"There was a young woman present who argued fiercely with the dealers, something about getting her 'leaf' back, it was very heated and I felt the dealers were intent on killing her but she just disappeared as did the two shady dealers shortly afterwards. The entry door then suddenly shut leaving me locked inside. It dawned on me that there had to be other entry exit points and a 'backroom' where the arms were stored prior to sale. I set about trying to locate one of these by following the tracks left behind by the electric carts that the dealers used to ferry the weapons located in multiple depots leading me to conclude that the mountain range was riddled with weapons"

"What sort?" The Major asked seeking more details.

"Handguns, automatic weapons, landmines, surface to air missiles, an assortment of aerial bombs ranging from small to the mighty Mk-84 2000lb variety"

"Oh my, it looks as if they are indiscriminately equipping all and sundry" The Major replied in a disgusted tone of voice.

"It would appear so" Marcus said in agreement.

"I take it you left nothing behind" The Major asked.

"Affirmative" Marcus answered without batting an eyelid.

"Are you quite certain of that?" The Major firmly answered pressing the point.

"Affirmative Sir....!" Marcus sharply replied as though he had snapped to attention.

"Why do you ask?" Brit curiously inquired.

"Because this morning's television news reported a large seismic event occurring around Roros with its epicentre in the adjacent mountain range which is very unusual for the region as it is considered to be geologically stable, also few aftershocks were recorded"

"What are you suggesting?"

"The most likely cause to my way of thinking was an explosion and depending on its size and extent it may well have put everyone out of business, for how long is another question that only time will answer" The Major explained

"It might also terminate our mission sooner than anticipated" Both Brit and Anya concluded simultaneously

"Not really"

"Why?"

"It is political in nature which means it could take forever as it twists and turns much like a venomous snake pandering to the needs of those who gave it life" Major Weir coldly replied as a matter of fact

"From what Marcus told us you were left out in the cold, what exactly are you able to report?" Anya inquired seeking to obtain a fuller picture of the events

"I couldn't follow Marcus because several heavily disguised trucks arrived making it difficult to remain obscure, consequently I remained in the shadows observed and took photos until the trucks were loaded and departed. I then scampered back to our vehicle and followed with lights off at a safe distance; about twelve clicks down the deserted road the convoy came to a halt and were greeted by a black limousine bearing Danderyd number plates.

For your information Danderyd is a municipality north of Stockholm where the affluent of all dispositions safely reside. Based on what Marcus, Anya and I have presented our course is clear, but before I chart it let me introduce you to the new member of our group" The Major said as he signalled Nils to usher in Nicoli's replacement who somewhat arrogantly glided into the room.

"Captain Gerhardt Jager on loan to us from a highly specialised unit belonging to the German KSK which prides itself in having the foremost knowledge in computer hacking. His first assignment will be to assist Brit and Anya unravel the Creed's computer dilemma, meanwhile Nils will resurrect Marcus's phone and download all of the relevant imagery whilst I shall obtain as much information as possible on the owner of the black limousine bearing Danderyd number plates, I suggest we reconvene in six hours" The Major succinctly answered leaving Marcus pondering what he should do. Anya recognised the desperation in his face and quickly said "Come join us it will be fun" An invitation that Marcus knew should not be refused.

The foursome relocated to the makeshift computer room that they had constructed a few days earlier but before they sat down to do business Gerhardt Jager decided it was an opportune time in which to relax and get to know each other.

"I am Gerhardt Jager. I was born in East Germany in the year that the infamous Berlin Wall came down namely 1989. It was not easy as the inhabitants were reluctant to allow the West's ideas and philosophies penetrate their ways consequently my thinking has been influenced by Russian ideology until I immigrated to West Germany and forged a new life for myself. In some ways I am thankful for my past as it has allowed me to advance my career largely because I think differently much like yourselves otherwise they would not have assembled us. This is a conclusion I reached from reading your individual dossiers that the Major supplied and although I am ranked a Captain I am not your leader I am just another cog to spur things along" Gerhardt said in a Berliner accent that was sprinkled with Russian overtones and a smile that Marcus thought was hardly warm and fluffy consequently he took an instant dislike to the Captain as he could foresee future conflicts between the two of them providing their areas of interests did not overlap. Marcus took a back seat as Anya explained the Creed of Tyr's problem to Gerhardt.

"We have an interesting situation based on your strong belief that everyone you interviewed is innocent, the question becomes how was the computer breached? Is it still under surveillance? If so is the offensive camera operational via wireless, hard wired or via the cloud? Furthermore how robust was the main computer's defence to attack whether overt or subtle, we need to physically examine the camera's connection to tell us how sophisticated our enemy is" Gerhardt analytically responded as he mentally toyed with the problem at hand.

"If Pastor Kristiasen is dead access is immediately compromised" Brit concluded

"Only if there is no second in command which I would find unusual given the ideologies of the Creed" Gerhardt reasoned

"It may not come to that, according to the Major you hail from a crack unit with the foremost knowledge in computer hacking, surely you are able to determine everything remotely" Marcus fearlessly challenged the Captain as he interrupted their conversation. Gerhardt responded by briefly looking at Marcus with an icy stare before saying "Which part of you said that, the backstabbing Englishman or dumb Pollack?"

"Perhaps it was a joint decision"

"Better than fighting each other" Gerhardt acidly replied in a way that suggested Marcus suffered with a split personality disorder. His comments did not faze Marcus who simply smiled and said "Hope you know a thing or two about RATS" His comment baffled both Anya and Brit.

"Absolutely, we have extensive knowledge on their habitats, reproductive cycles and migratory behaviour" Gerhardt arrogantly answered

"That being the case you should have no difficulty in catching anyone of them" Marcus boldly insinuated

"Will someone please tell us what rodents have to do with our situation?" Anya asked as she did not understand the hidden meaning of the subject at hand.

"RATS in computer language is an abbreviation that stands for Remote Access Trojans a form of malware that allows a hacker to take control of a computer" Gerhardt smugly answered

"Usually via an email if the user is gullible or stupid enough to open it, which means people like us, I think I will leave you to play the Pied piper whilst I do other things" Marcus replied making reference to himself and dumb Pollack's.

"Where are you going?" Anya asked

"No where important, I shall return within the allotted six hours" Marcus vaguely said and quickly left, not satisfied with his answer Anya jumped to her feet and followed closely behind intent on finding out more.

"What are you doing?" Marcus asked as he felt Anya's breath on the back of his neck.

"Seeking more details"

"It is I who should be doing the asking, you weren't exactly forthcoming earlier!" Marcus accurately stated

"What do you mean?"

"Where was your last meeting with Kristiasen and were you targeted?" Marcus fired back as he noticed numerous bruises on Anya's forearm which she quickly concealed.

"You're not exactly an angel either you lied to the Major about sabotaging the weapons depot!" Anya angrily countered

"What of it?"

"You exceeded your authority!"

"Let us say that my hatred of arms dealers got the better of me" Marcus firmly replied

"What will your hatred cause you to do next?"

"I don't know I haven't given it much thought, it will depend upon circumstances, this is where I need to be alone to mull things over" Marcus replied as his mood started to mellow

'Which makes me think that your sabotage was done quite eloquently" Anya deduced as she smiled

"Beauty is in the eye of the beholder" Marcus softly replied

"Five hours and thirty one minutes to kill, what shall we do?" Anya asked with a cheeky smile

"Analysis would be appropriate" Marcus suggested

"Lead on" Anya replied as they walked along the corridor that would ultimately take them outside to where his BMW motorcycle was parked

"Five hours and twenty eight minutes is a long time to spend analysing and coming up with dead end propositions, why don't we find somewhere nice and cosy and mull things over coffee and lunch, surely there is a cafe close by that we can go to?" Marcus romantically said once they stepped outside into the warm sunshine which prompted Anya to eagerly seek one out on her mobile phone

"Urr-ekka is situated 5km from here, we can walk there it will take us about 50 minutes sooner if we pick up the pace"

"Lead the way I'll try to keep up" Marcus replied knowing full well that he didn't stand a chance especially if Anya activated her ARSE

The time proceeded at its own pace which allowed the couple to reach several conclusions namely that it was futile to visit the Creed of Tyr administrative offices as they were most likely under constant surveillance this explained why Anya even though heavily disguised became a person of interest in the library, what worried them most was the idea that the rental car that she was given may have been 'tagged' with a tracking device when she visited Kristiasen at the Creed of Tyr's complex. Whoever they were easily recognised Tanya's disguise and were intent on questioning her in the library. Considering how much damage she had inflicted on her would be assailants plus the fact that she did not return to her car which was parked in Onepark Oslo SP it would most likely cause the same people to visit Norwegian Ice or keep it under surveillance. Marcus and Anya would need to bring up this security issue when the group reconvened that afternoon.

"Well ladies and gentlemen I hope you have had as much success as Nils and I" The Major openly said as he surveyed the blank faces before him, he paused for a moment and then said" Perhaps not it would seem. Never mind we have enough to go on with thanks to our collective efforts. Marcus you took some very nice and precise photographs which enabled us to identify the 'purchasers' of the weapons as belonging to the bikie organisation known as the Bandits form Hell. The 'sellers' however do not appear to be on any criminal data base. Somewhere along the line your phone switched from camera to video mode consequently it recorded some audio which I will now play and let you decide if it is of any value"

"It confirms what I reported earlier, fluent English, broken Swedish....." Marcus attempted to say before being cut short by the Major who corrected him.

"Norwegian actually"

"Pardon....?" Marcus queried

"The bikie members were Norwegian" The Major confirmed

"And the Arabic....?" Marcus asked

"Sounds more like Modern Hebrew" Brit determined from her library days when she briefly dabbled in linguistics

"Excellent" The Major applauded and then continued to present his findings "The black limousine bearing Danderyd number plates belongs to a Yugoslavian gangster with affiliations to numerous European bikie groups that supply the Continent's drug cartels with their armoury needs. On the night it was driven by a women most likely his wife who according to the authorities is squeaky clean which suggests she has a unique way of keeping them satisfied. There is a suspicion that the Bandits from Hell use the dark web's Telegram It to foster their activities in the Middle East thereby allowing the Israeli's to continually siphon off 3.8 billion dollars a year plus and additional 500 million dollars for missile defence from the gullible Americans as foreign aid to ensure the survival of Israel and its continual creep into Palestine"

"Bet they have more nukes than the Americans" Marcus cynically mumbled

"That is the general belief amongst the world leaders, makes you wonder why they constantly pick on the Iranians" The Major replied

"Someone has to look bad in order to justify the other one's position" Marcus acidly replied as he had seen so much of it before.

"We have nothing on your woman and as for her demanding, at this stage the 'leaf' is either biblical, botanical or something fashionable. How did you and Gerhardt fare?"

"It will take longer than I anticipated" Gerhardt sadly answered

"We independently came to the same conclusion plus Anya may have caused a security breach" Marcus regretfully replied

"In what way" The Major asked a little concerned

"We believe that the Creed of Tyr remains under constant surveillance largely because it is a tenacious organisation organization that actively seeks to recruit new idealistic individuals to maintain and further its cause. We think that Anya was photographed either there or during one of her prison visits and that the hire car she used may have been fitted with a tracking device. If the latter is true and taking into account how well she defended herself against her would be assailants in the public library it is fair to say that the hire car movements will be of interest and we can expect a visit" Marcus slowly explained

"Where is the car now?" The Major asked

"To the best of my knowledge still parked in OnePark Oslo SP" Anya correctly answered

"Your thoughts Marcus......?" The Major inquired

"We report the car as stolen and check our external perimeter"

"Very eloquent in fact as eloquent as the seismic events at Roros" The Major replied with a glint of approval in his eye

"If they do come snooping and we apprehend them" Marcus thought out aloud

"They may or may not help us especially if they are hired thugs we will be none the wiser it's up to Gerhardt to identify and locate the faceless hackers" The Major determined

"Reporting the car as stolen will serve no purpose" Anya unexpectedly said

"Why is that?" Marcus coldly asked seeking further clarification

"I suspect it was 'tagged' at the Creed's compound whilst I was with Kristiasen, I returned to it around midday and then returned to Norwegian Ice and stayed for about an hour. Norwegian Ice has tasting rooms and a restaurant therefore my movements are suggestive of meeting a friend for lunch, I think it might be better to think of the car as being abandoned by a person who has fled the scene" Anya cleverly argued

"That is the best case scenario, but if the car was 'tagged' at the prison then our friends will definitely visit us, did you leave anything behind in the car?" Marcus asked

"It's clean"

"What about fingerprints?" Marcus persisted

"I wore gloves at all times" Anya truthfully replied

"It's not a crime scene!" Brit interrupted coming to Anya's defence

"That's where you are wrong" The Major announced as he displayed on his mobile phone the latest news complete with a photograph of Anya as Aino Koskinen courtesy of Oslo Today.

"Two holidaying Israeli architects were savagely beaten in an unprovoked attack in the public toilets at Deichman Bjorvika library yesterday. Both remain in a critical condition at Oslo's general hospital. Police wish to question the following subject, if anyone knows of her whereabouts please telephone 1350"

"You know what this means?" The Major asked his squad

"Potentially anyone and everyone who came into contact with Anya as Aino Koskinen will be questioned, prison staff, the psychiatrist even his phone records might be checked etcetera, etcetera, especially if one of the Israeli's dies" Brit regretfully answered

"Thankfully whereabouts are unknown, Aino Koskinen has disappeared into thin air" Nils confirmed

"What about the car?" Marcus asked

"Registered under a false name and address, supported and complimented by expertly forged documents and paid for in cash by one of my heavily disguised staff" Nils confidently answered

"That only leave's DNA as a possible lead" The Major suggested

"Not so! My DNA is highly restricted" Anya said with an air of authority

13

MY HOUSE OR YOURS

"You should think of a computer as being a house, the bedroom where memory is stored, the bathroom and laundry where things are washed clean and the unwanted deleted, the kitchen where things are created, the dining room for all interactions, question is how can an intruder break in and remain undetected while everyone goes about their daily routines. What will make the intruder flee and take the most dangerous pathways until he has nowhere to run? Is death the ultimate incentive? If so what form does it take? The intruder stands with pictures until he becomes one sufficiently small enough to be posted, return to sender a most satisfying prospect" Gerhardt cryptically mumbled as his fingers danced on the keyboard of the computer in front of him.

"Are you neutralising the malware?" Brit asked

"Not in the slightest, my approach is one of reduction and expulsion, in other words shrink the bastard and kick him out the front door with I add a piece of pink ribbon stuck in his arse so I can follow him" Gerhardt coarsely answered without taking his eyes off the computer screen.

"How's it going?"

"Good very good, just need to determine how long I want the

ribbon to be, too long and he will trip, too short and I will not find him, it has to be just right for me and he" Gerhardt replied as his fingers it seemed played the overture to one of Verde's comic operas. "Okay now we go, ready, steady, kick" He then said as he pressed the enter button that would start the process off. Both Brit and Anya watched in awe as the computer screen went from displaying endless reams of digital sequences to a geographical map of Scandinavia which light up the cities that the intruder had passed through." So far so good" Gerhardt gladly said as he watched and knew that it would be a convoluted journey before the intruder's home address would be found.

"Impressive" Brit said in admiration

"Thank you, this is my programme, it took quite a while to perfect although I must confess I did get a little help from my friends the Russians"

"They do have a wealth of experience interfering in the American elections and its infrastructure" Anya commented

"Absolute nonsense, it is the Americans themselves who are doing all of the interference, that is one screwed up nation!" Gerhardt without any qualms openly disagreed

"Too much freedom" Brit suggested

"Absolutely" Gerhardt concurred and continued to monitor the intruder's travels

"What's happening?" Brit asked with a sense of excitement as she always enjoyed a thrilling chase

"He has left for parts unknown, so we have to use something else as the pink ribbon has been discarded, clever fellow obviously found it too uncomfortable, next time I will tie it around his testicles" Gerhardt said with an air of temporary frustration

"Can you still track him?" Anya asked

"Of course, the ribbon was an annoying distraction the real tracking device is in his head"

"Pardon....?"

"I've caused him to whistle" Gerhardt blankly replied

"How does that help you?" Brit inquired thinking that it referred to an auditory phenomenon

"Whistle stands for White Hot Instant Service Tumble Lag Execute which means as the intruder skips from one server to another it causes that server to instantly drop out and cause a black spot which allows me to track his movements and as you can clearly see he cunningly adopted a spaghetti route before landing in the Israeli embassy in Washington DC" Gerhardt proudly replied as he savoured another successful mission.

"Well done!" Both Brit and Anya complimented their new colleague not realising that it was not an instant result but one that had taken in excess of four hours to complete

"I suppose we should tell the Major providing the result is accurate and not a false positive" Brit then said

"No chance of that!" Gerhardt arrogantly replied

"Very well then let us proceed" Anya proposed

The trio found the Major, Marcus and Nils in the boardroom down the corridor all were seated with cups of coffee in the hands that did little to relieve their mental fatigue.

'Can we disturb you?" Anya gently asked after knocking on the door and entering the spacious well appointed room.

"Come in I'm glad you are here, we need to go over all of the information together, I gather you can confirm that the Israeli's are most probably behind all of this?" The Major calmly inquired

"Affirmative Sir......!" Gerhardt said in a loud voice as he came to attention and clicked his heels

"Take a seat, we need to discuss what we know so far" The Major placidly said and waited for the trio to act accordingly before he described the gravity of the situation before them. "As you know our mission was to discreetly uncover how and who influenced the Norwegian parliamentarians into allowing American troops onto sovereign Norwegian soil. It was meant to be a simple task that would allow our superiors sufficient leverage to reverse the situation and put an end to Operation Anaconda. Unfortunately a series of events have occurred that place us in an unenviable position. The Israelis are once again playing the victim card and are attempting to link four separate incidents starting with the explosion at Hell's David's Camp retreat which claimed the life of Nicoli. The Israelis are calling it an act of terrorism perpetrated by Nicoli who they claim was seeking revenge related to legitimate business dealings that involved his family and Croatian Jews prior to Nazi occupation.

They believe he had an accomplice who orchestrated the bombing of the Israeli embassy in Oslo the following day and that the same accomplice assassinated two CIA agents who were undercover Mossad agents. Last and not least we have the two Israeli 'architects' who were severely beaten to near death at the state library. Needless to say the Israeli's are hopping mad and are demanding answers and immediate action to this wave of anti-Semitic behaviour. They are suggesting that the Neo-Nazi's movement never disappeared from Norway, it is widespread and deeply entrenched and Norway as such should be expelled from the United Nations all of which has caused unprecedented turmoil in the corridors of Norwegian power"

"What makes the Israeli's so important?" Brit asked as she had never taken an interest in the geopolitics of the Middle East.

"They have a baseless over inflated opinion of themselves, make no mistake they are extremely cunning and ruthless in getting their own way, that's why we have to be extra diligent when it comes to our welfare" The Major grimly explained as he looked around the room to gage the reaction of his fellow operatives.

"There are approximately thirteen hundred Jews presently in Norway many of which hold high places in the government and its bureaucracy, they have wormed their way in by blackmailing the Norwegian Government's failure to protect their families during WW2 to satisfy one purpose and that is to siphon funds from Norwegian Gas to finance the State of Israel, furthermore these Jews belong to the Mozaic Centre which actively lobby's and irritates the government no end on all manner of seemingly important topics, needless to say they are a thorn in the Government's side. We believe the recent events has shaken the Mozaic's to the core but as money is the key issue they will be reluctant to leave, you can expect more Mossad agents to invade our beloved Norway to protect their investments however it might be all in vain" Nils slowly said as he drew on his knowledge of local and international affairs

"I have a feeling that the Mozaics are the one's pulling the strings. The Creed of Tyr dismantling having nothing to do with the Americans gaining access to Norwegian soil in order to set up their proxy base. The Mozaics with their members in high places especially in taxation may have unearthed sensitive information of the unexplained wealth of certain politicians considering their fanatical preoccupation with what rightly belongs to the Jews no matter how far back one goes in history, it is fair to say it was this avenue that they used to coerce the Minister for Justice and the Minister for the Interior into supporting the Americans presence in Norway, visiting the said politicians will be of no consequence, they are most probably under greater surveillance to make certain they do not stray from the path. This will become a battle of pressures meaning theirs and ours" Marcus analytically deduced.

"What are you suggesting" The Major asked most intrigued by Marcus's thoughts

"It is fair to say that all media content in one way or another is determined by the Government of the day even to the extent of selecting the most appropriate words. The 'seismic' event which I had a hand in did not have its epicentre at Roros, it occurred at 62-6472N 11-8669E on the Swedish side" Marcus reluctantly admitted even though he knew that the Major had suspected as much

"What of it?" The Major sternly asked

"Perhaps the Swedes are freer to report as they see fit"

"Are you suggesting we play the wait and see game?" The Major asked growing rather impatient

"On the contrary I think it is time we placed a thought provoking phone call tinged with an element of conspiracy" Marcus cleverly retorted

"To whom....?" Gerhardt abruptly asked

"The Swedes" Marcus succinctly answered

"Precisely which ones...?" Gerhardt once again abruptly if not arrogantly asked

"The television media, Stockholm Today is a good bet and we should contact Safeguard Nordic Purity group"

"Who are they?" Brit asked not having any prior knowledge of their existence

"A violent highly influential Neo-Nazi group" Marcus calmly answered

"Why...?" Brit asked confused by Marcus's suggestion

"In keeping with the Israelis narrative that the dark undercurrents of Norwegian society past and present go largely unnoticed thus fulfilling their fantasy, except are they prepared for intervention by the Swedes" Marcus explained

"I'm a bit confused" Brit freely admitted but could see that the Major in contrast to the others wasn't

"The Norwegian chapter is small with no political clout, at a pinch the best it might muster is fifty or less individuals a number that is difficult to predict as the chapter is secretive and employs tight membership regulations, in other words it is ill equipped in contrast to the Swedes who have undergone military training with Russian ultra nationalistic forces"

"What is the name of this chapter?" Brit asked

"Safeguard Nordic Purity" Marcus replied in a poetic tone of voice

"Does it have any affiliation with the KNN?" Anya asked Nils directly

"Minimal" Nils briefly replied

"But extensive in other ways" Gerhardt was quick to add

"Precisely as the name implies it is active in Denmark, Finland, Iceland, Norway and Sweden" Nils further explained

"Highly organised, motivated, fearlessly focused" Gerhardt said as though he had personally dealt with several of its members before

"That's all very nice but why should it show any interest in what we are doing?" Anya critically asked

"Because what happened in Norway threatens to defile Nordic Purity in more ways than one" The Major wisely answered

"I thought the Governments were doing a good enough job of that by allowing undesirable refugees into their respective countries, after all some extremists predict Swedes will be strangers in their own country by 2040" Gerhardt said straight to the point

"This is not the time to discuss matters of ethnic cleansing" The Major sharply rebuked the East German who did not flinch in the slightest

"That may not be strictly true" Brit unexpectedly said coming to Gerhardt defence

"What are you driving at?" The Major barked

"We have never been informed as to whom we are answerable"

"What of it?" The Major growled

"I cringe at the thought that the Danes might be involved"

"Why...?"

"They do not have a particularly good reputation when it comes to being trusted. I believe one of their favourite pastimes is spying on European leaders for the benefit of the Americans, I hope none of your superiors are Danish or have Danish connections" Brit bravely countered

"I cannot say with absolute certainty" The Major was forced to admit

"Then the list of those against us grows" Anya grimly concluded as she swallowed hard

"Americans, Jews; Danes what a wonderful trilogy of absolute bastards...!" Brit bitterly said as she considered how the group was likely to act next

"Something we Germans have thought for a long time, which I must add will work to our advantage" Gerhardt smugly whispered

"How do you mean" The Major asked

"The Americans have all the gear but no idea, the Jews are blinded by their arrogance for world domination and the Danes are emotionally bankrupt" Gerhardt quickly responded

"That's all very nice but what of it, how does it help us" The Major bluntly asked Gerhardt who appeared to shrivel up and die on the spot which plunged the room into abrupt silence

"I think we should act on your achievements to date" Nils quietly said with a warm smile as a way of encouraging further dialogue

"What did you have in mind?" The Major asked

"Conduct a fact finding mission at the Yugoslav's house in Danderyd, visit the Bandits from Hell on the pretext that you want to buy arms and send out search parties to see how many mountain-eers and hikers were injured on both sides of the mountain range during the 'seismic' event, report your findings onto the net because it appears that even the Swedes are reluctant to report anything con-troversial" Nils replied in a hushed voice as though someone might be listening in on their conversation.

"Before we venture forth I would like to know if your superiors were informed as to our identities" Marcus intensely asked the Major with a cold stare

"The people who put this project together are no fools, they remain highly secretive and cautious in their every move, selection of agents was my domain under the guise of conducting a new approach to counter terrorism which I fabricated and had bound into a written manual that embraces techniques not seen before, it is a think tank exercise that is not meant to attract any attention to itself, do I make myself clear?" The Major carefully explained as he left his chair and paced about the room

"So we remain relatively safe, under the radar and can go freely about our business" Brit concluded

"Relatively speaking..." The Major hesitated to agree but before he could add anything further he was interrupted by Nils "Excuse me David, we have guests"

"With big ears...?"

"Precisely"

"They didn't waste their time, where are they?" The Major asked sensing excitement in the air

"Across the road behind the bushes for the past four hours"

"Means of listening?"

"Laser plus binoculars"

"Ethnicity..... ?"

"Most likely Nordic" Nils postulated

"In other words hired thugs...!" The Major concluded

"Affirmative"

"Course of action Ladies and Gentleman...?" The Major openly asked his group

"If we engage and dispose of them it will draw attention to us and confirm our whereabouts and guilt, doing nothing is the safest option, they can only stay for a limited period of time before a civic minded individual will ask why they are loitering there" Anya thought out aloud

"That may not happen before tomorrow, after all it is 8.15pm and they have darkness to keep them covered" Nils suggested

"Or sooner as they may decide to break into Norwegian Ice once its restaurant has closed for the night" Gerhardt postulated as that was what he would most likely do

"I suggest we sit tight and allow our well hidden security and the police to deal with these annoyances" Nils vaguely said with a wry smile much to Gerhardt's disappointment whereas the remainder of the group's members accepted what Nils suggested and whilst they waited for the inevitable commotion to start they enjoyed a light dinner and discussed which targets each member would tackle in the days ahead. Once they had finished eating and it neared 11.15pm Nils activated the boardroom's wall mounted television, selected security on the remote and flicked through the various camera angles to view any activity in and about Norwegian Ice's fenced off complex. By 11.30pm the group watched as a black SUV drove along the southern perimeter, stopped in a poorly lit area and its two occupants dressed in black with matching balaclavas climbed onto the SUV's roof and scaled the three meter high fence to descend on the other side, to them the would be assassins there was no security to contend with, no motion detecting flood lights, no guard dogs, no security guards on foot, everything was still, ripe for the picking. Armed with crowbars the duo approached a side door marked 'authorised entry only' which was flanked on each side by what appeared to be large brick pillars. The lock on the door appeared simple, easily jemmied by a crowbar but as soon as one thug inserted the crowbar's tongue the brick pillars sprung to life and two menacing robots equipped with stun guns confronted the would be intruders who stupidly lashed out with their crowbars only to be dealt 100,000 volts of electricity.

"Remind me never to come home late and try that" Gerhardt flippantly remarked as he mentally applauded the complex's so-phisticated defence system and watched as the intruders' bodies quivered with defeat.

"What's next?" Anya eagerly asked

"The robots alert the police once they have secured the intruders" Nils happily commented

"And then...?"

"They are carted away and processed according to the video evidence we supply on the following day" Nils replied

"So this has happened before?"

"On numerous occasions by wayward alcoholics and those wishing to steal our commercial secrets" Nils replied

"Surely they could side step the system by taking the power out" Marcus suggested

"Not so easily, the robots are autonomous and the auxiliary emergency power steps in within seconds of a power failure" Nils proudly answered

"I think we can safely say that this threat has been clinically resolved, Marcus it is time for you to make contact with the Bandits using Telegram It on the dark web on the pretext that you wish to purchase arms, Gerhardt can act as your personal bodyguard. Brit, Anya you will attend to the Yugoslav and pump him for information relating to the identities of his suppliers, Nils and I will look for 'survivors' of the 'seismic event' it appears the authorities on both sides are reluctant to exercise their respective duties, that's all for tonight, hope you enjoyed the 'show'" The major cheerfully concluded and allowed his troops to disperse for the night.

The thought that he should contact the Bandits from Hell did not sit very well with Marcus for it caused him to have a disturbed night's sleep full of vivid nightmares in which he saw Anya captured and violently tortured by the Bandits from Hell before her lifeless and mutilated body was dumped on a rubbish heap deep in the forest and left to rot and be eaten by wild animals.

It was inevitable that this should happen as Marcus very quickly spiritually bonded with those he worked with and because of this he cursed himself for not having spent more time with Nicoli for he thought he might have saved him but it was not meant to be.

The following morning would be an emotional turmoil, nothing pleasant to wake up to, a decision needed to be made, blindly follow the Major's order or shadow Brit and Anaya. Marcus was not comfortable with the Major's thinking, something was not quite right but Marcus would obey for one purpose and that was to demonstrate its futility and so it was that in the early hours of the morning Marcus left his warm bed to contact the Bandits from Hell using one of the anonymous computers the group had previously assembled. As he briskly walked towards the computer room in his suit of 'armour' Marcus determined that it was highly unlikely that any merchandise was stored at the Bandits' club house in all likelihood the weapons that he recently saw in the mountain caves were already in transit and would most likely be shipped out of an insignificant sleepy Swedish port such as Gavle which was ideally situated for such things.

Marcus was no stranger to the Dark Web he had entered it many a time before as part of conducting military exercises of the cyber variety. Once comfortable inside the computer room he systematically went about ensuring that the computer he had selected was up to the task of engaging the enemy by performing a systems check, some of Marcus's best work was done when he was alone.

"VPN number check, encryption mode active, TOR engaged, all apps nonexistent, most importantly Shallot Router intact, good, now time to dig" Marcus whispered to himself as he carefully tapped away at the computer's keyboard and spelt 'violent concierge' into the search bar. The no frills website appeared in an instant and offered no assistance apart from a search bar into which Marcus typed Bandits from Hell. Apart from one or two glowing reports the majority were adverse in nature with headings such as 'Gang Warfare Specialists', 'Double crossing Mother Fuckers', 'Never Again'

The theme behind each negative posting was similar, rival gangs would turn up at exactly the identical predetermined time and collection site to take possession of their illegal arms, however without any documentation or proof of purchase or contact telephone numbers to support their claim the situation rapidly descended into chaos with one group accusing the other of theft resulting in a gun battle with multiple casualties on both sides. When it came to ascertaining what went wrong the Bandits accepted no liability washing their hands by saying their role was to supply the weapons nothing more the deal was conducted by an obscure third party and faceless couriers with no further recourse leaving both parties frustrated, out of pocket and to make matters worse the arms shipment invariably turned out to be defective.

At worse the Bandits were repeatedly rapped over the knuckles for being careless and unprofessional in which event they eventually capitulated and reluctantly offered the identical shipment to each gang at a heavily discounted price but it still meant they had been paid three times over.

Under these circumstances Marcus was reluctant to contact the Bandits as it appeared to him that he might be channelled to people who would prove to be useless, nevertheless it was something he had to do in order to prove that this criminal group would yield nothing of importance. The Bandits from Hell were brazen in their internet presence promoting themselves as a charitable organisation looking after the needs of the fallen and cursed, there was neither hint nor whisper of their nefarious activities. Several officers within the group were according to their website available twenty four hours a day for consultation.

"A clever diversion much like the obscenely mega rich who set up charitable organisations to make themselves look good whilst they continue to rape the public at large" Marcus cynically grumbled as he studied the contents of the Bandits 'clean' website and then he thought that perhaps it was not the gang as such but one or two members within who were hiding behind its facade and conducting their illegal arms dealings which the Yugoslav businessman from Danderyd might be persuaded to confirm or deny.

None of this was done in a hurry, Marcus was diligent, patient and paid close attention to detail, haste makes waste was his motto, things could not be rushed if one wanted proper irrefutable results, 3am quickly became 7.30am and with it a shock announcement that even he did not foresee.

"Pack up whatever you're doing!" Anya abruptly commanded as she burst into the computer room without knocking.

Marcus looked up and saw that Anya looked rather distraught

and distressed, obviously something was wrong but before he could ask or shut down his computer Anya went about violently disconnecting all and sundry.

"Come with me, first we collect all of your personal items then we exit"

"Why the urgency...?" Marcus asked confused by her actions

"We're under attack!"

"What! By whom...?" Marcus asked further confused by her actions

"Fake policemen"

"Pardon...?"

"You heard me, fake policemen, those two intruders from last night were found shot dead this morning, Norwegian Ice has been declared a crime scene, no one to enter or leave until further notice" Anya explained as they ran to Marcus quarters where he gathered all of his identity papers, Glock and jacket

"How do you know they are fake policemen?" Marcus asked

"Nils checked with his contact in the police department, no murder has been called in. The two intruders were decoys conveniently eliminated to provide an excuse for police intrusion, Nils checked the surveillance tapes, the intruders were shot from a distance" Anya explained

"Classical military tactic, kill one of your own and make it look as if it was the enemy, then destroy any evidence to the contrary" Marcus replied and mentally cursed himself for not foreseeing such an event especially when the Major had previously hinted of Mossad's involvement in Norwegian politics, he then stopped and asked "Are there many?"

"Four to one ratio"

"Twelve?" Marcus guessed as he did not consider the Major or Gerhardt as members of the team.

"Affirmative"

"Strategy....?"

"First line of defence...?"

"Run away to fight another day" Marcus once again guessed

"Affirmative" Anya answered as she gestured that they start walking again

"Secure means?" Marcus asked as he realised that he was completely in Anya's hands

"Time to put you on ice" Anya cryptically answered as she steered them towards the cool room where a sanctuary lay waiting. Once there she activated the double insulated doors to open and they entered the equipment room where they both donned severe weather clothing complete with face masks suitable to survive 50° below freezing.

"Right here's your clipboard, once inside I want you to walk about to make certain everything is working within the expected parameters, check and record the readings of the various instruments listed, Brit is already here" Anya warmly said

"And the other two" Marcus asked

"Can look after themselves..." Anya unemotionally answered as she ushered Marcus into the artificially contrived frigid Artic conditions that ensured Norwegian Ice's dominance of the spirits market.

"So this is where the magic happens" Marcus whispered to himself as he stood in awe of his surroundings

"Just don't stand there get on with it, don't want to attract any attention to yourself. I'll be in the control room with Brit, managers don't arrive before 8.30am so we have to survive for one hour, also unless they have codes the fake police wouldn't be able to access this part of the operation" Anya said as she prodded Marcus into action. He gingerly studied the paperwork on his clipboard and went in search of his first reading.

The fake police meanwhile went about the complex asking anyone there if they had encountered Anya in the disguise of Aino Koskinen. Nils kept himself scare by hiding in the locked surveillance room, he monitored the fake policemen movements and relayed his observations to Oslo's police department who despatched several squad cars plus their specialist tactical response group. By 8.30am the sound of sirens filled the air from every direction causing the fake policemen to abandon their operation, regroup and make a hasty departure, all but one of the cars that they used managed to escape the last in line was thwarted in its attempt by being rammed by two Oslo police cars at Norwegian Ice's main entrance. Instead of surrendering the fake police decided to engage in a running gun battle with the Oslo police who were instructed to shoot to kill by both the Minister for Police and Minister for Justice. There was no question of the fake policemen abilities they fought with ruthless tenacity and accuracy wounding several Oslo policemen in the process as they ran from one point of cover to another in their attempt to elude capture. However irrespective of that they were no match for Oslo's tactical response group highly trained personnel and their powerful sophisticated weapons which despatched bullets that easily penetrated any means of defence. When the fake policemen realised this they scattered in every direction and sought safety behind parked cars or laid prostate on the ground to no avail as the tactical response group picked them off one by one for Norwegian Ice's parking lot became their tomb. Nils had remotely sealed off the building and the surrounding wire fence was too high to scale. Within twenty minutes the forensics team had arrived followed shortly by the coroner and television crews in hot pursuit. Three fake policemen lay dead, one unrecognisable as his face was a splattered mess, the fourth lay dying in a pool of his own blood that continued to increase as his body emptied itself of its contents. Only Nils was made privy to these events, Marcus, Brit and Anya were isolated, but not totally as the sound of gunshots reverberated around the complex causing them to draw their weapons in anticipation of being attacked, even when the noise abated they remained 'en garde' and did not relax until Nils gave them the all clear.

"In view of the events early this morning the Major has decided to transfer us to a safe house not far from here. It is his feeling that another wave of sinister intruders will eventually come even though the last group obtained nothing, needless to say we cannot leave via the front gate for obvious reasons however a well hidden emergency exit is available to us at the rear of this complex where two non descript vehicles will be waiting. I and Brit will occupy the first car and lead the way as it has had the route programmed into its GPS. Anya, you and Marcus will follow closely behind, we will vacate the building in fifteen minutes giving you sufficient time to collect your belongings, we will reconvene in the computer room before setting sail, is that clear?" Nils asked

"Affirmative" Brit answered

"Copy that" Both Marcus and Anya replied as they looked at each other

"Good then go to it" Nils sharply said and proceeded to leave. Marcus waited until Brit and Nils were out of earshot before asking Anya "Have you got everything?"

"Certainly have, all of the important stuff, I like travelling light"

"Good then let's depart, enough is enough!" Marcus acidly replied

"What are you up to?"

"Taking steps to resolve the issue at hand" Marcus answered as he made certain the coast was clear

"What about the Major?" Anya asked

"He can bugger off back to Scotland and play the bagpipes!"

"I see" Anya replied with a sparkle in her eyes as she sensed and admired Marcus's determination "Know where you're going" she then asked

"Ultimately yes, presently no" Marcus glumly answered

"Then let me show you the way" Anya brightly said

"You've been here before" Marcus guessed as he frowned

"Once or twice" Anya replied without being specific

"On official business...?"

"You could say that"

"Which means several of your colleagues might be outside" Marcus speculated

"How astute of you, let's find out shall we?"

"After you" Marcus replied with a sweep of his hand and allowed Anya to lead the way which she did smoothly and efficiently.

Outside the car park resembled a war scene with bullet riddled cars languishing on flat tyres, bloodied dead bodies in awkward positions and three Oslo policemen heavily bandaged lying on stretches waiting to be transferred to hospital. The tactical response group had swept the area and had taken up positions in case of any further attack.

"Judging by the number of spent cartridges they came well prepared" Marcus said off the cuff as he followed closely behind Anya who walked authoritatively towards an officer seemingly in charge, he immediately smiled once he laid eyes on Anya.

"Hello stranger what brings you here? I thought you were on special assignment" The officer said as Anya neared him

"Precisely that"

"So it would seem. Tired of protecting oil installations?" The officer inquired

"You could say that" Anya coldly replied

"Care to tell me more?"

"Afraid not, rather classified and top secret if you know what I mean"

"I will once we learn who and what these people were doing here" The officer answered making reference to the dead gunmen.

"Good luck" Anya bluntly replied knowing full well that his efforts would prove fruitless

"Who's your friend?" The officer asked as he looked directly at Marcus who avoided the officer's gaze instead mentally analysing those that were present to see if anyone did not fit in.

"Can't say...we are in need of transport as you can see our vehicle has been severely incapacitated" Anya boldly stated straight to the point even though it was untruthful,

"Sorry can't spare anyone, perhaps you could hitch a ride in one of the ambulances, I'm sure the paramedics will be only too pleased accommodate you" The officer somewhat rudely replied

"Very well" Anya succinctly answered and abruptly turned leaving the officer wondering why she was there.

The ambulance paramedics were more than accommodating and made room for both Anya and Marcus under the proviso that the ambulance was not a taxi service therefore there would not be any deviations from their intended course, the end point being Oslo's General Hospital which was fine by them.

"Do you and that tactical response policeman have history?" Marcus asked out of curiosity as the past rapport between the two did not escape him

"A fleeting encounter, nothing more..." Anya slightly embarrassed replied

"You made it and he didn't, no wonder he's impotent" Marcus glibly answered which caused Anya to go silent and blush slightly

"Viagra was out of the question, would have failed the drug test, hum, physically incapable and mentally fragile, pity that" Marcus sympathetically reasoned as he studied Anya's facial features but she refused to give anything away, remained stoic in appearance and said nothing until they reached their destination.

"Do you need a hand with the casualties?" Marcus asked once the paramedic had parked the ambulance in one of the docking bays at Oslo's General Hospital

"Very kind of you, we are used to this, in any case you are not covered by our insurance policy" The paramedic who was seated with the casualties warmly replied

"Understand, thanks for the lift" Marcus genuinely said and waited until it was safe for all concerned to vacate the ambulance

"Where to now....?" Anya impatiently asked once they were alone

"Taxi to Oslo's International Airport"

"Where are we going?"

"Reykjavik.....Iceland"

"What's there?" Anya asked confused by his answer

"Free press I believe"

"Oh yes, besides our word what exactly do we have to show them and by the way are our Norwegian tabloids not good enough?" Anya playing the devil's advocate firmly asked

"Not all the time and lots to answer your question. This is neither the time nor place to show you it will have to wait until we are safely squared away in Iceland" Marcus forcibly answered as they walked towards the taxi stand near the main entrance to the hospital. Marcus hoped there would be sensible drivers on duty and not the type that offered drugs of addiction, luckily one fitted the bill.

"Oslo Central" Anya much to Marcus's surprise blurted out once they were inside the cabin

"80 kroner" The driver announced as a no bargain deal

"Akseptabel" Anya replied in Norwegian as she made herself comfortable and joined hands with Marcus making it look as though they were a couple in love both remained silent throughout the journey to Oslo Central. Once there Anya thanked the driver and paid him his money, once inside the complex she led Marcus to a vending ticket machine and purchased two Flytoget express tickets to Gardemoen Airport situated 35km north east of Oslo.

"We'll be there in no time, the high speed trains leave every ten minutes" She chirped as she glanced at Marcus who was impressed by her bold initiatives.

"Nothing like having local knowledge" Marcus admirably stated

"Exactly, I don't know about you but I am famished, let's grab a bite to eat and hot coffee before we board the train, I know of a quaint cafe down below" Anya brightly suggested and continued to lead the way. Marcus had to agree, food and water were a welcome relief for his exhausted and dehydrated body which could gone another thirty six hours with sustenance thanks to his survival training but then this was not some outback wilderness where provisions were scarce. Two fruit Danish's and a mocha coffee hit the spot, a mellow mood engulfed him all was right with the world for a brief moment or two.

"Your train ticket gives the flight times available for booking, clever don't you think?"

"Very convenient"

"We can make the 1.45pm flight, I've already booked us on line no need to rush haste makes waste" Anya warmly said

"Agreed"

"Flight time is about two hours forty five minutes, the only qualm I have is what are we going to do with our hand guns?" Anya asked in a concerned tone of voice

"Depends upon whether we want our whereabouts traced" Marcus thoughtfully replied

"By whom....?" Anya inquired

"The Major I would think, our sudden disappearance will make him wonder about our whereabouts and more importantly why we decided to ignore orders"

"Then let's be open and declare our identities, do you have your Grom ID on you?"

"Never leave home without it plus that useless one the Major supplied" Marcus quietly confirmed

"Likewise, together with my FSK ID we should have no difficulty with security or boarding the plane" Anya put forward

"Agreed"

"Time to make tracks" Anya responded before she downed the last dregs of her coffee.

The high speed train ride to Gardemoen briefly took nineteen minutes during which time Marcus and Anya continued to behave like a couple in love.

"Seeing that you are so efficient have you booked our accommodation in Reykjavik?" Marcus whispered with a smile when the train slowed and came to a stop

"Not yet, I thought we might do that on the spur of the moment once we land" Anya purred

"Why not......" Marcus answered with a sense of adventure and allowed Anya to continue navigating. The airport Marcus found was seamlessly integrated with the other forms of transport namely, trains, bus and taxi, everything was simply laid out and easy to find, Norway being part of the European Union visas were unnecessary however security could not be avoided prior to boarding the aircraft, Anya did not consider it to be an issue consequently she went about logging herself and Marcus onto the 1.45pm flight to Reykjavik and obtained the required boarding passes and seat allocations. With these in hand she confidently approached one of the police officers stationed at the security check point to declare their identity and the fact that they were armed.

The policeman looked very carefully at Anya and Marcus comparing their physical appearance with the photographs on their respective ID's.

"Your documents appear to be in order but as you may understand we are required to do further checks before you are permitted to board the aircraft, follow me please" The policeman quietly said and escorted them to a discrete interview room which was equipped with the latest anti terrorist electronic equipment operated by a battle scarred senior officer who sat wearily behind a desk and craved a bit of excitement to make his day.

"Who do we have here?" He unemotionally asked as Marcus and Anya entered the room and seated themselves before him

"FSK agent Anya Betts and Marcus Rhodes Grom operative" The policeman answered, took up position behind them and placed a hand on his pistol should any trouble arise. Both Anya and Marcus handed their ID cards to the senior officer who signalled that they surrender their weapons as well which they did without any reservation.

"We can't be too careful these days considering how easily documentation can be falsified by all manner of digital equipment. Would you like to go first Miss Betts, three simple tests, firstly retinal scan, second voice recognition and finally arms check, stay where you are I shall bring the equipment towards you" The senior officer said as he produced a compact piece of biometric equipment and manoeuvred it before Anya "Stay perfectly still whilst it does its job, do not be afraid. Excellent, now for phase two which I hope you will find quite amusing, but then considering our line of work we could all use a little divine protection" The senior officer dryly said as he produced a laminated copy of the Lord's Prayer written in Norwegian on one side and English on the other.

"Recite in your normal voice into the microphone that I am about to give you in both languages please" The senior officer softly instructed Anya as he studied the computer screen in front of him and compared the serial number on her Glock with that which was recorded. His actions although congenial were nonetheless irritating to Marcus who could not contain his frustrations.

"Everything in order.....?" He impatiently asked

"Apparently so, growing restless?" The senior officer accurately deduced as he was a good judge of character

"It's complicated"

"Isn't everything?" The senior officer answered as he gestured that it was time for Marcus's appraisal

"Same procedure as Anya's with one variation, the Lord's Prayer is written in English and Polish"

"You must cater for all kinds" Marcus acidly commented

"In smaller numbers than what you might imagine" The senior officer replied suggesting that very few nations had developed highly sophisticated secret services, a point that Marcus recognised only too well, not wishing to inflame the situation any further Marcus went through the motions, relaxed his posture and patiently waited for the outcome.

"Thank you for that, both of your identities have been verified, you are free to travel to Iceland under one condition due to the fact that neither one of you has been psychologically assessed in the past three years. Your guns will be stored by the flight crew and returned to you on your arrival in Reykjavik, we don't want anyone going berserk during the flight, safe journey it was a pleasure meeting you" The senior officer genuinely said with a touch of jealously in his voice as he stood up to shake both Anya's and Marcus's hands and wish them farewell.

14
GROM – IT

The aircraft flight to Reykjavik was fully booked which meant that Marcus and Anya could not discuss any aspect of their operation in private consequently Anya decided to while away the time by watching some of the light and fluffy in flight entertainment whereas Marcus opted to close his eyes and formulate ways of completing their assignment in the quickest possible manner which became almost impossible as the hostesses constantly bombarded the passengers with what it seemed was a continuous avalanche of tasty foods and inebriating drinks. Whilst the majority eagerly gorged themselves Marcus and Anya partook of the culinary delights in a restrained and modest fashion so as to preserve their mental and physical sharpness.

"Noisy lot" Anya commented as she removed her headphones and resigned herself to the fact that the onboard party was winning the decibel stakes

"That's an understatement, perhaps they all belong to the same tour group"

"Hostesses are coping well" Anya calmly observed

"With crowd and consumption control" Marcus sighed as he gazed about and wondered how long before the drunk and disorderly would start singing, fortunately they didn't as the Captain announced he was about to commence the planes descent which meant everything had to be squared away. There were no groans of disappointment only acceptance of the fact and instant calm.

Within twenty minutes they had safely landed and berthed at Keflavik International Airport situated 50km south west of Reykjavik. Once they retrieved their handguns from security Marcus and Anya boarded a shuttle bus that travelled along route 41 to the capital city where they managed to secure a luxury suite at the Grand Reykjavik Hotel under the name of Mr and Mrs Rhodes.

"What a wonderful room. It's been a while since I slept with a man" Anya erotically said as she cast her eyes on the suite's luxurious king sized bed

"It will be purely platonic I assure you" Marcus chivalrously replied as he casually walked about the spacious room

"We might need a change of clothes whilst we have these ones washed" Anya said making reference to the clothes they stood in

"Agreed I wonder if the stores are still open?"

"Unlikely the hotel's handy reference book says they close at 5pm" Anya replied

"Which means room service tonight and shopping tomorrow morning after breakfast" Marcus thoughtfully replied as he looked over Anya's shoulder to confirm what she had just read

"I like it when you are close" Anya purred which caught Marcus by surprise as he had up until now no romantic inclinations towards the FSK agent

"Promise you won't bite" Marcus softly said as he remembered how expertly she had defeated him physically when they first met

"I do have a soft side"

"Does that extend to fine dining and wine?" Marcus asked

"Test me"

"Very well" Marcus replied as he took hold of the hotel's information booklet, flicked through its pages to locate room service and then said "Not as extensive as I had hoped but it will do"

"Why don't you freshen up in the bathroom and I will order for both of us" Anya replied with a broad smile

"Very well" Marcus answered as he let go and walked away. He returned within ten minutes feeling somewhat better after having brushed his teeth, combed his hair and slashed on complimentary cologne all courtesy of the hotel's management.

"Care for tea and biscuits helps take the edge off I sometimes find" Marcus asked as he perused the tea and coffee selection

"Lady Grey with a little milk for me please..." Anya replied as she sat in a chair overlooking the city which had begun to put on its sparkling evening clothes

"Sugar...?"

"Pass"

"Very well, chocolate or ginger nut biscuit?"

"One of each" Anya replied as she felt her stomach grumbling

"Won't spoil your appetite?" Marcus inquired as he poured the teas and arranged the biscuits

"Hardy I'm famished, come sit next to me, I want to find out more about you"

"Personally or professionally" Marcus inquired wishing to know the scope of Anya's understanding which he would not immediately discover as a sudden loud rap on the door halted their conversation

"That was quick, what did you order...sandwiches?"

"I will check" Anya feeling a little insulted by Marcus's attempt at humour.

Marcus watched as Anya expertly walked towards the door, avoided using its eye piece to see who was on the other side and simply asked as she stood next to the door frame "Who's there?"

No answer was forthcoming which made Marcus draw his weapon in readiness for any unwelcome intruder.

"Who's there?" Anya once again asked as she strained her ears to detect if a person or persons stood on the other side of the locked and chained door. Marcus did the same even though he was further away. Both stood very still and regulated their breathing anticipating danger. The seconds ticked away, they both thought someone was playing a game of dare to blink with them until the house phone rang. Marcus gingerly picked it up and said nothing which the person on the other end of the line did as well and then another loud rap on the door sounded.

"Who is it?" Anya demanded to know after a lengthy pause

"Room service"

"One moment please" Anya answered as she unchained the door, carefully opened it in such a manner that convinced her it was indeed room service.

A tall but stocky Icelandic girl with flaxen hair and a ruddy face greeted Anya and when given the signal nervously wheeled in a trolley ladened with Icelandic specialities. She then proceeded to serve the food and pour the wine which Marcus clearly approved of. Anya very generously tipped the girl with Norwegian coins as she left.

"What do you think?" She asked

"Nothing here is on the menu" Marcus observed

"Precisely, I instructed the chef as to our needs and he gladly obliged, so what do you think of me now?"

"Elegantly sophisticated"

"I'm flattered"

"You shouldn't be I was telling the truth" Marcus genuinely said as he took a sip of the white wine which complimented the meal in front of him and then asked "what do we have here"

"As you can see we start with a fish stew made from freshly caught boiled cod, potato mash and onions in a white sauce, then the main meal is boiled smoked lamb served with green peas, sour red cabbage and potatoes in a white creamy sauce. A little rye bread on the side to help mop up the rich sauces and finally a glass of Black Death to relax and aid the digestion"

"Black Death...?"

"An Icelandic spirit distilled from potato mash, fermented grains and caraway seeds, it's what keeps the locals warm and in the mood during their harsh winters"

"That's one way of ensuring the populations survival" Marcus smirked as the wine started to exert its mellowing influence on him

"Well it's not winter yet so shall we eat before the food gets cold"

"An excellent idea" Marcus replied and seated himself at the casual table by the window and poured a glass of wine for Anya.

"Thank you, now that we are alone perhaps you could tell me more about Grom apart from what I remember Major Weir telling us earlier on" Anya sweetly asked which Marcus was prepared to do as he had been fully briefed by his superiors as to her identity prior to accepting the assignment.

"We are known as Jednostka Wojskowa 2305 operating under the nickname 'The Surgeons' as we receive extensive medical training and knowledge which we use to coordinate and execute special operations with surgical precision. Ours is a highly secret organisation performing major strategic manoeuvres that were accredited to other forces we have played extremely vital roles in Iraq, Afghanistan, Haiti, Pakistan and strangely enough part of our training is with the Swedish Navy's Special Command based in Karlskrona" Marcus explained

"In other words you act in unconventional ways"

"One could say that" Marcus agreed

"Which might explain why we are here in Iceland" Anya put forward

"There are many forms of battlegrounds"

"Some better than others" Anya suggested

"That only time will tell" Marcus reluctantly said as he spooned the last of the fish stew into his mouth

"Which is the case with the freer press I think you called it....?"

"Correct"

"How successful do you think you will be" Anya asked

"Depends on their mood what acceptable evidence I provide and who might be tilting the playing field" Marcus morbidly answered

"Spoken like a true surgeon"

"One has to know what one is dealing with and the possible complications" Marcus analytically remarked

"Prognosis.....?"

"That depends on the severity of the disease" Marcus replied as he started to carve his portion of smoked lamb

"Does it have a name and have you encountered it before" Anya asked as she followed suit with her meal

"Psidium leprosus" Marcus said after a brief pause much to Anya's delight

"You just made that up"

"Sounded convincing to me" Marcus said in defence

"What does it mean?"

"It's Latin for invasive disease" Marcus explained

"Chronic or acute....?"

"Good question which is answered by the severity and duration of its symptoms"

"You really are highly medically trained" Anya readily applauded her companion who nodded in response, remained pensive for a moment of two whilst he enjoyed his supper and looked out of the window "You don't by any chance do private consults?" She then cheekily asked

"Strictly accident and emergency, however having said that I wondered how strong and resilient your body is and how well it can endure injury when you activate your ARSE" Marcus replied

"Everything has its breaking point, that is why I have been taught to use the strongest parts of my hands, feet and elbows to inflict maximum damage to the most vulnerable areas of my opponent, would you like to examine me?" Anya continued to tease Marcus who remained impervious to her advances

"Perhaps another time when you are properly injured" Marcus as a matter of fact replied as he prepared to down his shot of Black Death

"First we clinker then we look into each other's eyes" Anya quickly said as she seized her glass of the fiery spirit and held it high. Marcus obliged, momentarily lowered his guard, clinked with Anya and downed his drink in one gulp

"I'm used to strong Polish Vodka but this stuff takes your breath away" Marcus gasped as he fanned his face with the palm of his hand in complete contrast to Anya who appeared unaffected. Embarrassed by his inability to handle the Vodka Marcus as a diversion started to clear away the dishes "We never did have that cup of tea or would you prefer coffee?" He tenderly asked

"Coffee please, there appears to be plenty of pods"

"Plus an abundance of chocolates" Marcus replied and allowed the automatic coffee machine to do the rest as he wheeled out the dinner trolley into the hallway

"It's been a wonderful evening" Anya purred once Marcus served the coffees

"That it has been, I was about to suggest we retire for the night and make an early start tomorrow morning" Marcus said after he offered a boxed selection of individually wrapped chocolates for Anya to choose from

"I'm happy with that" She replied as she chose what appeared to be a hazelnut praline which she delicately placed in her mouth and then took a sip of her crema coffee. Six chocolate wrappers later Anya was primed ready for bed and a good night's sleep. She lazily stripped down to her panties and climbed into bed and quickly fell asleep whilst Marcus brushed his teeth. Once he had finished he methodically undressed and hung his clothes in the wardrobe unlike Anya who had scattered her clothes around the suite. Marcus then placed his Glock under his pillow before dimming the lights and climbing into bed. Anya instinctively rolled over and snuggled close to Marcus.

"Tough as nails but still a little girl" Marcus thought as he also fell asleep

The next morning found the couple in exactly the same position as when they fell asleep, neither had moved, it was nearing 7am, time to enjoy a hearty breakfast, Marcus gently stroked Anya's forehead before gently touching her nose

"What......is it time to get up? Can't I stay in here a little longer, it's so nice and cosy" She pleaded

"We have important work to do, I'm sorry to say"

"It's always work can't I have a normal quiet life?" She grumbled before rolling out of bed and staggering into the bathroom allowing Marcus to quickly don his crumbled clothes and examine the extent of his facial stubble in the wardrobe's full length mirror

"Rough and ready" He mumbled to himself before sitting down at the foot of the bed

Anya emerged looking quite radiant and started picking up her clothes off the floor whilst Marcus kept his head low out of respect for Anya's modesty and remained so until she was fully dressed.

"Ready when you are" Anya brightly said as she approached Marcus

"Level 3 I believe it is"

"Correct" Anya happily agreed

"Have you been here before?" Marcus suspiciously asked as he opened the door and allowed Anya through

"Not really, I just remember reading about it in the directory. Shall we hold hands?" Anya sweetly asked as they walked towards the lifts

"Only too pleased to do so" Marcus softly replied and allowed Anya to intertwine her fingers with his.

Breakfast was served in The Pristine Cafe as it was known, a reflection of Iceland's ruggedly handsome landscape.

"This is nice!" Anya enthusiastically exclaimed as though she was on a first date with a handsome stranger

"Table for two....?" A waitress asked as she passed them by

"By a window if that is possible" Marcus answered

"Room number...?"

"427" Anya sweetly replied

"Doctor and Missus Rhodes" The waitress knowingly asked seeking confirmation

"That is correct" Marcus replied with a nod of his head

"I believe you have a guest waiting for you, come this way, we have put the three of you in a nice and private booth so that you can discuss your presentations at the medical conference to be held in a few days time" The waitress explained as she led the way

"Very thoughtful of you" Marcus thanked the attractive woman as he followed closely behind

"Ah Doctor Rhodes nice to see you again, I see you have brought along your lovely wife" A very fit middle aged man with greying hair said as he stood up to greet the pair

"A pleasure to see you as well, excuse me darling this is Professor Psi Williams head of the surgical unit that I trained in" Marcus said as he introduced his superior to Anya

"A pleasure to make your acquaintance Sir" Anya respectfully said as she offered her hand

"Thank you, shall we partake of the glorious food whilst we discuss matters?" Psi asked as he coldly calculated Anya's unlikely contribution to the morning's proceedings not realising that she was an excellent judge of character, had already summed him up and therefore knew exactly how to act.

"I'll let you learned men tackle the heavy stuff, my delicate stomach is crying out for fresh fruit and muesli" Anya said with a smile as she drifted off towards that section of the breakfast buffet which allowed her to scan the remainder of the restaurant for any undesirables. When she returned Anya was surprised to see that both the Professor and Marcus had forsaken the greasy bacon, fatty sausages and over cooked hash browns, instead they had piled on the fluffy scrambled eggs, smoked salmon and croissants accompanied by a generous mug of black percolated coffee.

"Survival food" She commented

"In keeping with our medical training" Psi somewhat arrogantly answered

"Pardon me for asking but is your name spelt sigh?" Anya asked out of curiosity

"Actually no it is P...S...I"

"The twenty third letter of the Greek alphabet"

"More along the lines of a bestowed abbreviation" Marcus's superior aloofly answered

"What does it stand for if not pounds per square inch?" Anya disrespectfully asked

"Precise Surgical Intervention....!"

"Based on your track record?" Anya insolently determined

"One could assume that!" Psi acidly replied not wanting his breakfast to be further interrupted

"How is it that you are here" Anya innocently asked as she frowned and deemed it strange that he had magically appeared

"In response to Doctor Rhodes request"

"Really....? I was led to believe we came here for another purpose" Anya subtly argued which prompted Marcus to explain in a hushed voice how it happened

"When we arrived I used my special Grom credit card to pay for the hotel suite. This card is constantly monitored by the unit, when used it sends a signal requesting help"

"Why do you need help, I thought we had everything under control?" Anya quite perplexed whispered

"We sort of do however I am not happy with Doctor Weir's treatment of the patients that we have seen who suffer with similar afflictions, it is far too airy fairy, I feel there is more to this disease than meets the eye in any event all of my suggestions and therapies are subject to my superiors rigorous evaluation and to the coroner at the end of the day" Marcus quietly explained in between mouthfuls of food

"Having said that are we still submitting the findings of our research to the Scandinavian Journal of Good Health?" Anya asked in a low voice as she played along by renaming the well respected internet news outlet 'Scandinavian Truth' to fit in with the medical jargon that they were using

"Unlikely as it is a highly sceptical publication with a particularly 'tough' cynical editor. Twenty five percent of research papers these days contain fabricated data thanks to the magic of the internet and highly sophisticated software" Professor Williams coldly announced

"So my husband's brilliant work with respect to the excision of spinal tumours will go unnoticed" Anya resentfully replied making reference to the destruction of the stored American arms in the mountain range separating Norway and Sweden

"As much as the recently reported seismic events in Norway" The Professor added

"Surely someone has to acknowledge his findings" Anya said with a deep sigh

"Only if it fits in with their agenda or the situation becomes explosive" The professor bluntly postulated

"So where does that leave us?" Anya asked out of frustration

"We allow Doctor Weir and his assistant to proceed as he wishes whilst we explore another avenue that promises immense therapeutic benefits which I will enlarge upon once we drive to the Blue Lagoon later this morning. I think we are entitled to do a little sightseeing before the conference" The Professor proposed

"What about our shopping expedition?" Anya protested as she looked at Marcus

"That's still on after all we will need swimsuits" Marcus willingly confirmed not wishing to disappoint the FSK agent

"Then I think we should reconvene at eleven o'clock this morning,

I will wait for both of you in the downstairs foyer the shops open at nine o'clock giving you sufficient time to properly deck yourselves out" Psi Williams said with a nod of his head before returning to the buffet and selecting a number of petite fruit Danishes

"The idea of shopping stimulates my appetite I think I'll copy what the professor is doing' Anya gleefully said as she rubbed her hands together and stormed away

By 9am Marcus found himself walking arm in arm with the delectable Anya down the main shopping avenue where Anya made a bee line to 88°South a clothing store which catered for people who wished to make a fashion statement by purchasing outdoor clothing with a sense of style, after all Iceland is not the warmest place on Earth at the best of times. The clothing designers extended their talents by manufacturing swimwear that was halfway between traditional and a wet suit with sacrificing neither style nor grace. Marcus was pleasantly surprised how quickly Anya decided which clothes suited her best as he struggled to match the speed of her decisions.

Once was all said and done they returned to the hotel, arranged for their dirty clothes to be laundered and proceeded to meet Psi Williams in the hotel lobby who greeted them by saying "Trust your retail experience was pleasant even though I gave you restricted time?"

"More than sufficient" Anya said without any qualms

"Excellent, what's in the duffle bag?"

"Bathers, microfiber towels" Marcus answered

"Then we are set, this way please" Psi said as he walked towards the main revolving doors and out into the fresh morning air where a white Saggar all terrain rental car driven by a highly trained and armed chauffeur awaited them

"This is nice" Anya commented as she opened its rear door and prepared to enter its luxurious interior, unlike Marcus who stowed away their luggage and took careful note of the vehicles three rooftop antennas and armour plated glass, a necessary precaution in Grom's eyes as the Americans had a more than subtle presence in Iceland and therefore exercised their 'in the interests of the nation' rights

"It's about a 45 minute drive to the Blue Lagoon sufficient time in which to brief both of you" Psi Williams calmly and quietly said as they set off in a south westerly direction towards Keflavik airport as the Blue Lagoon is located 20km from there.

"Before I do that I must apologise to you Anya as I wasn't fully informed as to your standing within FSK and the level of your intelligence" He then said

"No harm done" Anya politely responded even though she wondered if he would take any notice of what she might say later on

"Marcus I was very impressed with all of the images that you sent me however they are useless in today's political climate which dictates what can and cannot be accurately reported or exposed. Whilst Iceland supposedly enjoys the reputation of having the freest press, the American presence says otherwise. The official story behind your sabotage of the American arms depot stored between the mountain range separating Norway and Sweden was one of a seismic event, but as you know an earthquake is usually followed by aftershocks that may last weeks, months or even years We believe that either KNN's sympathisers or the Bandits from Hell on the Swedish side are responsible for these"

"What about the Russians" Anya asked as she thought they might be of assistance

"You mean our Eastern comrades whom the Americans are busily demonising?" Markus remarked

"Pardon....?" Anya asked quite surprised

"We Poles have a fond dislike for the Americans for what they did to us after WW2 namely abandon us and our right to independence and self governorship, USA betrayed Poland as it was not in the American interests, I think it backfired on them for although Poland is now independent it still harbours close links with the

Russians in all respects" Marcus softly explained

"I didn't mean that!" Anya a little annoyed replied

"I'm sorry you probably meant do the Russians know what the Americans are up to? The answer is yes but no to sabotaging the arms depot" Marcus coarsely replied

"Why...?"

"Because they don't behave in such a way" Marcus coldly replied signalling that their lovey dovey relationship was over

"I suppose they only resolve things diplomatically" Anya cuttingly answered

"Let us say that your combined efforts have given the Russians considerable leverage" Psi Williams said interrupting the warring couple

"At what level....?" Anya asked in raised tone of voice

"Locally and internationally at the very highest"

"Oh yes...how so?" Anya loudly jeered much to the discomfort of the driver who was driving cautiously and taking note of any potentially suspicious vehicles

"That is presently highly classified information" Psi Williams abruptly said thinking that his statement would end the matter

"Not good enough! Here's what I think! When Marcus stumbled across the secret arsenal of American weapons and alerted the Swedish authorities, the evidence it was postulated would cause a political storm in the corridors of Norwegian power and the Americans would be politely asked to leave. That did not eventuate! Why? Because all of the political parties whether socialistic, green, labour, far left, left, center, right or far right have something to hide. I am more than certain the KNN had amassed sufficient damning evidence to expel the Americans, sadly this will never see the light of day. So the tried and tested technique of expose, embarrass and expel was doomed to fail. Marcus's sabotage of the arms depot caused a ripple of concern as it preceded a predetermined series of orchestrated explosions designed to coerce those who had 'the leaf' illegally in their possession resulting in confusion amongst those who had organised the explosions and in those who had 'the leaf' leaving them wondering when would the explosions stop. Irrespective of that the official story remains the unchanged namely a seismic event, business as usual. Fundamentally we need to rethink our strategy especially if we are serious about ousting the Americans from Norwegian soil" Anya forcibly said as she confronted a very quiet Psi with her solid deductive argument

"Sometimes it is necessary to mix with the criminally predisposed in order to achieve results" Psi replied in a hushed tone of voice much to the drivers delight

"Are you suggesting something different to what the Major had intended us to do? Wait a minute this was never about driving out the Americans" Anya cleverly deduced

"Correct" Psi admitted and said no more

"It's bigger than that, it's about energy and satisfying Europe's needs" Anya thoughtfully said as she looked outside at the passing scenery which was largely devoid of vegetation

"Very astute of you" Psi replied indifferently as he looked straight ahead leaving Marcus to ponder the outcome of their discussion

"Thank you" Anya answered somewhat flattered

"Your comment about involving the criminally predisposed what exactly did you mean by that?" Marcus asked seeking clarification

"Before Psi deals with your inquiry answer me one question, do you still carry the mobile phone that the Major gave you?" The chauffeur asked out of the blue

"I do" Anya answered as she retrieved it from her coat pocket

"I don't" Marcus in complete contrast unashamedly said

"Wise decision Mr Rhodes" The chauffeur verbally applauded Marcus as he gestured for Anya to hand over her phone to Psi Williams

"Where is it?" Anya asked feeling betrayed

"Scattered throughout Lillehammer"

"Lovely place" The chauffeur quipped as he quickly glanced at Psi who examined Anya's phone devoid of its backing and muttered "Interesting piece of bait"

"To the seaside cottage Sir...?" The chauffeur asked as he gunned the SUV's engine

"Worth a try never know what one might catch at this time of the year" Psi Williams vaguely answered

"Your comment about the criminally predisposed.....?" Marcus subtly reminded his superior

"Remind me as to Major Weir's wishes" Psi Williams softly requested

"I was to contact the Bandits from Hell via Telegram IT. Anya and Brit to locate confront and pump a Yugoslav arms dealer for information relating to suppliers and clients whilst the Major and Nils sought out survivors of the 'seismic' event. My initial investigations revealed that I would most likely end up in a cul-de-sac full of undesirables" Marcus explained

"Then it's time to explore the other avenue I hinted at over breakfast" Psi warmly said as he watched the chauffer deviate from the main road onto a nameless side street that headed towards the ocean.

"Not as smooth a ride as you had hoped for...?" The chauffer dryly asked

"As long as it's not an omen" Marcus replied

"Oh but it is Mr Rhodes" The chauffer answered as he maintained his concentration and kept his eyes on the twisting road that rose and fell according to the topography of the rocky sand dunes which formed a convenient means of hiding a private residence from prying eyes.

"Quite extraordinary" Anya commented as a well maintained and picturesque cottage came into view

"Our meditative retreat" Psi happily announced as he reflected on many a wise decision made there

"Is that what we will be doing" Anya asked

"Amongst other things"

"Such as....?"

"Getting rid of annoying insects" Psi replied

"The nocturnal variety I imagine" Anya cleverly said in response

"You catch on quick" Psi replied acknowledging the fact that Anya understood that the phone supplied by the Major had been compromised making her a person of interest and that it most probably happened when she first visited the Creed of Tyr's complex.

As they neared the cottage Psi activated his Grom issued mobile phone, selected the security application to obtain an integrity status report of the cottage and its surroundings. Satisfied that all was well he gestured for the chauffer to park the rental car next to the building. Outside a fresh and blustery westerly 40km wind greeted them.

"No place for drones" Anya said once she stepped out of the vehicle

"Nor expensive hair do's" Marcus joked as he familiarised himself with their surroundings

"Follow me, it's a bit of a challenge getting inside" Psi said as he made certain that he had a set of house keys in his possession. The chauffer meanwhile collected a picnic hamper from the rental car and secured it.

Side entry into the cottage was from the eastern aspect away from the harsh elements. The main door could only be accessed after walking down a L shaped narrow corridor and unlocking two opposing wrought iron gates. All external lights were fitted with discrete integrated high definition digital cameras.

"Welcome to our seaside fortress" Psi chirped once he had unlocked the main door to reveal a cosy interior decorated in a minimalistic rustic theme

"Nice ocean views" Marcus said as he looked out of the panoramic windows which he sensed were more than double glazed

"Menacing and mesmerising at the same time" Psi suggested

"In other words a distraction at the best of times" Marcus also suggested

"A situation that we presently find ourselves in" Psi answered as he switched on a large LED television that monitored outside activity along the entire perimeter of the cottage near and far

"I am certain we will find a suitable remedy" Marcus confidently answered

"Is there such a thing given the complexity of the geo-political world?" Psi asked as he signalled for his chauffer to brew coffees for everyone and then he philosophically said "Much like funerals and weddings where someone invariably becomes upset over trivial things such is the nature of petty minded individuals"

"What is today's agenda or do we sit around waiting for our uninvited guests to arrive?" Anya asked as she found a comfortable armchair to sit in

"You inadvertently hit the nail on the head when you concluded that the nature of our operation was about energy and satisfying Europe's needs. Tell me do either of you know much about syngas?" Psi asked both operatives who appeared rather vacant

"Can't say we do" Anya confessed on behalf of the duo

"I didn't expect you to. Syngas or synthetic natural gas is used as a replacement for gasoline it can be produced from many sources including natural gas, coal, biomass or any hydrocarbon feedstock all of which require complex chemical reactions and sophisticated industrial equipment. In Germany during WW2 for example half a million cars were built to run on wood based gasoline. All quite primitive until now thanks to a collaborative effort between Iran, Russia and Germany, the contribution made by Iran was understanding what role light plays in natural nuclear processes that occur at the cellular level within vegetation whereas the Russians provided the working model using their space programme technology and the Germans the necessary state of the art computers and quantum mathematicians. The project is called L.E.A.F which stands for Light Emitting Artificial Fuel. A standard unit is made up of two cobalt infused light absorbers one produces oxygen and the other conducts the chemical reaction that reduces carbon dioxide and water into synthetic non polluting high octane gasoline. The development of this technology was meant to serve a number of purposes maintain Iran as a major supplier of clean fuel to the world and allow Russia to become a member state of the European Union which it could easily do under the Accession or Copenhagen criteria which require a candidate nation to demonstrate a guaranteed democracy, the rule of law, human rights and respect for and protection of minorities, a robust flourishing economy and the necessary administrative institutions capable of implementing the obligations of membership. Needless to say the West has for decades waged all manner of disinformation and economic measures to hamper this from happening and demonize both Iran and Russia in the process. Marcus the man you encountered in the mountains near Roros we believe was an Iranian Secret Service agent"

"And the woman I overheard demanding the return of the 'leaf'" Marcus asked interrupting Psi's description of events

"Don't have much info on her at this stage, she might be a double agent in which case means she is likely to sell to the highest bidder should she be successful in retrieving the device" Psi grimly admitted

"Do we know of her whereabouts?"

"I can only speculate which is dependent on the location of the 'leaf' Psi reluctantly answered

"Unlike our situation where Mossad is likely to pounce at any given time' Anya grimly concluded

"Unlikely given the circumstances"

"I don't understand' Anya replied as she looked intensely at Psi who remained calm and pensive

"I do not believe in waiting around for something to happen. Your phone has gone for a swim in the murky depths of Davy Jones Locker thus creating a dead end by cutting short the time available to mobilise troops and give pursuit. They are effectively out of the picture with respect to your security our major concerns presently are to determine the most effective way or ways of causing the Americans to leave Norway and to recapture the 'leaf'. We need to be creative and surgically precise in such a way that minimises trauma to the patient" Psi put forward in a manner that was intended to coax imaginative answers out of Marcus and Anya

"Occupational health and safety might be the way to go" Marcus replied after a brief silent interlude

"Please go on" Psi politely said

"The American soldiers are present in Norway to supposedly train under harsh winter conditions. What if it became unsafe for them to do so?"

"How so...?"

"Avalanches and rock falls are appropriate convenient ways of scattering the troops"

"Agreed....what else?"

"Divide and conquer, a terrorist attack on the marine base using American arms by 'terrorists' dressed as American marines"

"What about the American embassy?"

"The next target"

"And finally....?" Psi asked

"The parliamentary offices of those weak ministerial buffoons who lobbied the government to allow the Americans in"

"Question is how well will it work?" Psi asked with a frown

"Success will depend on timing" Anya thought out aloud as she pondered the likely Norwegian response

"Can you enlarge on that?" Psi asked

"Avalanches and rock falls will hamper and frustrate training until it is declared safe or relocated to another region. Presently the

Americans train in Setermoen on a rotational basis all year around but can also be found in a number of different locations where they are actively building barracks and administrative offices on a permanent basis these include Vaernes air station, Orland main air station, Rygge military air station, Sola military air station on the south western coast, Evenes military air station and Ramsund naval station. There is no point conducting the exercise piece meal I suggest we hit five targets simultaneously"

"How do you think the Americans and Norwegians government will react?"

"It will depend upon what sort of narrative is fed to them" Anya intelligently answered

"And how devious their minds are" Psi said finishing off Anya's statement

"Agreed"

"Considering the fact that the Israeli embassy in Oslo and its holiday home have been bombed do you think that the military bases you mentioned might already be on red alert?" Marcus asked Anya

"Perhaps not as these attacks have been labelled anti-Semitic and not anti-American"

"Point taken but isn't America Israel's greatest ally and as such opens itself up to both criticism and conflict. I anticipate base security may already have been beefed up" Marcus wisely countered

"Conclusions....?" Psi asked

"A single operative would be foolish to penetrate and plant incendiary devices inside the base without being caught, a better option is to fire several rounds from outside the compound preferably from a high vantage point using a compact reusable rocket launcher with a decent payload" Marcus intelligently proposed

"The likely targets being...?" Psi asked

"Can't make it too precise otherwise we will lose the 'terrorist' label, perhaps fuel depot, administrative offices, mess hall"

"In other words minimise casualties" Psi suggested

"Correct" Marcus confirmed

"I think we can safely say that an attack on one facility will cause it to alert the others, however it follows that their response may not be instant giving us sufficient time in which to inflict damage on the remaining bases. I suggest we omit Vaernes as it is too big a target for amateur 'terrorists' and more importantly over stretch your resources" Psi proposed

"Before we run away with ourselves we should consider how the Major is going to react, after all most things in life are territorial, our course of action is completely different to his agenda and will cause friction, irritation and even outrage" Anya said casting a shadow on their proposals

"That is where your feminine charm comes into play. I am more than certain you will be able to win him over in all respects" Psi answered in a charming and flattering manner

"A technique I suppose you want me to utilize in order to obtain compact rocket launchers from the Yugoslav arms dealer in exchange for his unfettered freedom to continue doing business" Anya intuitively replied

"The thought had crossed my mind" Psi freely admitted

"You're rather predictable"

"Really...? Hazard a guess as to what I might say next?"

"Lunch is served" Anya brightly said

"Not very original"

"Doesn't have to be, it is that time of day and your chauffeur has been busy in the adjoining room" Anya deduced as a result of her keen observations

"Very well you win. Let us retire and relax before visiting the Blue Lagoon" Psi replied and turned to lead the way.

After a relaxing meal that stretched over two hours Anya and Marcus found themselves at the blue Lagoon which is located in a lava field near Grindavik in front of Mount Porbjorn on Reykjanes peninsula. Even though it was late in the afternoon both Anya and Marcus were fascinated by the lagoon water's milky blue colour not to mention its 39°c temperature and high silica content all of which were manmade to some extent thanks to the nearby geothermal power plant Svartsengi. Here their troubles, woes and concerns were replaced by success, happiness and indifference bringing them a measure of transient relief and solitude. Psi and his chauffer did not join them instead they remained in the car park and stood 'guard' by aimlessly walking about appearing as anxious private tourist guides who constantly checked their watches.

"If I stay in any longer I will surely begin to cook" Anya said as she felt her body begin to rebel at being in a hot environment with little chance of losing heat through perspiration

"I agree the novelty has worn off" Marcus concurred and slowly walked towards the change rooms where they had stored their clothes in a secure locker. Once there they washed away the lagoon's influence and returned to active duty which meant Marcus as the chief physician faced the challenge of ridding his patient Mr N Orway of an aggressive primary tumour plus five secondary's without inflicting any long term damage. Precise radiation therapy was the treatment of choice using laser guided projectiles. He wondered whether Psi would provide such equipment or leave Marcus to source his own as no further mention was made of it during the journey back to the hotel which ended half a kilometre from its main entrance.

"This is where I leave you. Nice meeting you Anya you appear to be a capable asset, I wish you and Marcus good luck in your ventures" Psi said as the chauffeur slowed their vehicle to a stop

"It was a wonderful experience" Anya warmly responded and exited the SUV

Marcus quickly joined her, they strolled arm in arm back to the hotel whilst Psi and his chauffeur did a U-turn to return to parts unknown.

"AWOL without a whisper of why" were the first words they heard in a familiar voice once Marcus and Anya re-entered the Grande Reykjavik Hotel

"A necessary diversion to protect one and all" Marcus replied in a low voice as he laid eyes on Brit who appeared relieved that she had located her friends and that they were both safe

"What did you do....swim here?" Brit asked as she spied the duffle bag over Marcus's shoulder

"Something like that but a little more sophisticated"

"What he means is that we visited the Blue Lagoon" Anya briefly explained

"I see" Brit pretended to understand

"Come join us, we will tell you all about our adventures, it's good to see you, it's been a long time" Anya gushed as if she was talking to a friend whom she had not seen for a year or two

"Love to" Brit said playing along as Anya gestured they should walk together and use the lift whilst they engaged in 'girlie' talk, but instead of exiting on their assigned floor Marcus took them to the roof top bar where he thought no one might be listening

"Interesting view" He commented as he approached the balustrade

"Might explain why we are here" Brit answered as her way of seeking answers

"The attempt on Anya's life in the library and the subsequent visit from the undesirables at Norwegian Ice made me think that Anya's phone had been compromised starting when she visited the Creed of Tyr's facilities. Someone did not like her meddling in their affairs. However it may be deeper than that meaning all of the phones given to us by the Major were equally compromised suggesting that we have been under constant surveillance and that there is a traitor in the midst of those who formed our fact finding unit, clearly trying to blackmail by exposure those who black mailed members of the Norwegian government is a futile exercise. In order to protect the integrity of the unit I decided that we should flee to Iceland" Marcus slowly explained as he looked about and periodically smiled, Anya also smiled as she nodded in agreement with Marcus's words

"I suppose that leaves me naked and vulnerable" Brit reluctantly guessed as she played with her mobile phone

"Presently yes until you decide to join our side" Marcus replied and waited for Brit to follow suit which was not to be immediately as an unexpected text message both distracted her and cemented Marcus's words

"Damn, shit, fuck!" Brit angrily exclaimed as she read the concise message sent by Gerhardt the resilient East German "Major killed, unexpected drone attack, Roros Mountains" before she proceeded to violently reduce her mobile phone to microchips

"I wasn't expecting my prognosis to come true so soon" Marcus grimly responded as realised it was time for him to exercise his surgical skills.

15
SAFETY IN NUMBERS

Twelve hours later which seemed more like a well oiled blur, Marcus, Anya, Brit and Gerhardt assembled themselves in a quality riverside hotel in the locality of Drammen forty four kilometres south east of Oslo on the pretext that all previous arrangements orchestrated by Major Weir were tainted. The focus of their mission had changed with Anya and Brit taking a profound dislike to what the Americans and who else was involved had done in Norway. Once they had swept the apartment clean and done away with anything supplied by or related to Major Weir no further mention was made of him. Marcus then spoke openly about his staggered solution to the problem at hand in contrast to Anya who advocated a more aggressive approach which the others thought to be a little drastic and challenging whereas Marcus's proposal allowed breathing space, time for a ground swell to develop and hopefully result in civil unrest much to the disfavour of certain individual authorities. With the sudden death of the Major the group realised they were now on their own with no supply chains available to them.

"I think to obtain our explosive needs from the mountains store house or from the Bandits from Hell or that Yugoslav business man in Danderyd is out of the question, far too dangerous and all of these are potentially part of a sinister web" Brit analytically argued

"Then we should do a day trip to Sweden and visit The Chosen One's the big Kahuna" Gerhardt flippantly suggested

"Really...?" Marcus asked as he raised his eyebrows

"Ja I have done business with these people on numerous occasions" Gerhardt cheerfully answered

"Who are they again?"

"Known as The Chosen One's a gang which specialises in Yugoslavian made hand grenades and rocket propelled varieties, they will even tailor the weapon to suit your needs"

"Where do we find them?" Brit asked

"Gothenburg industrial area, Scrap Yard Incorporated a legitimate business I will call them and make an appointment" Gerhardt convincingly said as he withdrew his personal mobile phone, selected the preset number and waited for his call to be answered

"Scrap Yard Incorporated!" a gruff voice abruptly answered after several rings

"I believe you have stocks of Pristina Pokers and Mostar Movers" Gerhardt smoothly said

"Limited, cash sales, personal pickup"

"Tomorrow okay....?" Gerhardt asked

"1.15pm sharp, know where to find us?"

"Affirmative"

"Come alone...." the gruff voice answered and rudely terminated the call

"Judging by your perplexed looks I guess you are wondering what I was talking about? Pristina Pokers are hand grenades and Mostar Movers are grenade launchers, specialities of the cities in which they were made. The Chosen One's deal only in American dollars lucky I came prepared for such occasions" Gerhardt answered on a job well done

"How much will they cost?" Anya asked

"Considering where they are made, not as much as say German or French, $3000 should start the ball rolling. All that I need is a run of the mill car and set off early tomorrow as it is a three and a half hour's drive from here"

"Are you going alone?" Brit asked out of concern for his safety

"Conditions of sale, in any case these people scare easily they are not as tough as their name suggests"

"Can they be trusted?"

"Absolutely, it's the good guys that you need to be wary of" Gerhardt answered based on his past life experiences

"Does that include us?"

"Can't say at this stage, if you will excuse me I have matters to attend to" Gerhardt coldly replied as he turned to exit the apartment much to Anya's and Brits annoyance

"Strange fellow...!" Anya commented once he had left

"Or just too efficient....?" Marcus suggested otherwise

"Where does that leave us?" Brit asked feeling a little lost and useless

"With valuable time on our hands in which to source suitable equipment for stages two and three, namely the American Embassy and Norwegian parliamentary offices" Marcus confidently replied

"What did you have in mind? That goose stepping Prussian seems to have stolen your thunder!" Anya annoyingly prodded

"The least expected means of attack" Marcus calmly responded with a smile

"What might that be?" Brit cynically asked

"Autonomous vehicles" Marcus succinctly answered which prompted Anya into action and she immediately contacted room service to have a laptop computer sent to their rooms post haste.

Brit however remained unconvinced and cynically asked "What are you intending to create, a robotic invasion?"

"Something like that...."

"Let me guess undermine the public's confidence in electrification and pollution free transport"

"A bit more sinister than that" Marcus wickedly replied

"Tell us more" Brit eagerly asked

"All will become apparent once we obtain all of the items on my shopping list. Anya, see if you can purchase a litre bottle of kerosene plus a 500gm jar of molasses from the supermarket. Brit can you investigate the availability of ammonium nitrate rich fertiliser in 5kilo bags from the local hardware or plant nurseries. Once we have determined that we can freely purchase these we can store them in Gerhardt's vehicle once he returns" Marcus explained

"In other words you expect us to assemble outlawed ANFO's (ammonium nitrate/fuel oil) for military or should I correctly say terrorist use!"

"Either is an appropriate description"

"Using autonomous vehicles?" Brit concluded

"Correct"

"Challenging"

"I thought so, makes it both dangerous and interesting at the same time" Marcus mischievously replied

'We need to act swiftly in order to avoid detection by the police who are still suffering from the lingering after effects of the 2011 Norwegian attacks known as 22 July" Brit heavily cautioned

"Something I was aware of"

"Any idea from where you might obtain the vehicles?" Brit asked

"Three come to mind, Silent Zoom, Roaming Eye and Autosolo"

"Hopefully situated close by and easily accessed meaning no high tech security or burley guards to contend with" Brit optimistically said

"I think I can answer that" Anya interrupted as her request for a laptop computer had just been delivered and she enthusiastically set about activating it. Brit and Marcus watched her face change as she thought and sought answers to her questions

"Okay, negative to building ANFO's as maximum ammonium nitrate content in commercial fertilizers is limited to 16% otherwise we will need to burgle the factory which will be in keeping with creating the illusion of amateur terrorists sympathisers of July 22 and its hidden ideologies. This seems relatively easy we only need two or three 25kilo bags. The autonomous vehicles is an ambitious project, many hurdles to overcome, electronic security is of the highest calibre to prevent intellectual property theft by foreign corporations, the cars are securely locked away and fitted with multiple anti-theft and tracking devices. I suggest we build our own which can be done relatively easily"

"I'm not so sure" Marcus replied casting doubt on Anya's proposal

"Let me explain it further, first we appropriate several electric cars, disable their tracking devices, modify their battery compartment and to hot things up surround them with ANFO's cutting off their air supply, once we have parked said vehicles at the strategic locations we turn on the air conditioning to maximum heat and walk away" Anya brightly explained in a simplistic manner. Marcus nodded his head to indicate that he understood. His mind meanwhile went into overdrive and visualised all that was needed in order to bring Anya's concept into fruition.

"I guess we will need a workshop of some description" He remarked

"I know just the place. Lier Psychiatric Hospital it has a workshop at the rear perfect for our needs as it is abandoned and rumoured to be haunted"

"Let's hope it scares people off instead of disguising their movements" Brit said out of concern

"As long as we have power" Marcus said from a practical point of view

"An abundance of, it's decommissioned not derelict"

"So what purpose does it serve?" Marcus questioned

"It presents a fine example of how not to design or build a mental health facility but more importantly a training ground for future FSK agents" Anya replied

"Oh great now we have FSK agents running around to contend with" Marcus grumbled

"Not exactly it's off season with no scheduled excises, I checked"

"Oh did you now....?" Marcus condescendingly asked

"Don't worry it will be fine"

"I'll take your word for it. What about the electric vehicles, I believe they are almost impossible to steal' Marcus correctly asked

"That is true of Tesla models however the Nissan Leaf is easily accessible as its system is quite fragile"

"And how many of these easily stolen vehicles exist in Norway?" Marcus harshly asked

"Only a handful" Anya reluctantly answered

"So it's back to square one again, the success of which will be reliant on Gerhardt's obtaining the hand grenades and grenade launchers" Marcus sarcastically uttered in a defeated tone of voice

"Guess so" Both Brit and Anya jointly answered

"This is frustrating I feel as though we have achieved nothing and lost two operatives in the process"

"Sometimes it goes like that especially when you play with the big boys" Anya bitterly answered

"They are no smarter than us, everyone has an Achilles heel" Marcus thoughtfully said as he paced up and down the hotel suite and considered their situation

"You do realise we haven't had breakfast, an army should never march on an empty stomach" Anya said as she looked directly at Marcus who forced a smile so as to say 'room service please' which proved to be excellent timing as Gerhardt returned that precise moment

"I left without having breakfast, this is not how Germans think or operate, never again! Are we going out or have you ordered room service? He loudly said in his East German accent

"We were about to" Anya warmly replied

"Sehr Gut! For me please order weisswurst, sweet mustard,

cabbage, pretzels, hot black coffee"

"Marcus?" Anya asked

"Scrambled fresh eggs, toast, smoked salmon, selection of pastries, pot of hot percolated coffee please" He quickly responded as he visualised the food before him

"For three, I shall place the order, meanwhile everyone relax, we have a busy day ahead of us"

"Nein we have no time for this, what did you discuss when I was away collecting our limousine?" Gerhardt asked succinctly

"Marcus presented his thoughts on acquiring electric vehicles fitting them with fertiliser bombs and then sending or parking then outside of certain strategic targets" Brit answered

"Ja this is a gut idea, I see no problem"

"Except it appears Tesla's are impossible to steal" Marcus said in the negative

"This is not true, you will find if you do your research that Norway has the highest rate of Tesla thefts in the world. Professional thieves have worked out how to make the vehicle believe it is the owner gaining entry by repeated relay attacks and specific circuits including passive keyless entry and start systems. Tesla has kept this quiet and it is frantically working on the problem. But you see it is all for nothing and I will explain why. In the same way that only the government has a mobile phone directory so it is with electric cars. Every vehicle has an access code attached or should I properly say hidden within its VIN number allowing authorised emergency personnel to open the vehicle and extract the injured or trapped or otherwise. A special number sequence presented by blue tooth forces the vehicle to display the VIN number on the front and rear windows obviously someone has leaked this information to the criminals. Luckily my mobile phone is programmed with this number sequence and I am trained to decipher the VIN number. So stealing a Tesla is easy any other concerns?"

"Tracking App and police alert comes to mind" Marcus countered

"Why you ask this question?" Gerhardt asked rather annoyed

"It seemed appropriate" Marcus smugly replied

"Nonsense, once open and start commands are given courtesy of VIN vehicle thinks you are the owner und tracking App und police alert are put on standby"

"Silly of me to ask" Marcus falsely excused himself

"Apology accepted. So tonight we are busy, steal three 25kilo bags of ammonium nitrate und three Tesla's. But where will we hide them?" Gerhardt comically asked

"Lier Psychiatric Hospital" Anya softly announced

"You think I am a little crazy?"

"No it's abandoned I mean decommissioned" Anya explained

"This is what they always say und then I find it to be quite different" Gerhardt jokingly said playing along with Anya's dialogue

"It has a workshop, we can go after breakfast" Anya said in defence

"Excellent then we are set" Gerhardt replied with a wry smile which caused Marcus to re-evaluate his opinion of the East German in a more beneficial light however it was not long lasting once he and the girls were introduced to their new means of transport namely a black Mercedes S600 salon fitted with a V12 twin turbo engine

"A real goer don't you think" Gerhardt openly asked as he introduced his work colleagues to his petrol guzzling monstrosity that could propel them to dizzy heights given the chance

"Does it come with armour plating and bullet proof glass" Brit off the cuff asked

"Ja this is an ex diplomatic machine driven in the past by an Eastern European Dictator who needed it for fast getaways"

"Seems in good shape" Marcus commented as he walked around the vehicle and examined its overall appearance

"In all respects" Gerhardt proudly announced as he was made privy to the extensive log book "Let's not stand around talking about it, we should go for a joy ride und see what this beast is capable of" he then said as he gestured for everyone to get on board

"Brit you can navigate" He said once everyone was settled

"A pleasure" the FSK agent obliged and directed him accordingly as she knew numerous ways of getting to their destination. It was a pleasant 40 kilometre drive until they reached the outskirts of the complex where the atmosphere became quite gloomy, oppressive and tragic.

"I wonder how many souls still roam about the grounds" Anya asked in a strained tone of voice

"Many I suspect" Marcus answered as he reflected on his religious teachings, beliefs and upbringing

"Slow down, there's an access road to the rear of the disused complex, its entrance is somewhat hidden from view by overgrown foliage" Brit instructed Gerhardt who slowed the powerful vehicle along the semi-rural road

"There turn right, it's more of a well worn dirt track than a road" Brit then said as she pointed to where they should go. Marcus and Anya looked about them for anything suspicious but all was serene no one in sight just animals enjoying their peace and freedom.

"Yes you are correct, perfect film sets for all sorts of movies which I believe has happened in the past plus many hold the view that it is a photographer's delight. Some buildings better than others, I'll leave the romance to the dreamers for now we have a mission to attend to" Brit rather philosophically mumbled as they drove towards a collection of buildings in very bad states of disrepair having been unoccupied since the early 1980's

"Might make a nice hotel one day for the super rich" Marcus cuttingly remarked as he thought they were all in need of therapy

"Funny you should say that" Anya answered

"Why is that?"

"Many inmates belonged to the ruling classes from foreign nations" Anya explained

"Is that what power and wealth does to a person?"

"Invariably" Anya grimly acknowledged

"Remind me to stay humble and poor" Marcus requested

"That brings its own problems" Anya remarked as they came to a stop

"Yah something that I know well" Gerhardt embarrassingly admitted as he carefully steered their vehicle along the track, through a narrow archway and then into a large court flanked on three sides by storage, laundry and maintenance buildings.

"This is well thought out, all amenities in one convenient cluster" Gerhardt merrily chirped as he parked the Mercedes next to the maintenance building

"Looks nice and cosy" Marcus concluded as he alighted to stretch his legs

"Away from prying eyes" Brit speculated as she carefully scanned their surroundings

"Best to work during the day using minimal tools and creating minimal sounds, hope there's adequate washing facilities" Gerhardt intelligently reasoned as he did not want to alert the natives

"No chance of that the other buildings are one kilometre away" Anya replied setting Gerhardt's mind at rest

"Das is gut what about inside?" Gerhardt asked as he attempted to peer through the maintenance buildings dusty windows

"The building it is rumoured is haunted and everything inside cursed, no stealing otherwise a great misfortune will descend upon you!"

"Like the Egyptian pyramid tombs?" Gerhardt guessed

"Something like that" Anya solemnly answered as she pushed open the main door to reveal a well appointed and fully equipped workshop complete with a variety of manual and precision power tools

"We will do well here" Gerhardt smugly acknowledged as he made himself familiar with the abandoned workshop and its offerings before saying "Plenty of space to park three vehicles end to end which I think we should acquire from parking lots this afternoon driving in moderate to heavy traffic instead of stealing them at night. We hide them here go back to hotel for dinner, acquire the fertiliser from the plant which I predict will have bags piled high out in the open und next to a wire fence making it easy for us. I am happy mit this arrangement so if you anything else to do I suggest we go fishing for Tesla's" Gerhardt said with a confident broad smile.

The girls nodded in agreement whilst Marcus simply grunted as he was preoccupied with his Grom issued mobile phone

"Looking at porn sites again?" Anya teased

"Almost as good" Marcus cryptically replied as he continued to flick through what appeared to be pages of irrelevant material

"Whatever you're reading has really captured your attention" Anya observed

"But hasn't distracted me fully, even though you come well equipped Gerhardt I don't think you can steal three cars in one go, surely your phone needs to be in the car for it to continue working" Marcus implied

"You are quite correct, Brit will need to drive me in, return and drive me back three times"

"And I guess you will vary the car parks from which you obtain the vehicles and further if the cars vary in year of manufacture does your phone compensate for this?" Marcus asked making certain that all variables had been taken care of

"Very astute of you Mr Rhodes perhaps you are not the dumb polack I initially thought you were, the best years are pre 2000" Gerhardt replied with a measure respect

"Hopefully you will not target the same parking lot and use the same clothes" Marcus continued to probe

"Exactly my coat is reversible as are my trousers also I shall wear a surgical mask giving the impression that I have some sort of highly infectious respiratory disease, there are about twenty car parks to choose from all accept cash"

"Well thought out" Marcus verbally applauded the East German

"Thank you, if you will excuse me I should get going" Gerhardt replied and nodded for Brit to join him and then said "Before we depart I leave you some bottled water and a few energy bars"

"See you in about one hour fifteen" Anya said as she waved the couple away

"That's a fair estimate, any particular colour?"

"Dark is preferable" Anya replied

"Then dark it is" Gerhardt merrily replied and made himself comfortable in the passenger seat whilst Brit familiarised herself with the Mercedes controls

True to his word Gerhardt returned in the allotted time with a dark blue metallic 2019 Tesla model with black upholstery. He did not waste any time storing it away inside at the rear of the workshop before racing away to secure his next trophy leaving Marcus to determine how easy it would be to plant an anfo inside its cabin next to the battery compartment, once again Gerhardt returned within the seventy five minutes

"All okay" Marcus asked as he approached Gerhardt who sat purring like a cat that had just caught a large rat

"All is in order" Gerhardt smiled

"Military Police....?" Marcus commented as he noticed an official American arm band on Gerhardt's left arm

"A simple diversion to cause confusion"

"You certainly are full of surprises"

"Always thinking of ways to baffle our opponents" Gerhardt mischievously answered

"Me too" Marcus replied

"Anything that I should know about...?"

"Too early to say, it's in the embryonic stage"

"In other words you are still fishing perhaps you should change your bait!" Gerhardt somewhat arrogantly answered as he prepared to leave and retrieve his last vehicle with a sense of urgency as it was nearing 3.30pm, end of day for some workers which meant he would most likely find a suitable vehicle near the docks where harbour staff worked late into the night. This time it took a little longer to return given the extra distance they had to travel which was a bonus for Marcus allowing him to work out the technicalities of fitting a suitably sized anfo next to the battery compartment in a Tesla and an opportunity to work on his secret project.

"What are you doing?" Anya asked out of frustration as she had difficulty accepting Marcus's sudden reclusive behaviour

"Searching the aetiology of certain diseases"

"Why...?"

"To determine the best available therapy" Marcus replied without saying anything more

"You really are becoming increasingly mysterious, I don't know if I like that in a man"

"Women can't always have it their way" Marcus rudely answered with respect to mystery and its enticing use. Anya was keen to add fuel to the fire but was interrupted by the noise of Brit's return

"How did it go?" Anya asked once Brit entered the workshop

"Bit messy we had to drive around until circumstances were just right, Gerhardt scored well, he is about five minutes behind me. I'm exhausted with all of this adrenaline output plus we haven't had anything substantial to eat since breakfast. These energy bars are tasteless crap, don't know where Gerhardt got them from" Brit grumbled

"I agree, being famished doesn't help cognitive function" Anya eagerly admitted as she dreamt of a full three course meal with matching wines

"Time to lock up and go home...?" Marcus warmly asked much to the girls delight

"Lead the way Mr Rhodes" Brit implored

"Can't leave without Gerhardt"

"Why not he can look after himself, plus he has wheels and

knows where to find us"

"That would breach our security, give him time" Marcus wisely answered as he popped his head out of the door to see if Gerhardt had arrived which he had just done. Marcus allowed the East German to park the car before sealing off the building and making their way into Oslo under his guidance and Brit's excellent driving skills

"Where are you taking us?" Anya asked once they had set off

"Upstream Salmon, a rather posh European style restaurant"

"That's your new name" Gerhardt said from the back seat addressing his remarks to Marcus

"Bit fishy isn't it?' Brit commented

"I was thinking more along the lines of Posh Polack a vast improvement on Dumb Polack"

"Why exactly does he qualify?" Brit asked

"British upbringing and Polksi refinement" Gerhardt explained

"That remains to be seen" Brit countered as she aggressively weaved the powerful Mercedes in and out of traffic whilst heading towards Oslo central where the posh restaurant was located

"I can understand why you Norwegians want the Americans out" Gerhardt said changing the subject

"More details please" Anya requested

"In Germany we have 55,000 GI Joe's stationed there, we are not a free nation. We are a satellite of the USA, much like Italy and even the United Kingdom although the numbers are lesser. Once you let this vermin into your country it is difficult eradicating it as Japan rightly knows, it wouldn't surprise me if the training under harsh winter conditions is a smoke screen hiding something more sinister than you had previously thought. Question is what?" Gerhardt surmised with an acid tone of voice

"In any event if we found the true reason who will listen to us?" Anya seriously asked

"Does it matter?" Marcus asked in a hushed tone of voice

"What are you implying?"

"Force a silent withdrawal precipitated by activities behind closed doors"

"Once again who will listen to us?"

"Whoever has the most or least to gain there is no honour in politics especially geo-politics" Marcus correctly answered

"Are we out of our depth, after all we are but soldiers" Anya groaned in frustration

"Serving a cause to defend our country, to ensure national security, to protect against foreign invaders, aggressors, anyone who might undermine the safety of our citizens whether they are friend or foe" Marcus philosophically answered and remained silent allowing his impressions to filter through into his colleagues minds.

His choice of restaurant did not disappoint in all respects except for one namely that Gerhardt had one Schnapps too many and insisted on driving them at breakneck speed to the fertilizer factory. Marcus was not troubled by his actions as he realised Gerhardt was trained to perform under all conditions including alcoholic inebriation.

"So we are here, wait while I do my duty" Gerhardt instructed his colleagues as he was about to leave the car, find a pair of pliers in the boot and snip his way through the wire fence to misappropriate three 25kilo bags of ammonium nitrate

"Just one bag please, 5 kilo Anfo's is more than enough for our purposes" Marcus whispered

"Your orders will be obeyed at all times, back in a jiffy" the East German succinctly barked in a strong German accent and proceeded to efficiently and cleanly execute his duty. Within minutes the thud of the boot lid being shut indicated he had completed his task without incident and he somewhat sedately drove them back to their hotel for a welcome night's rest.

16
CHOSEN, FERTILIZER, DRAMA

After much bickering and heated debate the next morning Gerhardt reluctantly agreed to allow Marcus to accompany him on his journey to the Chosen One's in Gothenburg which would take them over three hours via highway E6 which gave amble time to discuss various issues facing the group.

Gerhardt made certain they left by 9am as his meeting with the Chosen One's was scheduled for 1.15pm in the afternoon giving them sufficient time to exercise comfort stops. The journey to Gothenburg was unfamiliar to Gerhardt but once there he would easily navigate his way around making certain that all was visually clear for an arms deal providing his mobile phone confirmed it as well.

"I think we have had enough of Scandi music" Gerhardt abruptly said one hour into their journey as he switched off the Mercedes audio system and activated his mobile phone

"You have better music on your device?" Marcus naively asked

"Nein, time for a little official entertainment"

"Meaning...?"

"We scan the local police radio channels and listen in on their conversation"

"Why...?" Marcus seemingly asked out of curiosity

"To see how much activity I mean importance has been given to the three stolen Tesla's, listen and learn" Gerhardt said as he activated his mobile phone's scanning software to bring up Oslo's police bandwidth 170.40 hertz

"Impressive is that it?"

"Nein we have three important channels to choose from, 170.40 hertz The Policeman, 171-1 hertz Dispatch and 171-25 hertz assigned for Car to Car. Between these three we will obtain a clear picture of how successful we were in bamboozling the police"

"You're very confident" Marcus replied with a tinge of admiration

"Which tickles your fancy?"

"I think Car to Car, it's always interesting to hear what the troops on the ground have to say" Marcus answered

"My sentiments precisely" Gerhardt agreed as he increased the speaker volume on his phone once the sergeant in charge of the investigation started to speak

"So far what we know is that yesterday three early model Teslas were stolen, two from public parking lots in the city and one from the waterfront in the mid afternoon. We have interviewed the owners concerned and find they are independent of each other in all respects. Information gathered from available CCTV shows military police wearing protective surgical face masks gaining access to and driving away in two cars, we suspect from eye witness reports that with the third car military police were also involved in its acquisition, what is strange is the fact that both American and Norwegian personnel were implicated judging by their respective arm bands suggesting a joint venture. None of the owners have any prior criminal records nor have their vehicles been outside of Norway in the past six months, there appears to be nothing suspicious about the individuals. The only conclusion that I can draw is that the owners are victims of organised crime pandering to foreign clients who have a liking for Teslas. Forensics has shown nothing as the owners cannot with any degree of accuracy remember the exact parking places which were later contaminated by other users I feel this case is a lost cause and cannot demand any further action on our part especially as all of the said vehicles are fully covered by comprehensive private insurance any questions...?" The sergeant asked on completing his findings which made Gerhardt glow with absolute delight

"Do we know the registration numbers of the cars" An eager police cadet asked who had been assigned to the case

"Yes, let me find them in my notes, here we are EV11968, Ay12035 and CF36126 why do you ask?"

"CF36126 offers us an opportunity of locating it" the cadet eagerly responded

"How so...?" The sergeant replied much to Gerhardt's dismay

"It is the most recent model, most likely fitted with tracking software that records its daily movements and reports the same to a central data bank for statistical purposes allowing for future car design and marketing to maximise profits and sales volume. Something that owners are unaware of and deliberately so otherwise they might view this as an invasion of privacy and avoid buying the product. I suggest we obtain the VIN number from vehicle records, shoot off an email marked very urgent to the manufacturer and hopefully they will reply within eight hours with the car's probable location, otherwise once night falls we will have lost any chance of retrieval for as we all know crooks like the cover of darkness"

"Scheisse....!!!" (German for shit) Gerhardt exclaimed once he heard these words

"Not so soon" Marcus replied

"It's all over" Gerhardt grumbled as he resigned himself to defeat

"What sort of German are you? I am ashamed of you! Consider the facts, multinational companies are notoriously slow to answer, average waiting time for a reply is 12 hours 10 minutes even longer when one takes into account time differences which is six hours between Oslo and Michigan, there is no problem"

"Yes there is and it's called a pimple faced cock sucking junior officer, full of ambition" Gerhardt bitterly argued

"You are wrong, this Norwegian didn't think it through it's more complicated than sending an urgent email"

"How do you mean" Gerhardt asked slightly relieved

"The car sends its movement details anonymously in an encrypted fashion. We have nothing to worry about" Marcus firmly stated with an air of authority designed to calm his colleague even though he knew time was of the essence

"We'll see about that later this afternoon around 5pm" Gerhardt replied with a hint of lingering doubt as he returned to the police conversation

"Anything else...?" The sergeant asked after pondering on the cadet's suggestion

"Yes there is which I think is related to the theft of the cars. There was a skilled entry into the holding yard of the fertilizer factory last night. Nothing it appears according to the staff was taken which I think to be a lie as their accounting procedure is sloppy therefore they would not miss a bag or two of ammonium nitrate which in my mind heralds future potential terrorist attacks of the nature that we have recently seen" The cadet enthusiastically said

"I'll stop you there this is pure speculation on your part. I am all for preventative crime but we cannot exhaust our resources chasing pies in the sky without concrete evidence" The sergeant rudely corrected the young cadet

"Yes Sir I apologize"

"Good then we will wait for the outcome of your urgent email to Tesla before taking any further action" The sergeant finally said before signing off

"Satisfied" Marcus asked Gerhardt

"Yes I'm glad to hear the sergeant exerted his authority and wisdom"

"In other words doesn't like smart arses"

"Or people who appear too bright" Gerhardt cynically replied as he gritted his teeth and concentrated on his driving leaving Marcus to briefly concentrate on his internet research.

"Still finding your way" Gerhardt asked after a while as he looked across at Marcus who was fiddling with his mobile phone

"More along the lines of fact finding"

"Difficult these days, the truth is heavily camouflaged and placed out of the way leaving finders frustrated and disillusioned"

"Well said, but then there is nothing like perseverance to win the day" Marcus countered

"Providing you are on the right track" Gerhardt calmly replied

"Having said that, you do know the way?"

"Ya vol mein herr, we are 20 minutes outside of Gothenburg, we deviate in 15 and make a bee line to the junkyard to conduct discrete business, slip away unnoticed, arm our cars and set off the fireworks early tomorrow morning around 3am"

"Seems like you have it all worked out" Marcus cuttingly replied

"Precisely" Gerhardt answered without any doubt which Marcus found a little disturbing based on his previous fieldwork experiences. Time as well as the scenery passed quickly by until they entered the industrial area of Gothenburg where The Chosen Ones Scrap Yard Incorporated was located on a sprawling lot which was piled high with disused items of all sorts.

The traffic suddenly became usually heavy for that time of day as they approached the yard and it was not until several "Event Ahead" road signs made themselves apparent that Gerhardt realised that something was going on at the scrap yard.

"So much for conducting discrete business" Marcus mumbled in a low voice as they limped along towards the main entrance where two ruffians dressed in studded black leather attire were directing traffic towards a muddy make shift parking lot that catered exclusively for all terrain vehicles.

"Let's not get bogged" Marcus dryly said as he felt their vehicle struggle to find traction before sliding to a stop "Quite the carnival atmosphere" He said once outside having smelt the fragrant air and heard the commotion generated by hundreds of happy voices.

"This is not what I expected" Gerhardt grumbled as he looked around

"Might be to our advantage just be on the lookout for pick pockets and undercover police looking for trouble" Marcus replied as they strolled towards the milling crowd underneath a large banner that shouted Exotic Trashed Treasure Bizarre.

"So do you know who and where you were meant to meet?"

"Not any more" Gerhardt sadly admitted as he tried to look interested in what was on offer at the various stalls

"Then all of this has been for nothing" Marcus surmised as he studied various faces that passed him by some of which bore resemblance to the African gangsters who extracted protection money from the restaurant that Marcus and the Major had dined at which caused him to conclude "Pristina pokers are for sale here, this is a carve up of a recent shipment heavily disguised follow the black faces"

"Very well, what are we looking for?" Gerhardt asked

"Novelties, this is no antiques show, look around you the scrap yard is a convenient location for a monthly event"

"That's why he said bring cash, no eftpos machines here"! Gerhardt agreed as he began to appreciate the variety of exotic Middle Eastern goods for sale that included herbs and spices

"Welcome to Africa with a twist" Marcus said as he stared at a stand selling Bunny Chow Chow which was a quarter of a bread loaf hollowed out and filled with a blistering hot curry mixture

"Can I try?" Marcus gently inquired as he pointed to a particularly red hot specimen

"This one burn you, not okay to try, only for super tough Africans, you need glass of milk otherwise you find yourself in big trouble" A middle aged woman with a strong Slavic accent nervously answered as she trembled slightly

"Maybe I can poke with finger to see how pristine I mean clean it is" Marcus said in code fashion emphasizing the words poke and pristine which the woman knew exactly what Marcus meant

"You can do" She replied

"You don't trust me, do you?" Marcus accurately determined from her body language

"You not my normal type of customer" The woman answered and began to withdraw her wares

"You have nothing to fear from me or my friend' Marcus convincingly answered and gestured for her to abandon her unfounded anxiety

"I take chance"

"Good do you have take home packs...?" Gerhardt asked sensing that she had what they wanted

"Only frozen, in fours and sixes"

"Excellent we will take two sixes please. How much for that...?" Gerhardt asked in a quiet voice not bothering to check who might be watching or listening to their conversation

"800$ American dollars, you put in bag I give you"

"After I cut Bunny in half" Marcus said as a condition of the sale

"Understand you come with me, he stay here, play guard" The woman submissively answered as she took Marcus by the hand and led him away to where she kept her portable freezers which were guarded by two heavily tattooed thugs with clean shaven heads. Marcus watched as the woman opened one of the freezers and then invited him to make his choice. Marcus produced a retractable army knife and proceeded to cut away at one of the Bunnies until he hit metal, not content with his find Marcus retrieved a black plastic bag marked Arun Balls much to the annoyance of the woman who immediately signalled for her henchmen to intervene. One of them suddenly grabbed Marcus by the scruff of his neck only to be met with a sharp blow to the base of his sternum which paralysed him instantly and he fell to the ground breathless and in acute agony.

The other reached into his back pocket to retrieve his pistol only to have it violently shoved up his back by Marcus until his shoulder was dislocated and his arm broken.

"I'll take these, one tray and one bag of Arun Balls for same price" Marcus coldly stated as he stared at the woman who briefly considered stabbing Marcus with the pin of her hair accessory but realised it was futile under the circumstances.

"No problem" She gingerly answered

"I thought as much, nice doing business with you" Marcus replied and walked away to rejoin Gerhardt who by now was surrounded by eager buyers of the coloured variety one of whom appeared particularly menacing

"That's dinner sorted, let's see if there are any after dinner delights available" Marcus brightly said only to be confronted by a well built Punjabi intent on blocking Marcus's path

"That black bag you are carrying belongs to me! I would be most appreciative if you could hand it over" The Punjabi roughly barked

"I don't see our name on it" Marcus as a matter of fact bluntly replied

"I am sorry to correct you I have a monthly standing order with this foreign woman and am not understanding why you are in possession of it unless you are a common thief or have picked it up by mistake" The Punjabi aggressively replied

"Arun Balls...is that your name?" Marcus flippantly asked tongue in cheek

"Precisely" The Punjabi vehemently replied

"My apologies, I thought it was concise for Arancini balls"

"Do not be joking with me!"

"Here you are then" Marcus without any resistance said as he handed over the black bag and watched it change hands several times before disappearing from view "I've heard of sleight of hand but this is at a whole new level" Marcus silently thought unaware that Gerhardt had not been so easily fooled and easily identified the Punjabi's mule responsible for transporting the package un-interrupted out of the scrap yard. Whilst Marcus attended to the formality of obtaining a partial refund Gerhardt slipped away and shadowed the mule who filtered through several layers of security before driving away unimpeded that was not the case for Marcus nor Gerhardt as during their stay the scrap yard's entry and exit points had been taken over by armed police equipped with metal detectors and portable X-ray equipment.

"This is going to be tricky" Marcus whispered once they decided to vacate the market

"Shall we ditch the bunny's" Gerhardt asked

"Nope let's bluff our way through" Marcus confidently answered as he chose a line that appeared to be advancing at a steady pace

"Got our official ID" Gerhardt asked thinking that it would be sufficient

"Always" Marcus replied as he readied himself

"Next!" A tall fresh faced policeman loudly said as he gestured for Marcus to step forward "Purchases on conveyer" He instructed as he pointed to his right. Luckily both Marcus and Gerhardt had left their handguns behind in the hotel safely locked away. The policeman then proceed to scan Marcus body for any offensive weaponry whilst his colleague examined the frozen six pack of bunny Chow Chow using the portable x-ray machine

"It always amazes me how they assemble the Chow Chow must have something to do with the metal ring inside" The fresh faced policeman said as he returned the Bunny Chow Chow to Marcus who was not at all surprised by the result

"You knew all along" Gerhardt remarked once they were out of ear shot

"So did you" Marcus suggested "Got any more reliable sources?"

"Where does that leave us" Marcus asked ashamed by the outcome

"We abandon attacking the American military bases and

concentrate on orchestrating 'terrorist attacks' on the US Embassy and members of parliament. Find us the nearest large chemist store plus a novelty one as well, I have an idea" Marcus replied as they neared their car.

The trip into Gothenburg was uneventful as were the purchase of the things that Marcus needed to prime the Teslas once they were individually fitted with 5 kilos of anfo which left Gerhardt rather perplexed when he saw them but it did nothing to alleviate his anxiety which continued to mount as time advanced towards 5pm which Gerhardt had postulated would make or break them. As a consequence instead of returning to the hotel to collect Anya and Brit he deviated and drove to Lier Hospital Complex, his negative mood did not go unnoticed by Marcus.

"I'm surprised at your inability to cope. I would have thought that the Russians would have trained you to be more stoic, resolute able to confront any situation and deal with it accordingly. What if the Teslas are found we adapt and find another way we don't even know what effect our attacks will have nothing by themselves I dare say that in itself suggests we have to do more" Marcus quite firmly said in a no nonsense manner so as to drive his argument home

"What are you suggesting?" Gerhardt asked abandoning his stupor

Once we reach Lier you will remove the offending Tesla namely registration number CF36126 and dump it somewhere far away from the others, semi rural I think, that leaves us with two usable vehicles. Next you will post on the internet a message that looks as though the Safeguard Nordic Purity group is responsible especially as the KNN has been compromised. The message will repeatedly hammer way at co-ordinates 62-6472N and 11-8669E as to what the Americans are secretly doing this should provoke an internet reaction followed by governmental knee jerks and media misinformation"

"I take on board what you have said and hope that you are right" Gerhardt with a slight degree of confidence reluctantly said

"Concentrate, visualise in the affirmative and all will be well. Drive carefully without saying another word, it's time for constructive contemplation" Marcus thoughtfully advised and switched on his mobile phone to continue his research as time was of the essence. By 5.15pm they had reached the disused Lier Hospital complex all appeared quiet and undisturbed no suspicious characters around. The same was true of the inside of the workshop where he has stored the stolen cars luckily the car in question was the last in line making it first off the rank. Gerhardt methodically went about gaining access to the vehicle before making himself comfortable behind the steering wheel. Marcus meanwhile attended to opening and closing the workshops main doors and then when Gerhardt had driven the car into the courtyard Marcus rubbed mud onto the number plates and threw a bucket of slurry over it making it more difficult to identify.

"I'll follow you at a steady pace turn right at the end of the track and favour the off roads until you think it is safe to ditch the car in a remote semi rural location, leave the door open and what else can be left running, we might even puncture a tyre or two" Marcus thought out a loud before following suit

Thirty minutes later the deed was done and the duo returned to the comfortable hotel to tell Anya and Brit of their experiences that day and the measures they took to remedy the various situations. The girls reciprocated likewise but their material was mundane in comparison. Brit however proudly announced that she obtained the supplies that Marcus had requested namely kerosene, three two litre round plastic storage containers with tight fitting snap on lids and a pair of long rubber gloves. Tonight's meal would be sushi on the run from a local Japanese restaurant before returning to the Tier Hospital and arming the stolen cars. Using limited light sources and having covered all windows Marcus mixed the ammonium nitrate and kerosene in the ratio of 9:1 in a bucket by hand and then packed the resultant firm paste into the round storage containers. He then punctured a hole in the centre of the lids that allowed a bundle of sparklers wired together to squeeze in nice and tight and then he snapped on the lids to seal the containers. In two separate plastic vials he first added crushed sparklers which contained potassium perchlorate, magnesium and aluminium fillings followed by a layer of potassium permanganate. These he wired onto the sparkler bundles much to the awe of his onlookers.

"Explain what is happening here" Gerhardt asked out of curiosity as he had not seen anything like this before

"We need a source of ignition to make the Anfo explode in the absence of using a detonator therefore I have made a make shift prototype. Potassium permanganate is a highly oxidising agent, dropping glycerine onto it rapidly generates heat and the mixture bursts into flames which in turn will ignite the sparkler bundle embedded in the Anfo paste. Once the intense heat measuring almost 2000 degrees Fahrenheit ignites the kerosene potassium nitrate paste it will explode with tremendous force. With the Anfo placed over the car's battery watch the whole thing burn like hell. Once you have positioned the Anfo and introduced the glycerine you have about ten minutes to exit the car before the catalytic reaction takes hold and proceeds to its end point" Marcus explained

"Very eloquent, based on simple ingredients easily sourced" Brit verbally applauded the man

"I am certain you have had training in this field" Marcus guessed

"Not in such an innovative fashion" Brit admitted

"It's basic chemistry"

"Things that are lost in this high tech world" Anya put forward

"Okay let's get dirty" Marcus said changing the subject and stepped aside to allow Gerhardt to drive the first car out without any illumination. Marcus then checked to make certain all were wearing military arm bands and surgical face masks before he muddied the car's exterior and joined Brit in the Mercedes in the knowledge that the US Embassy would be the first target which was located at 36 Morgedalsvegen Oslo.

Gerhardt set the address and allowed the car to navigate itself, within 200 metres of the final destination he stopped the vehicle and set it to autonomous and allowed it to finish the rest of its journey without any passengers on board once he had primed the plastic vial containing the ground up sparkler and potassium permanganate with glycerine. Within thirty meters of the Embassy's main gate Marcus's ignition system was well and truly ablaze and within a further thirty seconds the entire car catastrophically exploded shattering windows within a five hundred meter radius.

"Glad I didn't make a bigger bomb!" Marcus wickedly mumbled as they sped away "Conclusions?" He then asked

"No extra police on the roads, they weren't expecting us which means our next target might also be relatively easy" Brit analytically concluded

"Gerhardt you are the electronic whizz-kid mit der super-duper toy, can you deactivate the CCTV cameras in the parliament square before we enter it" Marcus asked

"Ja that should not be a problem, I need about twenty minutes before we breach its perimeter" The East German confidently answered

"Excellent.... how are you proceeding with the internet announcement....?"

"Back ground, characters, text has been done, just need to add voices and we are ready for transmission" Gerhardt modestly replied with a sly grin

"Everyone happy....?" Marcus asked and was met with a wave of smiles and grins "Good then let's continue to agitate"

The second stolen car had already been fitted with the Anfo it was simply a case of driving back to the abandoned hospital and using the vehicle to attack the Minister of the Interior and Minister for Justice parliamentary offices.

Whilst they drove back Gerhardt tuned into the police radio channel to monitor the law officers plus other agencies response to the 'bombing' outside of the American embassy so as to determine whether or not they would mobilize security to protect other sensitive targets and whether or not the group could proceed with planting the next 'bomb'.

The authorities' reaction was subdued to say the least especially as it was 3.30am in the morning and there were no reports of any casualties suggesting that in all likelihood the event was nothing more than an electrical fault causing a random car to burst into flames. As for the severity of the explosion that required further forensic investigation, emergency vehicles are on the scene, fire, ambulance, police, the area cordoned off the light of day would reveal all. The owner of the vehicle was absent but would most probably be found once the vehicle's registration details were retrieved. No extra patrols were called into play, all of which was sweet music to the group's ears as they powered back to Tier hospital which had not attracted any visitors including the homeless.

"Brit, you and Anya will travel in the Mercedes, I and Gerhardt in the Tesla, we will stop and park somewhere insignificant ten minutes outside of the parliamentary square allowing Gerhardt to remotely incapacitate its CCTV network and lighting system. We will have twenty minutes in which to plant the 'bomb' and swiftly leave. One final item, do a thorough clean sweep of the workshop, leave nothing incriminating behind, nothing that can be linked back to us" Marcus said just before they were about to exit the workshop. Like before being the highly trained professionals everything proceeded smoothly without hiccup or incident. They easily located the ministerial offices, strategically parked and activated the car in complete darkness and silently walked away, the ensuing explosion mirrored the first bit caused more damage due to the proximity of the surrounding buildings. This time the authorities' reaction was not so lackadaisical, police, ambulance, fire and anti-terrorist squads arrived on mass as it was feared that certain night workers might have been injured. Norway's corridors of power had been rocked to its foundations there was a new group in town one that meant business and demanded to be heard.

"Let's go home ladies, gentleman and grab some shut eye if you can once the adrenaline subsides. There's nothing like a good explosion to clear the air" Gerhardt mischievously said as he reflected on the day's achievements and indicated he had posted on numerous internet platforms Safeguard Nordic's Purity claim to fame.

By 4am they had returned to the hotel and behaved in a somewhat raucous manner as though they had just returned from a noisy nightclub or private function and made much ado about the enormous fun they had just experienced much to the disdain of the night duty manager. Once inside their hotel suite it was a different matter, the men became more reflective and analytical whereas the two female FSK agents descended into a sea of guilt thinking that they were likely to be branded domestic terrorists should they be found out, accordingly disciplined and harshly prosecuted. Sleep for them became impossible whereas both Marcus and Gerhardt slept soundly, thoughts of companionship filled Anya's and Brit's minds, it became a choice of whether to sleep together or climb into bed with one of the men without giving them the wrong impression. Either way it most likely would strengthen the unity of the group and cause them to further care for each other. Anya made the first move and teamed up with Marcus using him as a human teddy bear, Brit reluctantly followed suit and softly cuddled Gerhardt much like a loving pet dog without going to the extent of licking him to death, the foursome sleepy soundly in contrast to their 'wild' night out.

Gerhardt was the first to awake at around 10.35am and was surprised to find Brit in his bed curled up in the foetal position. He checked to see if his underpants were still on as a sign that his virginity was still intact and then he rolled out of bed and walked into the living area in the hope that one of the others had also arisen.

"Good morning" Marcus warmly whispered as he joined Gerhardt's side

"Where did you come from?" Gerhardt asked quite surprised

"The bathroom of course"

"You were very quiet"

"Either that or it's soundproofed"

"To ensure discreetness and preserve the pleasant ambiance" Gerhardt concluded as he held his nose

"Today's motto"

"I agree, we deservedly need a rest day" Gerhardt sighed before he activated the suites wall mounted television

"Time for fake news....?"

"No I prefer to call it cleverly crafted with every word meticulously selected to serve its purpose"

"That's a very eloquent way of describing it" Marcus acidly retorted as he watched Gerhardt use the smart TV to locate Gonorski.com an English speaking news channel manned by an attractive middle aged blonde woman

"Earlier today in unrelated separate incidents two Tesla automobiles caught fire and exploded in what some people would describe as politically sensitive areas, namely outside the American embassy and secondly in the middle of Oslo's parliamentary square, neither was considered to be an act of terrorism, both cars it seems were fitted with defective batteries from the same batch, no one was hurt according to authorities" she said as images of the wrecks' debris and damaged buildings were televised

"All swept under the carpet" Gerhardt prematurely remarked

"However according to our reliable sources there is contrary evidence that suggests otherwise. On certain social media platforms a group known as the Safeguard Nordic's Purity is stating the opposite and is demanding that the co-ordinates 62-6472N and 11-8669E be thoroughly investigated as it is a blatant violation of Norwegian sovereignty that threatens its national security. Needless to say the authorities have dismissed this as the ramblings of a drug fuelled extremist group and have vowed to bring it to justice for inciting neo-Nazi propaganda"

"Good luck" Gerhardt said with a smirk

"Why do you say that...?"

"Because it's fictitious, imaginary, it doesn't exist"

"Except in cyber space" Marcus wisely concluded before asking "How secure is it...?"

"Impenetrable!"

"So you can continue to agitate?" Marcus asked

"No problem"

"Are you sure of that?"

"Absolutely" Gerhardt replied with a wonderful sense of Germanic confidence before returning his attention to what the news presenter had further to say

"Unfortunately this may never happen, the area concerned is off limits to the public, it is currently being used for military manoeuvres" she grimly announced

"Bugger.....!" Marcus blurted out aloud annoyed by the set back

"The deception and cover up is bigger than we imagined Gerhardt surmised

"Obviously developing a ground swell of public unrest and disfavour is not going to succeed, the powers that be are able to quell any murmur instantly and prevent the light of day exposing their nefarious dealings"

17

ROYAL LOYALTIES

Disappointed by the fact that their efforts had not made any significant headway the group decided to seek solace at Drammen's seaport where several fashionable cafes and restaurants had sprung up to cater for the tastes of those who saw the ocean in all of its glory as the solution to all of their troubles and woes. It was no different for the group who decided to forsake breakfast at the hotel and investigate what the waterfront had to offer.

Eloquent open faced sandwiches, freshly brewed coffee and warm penetrating sunshine in the outdoors was just the right recipe to restore harmony, balance and optimism within the group, all was not lost, in fact, their failure would spawn success in subtle ways, it was just a matter of finding the right avenue.

"Marcus perhaps you could share with us the fruits of your somewhat guarded research" Anya earnestly implored her colleague who appeared reluctant to do so but nevertheless agreed to do so

"I suppose I should given the gravity of the circumstances, everything that we have encountered so far I believe have been multilayered distractions which appeared to me were lingering ramifications as a consequence of WW2. There is no doubt in the historical sense that war brings forth progress and innovation, electronics rose to prominence very quickly during WW2, transistors, semi-conductors and even primitive computers based on germanium and silicon were developed including their purification processes all of which have rapidly proliferated in our modern digital world which has an insatiable appetite for rare earth metals. China controls 90% of the market a rather unpalatable situation for the Americans and their imperialist agenda, they have reacted by signing into law a provision in the National Defence Authorization Act barring their Dept of Defence from buying permanent rare earth magnets and other sophisticated equipment made in China. Thus forcing the Dept to look elsewhere, Norway it was discovered has the geological goods therefore the military presence in Norway to the informed casual observer is to guarantee safe passage of processed rare earths from Norway to the US much like the shipments of heroin/opium from Afghanistan all of which is kept hush-hush so as not to alert the Chinese as they are keen to thwart the Americans economically and militarily in the latter aspect neodymium and samarium are the most important elements, this of course exposes Norway to attack hence the need to squash all public knowledge surrounding the nefarious operation. Dark Pebble an enormous hedge fund is financing the venture and surprise surprise Mossad appears to have seats on the board courtesy of our friends in Norway namely Mozaic who through its obsessive examination of WW2 records either blackmailed or bribed certain politicians into allowing the Americans to build bases on Norwegian soil. The storage of excessive amounts of military hardware in the mountains' caverns and its subsequent sale to black market operatives is nothing more than a fine example of official corruption. The creed of Tyr's members arrest is payback for its covert operations in Yemen and its desire to restore peace, prosperity and safety for its inhabitants. None of these scenarios are sufficiently controversial enough to oust the Americans which leaves us powerless or should I say more determined, Operation Anaconda may hold the key" Marcus slowly said so as to allow his friends to critically analyse his findings and postulations

"So you are strongly suggesting there is more involved?" Gerhardt abruptly asked knowing full well that many military objectives are highly convoluted to the point that the primary objective is often lost

"I am"

"Besides training in sub zero conditions and protecting cargo what is there?" Gerhardt prodded

"The US has presently under its imperial control around thirty countries in which it has around three hundred odd biological warfare labs involved in weaponizing all manner of microbes"

"Are you suggesting that one if not more of the American bases in Norway conceal such labs?"

"Perhaps"

"That is a rather elusive answer"

"Not really as a private interest may be involved" Marcus sadly answered

"Sounds somewhat sinister" Anya fearfully said

"Disturbing in the least"

"Care to share your suspicions" Brit asked

"The King of Norway has received considerable 'charitable' donations from Dark Pebble to 'restore' all of the medieval villas in disrepair on his royal estate located on the Bygdoy peninsula. The estate originally belonged to a Cistercian order of monks an most likely has an underground cellar" Marcus began to explain

"Are you suggesting it has been converted into a clandestine operation?" Brit asked a little shocked

"That is a distinct possibility especially as Black Pebble has heavily invested in multinational pharmaceuticals companies which we know from past and present experience how unethical they are" Marcus replied

"With royal approval he forgot to mention" Gerhardt said much to the girls' disgust

"Our King is not like that!" Brit strongly protested

"The Nazi invasion of Norway during WW2 was not only a breeding programme to promote the Aryan race, the Germans were after a reliable supply of heavy water for their experimental nuclear advancement, sadly the Royal family was involved" Marcus grimly reported

"To this day I suppose you are going to say" Anya viciously retorted

"Any else to report...?" Brit sternly asked as she placed her hands on her hips

"Ramsund naval base has seen frequent comings and goings of American naval vessels supposedly exchanging 'troops' who in reality are expertly disguised mules" Marcus calmly replied

"Carrying....?"

"Goods out refined rare earth metals in discrete quantities, goods in laboratory needs, some in sealed thermos flasks" He accurately answered

"Therefore we have two likely sites" Gerhardt concluded

"It would appear so, either we target one or assault both, one will be heavily guarded and the other less, relying on its innocent appearance even though it is on hallowed ground" Brit suggested

"The latter is particularly appealing to me for one reason namely that it was a Cistercian hot spot" Marcus said drawing attention to the religious involvement

"What of it?" Anya asked still fuming over the allegation that the Norwegian Royalty was corrupt

"The Cistercian monks were a highly intelligent order which advanced with or without divine aid, crop yields, animal husbandry, treatments for various diseases, they were the first to develop natural antibiotics the knowledge of which they extended to the Knights Templar, their laboratory and work books would be interesting to say the least" Marcus put forward

"That's all very well but Ramsund being naval can get goods in and out very quickly as opposed to Bygdoy plus it will have water tight security" Gerhardt countered

"Making it difficult for us" Marcus argued

"Unless one of us becomes a mule" Gerhardt cleverly suggested

"I suppose you will volunteer for the role" Marcus teased

"Absolutely....! We East Germans are masters at chess we know how to bluff and checkmate quickly this will be a walk in the park for me!" Gerhardt coolly replied

"Leaving us to infiltrate the King's farm which I coincidentally visited on many occasions to enjoy afternoon tea in the cafe located in the gardener's quaint house, purchase some delicious homemade organic jam and generally stroll about the extensive grounds. Being heritage listed I suggest we obtain site drawings and building speci-fications from the State library to pinpoint the exact location of any likely laboratory on the royal estate" Brit suggested

"An excellent idea" Gerhardt said with his full approval

"The stables and diary are possibly the most promising allowing the flow of people dressed in white coats to come and go freely" Anya postulated

"I agree" Gerhardt said having reached the same conclusion. Marcus however remained silent and concentrated on using his ultra sophisticated Grom issued mobile phone to access the royal farm's site map complete with technical specifications.

"So mein herr what have you found?" Gerhardt asked Marcus as he peered over his shoulder

"The cellar or more correctly the labyrinth of tunnels and chambers occupies an extensive area" Marcus replied showing his findings to his fellow colleagues

"With access from the dairy and stables it would appear" Brit determined after superimposing her recollection with that of Marcus findings

"Do they produce cheese?" Marcus asked

"Yes I believe so"

"Then that is the perfect cover to hide cultures of all sorts"

"Agreed" Brit said with a nod of her head

"Shall we strike tonight?" Marcus eagerly asked

"I think we should Ramsund is 1450km way at least nineteen hours by car" Gerhardt replied

"White coats or as we are?" Marcus asked

"Neither this is rushed, first reconnaissance, gather Intel then action, I know you want to bring about a rapid conclusion but we cannot abandon established basic protocol" Brit firmly cautioned as she sipped her coffee

"Very well, then we visit the extensive Bygdoy Royal farm and stay until closing after which we find several well camouflaged strategic viewing spots and gather Intel, pool all of it and devise a plan of attack once we have reconvened" Marcus quietly proposed much to Brit and Anya's delight which quickly turned into anguish as Brit remembered "It is only opened on the weekend"

"Half an equation is better than nothing we walk around its perimeter take notes and return later tonight" Marcus reassured his colleagues

"Binoculars would be nice" Brit commented as they were short on equipment

"There is an army surplus store in Oslo, we can easily pick up whatever we need" Anya vividly recollected as it was one of her favourite stores a thirty minute drive away from their present location. Eryk Sanstorm's Hunting for Survival housed all manner of goods specific to its trading name. The owner although battle scarred was a bright and breezy non judgemental soul ready at all times to share his knowledge and experiences with anyone.

"Ah Anya a delight to set eyes on you again" He merrily said as Anya and the group entered his well appointed shop

"Likewise" She warmly answered

"Window shopping for something special.....?" Eryk eagerly asked as Anya was one of his prized customers who invariably sought the unusual and expensive

"Powerful night n day not made in China binoculars times four"
Anya answered

"American, British, German....?"

"The latter please"

"At once, I have three to choose from" Eryk replied as he signalled
for Anya and her friends to follow him to where the exclusive were
catered for

"You must spend a lot of money here" Marcus dryly said as he
scanned the shop's surveillance system

"Yes and no, Eryk was a fellow FSK agent, we were involved in a
number of dangerous missions together unfortunately one of which
went terribly wrong and caused him great bodily harm" Anya sadly
reported

"Yet it hasn't outwardly dampened his spirits" Brit observed

"It would appear so" Anya agreed yet she knew differently as it
was a matter of Eryk not knowing when to let go

"Here we are ladies and gentlemen the good stuff kept under
lock and key for privileged eyes only, military grade designed to spy
and not be spied upon, excellent for tracking wild life and the occasional nudist if that is your fancy" Eryk brightly said as he displayed
what he had on offer

"Behind that door is that where you keep the latest advances"
Marcus asked as he pointed to a door to the left of them

"Perhaps you could be more specific"

"Russian made blue ray listening device" Marcus flatly replied

"Does such an animal exist?" Eryk asked playing dumb

"Only if you attended by invitation only the most recent M.I.N.T
convention" Marcus explained

"M.I.N.T standing for military innovative novel therapeutics"
Eryk appeared to guess

"Precisely"

"Can't say I have"

"Then obviously it comes to you by alternate routes" Marcus

said in a fashion that insisted on finding out more

"The purpose of acquiring such an instrument....?" Eryk forcibly asked

"Certainly not to record the mating call of the one legged Norwegian kingfisher nor the scrawny Scandinavian mallard" Marcus cuttingly answered

"What then....?"

"More along the lines of detecting voices associated with different cultures" Marcus cryptically replied

"It is unfortunate that we have become a multicultural nation"

"Irrespective of that, do you have the said item" Marcus bluntly asked

"In a variety of colours designed to match the clothes one is wearing, but I warn you it is expensive!"

"One always expects to pay for quality" Marcus quietly replied

"Speaking of which the instrument is extremely sensitive and will pick up all noises up to two kilometres way, thankfully it has features that filter out background noise for improved clarity and accuracy" Eryk proudly confirmed

"Trust the Russians, speaking of whom, what do you know about a 'leaf'?" Marcus asked changing the subject

"I have heard rumblings" Is all that Eryk was prepared to say

"I thought as much" Marcus said in a neutral fashion

"Perhaps we can talk about it another day when you have completed your little operation, where was it you were going?" Eryk foolishly asked

"That's classified information"

"Thought as much" Eryk answered as he left Marcus to walk into an adjoining room in which the latest advances in warfare were stored and heavily disguised. He returned within a short period of time carrying a back pack specific for outdoor adventures "Here we are your latest toy cleverly assembled to make it look as innocent as possible. The power source and electronic recording equipment are securely housed in the large compartment, the off/on switch sewn into the front straps, lastly emitter and receiver are located in the front panel of your deerstalker hat, completely wireless, with binoculars you look the part"

"What might that be?" Marcus asked

"Bird watcher of course all you need is some nice turf to explore of which there is plenty about" Eryk replied as though he knew of something secret and sinister

"Care to enlighten me" Marcus asked

"I believe we both know where sir and his group will be going" Eryk smartly replied

"Then it's hunting hats all around...." Anya suggested after over hearing part of their conversation

"If you could step this way I am certain we can find you suitable attire to complement your appearance, a shirt of two would be in order to give that rugged outdoor appearance" Eryk said as he rubbed his hands together and took Anya and her friends to the clothing section.

Twenty minutes later they were ready to depart and did so in Gerhardt's powerful Mercedes. It was a pleasant 40km drive to the Bygdoy peninsula. The farm was situated in the middle of the landmass which was mainly for the obscenely wealthy and fashionable but not entirely as the peninsula has many parks, forests and beaches that included a nudist colony which Eryk had previously subtly alluded to. Gerhardt drove in a south westerly direction until he accessed Christian-Frederiks Drive which bordered the western aspect of the Royal farm and then he parked the car in a heavily wooded area close to the stables and dairy. Once out of the car Marcus fitted the earpiece supplied with his unit into his left ear and switched on the listening device to gauge its sensitivity as he slowly turned 360 degrees on the spot. Satisfied with the results he switched the unit off to conserve power and joined his colleagues.

They walked slowly about using their binoculars now and then as though they had spotted an interesting bird or two and then discussed the merits of their find.

The occasional horse and rider passed them by as they neared the stables and exercise area but paid them no heed apart from the customary nod of the head.

Marcus stopped and focused his binoculars on several trees surrounding the complex and then lowered his head to listen into what might be occurring of importance at the stables. A window of opportunity presented itself when he heard a brief fragmented discussion about the use of ethanol with respect to rabbit fever and its spread.

"We are definitely in the right place" He whispered without letting on why "Let's keep moving and see what the dairy has to offer"

It was quite a trek to the dairy, this time they walked on the other side of the road and stopped now and then to study the birdlife in the adjoining forest so as not to attract any undue attention. The dairy was situated further away from the fence bordering the complex just over the 2km distance the blue ray listening device was capable of reaching which meant Marcus had difficulty in making out any sense of what he had faintly heard, it didn't matter however as the team could speculate on what was recorded in the confines of their car later on especially as dusk was starting to fall.

Knowing full well that the affluent peninsula would be heavily patrolled by police and private security the foursome headed back to the hotel for a well deserved rest, Aperol spritz and an elegant meal in the hotel's restaurant before attempting to analyse the evidence gathered. They listened to the recordings a number of times making notes and drawing conclusions before they entered into a debate as to the context of the material and their likely next step.

"It is quite clear from the horse stable recordings that experiments are being conducted with respect to ethanol and its effect on rabbit fever which I believe is caused by the bacterium

Francisella tularensis and can be spread to humans via ticks, deer flies or contact with infected animals. The bacterium under investigation is genetically altered in essence a bio-weapon and the concentration of ethanol between 40% to 95% concentration. The altered bacterium it appears is antibiotic resistant unlike the natural one which is easily treated with streptomycin, gentamicin, doxycycline or ciprofloxacin. There are no vaccines available against tularaemia and possibly against the genetically modified one which is likely to be more vigorous and aggressive. Are we all in agreement with my conclusions?" Brit asked as she studied her hand written notes

18
EASY BREAK IN

The responsibility of guarding the Royal family, all of its members and locations was assigned to the Royal Guard an elite subdivision of Norway's FSK. These troops were not to be trifled with and accordingly Anya, Brit, Gerhardt and Marcus would have to be extra careful and diligent in their attempted break in. The Royal farm was not considered to be a prime terrorist target as the Royal family behaved in an ultraconservative manner publically. The group therefore reckoned that there would only be minimal security to patrol the estate as it was portrayed as being low key in its operations.

It was 2.30am in the morning Gerhardt parked the car in a dark secluded spot amongst the trees and the foursome proceeded on foot in a stealth full manner allowing Brit to lead the way as she was familiar with the place, Gerhardt brought up the rear and was determined to stand guard once they reached the dairy. The air was fresh with the smell of animal manure everything was black the only hint of light came from dwellings far away. The group walked on the grass so as not to disturb the flora and fauna, nothing stirred and yet Marcus was doubtful of an easy entry into the facility as a consequence he activated his blue ray listening device, periodically stopping now and then to listen if any danger stood nearby ready to attack them to his right stood horses with menacing eyes to his left docile cows but not one bull. Ahead the building was less inviting the sound of heavy breathing filled is ears, the volume indicated at least three individuals not exactly snoring but then again not exactly breathing normally either.

"What on earth are they doing?" He mentally asked himself as he tried to make sense of the obscure noises

"Why did you stop?" Anya whispered as she turned around

"Bogies ahead not the time for engagement"

"Course of action.....?" Anya asked

"Try alternate entry point" Marcus replied as he continued to check their safety

"Side doors are a go" Anya said as she prodded Brit into action

"Copy that" Brit answered and pointed they change direction to avoid detection. Gerhardt meanwhile studied the horses and cows for any unusual movements. Brit took them via a convoluted path that used obstacles and greenery as cover.

"One side entrance" Brit softly said once they arrived

"Check for booby traps" Gerhardt suggested as he briefly examined the door frame and overhanging eaves

"Affirmative..." Brit answered "Nothing to merit except the door won't budge, it's not locked, just difficult to push open!"

"Perhaps stuff is piled up against it" Gerhardt said as he lent his weight

"Negative it's an emergency fire exit" Brit answered as she and Gerhardt exerted their combined force

"Actually it's a body" Marcus surprisingly said

"Dead or alive....?" Brit asked

"Alive lots of heavy breathing, three of us should be able to shift him sufficiently enough for one of us to squeeze through" Marcus explained as he visualised a male guard lying prostrate face down on the floor

"Won't we wake him?" Brit anxiously asked

"Unlikely he's under the influence of alcohol or drugs or both" Marcus confidently surmised as he remembered reading in a controversial tabloid that off duty Royal guards had engaged in illegal drug parties. Marcus instructed Gerhardt and Brit to line up in front of him and together they exerted their collective strength backwards without any regard for the 'fallen' soldier. The strategy worked very well and soon all four were inside the dairy. There was no need to restrain the Royal guard as he was under the influence of heavy illegal drugs which was also applicable to the other three behind the front entrance. Having adjusted to the darkness Marcus took charge and soon they located a lift and stairwell that would take them into the underground tunnels. He decided on the steep set of stairs as it would not draw any attention unlike the lift irrespective of whether or not the motion sensitive automatic lighting came on. As soon as they stepped inside and the door closed behind them they were immediately bathed in purple light.

"I think we are in the right place" Gerhardt happily deduced

"Disinfecting light" Brit correctly added as she grabbed hold of the handrail and closely followed Marcus who led the way. Three hundred and sixty five steps later they found themselves in the middle of a dusty antechamber from which numerous arms radiated.

"It's not a case of eeny meeny miny, moe, but then one never knows whom we might catch by the toe" Marcus dryly said as he peered down each of the tunnels seeking clues as to their purpose only to discover that the answer lay in the relative cleanliness of the floor." This will do nicely" He said after a while and stepped aside to allow the others to concur.

"I think we all agree" Brit was the first to reply and watched as Marcus stepped into the darkness beyond the passage's mouth. She gingerly followed her eyes straining to capture Marcus's outline which moved smoothly before her unphased by their claustrophobic surroundings, Anya followed a little less troubled whereas

Gerhardt secretly revelled in their surroundings. The tunnel was a good 500meters in length that ended in a bifurcated antechamber.

"Left or right is the question, floor's equally clean, need to look for other clues, no noise please, time to listen down each tunnel and detect clean sounds from afar" Marcus muttered to himself as he stood motionless in front of each bifurcation and allowed his listening device to show him the way "Left it is" He determined and realised how easily he could see in their present location which was beyond his natural abilities "Pilot or standby light of sorts is the only conclusion, cleverly concealed as is its intended operation, sinister or not?" He thought as he considered the safety of the others "Safe to proceed or not, is this a check point before entry?" He wondered as he looked about the antechamber for any wall mounted electronic device that fitted his suspicions

"Was machst du?" Gerhardt asked forgetting that Marcus didn't understand German or so he thought

"Looking for the source of light and maybe an electronic check point" Marcus quietly explained as though the walls had ears something that Gerhardt had already considered consequently he signalled for everyone to say nothing as he realised they had entered a voice recognition chamber which required authorised individuals to repeat a specific descriptive phrase before being allowed to enter the final access tunnel to the underground secret laboratory. Gerhardt communicated his findings to the rest of the group using the appropriate sign language which included the threat of death. He also determined that individuals entering the chamber only had a limited time in which to say the secret phrase which if not done would close off the access tunnel for at least one hour during which time security would come stampeding in. The sound of a door closing indicated that the time was over. The group had two options retreat to where it had come from or wait, see and decide if it could overpower the unknown number of guards that might appear. The question was how many were likely to turn up? Were the drugged four in the dairy above the only ones on duty if so when would they be revived or were more guards idly walking about the estate would they be summoned by an alert code? In any event it was a frustrating waiting game that taxed the group's patience and the urgency of getting things done.

Marcus decided they should all retreat into the access tunnel away from the antechamber in case it was equipped with debilitating laser beams Gerhardt however raised many objections by saying "We will achieve nothing in here, this is a silly move decided by a dumb polack obviously you lack IT knowledge!"

"Considering our circumstances there is no other course of action" Marcus acidly replied

"That is where you are completely wrong. We do not need to know the exact phrase in order to deactivate the shut down and activate the access. We discovered years ago that blah, blah, blah, blah...........creates a repetitive digital sequence usually 1,1,1,1.......... or 2,2,2,2...........or 3,3,3,3.......right up to 9 repeated 7 times that the voice recognition software readily accepts guessing that the people behind the conspiracy think themselves to be superior I suggest we start with number 1 and advance from there....."

"Providing we don't get fried" Marcus interrupted Gerhardt who aloofly ignored Marcus's statement and scrolled through his phone's data base until he located the appropriate digital sequence which he elegantly presented to one of the many concealed wall mounted microphones an exercise that Marcus considered to be more than farfetched, once prompted Gerhardt's phone sung its message of authenticity and the left bifurcation magically came alive an event that almost defied mathematical probability which caused Marcus and Anya to question Gerhardt's true allegiance even more.

The tunnel leading to a door that heralded it was the only entrance into the laboratory was filled with disinfecting light sources sufficiently strong to achieve its goals without permanently blinding any individual Marcos expected another check point at the door which proved correct, a digital keypad required a specific number sequence which Gerhardt easily satisfied an act that fuelled Anya's and Marcus's suspicions no end, they both drew their weapons in readiness for any confrontations once they entered the laboratory. Inside everything was relatively peaceful incubators went about their business generating copious amounts of modified bacteria, whilst banks of refrigerators stood to attention and kept hundreds of filled vials safe in readiness for distribution whereas the packing equipment lay idle. Gerhardt signalled that they should fan out and gather as much evidence as possible and then reconvene within 20 minutes or so. Brit acknowledged his request and immediately starting taking photographs of the manufacturing equipment whereas Anya was more curious about retrieving computer records leaving Gerhardt to stumble about aimlessly and Marcus to follow his instincts all of which was well and good until Marcus in his observant fashion recognised the presence of motion detectors which suggested they had a limited time in which to act before security arrived providing it thought that everyone had left for the day. Having gone their separate ways locating the others would be difficult considering the complexity of the underground complex it was not the time to act chivalrously Brit and Anya could use their FSK badges to bluff their way out saying they were on official business whereas Gerhardt and Marcus needed to utilize other methods of avoiding detection and escape from an area that housed the most sensitive information and most dangerous variants of the bacterium which had not proceeded to the next stage of their development namely large scale production. Marcus per chance found a series of log books pertaining to daily dark experiments that detailed unique ways of weaponizing the bacterium never conceived before which if not recognised earlier enough would cause the rampant disintegration of the society in which it was released.

The data was mesmerising it begged to be devoured which was not appropriate under the circumstances until Marcus paused for a second and remembered his training "do not panic until you see the whites of the enemies eyes" accordingly he re-evaluated his situation with respect to the motion detectors concluding that the Royal guards were not part of surveillance that was privileged information for the villains at play who most likely were housed off campus and who might be so arrogant as to suppose that anyone in the laboratory after hours were bona fide personnel.

The room that Marcus found himself in was an open plan design to allow free flow of information between its occupants, it became apparent to him that it was not restricted to microbiology but included geo-political strategies and military manoeuvres all of which needed to be opened and photographed. Marcus shifted through the bundles of typed data efficiently looking for conclusions and intended actions rather than suggestions and nebulous maybes. It did not escape him that it was heavily influenced by the CIA and Mossad's hidden agendas which he had previously encountered during his active career. This time there was no fancy dossier marked 'Top Secret' instead a handbook entitled 'Eastern Disruptions' authored by Nancy Newdale Secretary of State which judging by its cover appeared to deal with botanical themes. Marcus opened the A5 sized booklet and glossed over the list of chapter headings seemingly innocent until he decided to read and discovered from page 5 onwards a world of double speak, smoke and mirrors and official codes that had been unleashed against defiant nations for decades with one purpose in mind, disrupt, pillage and control using countries both loyal to the west and those who projected themselves as being neutral in order to achieve these ends. Norway was no exception, targeted by the CIA and blackmailed by Mossad into secretly assisting the development of highly infectious bacterium and then facilitating its spread into Russian society to thoroughly demoralise its people, cause widespread fear, panic and distrust of all authority whether it be civil, military or religious, in essence anarchy and the dissolution of society allowing it to be invaded by thieves and vagabonds. Marcus whipped out his Grom issued mobile phone selected a suitably illuminated table with little clutter, set his phone to ultrafast camera mode and proceeded to furiously photograph all of the documents he considered of paramount importance whilst remaining fully alert and vigilant as to his immediate surroundings and beyond.

'Eastern Disruptions' was definitely in Marcus's mind the blueprint for using modified rabbit fever to disrupt Russian society which various chapter headings both suggested and confirmed.

'Psychological abilities of plants'

'Roots that easily fragment avenues'

'Winds that destabilise'

'Gentle dew'

'Manchurian Hills'

'Techniques of sowing malignant plants'

These he read with much disgust until the entire underground complex was plunged unexpectedly into darkness sending Marcus's mind into battle mode which analysed his circumstances no end and came to the following conclusions.

"Most likely a pincher movement, one from each side, activated sleeper cell either two or four assets, donned with night goggles and thermal imagery, hope the others stay still, use their binoculars set to night vision and near field. Best find somewhere warm to stand next to as cover, remain motionless, blend in, to suggest nil intruders, false positive, rat or mouse, security squad moves quietly, special sound minimising footwear, expert at what they do, difficult to detect where they are, except for intermittent strange yellow lights, not red lazar, something different, once broad then narrow, move slowly, predetermined sweep of sensitive areas, routine or a response to our presence, robotic or human, crawling or flying, the former, drones, multiple drones, best avoided until exercise is over, one is here entered my space hope this is low key area not as important as manufacturing and packaging, upright mega-computer shields me well, it's looking directly at me, I return the gaze, binoculars confuse it, reflections of itself befuddle it, it hovers, hesitates, seemingly I fit in, like a jacket hanging on a coat rack, one, two, three it's gone, will it return, unlikely, peace at last, wonder if the others avoided detection, no evidence to the contrary. Most likely a spot search, will our presence set it off again, need to act faster, gather damning evidence and depart, once lights turned back on. Wait, drone is back with its partner, damn, not confused wants clarification from its superior! Difficult to ascertain how well drones are armoured, can't move, must stay put, show no fear, no physiological reaction, coat on hanger that's all I am, boss drone coming my way, multiple beams shot at me, heart rate steady, no panic, no fight, flight or fright response, no adrenergic output, completely relaxed, almost like stuffed animal, no animation, coat and trousers on a rack, nothing to see, go away, the rats want to play, it's agony being here, no time to waste, things to do, people to expose, bloody hell you're being persistent!" Marcus mentally agonised as the boss drone considered its next course of action much like Marcus who realised how important it was for him never to be identified therefore if the drone would not relent he would neutralise the flying robot, its slave and destroy all of its surveillance equipment in the hope that his actions would not cause it to emit a distress signal which it couldn't do once its power supply was disconnected.

Marcus sensed that the boss drone was about to discharge a projectile in order to elicit a response from him but he pre-empted its move by lashing out, seizing the drone by the scruff of its neck and ripping off its externally mounted battery before throwing it at its slave severely disabling it and then violently detaching its external power source without any sense of regret as he knew that his actions in all probability would prevent the lights from coming back on. Marcus then activated his blue ray listening device and went in search of his colleagues whom he hoped were well and intact. He searched high and low in the areas that he last saw them without any success which caused him to think that they had aborted their missions once the lights had gone out and the drones appeared

"Did they evade the electronic assassins or were they captured, confined or worse?" He thought as he slowly scanned all and sundry and reflected on the use of intense yellow light by the boss drone which he had instinctively avoided.

"Two life forms ahead groaning about the dark and not being able to see, perhaps they have lost their binoculars" Marcus thought as he carefully made a beeline to where his comrades had fallen. Both Anya and Brit lay on the ground in the foetal position next to each other in a distraught manner not knowing where they were, what they were doing and who Marcus was.

"Come let's get you on your feet" He gently said in a familiar voice as he helped each one up and then reassured both that they were in safe hands which they gingerly accepted given their fragile status.

"Is it pitch-black in here because I can't see anything?" Brit asked in a shaky voice as she fought back the tears

"Not entirely" Marcus had to say

"Who are you?"

"A friend" Marcus warmly answered realising that both it appeared suffered with memory loss brought about by a traumatic event that begged for urgent attention "Let's get you out of here" He then said forsaking any further evidence collection as he activated his phone to access the site plans he had previously downloaded off the internet. Marcus studied these intensely and formulated the shortest possible way out based on where he thought they were positioned within the underground complex. He sharp analytical mind did not fail him and soon they were able to savour the sweetness of the dew ladened early morning air. Satisfied that there were no impediments to their escape Marcus led both Anya and Brit by the hand out of the farm complex without any respect for Gerhardt as his loyalty was questionable the only hurdle was the fact that Gerhardt had the car keys in his possession. Undaunted by this Marcus arranged for a taxi to ferry them back to the hotel on the pretext he and the girls had too much alcohol amongst other things that night at one of the numerous parties that populated Bygdoy's peninsula such was the lifestyle of Oslo's rich and idle. The driver who turned up was used to such occurrences and made the early morning hours his preferred working time as it allowed him to charge inflated taxi rates which was neither here nor there to Marcus who valued safety over anything else.

"Good party?" The taxi driver jovially asked once Marcus and the girls had made themselves comfortable in the rear seat

"Rather" Marcus dryly answered in a slurred voice

"So I can see" The taxi driver said making reference to Anya's and Brit's blind, paralytic subdued appearance

"Time to put these lovelies to bed"

"A threesome hey......?"

"I wish" Marcus lecherously replied

"Where to....?" The taxi driver asked expecting the destination to be a raunchy nightclub which wasn't the case at all, nevertheless it didn't stop him from making idle chit chat as he drove along much to Marcus's annoyance as he wanted to be back at the hotel sooner than later as it was nearing day break and Marcus had a number of urgent things to do which included obtaining cash for sundry items.

Satisfied that both Anya and Brit were secure and relatively comfortable in the hotel suite master bedroom Marcus sought the services of the hotel's duty manager who greeted him as Marcus approached him

"Good morning Sir"

"Morning, I am in need of some cash" Marcus as a matter of fact said

"Yes Sir we can accommodate your needs, what sort of currencies were you after? The exchange rates are listed on the board behind me"

"Four hundred and thirty seven dollars and seventy nine cents American"

"That's an unusual amount wouldn't Sir like to round it off to say four hundred and forty dollars?"

"Actually no, the person I am doing business with is very peculiar when it comes to sums of money I don't won't to upset him"

"Very well Sir I am certain we can meet your needs once the banks open" The duty manager assured Marcus

"Can I perform the transaction now meaning I make a withdrawal and collect the monies later so as to save time" Marcus suggested

"I cannot see why not just place your card here on the eftpos machine select your account and I will do the rest" The duty manager instructed Marcus as he placed the eftpos machine before him.

As soon as he had performed the transaction Marcus received an encrypted text on his Grom mobile phone which when translated indicated help was on its way and that he should stay put, Accordingly Marcus thanked the duty manager walked to the casual open all hours cafe in the lobby and ordered a double espresso to perk himself up considering how little sleep he had had that day. He reflected on the different possibilities of what might have happened to Gerhardt and couldn't come to a conclusion as to whether or not Gerhardt was an asset or otherwise, he also wondered what complications if any their abandoned Mercedes might create it certainly was not a vehicle of interest nor associated with any crime according to local and international authorities. However one could never be absolutely certain about such matters all that he knew was that time was running out as he felt opposition forces were rapidly increasing in numbers, but then he as a Grom inclusion in the special ops team guaranteed that his movements and safety were at all times closely monitored needless to say help was never far away.

"Good morning Dr Rhodes I believe you requested a second opinion?" Psi Williams said in a low voice as he approached Marcus from behind

"That I did" Marcus truthfully answered as he turned to face his superior

"Have your patients been admitted to hospital?"

"Negative they are confined to our hotel suite"

"They're meaning two or more" Psi Williams asked as he waited for Marcus to stand up

"Affirmative"

"How serious....?" Psi inquired as they walked towards the elevator

"Difficult to say, possibly neurological in nature' Marcus answered once they were inside the vacant lift

"You did the right thing in contacting us" Psi replied with a frown before adding "I need you to fully brief me about where you were and what you were doing"

Marcus instantly obeyed and described the events which he thought were pertinent to the girls afflictions namely the drones seek and destroy mission and how he thought he had evaded injury. Psi listened carefully but did not offer any diagnosis until he had thoroughly examined each FSK agent individually. Both were silently lying in the foetal position and appeared to be in a degree of agony which did not prevent either one from responding to Psi's wishes.

"Can you identify anyone in the room?" Psi asked

"Vaguely" Brit moaned as she struggled with her affliction

"Likewise" Anya whispered as she lay quite still

"What time of day is it?" Psi then asked

"Midnight it's so dark in here "Brit answered in total contradiction to the morning's sunlight as Psi shone a bright pencil light firstly into her open eyes and then into her ears.

"Ouch that hurt" Brit gravely exclaimed much to Psi's surprise as he hadn't touched any part of her ear and consequently it confirmed his suspicions about her condition

"Apart from a diagnosis we can't help these two damsels immediately" Psi concluded

"Hospital transfer....?" Marcus guessed

"As soon as possible"

"Life threatening.....?" Marcus nervously inquired

"If left untreated perhaps, otherwise reversible"

"Diagnosis"

"Total retinal blackout caused courtesy of Yellow Peril Resources"

"Who are they?"

"Experimental weaponry company based in Taiwan which concentrates on manufacturing light based weapons of incredible intensity which you experienced and thankfully avoided but not so for your colleagues. Pulses of intense yellow light freeze retinal rods and cones and paralyse the optic nerve resulting in total retinal blackout hence no images reaching the brain's visual cortex and furthermore scrambling the sensory cortex which in turn adversely affects the memory centre resulting in the past twenty five days of memory being erased. The antidote is one of counteracting this phenomenon by exposing the patient to red light in the near infrared part of the light spectrum followed by green light in the ratio of 7 to 3 providing it is done within twenty four hours of exposure luckily we brought with us the appropriate equipment as these assaults are becoming increasingly frequent" Psi explained as he stood up to face Marcus who could not hide his anxiety

"Don't worry they will be fine by tomorrow" Psi reassured Marcus

"What now?"

"We take the girls downstairs to the SUV and transport them to our secret hideaway" Psi calmly answered as he gestured for Marcus to help Anya out of bed and carefully assist her by walking arm in arm out of the hotel whilst Psi attended to Brit. Their movements attracted no undue attention and soon Psi's chauffeur whisked them away allowing Marcus to breathe a sigh of relief.

19
LIGHT SPARKLES

When Psi said secret hideaway Marcus instinctively knew he meant somewhere lavish most probably an exclusive secluded clinic catering for the likes of the vain and rich. Light Sparkles was exactly that, a cosmetic retreat that guaranteed to take years off your appearance irrespective of your age. It was one of Grom's many retail outlets that tapped into the persistent vanity of middle aged corporate individuals in order to siphon off funds for more noble causes. Psi instructed his chauffeur to discretely park in one of the allocated bays reserved for wealthy clients at the rear of the clinic, within minutes of doing so two orderlies dressed in immaculate white uniforms emerged pushing empty wheelchairs intended for Brit and Anya. Marcus watched as the girls were taken away and wondered if he would ever see them again.

"Fretting about them will not get the job done" Psi said in a fatherly tone of voice once he returned from instructing the orderlies as to the girls needs

"I suppose not" Marcus reluctantly replied angry that he had lost three operatives and that he could have done more to prevent that from happening

"Then let us begin, we have yanks to kick up the arse and a LEAF to recover" Psi said with a wry smile as he gestured for Marcus to re-enter the USV

"Where to now...?" Marcus asked

"Depends on what you brought us from the lab, you did acquire some physical evidence I trust?" Psi strongly asked

"In a manner that reflects my training, however is now an inappropriate time and place to exhibit my wares" Marcus cryptically replied

"Very well we will endeavour to find you somewhere more suitable away from prying eyes" Psi replied and grinned at the chauffeur who knew exactly where to drive which Marcus expected would be glamorous. The chauffeur did not disappoint and soon they were in the more exclusive part of Oslo where they parked outside of Hamaritz Surgical House where the experts went to purchase the latest in operating theatre equipment.

"Just what the doctor ordered" Marcus quipped as he gazed at the impressive building made more so by its large window displays and the merchandise inside

"Our Scandinavian flagship" Psi remarked as he led the way into the building and up a flight of stairs at the top of which sat a brooding security guard well equipped to deal with any situation. The security guard and Psi locked eyes, acknowledges each other like old school chums and continued on with their business.

"In here gentlemen" Psi said as he opened a door belonging to a large presentation room before saying "Make yourselves comfortable whilst I organize coffee, Marcus give Patryk your phone and he will download and print off whatever you recorded in the secret underground laboratory, thank you" Marcus obliged, unlocked his phone and handed it to the chauffeur who expertly connected it to a computer before sitting down. Psi returned shortly afterwards with a tray ladened with fresh pastries and Vienna coffee.

"Marcus you have the floor...enlighten us" Psi said as the chauffeur handed a remote control to Marcus who clicked on import pictures and waited for the computer to respond

"What we are about to see and read is also new to me. Our preliminary findings based on audio recordings at the royal farm according to Brit's understanding is that biological experiments were conducted which altered rabbit fever bacteria into becoming totally antibiotic resistant but more importantly enabling the same bacteria to use ethanol as a food source ranging between 40% to 95% content without any negative effect on the bacteria. In essence the use of ethanolic hand sanitizers will facilitate the spread of the disease once released into the community causing widespread panic and distrust of all authorities. After we penetrated the underground facility with the invaluable help of Gerhardt we discovered a sophisticated microbiological manufacturing facility. Britt went about photographing it Anya I believe preoccupied herself with obtaining computer records whilst I concentrated on the tactical room"

"I'll stop you there for a moment, I have both of the girls mobile phones we can examine these later, please continue" Psi said pausing Marcus's presentation

"In the tactical room I came across a book titled 'Eastern Disruptions' by Nancy Newdale Secretary of State arguably a CIA blueprint for regime overthrow as these photographs demonstrate. From the following slides we can read that the tacticians kept a close eye on the weaponisation of the rabbit fever bacteria which it appears has reached a critical stage of development. The associated tables and graphs clearly show the exponential growth in numbers with increasing ethanol concentration there is no plateauing. The bacterium can easily be spread by drinking contaminated fluids or in this case alcoholic drinks which this slide suggests, at the bottom of which the death rate associated with this disease increases from 60% to 95%. Furthermore from a military aspect aerosols are another avenue of delivery, highly infective needing only two to ten bacteria to infect individuals either orally or nasally, highly incapacitating, on the downside it needs to be treated very carefully by soldiers carrying the weapon otherwise they will exterminate themselves. In comparison to the previous Schu S4 strain known as 'Agent UI' it is superior in all respects, a proper killer microbe! The primary target is Russia, means of delivery, bottled vodka, no one will suspect vodka as being the causative agent as ethanol has always been considered a disinfectant, Any one suggesting otherwise without laboratory proof will be laughed at, this slide shows numerous disjointed notes, scribbling which I can read are preoccupied with blackmailing a distiller into supplying the bottled vodka. 'Fjord Fantasy' has been ticked as a likely assist. Also note on another piece of paper the doubling rate for the bacterium, at room temperature it various between ten to forty minutes, between 5° and 8° it is between three to eight hours, once the food source is exhausted it will slowly die or encapsulate itself and leave a sediment which in all likelihood will render it unattractive in any case there may be nothing more than water left behind. Hence a technical hurdle to overcome. One solution lies in a lid which is specially designed to accommodate inoculums and sealed over with a fragile hymen much like a virgin. Unscrewing the lid breaks the seal and seeds the vodka allowing the germs to proliferate and infect the unsuspecting individuals" Marcus said as he flicked through the various photographs he had taken.

"Perhaps the Achilles heel of the entire operation" Patryk deduced

"Yes and no, the trick will be to get the size of the inoculums correct, it needs to be small as the bacteria is particularly virulent. Remember it only needs two to 10 microbes to infect people and later on those who develop pneumonia will spread it aerially. Another delivery device is the inclusion of an object resembling a miniature potato, a clever marketing tool to stimulate sales much like the worm in tequila. Potato Palinka is something I came across whilst shifting through a pile of papers"

"Such a name would be very appealing to the Russian mentality" Psi interrupted visibly pleased with Marcus's efforts "Especially if appears to be a home grown product" Psi determined as he gestured for Patryk to download whatever Brit and Anya had managed to record on their mobile phones prior to being compromised by the killer drones. This allowed Marcus to take a break and appreciate the fact that under duress neither girl had 'lost' her phone but he wondered why Anya hadn't been able to activate her 'arse' system of defence. Within minutes a kaleidoscope of high definition images showing all aspects of rabbit fever incubation, separation and packaging flooded the large LED display screen culminating in a photo that said it all namely hundreds of nugget shaped baby 'potatoes' awaiting delivery.

"Quite a neat operation, if you will Patryk let's see what Anya found" Psi said as the photo show came to a close and they waited for Patryk to present Anya's findings which did not disappoint but rather complimented and cemented that the delivery device was in fact Potato Palinka assembled on the outskirts of St Petersburg using Russian vodka making it look as though the terrorist act was orchestrated by separatists.

"A very clever design, 'potato' dangling by a thread in the neck of the bottle, once it is unscrewed 'potato' falls in, disintegrates and reproduction is activated producing a lethal cocktail. Did you by any chance obtain samples of the 'potatoes'"? Psi asked Marcus who responded in the negative

"No matter we can use the images as a template I can safely say that you have completed your mission extremely well"

"That's it? I feel as though I have achieved nothing!" Marcus replied a little disgruntled

"Precisely, we operate to make someone else look good" Psi reminded him

"Who might that be?" Marcus asked fishing for answers

"Leave that up to us, your mission however is not over, you are merely being reassigned"

"To what" Marcus asked aggressively

""Retrieve the LEAF"

"Surely it must have disappeared by now?" Marcus concluded

"Not necessarily, there are many players each wondering what the others know in relation to the LEAF's whereabouts' Psi answered

"What sort of information will you give me before I am thrown to the dogs" Marcus cuttingly asked

"23 Malmskill Crescent Stockholm"

"Where I will find?" Marcus abruptly asked

"Dark Pebble offices occupied by several shady characters of the extinguishing variety" Psi replied matter of fact

"Mossad in other words"

"Whom we have been shadowing with limited success sufficiently adequate to suggest the LEAF resides there and will do so until things quieten down. You won't be going alone as it is one of our primary targets now that we have discovered the importance of the potato 'nuggets'" Psi answered unsympathetically

It did not come as any surprise to Marcus that the likely residence of the LEAF according to Psi was Stockholm because it all made sense in that even the Swedes had not made much ado about the extensive mountain weapon depot they were obvious partners in crime with the Americans and most probably the Israeli's as well and therefore Marcus questioned the significance of his supposedly 'secret' unit and its true purpose which he concluded was to test the security of what was truly happening in Norway. Furthermore he could not discount the fact that his selection was most probably payback for all of the past successful missions that Grom had conducted in Syria, Yemen, Iraq and Iran which were considered as contrary to the wishes of the west. This exercise was no different, like it or not, Marcus was involved in protecting Russia as a consequence he needed to be doubly vigilant about his safety and those around him so he thought. Marcus watched in admiration as Psi Williams' technical group worked very quickly and diligently in one of the secluded back rooms of Hamritz Surgical House using all manner of established and new techniques that incorporated 3D printers to generate the 'potato nuggets' and kanvas software to print off a ritzy Potato Palinka authentic label for the spirit bottles which were filled with 45% ethanol made by diluting 95% laboratory ethanol with triple distilled spring water fit for any discerning spirit connoisseur. Once labelled and loaded the bottles were carefully packed into straw filled wooden boxes that featured a sliding Perspex lid with a large skull and crossbones imprinted upon it suggesting death lay within.

Marcus mentally applauded the technical efforts as he considered his own strategy in rescuing the LEAF and or its owner but as it was nearing 2pm and his blood sugar had fallen his thinking became a little clouded and he nudged Psi in the hope that lunch was not far away.

"My apologies I forgot that an army only marches well on a full stomach. Come with me" Psi warmly responded as he indicated for both Marcus and Patryk to follow him to the complex's well equipped common room which offered numerous culinary delights plus intimate dining areas. Marcus and Patryk chose carefully as each knew that hunger causes bad choices. Psi waited patiently for his operatives to regain their mental clarity before engaging in any further conversation.

"Tonight gentlemen we play the Grim Reaper dressed as Santa Claus albeit delicately as Marcus's previous actions have complicated matters to some extent meaning we cannot deliver any 'gifts' to various Ministers offices as a car bomb made a mess of parliamentary square leaving us with the daunting task of home delivers under a cloud of uncertainty as security might remain tight. The targets to be precise that we had in mind are; the head of the cult Disciples of Tyr, the Minister for the Interior, The Minister for Justice, the offices of Mosaic and Dark Pebble, each 'gift' will have an appropriate greeting card attached neither religious nor wishing the recipient 'happy holidays' instead somewhat sinister along the lines of 'Leave!', 'Traitor!', 'Resign!', 'Bad Investment!' All 'gifts' must be delivered simultaneously, Marcus Patryk will drive you to Stockholm tonight you will leave around midnight, a six hour journey by car, no plane flights available, train and bus is horrific almost twelve hours with multiple changeovers" Psi slowly said as he observed Marcus and Patryk's reaction to his proposals

"That's all well and good providing every recipient had full knowledge of what is brewing beneath the Royal Diary if not then their reaction might become one of collectively shouting 'terrorism' on the other hand if they are actively aware and engaged our efforts may strike a nerve causing them to realise their plans have been exposed and therefore an alternative is needed including doubly their efforts in all departments concerned in effect we will achieve nothing!" Marcus coldly answered

"Rather good predictive thinking on your part"

"Thank you" Marcus replied accepting Psi's compliment

"Anything else to add...?" Psi asked with a smile

"There is no evidence in the official Norwegian parliamentary records of any opposition, protest, argument or dissatisfaction in allowing American troops to inhabit Norwegian soil, nor invitation for public comment, submissions or any media reaction of any sorts, it's almost as if the entire operation has been designed as an extended visit by foreign troops. I understand you want me to visit Dark Pebble offices and it would seem without Intel or backup, question, how tight is its security and how many Mossad agents will I encounter?"

"That is a matter for you to determine, our resources in Scandinavia are light on" Psi replied much to Marcus's annoyance

"Very well then it would seem that I shall have to rely on myself" Marcus emphatically stated

"You have my full blessing" Psi Williams said abruptly leaving Patryk rather amused

"Guess it's your call" Patryk said

"Hasn't it always been?"

"Can't say since I don't know you that well" Patryk correctly answered and also abruptly took his leave leaving Marcus the opportunity of further predictive thinking which he quickly slipped into inorder to devise a move that took into consideration all gathered evidence and strategies. It was a very satisfying and rewarding past time much like creative writing with a twist namely reality and not fiction. His well conceived modus operandi would take place at exactly the same time that Psi had instructed his other agents except Marcus would not be travelling to Stockholm instead he would concentrate his efforts in Oslo. Content with his plan Marcus spent his time accessing the access points of the estate he would ultimately penetrate until Psi and Patryk joined him for dinner.

"All sorted?" Psi asked as he approached Marcus

"In detail"

"Excellent....equipment needs?"

"Backpack, four bottles of Palinka, night goggles, tempered stainless steel multifunction knife, extra magazines, jacket that the Major gave me run of the mill middle class car"

"Is that all?" Psi asked

"Minimal needs maximum results Sir!" Marcus replied deadpan

"Very well, join me in the technical room after dinner, I'm certain we can accommodate your needs" Psi answered before seeing what was on offer which was designed to satisfy the appetites of at least fifty healthy workers who rapidly formed a queue once they had finished work for the day

"I don't think that so many worked here" Marcus said as he counted heads

"It's a big operation, goods in, goods out, internet sales, telephone sales, field reps, etc, etc"

"So I gather' Marcus said acting quite surprised as he accepted a dinner plate offered to him by Psi

"This better not be your last supper" Psi said off the cuff as he hoped Marcus had not bitten off more than he could chew

"The same thought had crossed my mind. Time will tell" Marcus genuinely answered as he admired the spread of food before them and wondered how well Brit and Anya were being cared for and their likely recovery.

Being highly self disciplined once Marcus had collected his goods and told where to locate his car, Marcus made himself comfortable in the common room to gain some rest in anticipation of an adrenaline filled early morning adventure.

20
WEED KILLERS

Whilst Psi's other operatives went about delivering complimentary bottles of Potato Palinka in all manner of ways that defied logic, Marcus made a bee line to the Royal Palace situated on a rise, the Bellevue at one end of Oslo's main thoroughfare Karl Johns Gate. Once there he carefully navigated his way around avoiding the Israeli, Estonian and Canadian embassies to park in a dark corner at Queen Sonya's Art Stable. Access to the extensive grounds was easy, a rusty waist high gate was all that hindered nothing more as there was nothing of value to steal apart from machinery which was securely locked away, most of the security was centred about and around the Palace in close proximity, it was there that Marcus would have to be careful as there were three units responsible for overall security. The Department of Security, the Norwegian Royalty Protection Unit and His Majesty the Kings Guard. Marcus determined that the Departmental Security patrolled the grounds leaving the other two to take care of the Palaces interior.

What was in his favour was the dreary weather, cold biting winds, dark cloud filled moonless sky sufficient to keep the hardiest at bay and yet not so for in the distance Marcus could make out various bright red tunics darting about.

"Just what I didn't need, interfering Canadian Mounties, why couldn't they just stay at home!?" Marcus cursed as he watched the exchanged law enforcers perform their simple assignments, which involved a squad of them jogging past Sonya's Art Stable dangerously close to where Marcus was hiding before tiptoeing through Dronning Park and jogging to the main checkpoint to make certain that the guard on duty was not asleep which they did by encircling the command post and proudly singing the Mounties Song.

"Nothing more than a diversion" Marcus reasoned as he carefully looked about for any stragglers who were the real danger to thieves and vagabonds. Three in total passed him by each meticulously examined everything in their path but not one detected his presence as he had blended into the background thanks to the gillie jacket based on octopus technology the Major had given him a few days previous complete with hood, balaclava and modified ski goggles. Marcus would not budge until the night returned to its deafening silence.

Marcus remained motionless and concentrated on the noises that the Mounties made as they left the command post and zigzagged their way through the Palace Park back to the Embassy for a quick debrief and hot coffee.

"So much for today's entertainment" Marcus mumbled incoherently as he waited for any further developments such as another cohort of Mounties coming from the opposite direction. After twenty minutes of waiting no such event was forthcoming.

Confident that it was all clear Marcus walked briskly towards Dronning Park where a variety of statues populated the greenery affording him numerous opportunities in which to hide but it also meant that it was ideal for sinister forces to inhabit and patrol. Marcus decided not to venture through the park but instead bypass it altogether and cautiously advance to the rear of the Palace where the staff entrance was located. As he neared the building the image of the Palace changed giving the impression to the casual observer that the lower ground windows somehow magically shifted to the right and then returned to their original positions. Knowing full well that he had not ingested any hallucinogenic substances Marcus quickly deduced that highly sophisticated guards awaited him wearing Gillie suits identical to his own and he instinctively fell to the grass and remained prostrate with weapon drawn. In effect he had become a mound of grass.

Even though Marcus was well camouflaged he was aware that his backpack might draw some attention accordingly he carefully drew it close to his body, wrapped his arms around it and strained his hearing to pick up the slightest noise that shouted 'Danger protect yourself'! Several of the statues unexpectedly came to life and systematically started scouring the grounds using intense headlamps mounted on top of their bullet proof helmets much to Marcus's frustration as he had wished for an uneventful entry into the Palace. Something had obviously spooked the come alive statues and he briefly wondered if he had done something carelessly wrong to cause it, irrespective of that Marcus made certain his trusty Glock would answer any threat in a clear and precise manner. Marcus chose to remain prostrate and thought he was sufficiently distant to avoid detection even though the headlamps' light beams could easily penetrate the darkness which they did so coming within centimetres of his body until several of them pinpointed the culprits' ironically wild foxes in search of a rabbit or two. Then and only then did the lights go out allowing Marcus a moment of respite, time in which to revise his strategy.

"Black is back, perhaps they ate changing to night goggles, what awaits me now from here to there, perimeter so far heavily guarded, I'm out in the open not a good place be, not a good idea to adopt an upright stance, need to keep low at all times and if necessary slither along until I reach the main building" He thought and started his arduous procession towards the rear of the Palace where he hoped no one was waiting for him. Marcus's decision to remain low proved immensely beneficial because with four hundred metres to go he encountered numerous low level laser beams designed to detect and neutralize.

"Cunning bastards, what lies next in store for me?" Marcus questioned as he admired the lengths to which the various departments had gone in order to protect the King or was it more than that? Did royalty really require this level of protection?

"Next question are the come alive statues in Dronning stationary or are they floaters in other words have I been detected and am being expertly shadowed? Am I safe or fragile?" He continued to think as he slowly crept along on his belly towards the rear of the Palace

Marcus occasionally raised his head in anticipation of a drone attack as these he considered to be the weapon of choice by spineless wonders those who were afraid to do battle face to face. He also looked for any concealed motion detectors which were none even though the rear car park was full of exotic and mundane cars, a perfect place in which to hide.

"Snap, crackle, pop is not the giveaway sounds I wanted to hear!" Marcus grumbled as he gingerly stepped onto the noisy gravel that covered the rear courtyard and parking lot

"No way of avoiding it, however side steps minimize the volume, one last detail unresolved, what is my exit plan considering how many bodies have swept past me in the last hour, furthermore are anyone or more of these cars before me inhabited by drunks, fornicators or snipers?" Marcus thought as he kept low and avoided vehicles that he perceived to be evil and did so until he determined the shortest possible route to a staff entrance which was reserved for kitchen hands and after hour's deliveries. Then and only then would he advance and make it look as though he had just emerged from one of the vehicles and was about to deliver a packet of goods, Marcus walked tip toe across the noisy pebbles so as not to wake up the dead or those who might be artificially nearing that phase of life, he held his back pack close allowing his jacket to perform its duty as he ascended the stairs to access the near porch which was adorned with potted shrubbery. Two heavily armed guards dressed in jungle greens emerged from either side of him, one immediately barked into his communications device

"Main gate one, you cleared anyone in past five minutes?"

"Nope"

"Possible code 2 bogey...... repeat code 2 bogey....!"

"Copy that" The main gate guard on duty acknowledged which made Marcus think that his equipment had failed and he decided to stay put where he was namely half way up the stairs a suitable platform from which to launch an attack consequently he crouched down to minimise his surface area, tensed his muscles in anticipation and closely monitored the guards' movements.

The guards strutted about the porch looking for the intruder who for all intents and purposes had suddenly disappeared. Thinking that his mate had over reacted to the medication he was on the other more rational guard signalled that they should abandon the exercise. In complete and absolute defiance his mate rudely put up five fingers to indicate five minutes more and continued to feverously sweep the area a behaviour that Marcus knew quite well would impede his progress.

Marcus needed a diversion, a distraction to facilitate entry into the Palace, causing a commotion was out of the question as it would encourage more guards to arrive, the waiting game was the best option until the genuine deliveries arrived to satisfy the day's needs. Accordingly when the coast was clear Marcus slinked his way to hide behind the shrubbery where no guard had taken up residence, luckily Marcus had timed it well in all respects, managing to avoid detection and being in the right place at the right time to piggy back food deliveries when they arrived.

The relentless cold winds eventually took their toll on the guards who suddenly gave up the chase once their adrenaline had run out and they retreated back into their makeshift home behind the shrubbery much like homeless people which amused Marcus no end. As the clock neared 5.45am Marcus could detect stirrings within the Palace, it was obvious that the kitchen came alive and wait staff came on duty to dust and set the tables for a royal breakfast, it also meant that fresh produce was not far away. By 6am the rumblings of a heavy duty food transport vehicle could be felt by one and all on the rear porch, Marcus watched as one of the Palace's rear doors opened as the truck reversed towards the Palace's rear steps and two young men emerged once it came to a halt to open up the rear of the truck and activate its hydraulic lift which was ladened with neatly packed boxes of fresh fruit, vegetables, dairy product, meat and fish. The young men were permitted only to deliver the produce to the porch no further, Palace servants stood ready to shoulder the boxes inside and store them in the cool room. Marcus emerged from his hiding place quickly inserted himself amongst the staff and slipped inside avoiding colliding with any of the staff as they industriously buzzed about shunting him to and fro causing him to think more deeply about how many guards inhabited the rear porch was it four and not two Marcus gravely concluded, he could account for two in jungle greens but what of the others were they with him now, in front, behind, next to, how would he deal with them. Luckily he had an advantage namely his multicoated ski goggles that identified life in its various forms.

Marcus severely criticised himself for not having worn these earlier for they would have shown him the number of adversaries he might have encountered but then he had a great deal to consider nevertheless he continued to chastise himself for not being 110% attentive in the most reactive way which became more urgent as the army of servants forced him to take shelter in the vast cool room. Marcus instinctively hid his backpack behind a stack of fresh fish packed in ice and waited for the commotion to die down before making his next move. There was no one else in the cool room so he thought until he caught sight of a whisper of water vapour from someone's breath not far away followed by a malicious snigger that suggested Marcus had walked into a trap. He slowly brought his hand up to his face and attempted to activate the ski goggles by pressing what he thought to be an on/off switch without any success.

"How can they see me? If I can't see them, is it thermal recognition that they are using? That can't work my clothes have been 'frozen' by the weather outside I blend in here, I am as cold as the rest of the goods stored in here, there is nothing to make me stand out" Marcus confidently concluded as he kept an eagle eye out for any sudden movement or water vapour trails. "Should be interesting when the lights go out" He postulated as he predicted once the cool room door closed the lights would automatically shut off after thirty seconds casting the room into pitch blackness it was then that his ski goggles worked and he could see everything in minute detail including the presence of two foreign speaking spies who stood next to each other one brandishing a special forces knife the other a rope with numerous bits of embedded scalpel blades designed to inflict the deepest cuts much like a shark attack leaving the victim to bleed to death. Marcus realised these were two very dangerous individuals, professional killers of the highest calibre, there was no room for error should he engage them, something that was unavoidable because sooner or later it had to happen if he were to succeed in his mission. Marcus was particularly afraid of the rope with the embedded scalpel blades because if it found itself around his neck it was game over, to a lesser extent if it attacked his upper arm or thigh and severed a major artery. His gillie jacket offered some protection but how much was a topic of conjecture.

Marcus stood quietly and observed the two highly trained assassins struggle with their night vision as their night vision goggles proved useless in the extremely dark conditions. They vaguely knew where he was but could not reach him without being exposed, they would have to rely on one point in time namely when someone else entered the room and the lights came on for a brief second or two their prey namely Marcus would stand naked before his gillie suit merged him into the background prior to that they could only guess where he was located and would have to rely on sounds as a way of tracking him something that Marcus was keenly aware of and as a consequence he edged his way towards the door as quickly and silently as he could for he calculated he had about three to four minutes before one of the cook's assistants came rushing in to raid the larder.

Marcus didn't have to wait too long, soon came the noise of the sliding door rumbling on its track, the footsteps of four chatty people plus a blaze of light sufficient enough to dazzle temporarily allowing Marcus to seamlessly blend in with his background and the uniforms of the kitchen hands and slip outside completely unnoticed leaving his assassins snookered, befuddled and behind.

Marcus kept his back to the wall and side stepped along though a series of corridors, stopping now and then to allow staff to pass without recognising his presence which included the most meticulous house cleansers who could and would notice the slightest thing out of place. Apart from one or two individuals who stopped to look twice and think hard about the anomaly they had encountered Marcus's progress was uneventful. His homework suggested he would have to reach the main foyer from which radiated several arms that led to different spheres of activity which included the King's private rooms for receiving distinguished guests and discussing all manner of political issues national and inter-national plus those of a dubious nature. Marcus knew that both the corridor and entrance to the King's office would be guarded whilst the King occupied them and to a lesser extent when he was absent.

Judging by the smells emanating from the kitchen breakfast was not far away which meant unless there was a dumb waiter servicing His Majesty's rooms a breakfast trolley accompanied by one or two waitresses would soon be coming Marcus's way. It also suggested that extra guards might accompany the waitresses to make certain no additions of any sort were made to the array of food on offer.

"Two's company three's a crowd, one that I need to get into" Marcus strategically thought as he calculated his chances of not only penetrating the King's rooms but dealing with an unknown number of armed personnel both inside and outside. Certainly a good ploy if he could not capture the King quickly would be taking one of the waitresses hostage whilst he made his case to a King who was either innocent or guilty, informed or ignorant of the facts surrounding the American 'invasion' of Norway providing Marcus was not detected beforehand in which case a gun battle was likely to occur. Such were his thoughts once he reached the main entrance foyer which was deserted in all respects much to Marcus's surprise, instead of relying on his memory Marcus decided to follow the breakfast trolley once it arrived as it was more than likely intended to satisfy His Majesty's insatiable desires.

From the right a solitary shapely waitress wearing a suspender belt, black stockings and no visible underwear appeared and gently pushed a breakfast trolley which was flanked by two immaculately uniformed King's Guards one of whom stopped at the entrance to the corridor leading to His Majesty's private rooms while the other walked to the end and stood guard at the door after he had determined that the rooms were secure. Marcus followed at a safe distance and then rapidly caught up when the King's Guardsman emerged from the Royal rooms. It was then that Marcus recognised the scent of the woman whom he had observed arguing with the arms dealers some days ago and he wondered if she was one and the same.

The King's private rooms were more like a series of interconnecting suites complete with luxurious carpets, furniture and priceless pieces of Scandinavian art. The windows double glazed with bullet proof glass allowed uninterrupted views of the spectacular rose gardens and the forests in the distance. The curtains were open allowing the early morning light to enter and entertain.

Marcus retreated to a corner that allowed him to hide and observe.

The King a handsome man in his early fifties emerged from one of the adjoining rooms and immediately flew to the waitresses, embraced her passionately whilst his tongue erotically played with hers and his hands fondled her private parts causing her to swoon with delight. She did not resist and allowed him to carry her to a couch where she took the initiative and performed expert fellatio until he could not hold back any further and he discharged his manly reproductive juices into her eager mouth.

Marcus remained unphased by what he had just witnessed as all it did was give him an insight into the Kings psychological profile.

Oblivious to the fact that someone was watching them the King and his waitress fondled and kissed in the afterglow of their love-making which came to an abrupt ending once Marcus cleared his throat and deactivated his unique gillie suit ,leaving him visible but not identifiable.

The King and waitress jumped to their feet, the waitress pulled her skirt down to hide her modesty and then wiped her mouth to remove any traces of her pleasure whilst the King holstered his sexual weapon and adjusted his clothing.

"What do you want?" The King bellowed fearing that Marcus had come to do harm

"A moment of your time"

"I don't deal with the uninvited never mind terrorists!" The King cuttingly replied

"You shouldn't rely on appearances" Marcus cautioned as he could see that the King was desperately trying to remember where the panic button was located

"Then why are you here?" The King calmly asked as he attempted to ascertain how many weapons Marcus was carrying if any at all in which case the King held the advantage. Marcus ignored the King's analytical stare and unbuttoned his tunic to reveal the Glock that was housed inside his trouser waistband

"You come well equipped!" The King nervously observed

"Sufficient for my survival needs, more importantly I am here to safeguard yours irrespective of your innocence or guilt!"

"I don't know what you are talking about!" The King falsely replied which Marcus easily concluded

"No knowledge whatsoever of American military weapons stored en masse in the mountains, the illegal mining and covert exportation of Norwegian rare earth metals and the establishment of an underground biological warfare facility on Royal farm land specialising in the development of a highly virulent and lethal man made variant of Tularemia!" Marcus coldly stated

"Tula.....?"

"Otherwise known as rabbit fever, deer fly fever or O'Hara's fever" Marcus as a matter of fact explained and watched as the King emotionally squirmed with the agony of having been found out

"Anything else.....?" The King arrogantly asked pretending that all he had just heard was nothing more than sheer lunacy and total bunk ham

"The theft of a highly sophisticated device designed to produce an abundance of clean fuel courtesy of the sun"

"News to me" The King bluffed as he tried to outstare Marcus

"So if I were to perform a thorough search of your rooms I wouldn't find such a scientific advancement in one of your diplomatic bags destined for Israel because royalty never lies?" Marcus sarcastically argued as he felt things were about to reach a crescendo accordingly he made certain he could easily retrieve his Glock in a flash if need be

"We are an impeccable breed of humans that is why we are born to rule, having said that I feel as if our discussion is going nowhere so unless you have anything specific or startling to tell me I suggest you leave and allow us to fulfil our duties for the day" The King aloofly said as he violently gestured for Marcus to depart

"Obviously safe guarding Norwegians in their own land is not one of them!" Marcus cuttingly replied and waited for the King's reaction which was cut short as the Kings Guard stationed outside at the entry to the King's rooms suddenly burst in, gun in hand which he first pointed at Marcus then at the waitress before discharging three bullets into the King's heart. The waitress instinctively fell to her knees, rolled to the right, magically produced her service revolver and shot the Guardsman between the eyes leaving Marcus dazed by the frantic events. He wondered if he was next.

The waitress frowned, lowered her gun, wiped it clean with a napkin and placed in the King's right hand and indicated they should vacate the rooms forthwith.

"Not without the LEAF!" Marcus stubbornly said as though he was giving an order

"Leave it, you don't realise its true purpose! We have to go!" The waitress quickly said with a sense of urgency. Marcus could see that she knew what she was talking about and reluctantly obeyed

"Activate your outfit, follow me!" The waitress forcibly barked as she looked around to make certain they were not about to be inundated by a mass of security

"Copy that" Marcus succinctly answered as he faded from view

"Stay close there is little room for error"

"Understood" Marcus replied and latched onto her apron strings convincing himself that this woman could be trusted especially if she was one and the same perfumed lady that he had encountered in the mountains at the same time Marcus felt utterly useless like a little boy being taken out of harm's way. What had this perfumed waitress recognised in him so as to take Marcus under her wing? Would Marcus ever find out? Should he ask the question or simply disappear after saying a polite thank you? Would that ever be enough? As far as Marcus was concerned the entire operation was a failure, Nicoli had been killed, Brit and Anya physiologically if not psychologically damaged, Gerhardt was missing and the Major killed by a drone attack near Roros. Whoever had orchestrated the

American 'invasion' of Norway was a formidable foe with apparently no Achilles heel, no weakness whatsoever unlike certain key individuals within the corridors of Norwegian power. Marcus was alone, certainly there was Psi but for all intents and purposes he was the administrative type reliant on the likes of Marcus for results.

Marcus's tactic of confronting the King, using him as a pawn was doomed from the start, Operation Anaconda was on track to succeed, a noose around Russia designed to sap its energy and feed it to America's cronies. Had Marcus succeeded his life would not be worth living, forever hunted in one way or another. So far he had eluded identification, unlabelled he was free and would remain so until circumstances changed and success brought his failure in the form of an early death for now enjoy being strung along by a perfumed waitress, a peaceful sanctuary awaits in the small town of Zakopane at the foot of the Tatra mountains. The town's name ironic in itself as it means 'buried' an invitation to bury one's woes or simply bury oneself in the immense beauty of the region away from geopolitical games and their dire consequences.

The perfumed waitress expertly led Marcus away from the killing zone into one of the deceased King's retreats where he enjoyed inspiring philosophy, light classical music and a generous serving of XO Cognac irrespective of the time of day. A dead end Marcus thought until the waitress 'touched' a window latch that opened a 'door' to a world full of wonder beneath the floor.

"Where are you taking me?" Marcus whispered

"Into Pan's paradise" The perfumed waitress seductively replied as the 'door' shut behind them and a group of eerie lights came on to reveal panpipes, life like goats, shepherds and hunters scattered everywhere

"This is surreal" Marcus said as he tried to a customise himself to their bizarre surroundings

"Here we drink the elixir from Pan's flute and acquire his enormous strength to instil panic into those who dare to impede our escape" The perfumed waitress confidentially confided as only a select few knew of this hideaway and its accumulated ancient treasures. Within minutes of consuming a small portion of the precious drink all of Marcus negativity subsided he was ready to do battle once again.

The perfumed waitress changed her clothes to resemble a chauffeur after which she led Marcus by the hand to an underground garage that housed several official automobiles all of which she ignored except for a dirty delivery van that bore the official Royal Crest and the signage 'Bygdoy Dairy'

"Are we going to the farm?" Marcus asked out of curiosity as he did not know what the rest of the morning held in store for him

"Nothing of much interest there" The perfumed waitress answered as she made herself comfortable behind the steering wheel

"Where to then?" he continued to probe

"Places"

"Is that it?"

"For the time being, don't worry no harm will come to you"

"That's reassuring" Marcus replied as he reflected on the fact that the perfumed waitress had eliminated the King's assassin dressed as a King's guard and had in fact potentially saves Marcus's life

"Stay low in the foot well until we clear the entrance, they're not used to seeing me with a passenger" The perfumed waitress instructed Marcus as she exited the underground garage

"Very well" Marcus replied and rolled his body into a tight ball

"That's impressive"

"Thank you" Marcus answered thinking that everything would go smoothly which it did until they reached the main gate where their progress was halted

"Problem....?" Marcus whispered

"Potentially" The perfumed waitress answered out of the corner of her mouth before stepping out of the vehicle

"Need to check you van!" A burley security guard grunted as he approached her

"Why it's empty I'm on my way to collect cheeses"

"Can't say following strict orders open the back and step aside" He rudely grunted as he threw his weight around

"As you wish" The perfumed waitress coldly replied and opened up the van to reveal nothing but space "Care to look underneath in case somebody is hanging from the exhaust pipe" She added which the guard did not find particularly amusing

"Clear to go" He rudely said and slammed the doors shut

"Amateur!" The perfumed waitress muttered under her breath before climbing back into the driver's seat and setting forth

"Where to now....?" Marcus asked as he nestled into the passenger seat

"Places"

"Thank you" Marcus dryly said and remained silent as the perfumed waitress expertly negotiated the back roads to reach their first destination namely the riverside hotel in Drammen where Marcus, Brit, Anya and Gerhardt had briefly set up base

"What are we doing here?"

"Acting as bait and collecting stuff" The perfumed waitress explained as she strategically parked the van "Go to the concierge and collect a bag of personal belongings which should be light on as you used hotel supplied toiletries and were on the run so to speak"

"Any outstanding bills....?"

"Already been attended to" The perfumed waitress responded which suggested she was working for Psi and was most probably a highly ranked operative. Marcus paused for a while to analyse his situation before following orders

"Back in a moment" He said then proceeded to exit the van and cross the street. The perfumed lady meanwhile remained seated and carefully took note of all those outside the hotel as well as those entering and exiting. Marcus returned within ten minutes bag in hand and realised the significance of using the Royal van namely as a decoy that shouted its occupants were working for the King nothing suspicious about that

"Where to now....?" Marcus asked glad that the experiment was partially over

"Noisy places"

"You don't give much away" Marcus commented as he looked straight ahead to determine what direction they were going in and their likely end point. The perfumed waitress remained preoccupied with looking around for any potential followers which so far were none but then they had another sixty kilometres further to travel and anything could happen, in essence remain vigilant

"I know silence is golden but do you suppose we could have the radio on for a bit of noise?" Marcus said after a little while

"Classical, rock, pop, middle of the road...?"

"Your choice" Marcus politely answered as his true intention was to discover the present level of peace within Oslo's borders

Within minutes of switching the radio on 'Breaking News' filled the cabin

"Norway has been rocked to its foundations this morning by the brutal assassination of our beloved King at his Palace. Details are sketchy. In separate developments there has been a flurry of activity on social media where scores of individuals have uploaded videos of biological incident response force teams invading the Minister of the Interior and Minister of Justice parliamentary offices, the surrounding areas are sealed off suggesting it is something very serious. A team has also been spotted at the Offices of Mosaic and furthermore a SWAT team is on route to the cult religion Creed of Tyr according to police radio hackers. Whether any of these incidents are related is speculation at this time. We will bring your further developments as they happen"

"Guess my 'bomb' isn't going to play a major role after all"

Marcus thought to himself and wondered what was likely to follow

"Should keep the media circus busy for the next few days" The perfumed waitress cynically expressed as she kept her eyes on the road and monitored those following closely behind

"Can I buy you breakfast, after all you are taking me places?" Marcus warmly asked

"Once we get there" The perfumed waitress replied as she reduced the radio's volume

"Excellent" Marcus feebly answered and closed his eyes in an effort to de-stress his tired body which easily fell into a deep sleep. Marcus dreamt of tranquil mountain lakes, fields of wild flowers in full blossom and gentle breezes that caressed his troubled cheeks, a contrast to the tension filled weeks he had endured in an attempt to bring about geopolitical change. The sound of low flying jet engines coupled with the smell of aviation fuel soon put an end to his idyllic interlude he woke bleary eyed to face a van devoid of its driver.

"What's this, dump and run?" He negatively thought as he familiarised himself with his surroundings and proceeded to exit the van which was parked in an area reserved for international cargo employees

"I suppose I am going to be packed into a cardboard box labelled return to sender" He thought as he wondered where his perfumed waitress had disappeared to then he decided to investigate whether or not she had entered the main receivals building which resembled a hive of activity but before he could take a step in that direction he was tapped on the shoulder from behind.

"Wrong way" The perfumed waitress advised as she indicated Marcus do an about face

"What about breakfast?" Marcus asked

"Another time perhaps, presently far too dangerous, airport security is very tight, everyone leaving is being triple checked. Best avenue for you is to go via cargo, not very comfortable but at least you will get there"

"Understood" Marcus replied as in the past he had done the very same thing

"Activate your suit, that plane over there is destined for Warsaw, it leaves in fifteen minutes, here is an open first class railway ticket, once you arrive access the central train station and go to wherever you would like. Good luck" The perfumed waitress instructed Marcus and walked away without saying anything further which saddened Marcus a little but then that was one of the pitfalls of his job.

Entry into the plane was relatively easy, as was locating a place to nestle into amongst the secured cargo. The plane was manned by a chief pilot and his first officer, no cabin crew to offer refreshments, flight time approximately two hours giving Marcus sufficient time in which to decide where in Poland he would to unwind and reflect on what he could have done differently in order to achieve a positive outcome. Marcus yearned to return to Zakopane a small town at the base of the Tatra Mountains where his grandfather once lived before he passed away and where Marcus and his mother enjoyed many summer holidays trekking through the forest, canoeing on the pristine lakes and interacting with wild animals. Total travelling time by train would be at least eight hours meaning he would not arrive before 5pm, hopefully he would find suitable accommodation at that hour given the popularity of the region and the day of the week.

21
NEVER

At 6.15pm Marcus after a brief five minute walk from the city's high street of Krupowki found himself in the foyer of the Dynamic Aries an iconic hotel in which to experience culture, art and fulfil one's passion for the mountains. Then using his Grom issued credit card which would instantly alert his superiors as to his whereabouts Marcus booked one of the remaining premier double rooms on offer, order room service and retired for the night to enjoy his food and watch a meaningless Polish Police TV series which he had no difficulty in understanding, he did not expect to hear from his superior Psi as Marcus considered the Norwegian mission to have been a total failure, he would only be contacted if his services were urgently needed by Grom which meant he was free to enjoy reliving his childhood memories in the interim period.

The following three days were filled with immense joy and satisfaction tainted to some degree by a lingering anxiety that he would be rapped over the knuckles by Psi who always demanded more, in other words around every corner was a bastard who wanted to ruin your day. Marcus kept his Grom issued mobile phone on him at all times in anticipation of Psi contacting him, strangely enough it remained silent to the point that Marcus thought it was either broken or there was no network for it to connect to. By day five Marcus thought that perhaps he had been excommunicated and that it was his duty to contact Psi much like the prodigal son returning to his father, Zakopane's magic was slowly losing its lustre and with it the 'black dog' started to show his ugly face and threatened to 'bite' Marcus infecting him with lifelong disillusionment. Marcus decided to tough it out for a further two days before returning to Warsaw and presenting himself to Grom headquarters. On the day of his departure things took an unexpected turn. Marcus was in the restaurant enjoying a hearty breakfast when Psi and the perfumed waitress appeared and joined him. A lump formed in Marcus's throat and he broke out into a cold sweat which he couldn't disguise.

"Don't tell me I make you nervous?" The perfumed waitress jokingly said

"Slightly...."

"Then I haven't lost my touch" She seductively purred

"Care to join me for that breakfast we were meant to have?"

"Love to but business first" She erotically responded

"It's always business first" Marcus grumbled

"Finish your meal soldier we have important matters to discuss!" Psi firmly said

"Actually I don't think I could eat any more" Marcus replied as a wave of dread swept over him

"Very well, is there a conference room in this fine establishment that we could use?" Psi asked

"I don't rightly know, I'll ask" Marcus nervously replied and went in search of the answer closely followed by Psi and the perfumed waitress.

The hotel's duty manager acknowledged their request and ushered them into a small room complete with sophisticated audio visual equipment. Satisfied that it met their requirements he took his leave and closed the door behind him which Psi locked. Marcus feared that the briefing he was about to receive was a damning indictment of his inability to deliver consequently he sat very quietly willing to accept the worse.

"Using your mobile phone as a tracking device we were able to track your movements as soon as Patryk alerted us that you had given him the slip. In other words you disobeyed my direct orders!" Psi angrily stated

"Did I?" Marcus blatantly questioned his superior

"I would think so"

"I remember you saying I had your full blessing"

"In regard to relying on yourself in Stockholm.......!"

"I didn't see it that way!"

"And managed to get the King killed......!" Psi fired back

"It wasn't intentional!" Marcus replied

"Are you quite certain about that?" Psi challenged his operative who frowned at the prospect

"Absolutely"

"Setting that aside we believe that your presence spooked the King's Guardsman who was an assassin most probably Mossad in disguise"

"What of it?" Marcus asked

"When he saw you in the gillie suit he wrongly assumed the King was about to make a run for it and therefore became a liability which needed to be eliminated that is why he shot the King dead"

"How did he come to that conclusion?" Marcus asked

"He was fitted with an ultra sensitive listening device capable of hearing through walls. The King's denial of everything that you threw at him was sufficient for the assassin to make an executive decision, you were his next target followed by the waitress luckily she intervened"

"For which I am eternally grateful" Marcus genuinely answered although he knew otherwise

"Your self reliance caused the King's death" Psi firmly said pushing the point

"Unfortunate collateral damage" Was all that Marcus was prepared to say

"Or a very clever chess move that predicted five moves in advance of the King's falling which suggests you knew something that we didn't!"

"Pure coincidence" Marcus softly replied as he slowly regained his self confidence

"Admit to nothing"

"Best way unless the torture becomes unbearable in which case make it sound plausible" Marcus replied in textbook fashion

"True to form, with the King dead the Norwegian parliament can continue unabated until his heir is installed according to their legal process. But supposing there is another avenue in which the deceased King can still exert his influence from the grave one that you may have come across, a treasure map of sorts?" Psi taunted Marcus who remained silent in order to force Psi to show his hand

"Today after a week of mourning the King will be finally laid to rest in the royal cemetery following a requiem service at Trinity church Oslo which can easily accommodate at least one thousand worshippers, it is therefore sufficiently large to carter for all members of parliament, select dignitaries plus their families. The Prince the King's sole offspring will deliver the eulogy. The service is expected to commence at 10am sharp and will be televised in approximately thirty minutes from now" Psi then added

"Will we watch it in its entirety?" Marcus asked

"I expect so, why do you ask?"

"Because I will need to alter my travel arrangements" Marcus explained stone faced

"They have already been cancelled you are coming home with us" Psi sharply answered which made Marcus wonder what they had in store for him for disobeying direct orders. How critical was the delivery of Palinka to Dark Pebble's offices in Stockholm?

"Perhaps I could have a toilet break before the ceremony starts"

Marcus politely asked as he suddenly found the room that they were in too oppressive

"But of course, my assistant will go with you" Psi answered making it sound as though Marcus was under house arrest something that had never happened to him before and he wondered how far from grace he had fallen.

On the way back from the bathroom Psi's assistant ordered a pot of Russian Caravan tea plus slices of poppy seed cake. While they were absent Psi employed the services of a Norwegian VPN website and was able to live stream the Kings funeral. The threesome whiled away the time in silence as they watched the church slowly fill to capacity. It was then that Psi un-muted the computer screen and the sound of ringing bells filled the room heralding the arrival of an elderly priest who took his place in the chancel and allowed the choir to sing an appropriate prelude namely a selection of solemn Sibelius music after which time he ascended the elevated lectern to greet the congregation.

"Grace to you and peace from God our Father and the Lord Jesus Christ. We ate gathered here by the coffin of our beloved King who was murdered by one of his own guards a week ago" The priest warmly said

"Mistruth number one" Marcus mumbled

"To be rectified sooner than later" Psi also mumbled

"A great man in all respects, a man of the people, a real champion of all that is Norwegian, our culture, way of life, belief systems, industry, tourism, the list is endless, generous to a fault but always had time for his family, his departure has created a huge chasm, but it is not for me o labour about his attributes and therefore I make way for his son our future King to present the eulogy" The elderly priest said before descending from the elevated lectern and exchanging pleasantries with the future King.

"Good morning ladies and gentlemen, much of what the pastor just said was meant to be the text of my speech. However recent events of the past few days have altered the narrative to include a dark side and why my father chose to obey it. As you know a number of Norwegians during WW2 collaborated with the Germans including certain members of my family but managed to keep it secret and discreet. They were not successful and soon found themselves blackmailed for all sorts of things. One would think that once the offending person had died that would be the end of it, but no, these self appointed victims never knew when to say enough is enough therefore my father found himself in the unenviable position of having to pay for his father's 'sins'. These are despicable criminal acts perpetrated by evil people; they have no place in our world especially when they threaten the safety and welfare of innocent women and children. My father learnt of the real reason behind the American military presence in Norway but was powerless to do anything about it. Not only did he have his back to the wall but many guns were pointed at him and members of his family without anyone of them knowing" The King's son words cut deeply into the hearts of some of those who had facilitated the American military presence in Norway whilst others remained arrogantly aloof and dismissed his wild accusations

"My father was no fool, his love for country and family knew no bounds. He set about devising a plan to free Norway one that would challenge Norway's parliamentary system and its consti-tution. It took me two days to come to grips with the realisation that my father, my best friend had been callously ripped away from me forever. Fortunately my wonderful mother a pillar of immense strength soldiered on and attended to the funeral arrangements as required by tradition. When she thought that I was sufficiently lucid she alerted me to the fact that there appeared to be no Will in place something that I found particularly confusing, in desperation I consulted the Will Registry where all valid Wills are required by law to be deposited only to learn that the Will had been cancelled. Question was by whom and on whose authority. This led me to conclude that everything would remain the same and would be transferred into my name after my coronation. Two days ago I received a communication from the Vatican's official lawyers in Rome stating that they held certain sensitive documents that could only be released to me upon my father's death providing I outlived him and I was of sound mind and body. These documents would be delivered to me personally and in private by the Swedish Cardinal who wished to attend my father's funeral along with members of the Swedish Royal family. I am pleased to say that I have received the paperwork without incident and that the Will was amongst it. As we know a will represents the wishes of the deceased with respect to the distribution of his or her assets, but can it be more than that? Can it include a command in other words what is included in my father's legitimate Will is the Norwegian Constitution and parliamentary system obliged to honour it? Specifically the following passage written in Latin:

'In perpetuum portantes sidera et verbera de terra nostra, ursam semper amplector, quia non est tibi nocumentum'

For the majority of you seated here today what I have just recited is meaningless gibberish however for the likes of our learned pastor and Swedish Cardinal it is easy to understand, translated it reads:

'Banish those bearing stars and stripes from our land forever, embrace the bear for it means you no harm'

One could argue that this is nothing more than eloquent ramblings of a delusional person until one examines the supporting documentation that detail the nefarious activities of the Americans on our sovereign soil and all those who allowed it to happen in such a manner that it threatens our national security. All attempts to previously expose these were thwarted, even our media was compromised those who could for a brief second or two were labelled conspiracists. I wonder if my father was amongst them. On the day of my father's assassination there occurred numerous biohazard incidents at the following locations; the Minister for Justice offices, the Minister of the Interior offices, the Disciples of Tyr headquarters and the offices of Mosaic, not one of these resembled terrorist attacks, they were in fact bold statements that shouted 'We know what you have done, you have been exposed' The biohazard came in the form of a bottle of Vodka that contained a virulent highly transmissible form of bio-engineered rabbit fever which was developed at the Royal farm. The bottle of Vodka had an explosive device attached to it.

My father did not die in vain, his death has revealed the underhanded, back stabbing corruption that has occurred in the highest circles of Norway's political elite" It was then that Psi muted the Prince's verbal delivery but allowed the ceremony to be recorded in its entirety for future reference on a USB stick inserted into one the computer ports that they were using.

"Done rather elegantly in fact so elegantly it smacks of your clandestine involvement" Psi said out of the corner of his mouth as he looked directly at Marcus who remained silent and stone faced waiting to see what further argument Psi might present

"As we know the Vatican has its own secret service of which several Cardinals are members. It is highly unlikely that the King accumulated any of the evidence as he would have been easily found out due to a lack of expertise and been eliminated far earlier than last week. I not believe that he had any affiliations with the Keep Norway Neutral party or any other conspiracists. I think that he accidentally stumbled across the Rabbit Fever facility once the Americans had settled in. The irrefutable evidence that the Prince has in his possession was most probably supplied by a reputable third party given to and couriered by the Polish Cardinal to the Vatican's lawyers along with a proposed new will doctored with the help of advanced artificial intelligence then collated and couriered back by the same Cardinal to the Swedish Cardinal over a period of several weeks in readiness for the King's demise which whether one likes it or not was inevitable. In true Grom fashion it will be the Prince and his deceased father that will receive all of the credit in rectifying Norway's political indiscretions once they banish all those associated with the stars and stripes by all means possible" Psi slowly said in such a fashion that was meant to force Marcus to admit that he was the third party but that didn't happen so Psi continued with his postulations

"Responsibility is something that Mossad currently will be reluctant to accept. According to unofficial channels a highly sophisticated clean energy device based on the photosynthesis principle that promises to solve the world's needs was illegally acquired by Mossad. This device exploded during its inaugural demonstration killing and maiming a number of high profile government officials in Israel two days ago" Psi said with a wry smile as he studied Marcus for any signs of admission

"I suppose they will blame the Iranians for it" Marcus cynically suggested

"Don't they always?" Psi agreed as he foresaw the inevitable dismissal of the Norwegian government by royal decree, the arrest prosecution and incarceration of guilty politicians, the expulsion of other key personnel, the dismantling of organisations that threatened Norwegian values and its national security all thanks to an 'unidentifiable' third party